DANTE
international

Sharon Kasanda

© Sharon Kasanda

First published in 2012

Published by
Wordweaver Publishing House
P.O. Box 11579
Klein Windhoek
Windhoek, Namibia
wordweaver@iway.na

ISBN 978-99916-878-2-7

To Dan and Joe,

This is for my family; my mom Miriam, my dad
Choshi, sisters Martha and Naomi, and brother
Chongo, for keeping me on track and supporting
my crazy dreams, no matter what they were. You
have been my little piece of heaven on earth. To my
partner Tshuutheni, who has never doubted me
and has wrapped me in love every step of the way,
and to all of the amazing people who have helped
me bring my dream to life; without you I would
not be where I am today.

Sharon Kasanda

Thanks for all the help (☺)
you guys are awesome, it was
a pleasure meeting you,
stay blessed!

3/12/14

CHAPTER 1

Sunday, 15 April

*T*he city that had once held such beauty and light for him, now held nothing but despair and torment. Every day was a nightmare. A nightmare of loneliness, of a perpetual coldness that was slowly growing in his heart, freezing out any other emotions that he could possibly have felt.

The serenity that was Windhoek was amazing; the desert protected the city from the cold harsh reality of a new future and forced its intentions on the inhabitants, creating a safe haven of quiet peace and bubbling expectations; it made him sick to his stomach. He had tried to move, he had tried to run away, but his city would not let him go, always calling him back until he returned to the sounds of the female kapana sellers, the hustling of the open markets and the bright glaring lights of the city centre. The serenity would return for a while, but then the desolation would hit; hungrily clawing, whispering and taunting him.

He would make them pay for what they had done to him; the despair that had become a part of him would become theirs and he would make sure their lives became a living hell of bitterness, unforgiveness and the sweetest of nightmares.

He shuddered now as he felt her skin grow cold under his touch, her body cooling like the heat had suddenly been switched off. He was kneeling beside her, stroking the curly black kinky hair on her head. It had seemed so alive a few moments ago and now clung to her lifeless body, shrouding the top of her head with its inky blackness. Tears of joy streamed down his face and he wiped them away hurriedly, the transparent gloves covering his hands absorbing the liquid before they could stain her perfect ebony skin. He had only been trying to take the pain away. He did not understand why she had resisted him so much. If only she could see how perfect she was now, how he had understood her and had seen her pain. He had made her whole so that she could be loved properly, by a real man. Her imperfections were gone and he forgave her for her depravity. She was so beautiful.

Her gold stiletto heels had gleamed wickedly under the flashing strobe lights, which raced across the bare length of her legs to the little gold skirt that barely covered her. He had stared at her in pity, wanting to remove his jacket and cover up her nakedness. The shirt she wore had almost brought tears to his eyes. With no back and made of such flimsy silky material that her nipples peered through it like a set of headlights, beckoning him to end her misery. He had done so gladly. Wrapping his jacket around her, placing a drink in her hand and whispering what a beautiful woman she was. It had been shamefully easy to pull her away from the crowd. She had eaten up his compliments like a woman starved.

He had not meant to end her life so soon. He had wanted to change her first, to free her properly. He had wanted to spend more time with her and tell her that she would want for nothing, that she would be free to be whoever and with whomever she wanted. She should have thanked him, instead of laughing and sneering at him. Halfway to his car, she had suddenly refused to leave with him. She had screamed at him, banging her fists against his chest, balancing precariously on her stilettos. The alcohol swirling and curdling through her system had been in full-force, slurring her words as it talked through her. It had possessed her, taking hold and twisting her into another being – the ugly being he was trying to get rid of. He had held her wrists firmly, watching with pity as she flailed against him, aiming kicks at him that rarely reached their mark, hurling verbal abuse and spittle at him, then resorting to begging him and crying to be let go. When she had finally resorted to sleazy sexuality, he had disgustedly wrapped his hands around her neck and forced all the ugliness out of her. He felt relief, and had watched as the life drained out of her. She looked beautiful in death. He wished he could keep her like this forever.

CHAPTER 2

Monday, 16 April

Dante prided himself on his appearance. He stood in front of the mirror, looking back at his almond-shaped eyes, his smooth ebony skin, the curly hair closely cropped to his head, the charcoal grey suit which moulded against his 1,85 metre frame.

I am irresistible, he thought, his mouth curving upwards sensually, *and I am rich*.

He bent over to wash his hands, absently tapping the top of the silver faucet lightly, frowning at the communal bathroom of the agency. Above all, he had always wanted his own private bathroom adjacent to his office. Something that was laid out in the finest of black marble, from the basins under the water faucets to the smooth bowl of the toilet. The tiles would reflect the light coming from the small circular bulbs embedded in the ceiling. The shower stall would take up almost half of the floor space and have multiple water jets that gleamed dull silver. Dante had shared a bathroom his entire life and now regarded a personal bathroom as a necessity. Although his bathrooms at home and at Dante International now came close to his dream, sharing a bathroom at HD Advertising still displeased him immensely. He glanced around the small room. The utilities were ceramic, and the wide mirror and toilet had been sheathed in the interior decorators love for wood – even the vase on the toilet cistern which held the potpourri was made of wood. The bathroom mats were maroon, the brown of the desert hung from the picture frames on the walls. Dante twisted his mouth, wondering when he had given his approval for these colours.

The ring of the phone in his jacket pocket startled him. He knew it could only be Roberta Erlichmann, his friend and partner. The ambitious thorn in his side who never let him rest – ever.

Dante sighed. He was genuinely fond of Roberta, but even she had begun to push him to his limit. Perhaps he was just tired. Work pressure was increasing at HD Advertising, where he worked as a partner, and managing Dante International Storage also demanded more and more of his time lately. His body had begun to feel the pull of the constant work demands. He sighed again. His phone hadn't stopped its insistent ringing. She knew he would pick up, he always did.

Straightening himself up, he reached into his pocket and pulled out his phone. He scowled as he stabbed at the green call button.

'What is it Erlichmann?'

'Dante?' Roberta trilled sweetly, her voice tiny over the phone's speakers. 'You're hiding in the toilet again, aren't you? I'm outside, open the door!'

Dante turned to look at the closed door, not flinching as it shuddered under Roberta's knocking. 'Go away Erlichmann.'

'Funny Dante. Like I'd ever go anywhere without you. Get out of the bloody bathroom!'

Dante stared at the door separating them. In his minds-eye he could see her green eyes flashing, her brown and blond curls dancing around her head. They had been lovers for ages and amongst their affairs and flirtations with other members of the opposite sex, the sexual relationship they had started in their teenage years had never disappeared. They had always been united in their loneliness at odd hours of night, when they both craved familiarity. He wondered if this is what they would still be doing in ten years, or whether one of them would find love and move on.

'What do you want Erlichmann?'

'The meeting's about to begin,' her voice became urgent. 'I have a list an arm long of things to brief you on! How many more crucial meetings are you going to miss?' Roberta sounded annoyed.

'Yes darling, I know. But I've been busy,' then he smiled to himself. 'Don't you think you look a little ridiculous standing outside the toilet door and talking on the phone?'

'Well man, open the door already. Like we've not been in a toilet together enough times!'

'Bring those green eyes in here and I'll show you what it really means to be in a toilet together.'

'This is no time to be naughty, Dumeno,' Roberta sounded irritated, but Dante could almost feel her blush through the closed door. 'Besides, I thought August might be in there with you – she's not at her desk.'

'I don't play with *all* the staff Roberta! At least not all the staff at HD.'

'You're bloody priceless, Dumeno,' Roberta snorted over the line, her banging on the door becoming invasive in the small space. 'Enough now. Get out of there. The meeting starts at nine. That gives us only forty-five minutes, and I still have to brief you on our final strategy.'

'Come on, Robbie,' Dante tried one last time. 'A quick one right here. In this closet of a space you call a bathroom.'

'Dante Dumeno,' Roberta was being firm. 'Out, now!'

Dante grinned, and drawing the phone away from his ear, pressed the red button to end the call. He checked his appearance again in the mirror before unlocking the door that held Roberta out.

She had a wry look on her face as she clicked her phone closed with a loud snap, moving the folders she was carrying back to balance in the crook of her arm.

'Finally! That took long enough. Let's go. Jaco's waiting for us in the boardroom.'

'I hope he's dressed appropriately for a change,' muttered Dante.

Roberta acted as though she had not heard Dante and did not miss a beat in her stride, only pausing briefly to hand a folder to the dark-skinned girl sitting behind the reception desk. 'Make sure that Chris gets this as soon as he comes through that door. And send him straight up. Also, bring some coffee up there pronto.'

Roberta didn't wait for the receptionist to answer, and continued on her way to the boardroom. Dante, with a smile on his face, shook his head and fell into step behind her. She kept talking, so he had to walk briskly to hear her.

'Remember what I was saying yesterday? Did you even look at the presentation? I guess not,' Roberta shook her head without looking back at him. 'Briefly Dante, and pay attention. As we all know, AIDS is big business.'

'Such concern you have for your fellow human beings Robbie,' Dante smirked.

'Ah shut it. Now, what we have here is five major AIDS funding organisations finally getting some sense and combining their money and time to concentrate on one awareness strategy. Freaking AIDS NGO's are all doing the same thing around the country, of course their messages are ineffective because they're not working in tandem with each other,' Roberta rolled her eyes. 'Anyway, so this is the big one. If we win this deal – no – when we win this deal, we can retire Dante! The beauty of it is that it's not just Namibia, but will expand next year to include the whole of southern Africa. Perhaps even the whole of Africa. We've never tendered for anything this big!'

Roberta took a breath, and checked to see if Dante was still following her. He nodded. The sensual smirk that had lingered on his face moments earlier had been replaced with a mildly serious look. She swallowed her annoyance. Dante would never look like he was paying attention to what anyone had to say, but his brilliance reared when put to the task. Roberta was counting on that brilliance now. She handed him a blue folder and continued, as they walked up the spiral staircase to the second floor.

'We're one of three agencies tendering for this job. DXV Imagery and Advantageous Solutions have already given their pitches; unlucky bastards think they did a good job. Remember Samuel and Toini? They're on the panel for the pitches, and it was time for them to pay back the favour they owed us. They told me how the presentations were going so far,' Roberta grinned. 'What we're offering is ten times better.'

Dante smiled. Roberta didn't play fair, that was true. But she did win. He found her irresistible in this frame of mind. Secure, competitive, brilliant. He also found her irresistible in that sky-blue jersey dress she was wearing, complimented by a white belt sash. It clung to her curves in all the right places, kissing her body to just below her knees. Roberta was tall, and had cause to boast the best of both black and white worlds. Her father, a German businessman and property mogul, had come to Namibia for a holiday, and the estate agent who had organised his accommodation got to know him on a very intimate basis. His three month business visit had turned into a three month long affair, after which they had parted on good terms. Which was just as well because nine months later Roberta had come into the world kicking and screaming.

As they climbed the stairs, Dante reached over subtly and pinched her bum, using the file as a guard against prying eyes. 'You are dressing to impress, Robbie. Although I can't help but wonder if what you are wearing will impress their minds or stroke their heads?'

Roberta, feeling slightly weak at the knees, lowered her voice and spoke huskily to Dante. 'The only head that's being stroked all by itself seems to be yours.'

Roberta had housed her brainchild, HD Advertising, in a stone-brick house on Jan Jonker Avenue, in a suburb called Luxury Hill. On being buzzed into the residence through a single gate, visitors would find themselves in the main foyer. The floors were outlaid in black tile, the walls a warm tone of brown, in sync with the warm red-earth tone theme that ran the entire length of the house. When entering the building, the first thing to view was a large reception desk, with two walkways that led off to the male and female toilets, and to the large kitchen. On the left on entry, abstract couches were carefully arranged to give the company a more relaxed look, and were complete with an artistic table sectioned into a magazine, newspaper and book stand. To the right was thick glass; the administrative employees behind it carefully arranged into cubicles that were designed to have minimal view of the entrance.

A spiral staircase, lined with carpet, twisted up to the second floor. This was were the creative director, graphic designers, production manager and CEO resided, most of their offices separated by glass partitions. Roberta was not a great fan of secrecy, and wanted to see what her staff where doing at all times of the day. Her office and Dante's, however, were private. They had earned the right not to showcase themselves to the staff.

As they neared the closed door of the boardroom, Dante touched her arm lightly, arresting her movement, and walked past her. He reached the door first and held it open.

As she entered, Roberta suddenly noticed how tired he looked. 'You are spending too many nights working late at that bloody park. Someone would think you were trying to hide something.'

Dante's smile stretched out slowly across his face. 'Jealous?'

'Are you even serious? I'm the one who gave you the money to start that stupid storage facility. I'm sure that's where you'll be tonight.'

Dante sighed theatrically, motioning Roberta to continue inside, watching the muscles underneath her dress move as she walked past him. 'I had to give you something constructive to do with your father's guilt-money.'

'All the same, you should take a night off,' she smiled suggestively at him. 'I can help you freshen up. Maybe I can watch you eat. Maybe we can eat together?' Roberta looked him up and down, her meaning clear.

Dante laid his hand over hers, his fingers caressing. 'If that's a dinner invite,' he said, 'then I accept.'

Roberta's smile turned into a grin of ardent delight.

CHAPTER 3

Naka 'Naks' Shikongo hurried through the doors of HD Advertising, walking past the sofa arrangement to the reception desk. His eyes were covered with sunglasses, his jeans blue and low slung, and his white t-shirt blazed with red and yellow.

'What's up August? I need to see my boy. Now!'

August nodded at him from behind the reception desk, acknowledging his existence. 'You need to give them some time. They're busy with their presentation. How many times have I told you to make an appointment?'

'Me? An appointment? Dante is my boy and Roberta is my girl. I don't need an appointment! I don't want to wait. Lemme go up quickly. I won't be long.'

August snorted, her hair bouncing on her head. The long Brazilian weave she was wearing hung down her back in curls, framing her heart-shaped ebony body, the red lipstick on her lips sneering at him.

'Listen Shikongo, you aren't going anywhere except sitting on that couch right now. Or just leave and come back later. They've been busy up there two hours already, so I doubt it will take much longer. But I ain't making any promises neither.'

Naks bared his teeth mockingly at her. 'You are always such a bundle of joy sista. I'll wait.'

'And take off those sunglasses, you look like a *botsotso*!'

Naks moved away from reception and settled on one of the squishy couches Roberta loved, trying to get comfortable. Although he was older than his two friends, his height and the way he held himself, made him appear younger for his age. What he lacked in girth, he made up for in personality. His head, shaved bald, shone with oil, and his sunglasses were a constant presence on his nose. He had gone to Jan Jonker Afrikaner School with a swagger in his step and more money in his pocket than met the eye – and that's where he had first met Dante. His charm had drawn the girls; and his money the boys, who all wanted to know where he got it from and would gather around his car during break-times, admiring its latest rims. Naks not only had a loud mouth, but his eyes had roamed the schoolyard, constantly watching. They had met during break-time in the smokers' lounge, a dirty area behind the science building that was a blind spot to teachers. The smoke curling from their mouths and around their heads was enough to grant them a place on the school's notoriety board.

'Can I have a light?' Naks had sidled up to Dante, holding out his joint. Dante had nodded, fishing his lighter out of his grey uniform trousers. The flame flared up between them.

'Where the fuck did you get your name, man? Yo parents can't be white – you as black as they come!' The other guys around them laughed and Naks chewed his gum a few moments more, moving his jaw up and down like a ruminating cow, before he spat it out onto the dirt between them, and put the joint between his lips.

Dante shrugged. 'Wasn't my choice.'

'Fucking Dante. Dante! An Ovambo called Dante! What the fuck was the *Sali* and *Bali* thinking?'

'You should check my siblings' names, bra.'

'What? Why didn't you argue? Get them to change the names?' Naks said, his eyes bright. He removed the joint from his dark lips and spat, the saliva a congealed brown between them.

'They're dead.'

'Man, that's fucked up. Did they leave you with anything?'

'They left me with family.'

'That's really fucked up!' Naks spat again, nodding in tandem with the group of boys around them. 'You taking care of them?'

'Yeah, bra.'

'With what, dreams?' Naks had laughed loudly.

Dante took the cigarette out of his mouth, grinding the butt on the wall they were leaning against. 'Since when did it become your business?'

Naks narrowed his bright eyes at him, the joint hanging between his black lips as the smoke floated up towards the sky. 'Do you want to turn those dreams into real money, bra?'

That moment was the turning point in Dante's life. He and Naks became business partners, and Naks had laughed at Dante's amazement at the different personalities that they sold to. From politicians to lonely housewives, from teachers to high ranking foreign officials, there was always money to be made with the drugs. Naks knew that Dante did not considered himself a dealer, but had luxuriated in how he was now able to provide for his siblings. Their constant motivator had been the weight of the money in their pockets which reminded them of where they had come from and what they had to do to get ahead.

Naks didn't have to wait long. Shortly after getting settled in his seat, the big shots were escorted out by Roberta. Once they'd left she indicated at Naks to follow her up the stairs.

'Robbie, baby, you missing the full colour?' Naks sneered good naturedly at Roberta when they reached her office.

'It's been a while. But I've been … otherwise entangled,' Roberta smiled at her friend as she sat down and stretched her legs out. 'Jealous?'

'Just feeling left out,' Naks mourned, pouring himself a glass of water from the jug that stood in the corner, his dark glasses still perched on his nose. 'God knows girl – the first day you came over to our place with that curly hair, those damn green eyes. You were meant to be my baby mama, only to find out you wanted everyone else as well.'

'You're still the dealer Naks, not me.'

'Ag, what you talking about? We're all dealers. I would've been too much for you on a more permanent basis. Anyways I like the friendship.'

'Friendship?' Roberta laughed. 'You still call it friendship?'

'I call it friendship with benefits. The three of us being friends is pretty screwed-up Robbie,' Naks leaned forward, the eyes of his glasses staring at her. 'So what is it? Dante on Mondays, me on Wednesdays and toyboy on Fridays?'

'You'll always remain the bastard won't you, Naks?'

'Whatever Robbie. Where is our boy? I'm worried.'

Roberta scoffed. 'Worried about what Naks? We cannot afford any problems now. We've got too much at stake. Just keep your worries to yourself and don't mess with the good thing we've all got going here.'

'Don't mess with what, Robbie?'

They turned simultaneously, towards where Dante stood lounging in the doorway. 'What are you two up to? Keeping secrets again?'

Dante advanced into the room, settling himself on the chair next to Naks.

Roberta shrugged her shoulders. 'It's nothing Dante, you shouldn't even bother yourself about it. Naks is just being strange again.'

Dante looked between the only two real friends he had in his world; he trusted Naks' instincts and adored the way Roberta would stand and fight for him in any corner.

When Dante saw his two close friends together, they reminded him always of how far they had come. How they had all changed and grown from the people they were previously destined to become. He owed both Roberta and Naks so much more than his life.

Growing up in Katutura, Dante could remember his mother working as a domestic helper in the Windhoek suburb of Avis, barely earning enough to sustain her children and alcoholic husband. Meme Priscilla Shiweda had become an old woman before her time. The stories that were told about the wealth his family used to have before Tate Petrus Dumeno squandered it on beer, meat and women seemed like fairytales compared to the harsh reality of life. All Dante saw and remembered was the small two bed-roomed house, the sad eyes of his mother and the ever growing pile of beer bottles in the corner of the kitchen.

She would wake him up early every Saturday morning, her *ondelela* rustling quietly. Her face bright with vaseline and the smell of sunlight soap wafting from her body and clothes onto him. Her mouth would smile at him, the curve of her lips not reaching the sadness in her dark eyes. She had always kept her hair natural and short, the small kinky curls framing the smooth lines of her face. He could smell the faint scent of perfume on her, one of the only treasures she possessed that she had guarded with an iron fist from his sister. Dante had watched her make it last longer by mixing a tablespoon of the concentrated scent with enough water to hold the scent together, creating a new bottle of the perfume. Her smell had never changed over the years, neither had her smile; it had been the foundation he had come back to despite the turmoil that was his life. Her maid's uniform was crisp; ironed and meticulously cared for, as if she knew that this was to be the last lifeline for her and her family.

The harder his mother worked, the harder his father worked at losing her hard earned money. The balding man with the bloodshot eyes and stomach spilling over his dirty jeans who sprawled on the couch all morning was a far cry from the Petrus Dumeno Junior in the childhood stories.

'I was forced to marry your mother,' his father would slur at anyone who came within hearing distance. 'That woman, she tricked me. She's a bad spirit.'

Then he would burp loudly, his bloodshot eyes angrily glaring. 'I was the man of this location, they respected me! That woman, she could not keep her legs closed. She opened them for every man at the shebeen! Her evil spirits, they ruined me!'

They learned to keep out of his way and eventually treated him like a disagreeable guest whose noise and abuse they had to take for an hour every day before he passed out, his face at times plastered in his own vomit. His mother would then patiently clean off the side of his face. Dante always knew his father was capable of violence but was just too lazy to inflict it, and so his tongue lashed back and forth between the three children and his long suffering wife. He remembered the nights he would sit awake shushing his sister to sleep, her round dark eyes staring at him in the dim light of a candle, trying not to look at the stony face of his younger brother who's eyes beseeched him to say that everything was going to be all right; trying to drown out the sound of their parents fighting.

'He used to be a good man,' his mother would whisper to him, her eyes on the duvet cover as she would busily tuck all three of them into the two single beds that she had pushed together to create a double bed in their small room. '*Osheeli*, don't hate your father.'

'Bra,' Naks' tone was serious. 'I heard that something might be going down at DI.'

Dante looked at his friend speculatively. 'What does that mean?'

'I've started hearing rumours. Something big is going to happen at DI.'

Dante shrugged. 'I really don't have time for this. Roberta and I have actual work to handle right now. Naks, come on bra.'

'Listen Dumeno, I am hearing whispers. Something is going down.'

Roberta sniggered, poking Naks in the shoulder. 'Are you sure you haven't been smoking your own stash?'

Naks shook his head at her. 'Just keep your ears and eyes open. You know I hate all this corporate bullshit that you guys got yourselves into. And Robbie, you're such a prick.'

Roberta stretched her legs again, pulling them back underneath the chair, her pink mouth opening at them in a yawn. 'Thursday is good for me, Naks. And this corporate bullshit, it puts a hell of a lot of food on all our tables.'

Naks shrugged. 'Anyway, that's all I heard, wish there was more.'

Dante exhaled noisily, dragging his hand across his face. 'Okay fine, I'll ask Hienry to look into it.'

'Yes, ask the bulldog,' Roberta snorted. 'With all the money you're paying him, Dante, he needs to start earning his keep.'

CHAPTER 4

'August *iwe*, what are you wearing!'

'You're just jealous because you're not my size Rabecca. Go on a diet, go to the gym and just stop harassing me!'

'I always wonder if you're here to work or if you're going to a fashion show.'

Farusja Mumba watched her best-friend and the secretary laugh good naturedly at each other, her fingers lying lightly on the counter, belying her nervousness. The woman behind the reception desk turned to look at her, smiling briefly.

'Miss Mumba? Mr van Reensburg will be with you shortly. Please have a seat.'

Farusja moved away from the large desk, towards the couches in the foyer. Rabecca followed her, continuing to chatter to the secretary. Farusja did not know what she was still doing in Namibia. Her plan had involved a brief holiday with Rabecca Mulenga before she made her way back to Zambia, to the painful memories of the two gravestones of her parents. And now, two weeks into her holiday Rabecca had promptly proceeded to organise a job interview for Farusja at the company where she worked.

Farusja settled herself into a couch ten times deeper than it looked. She expected Rabecca to head straight off to her office, but instead she squished her bulk in next to Farusja, grunting and groaning as the chair almost swallowed her.

'Don't you need to go work Becca? It might not be the best idea for everyone to know you got me this job.'

'Ah, *iwe*, what are you talking about? All the people here were hired on say-so from relatives and rich parents. Every corner of this place is crawling with nepotism. Besides, except for this report I have to hand in tomorrow, things are a little quiet in my office. At least until we win this tender, then neither of us will have time for chit-chatting.'

'What makes you think they'll employ me?'

Rabecca laughed heartily. 'What are you talking about *mami*! The post in design has been open for ages now, even if you're a foreigner. The least they can do is give you an interview. Who knows, it might even be fun.'

'And I came here for a holiday…'

'Think of it as an extended working holiday,' Rabecca's whole body shook with glee. '*Iwe*, we both know that there is nothing you need to rush back to Zambia for.

Your home is with me. I told you, earn some money before you decide too quickly on what you want to do with the rest of your life!'

Farusja sighed, twisting her portfolio folder in her hands nervously. She had now been waiting over an hour for her interview, her cell phone cheerily winking the time at her: 12h30. She had gone through all the magazines and newspapers on the table in front of her, twice over. These people had some nerve. She was contemplating walking out of the building without the interview, although Becca would kill her. She was not this desperate.

'Miss Mumba? You may come up.'

Farusja looked up startled, and the tallest man she had ever seen filled her view.

'I am Kobus van Reensburg, HR Manager. Follow me,' he turned on his heel and walked back up the spiral staircase, not looking back once to see if she was behind him.

Farusja, after struggling to get out of the chair that had trapped her, scurried after him. He led her up to an office that had, on first glance, a large painting of a savannah landscape hanging from the wall directly above his desk, at least she assumed that his desk was hiding under all those stacks of folders and millions of post-it notes. By the time she had brought her eyes back down to his, he was sitting and looking her up and down, his gaze penetrating. He motioned for her to pass over her portfolio. He glanced at it briefly, appearing uninterested.

'Ok, you now have five minutes to tell me why we should hire you.'

Initially a bit taken aback, Farusja quickly found her composure and spoke eloquently of the assets her creativity would bring to the company. At least she thought she was pretty damn eloquent. However, a few minutes into her speech on how brilliant she was, he dismissed her with a casual wave of his hand.

'That will be all, Miss Mumba.'

Farusja paused, her mouth still open in mid-sentence. 'What?'

'I said that will be all, Miss Mumba,' Kobus stared at her, his gaze stern and unflinching. 'I am sure you can find your way out.'

Farusja stared at him, a hot flush beginning to spread from the tips of her toes to burn in her face. She collected herself and deliberately reached forward to take her portfolio off his desk. She turned on her heel and left the office, keeping a smile firmly plastered on her face. Farusja stood at the top of the staircase, biting her bottom lip to stop it from shaking as she began to descend, her eyes rapidly blurring as the lump in her throat grew larger. *How dare he treat me like that?* She fumed, the lump of anger in her throat blossoming. *I should have used my portfolio to give him a smack in the face!*

She did not see the man in front of her, and connected solidly with his chest. The impact made her cry out in surprise as she grasped at the open edges of his jacket and felt one strong arm wrap itself around her, as the other one shot out to grasp the railing, steadying them both on the perilous staircase.

She looked up at her rescuer, alarmed at what falling down the staircase would have done to her image, her reputation and her neck. Dark eyes stared back down at her, and the slight smile on his face curved his lips upwards. 'Dreaming on these stairs will get you killed.'

She could not place if he was Namibian from his accent, which did not sound native to any country. He was handsome, it shouted from the almond slant of his eyes to the strength of the arm around her, and despite her disaster of an interview, her heart quickened.

'Thank you,' she kicked herself inwardly as her voice came out breathless and husky, and by the way his smile widened into a full set of teeth, she felt sure that he knew exactly what she was thinking.

'You're welcome.'

They were both startled by the cough at the bottom of the staircase. It was August, the receptionist, with a tray of steaming coffee, standing undecidedly at the bottom of the stairs. With the realisation that they were still holding onto each other, Farusja felt the arm that was wrapped around her release itself slowly, moving up to hold her shoulder firmly. 'Are you sure you're okay?'

Farusja nodded. She released the black lapels of the suit she was clutching, smoothed down her own suit self-consciously and retrieved her handbag which had fallen down her arm and now hung from her wrist.

'Bad interview?' he asked as he let go of her. He turned around to motion to the receptionist. 'Come on up August.'

They stood quietly as the receptionist crept cautiously past them, the cups on the tray wobbling precariously. As she walked past, Farusja saw the look that August gave them both. It was a look that promised she would make Farusja a ripe grape on the rumour vine.

'Good luck,' he smiled at her one last time, walking up the stairs past her and leaving a whisper of musk in the air behind him. 'And hold on to that railing, I cannot catch you twice.'

Rabecca treated Farusja to lunch at Oshizizi, a new upmarket restaurant that offered everything green and organic. Rabecca was only officially on her diet at Oshizizi, and Farusja laughed as her friend ordered a large chicken salad with an orange juice, knowing by the look in Becca's eyes that in an hour she would be hungry again. It was the first restaurant Farusja had been to in Namibia and she marvelled at the serenity of the place. It was set outside, the trees had been grown to strategically provide shade, the sound of the water trickling in the fountains was peaceful, creating a relaxed and happy atmosphere. She brushed the leaves off the table that had fallen from the massive Acacia tree they were sitting under and ordered her meal.

Rabecca was a loud outspoken Bemba woman from Zambia. Her tightly curled natural hair sprung merrily around her head. Her skin was smooth ebony, and her wide-set brown eyes, small flat nose and full, ever smiling lips gave the true impression of her open personality. Even her 1,55 metre frame could not contain the vivacious bundle of energy. Rabecca's curves hugged every inch of her body, and although her wide hips and large breasts were carrying more than their standard weight, her boundless energy remained intact.

Rabecca laughed heartily as Farusja related the events of the interview to her.

'And you think that's bad! Ha, you should have been at my interview. So when do you start? Did August call you already? And why are you causing drama already with that heartbreaker Dumeno? I told you to do your homework!'

Farusja laughed nervously. 'It wasn't him. No way it could've been him. It was probably just some other random employee.'

Their conversation stilled as the tall waitress returned, balancing a tray that held their drinks. She smiled at Rabecca as she handed her an orange juice and passed the same over to Farusja. 'I have made it just the way you like it, Miss Mulenga,' she said, standing next to the table. 'Anything else?' She left as they both shook their heads at her.

Farusja stared at her friend in curiosity. 'What does she mean *just the way you like it*?'

Rabecca sighed dramatically. 'When you work at HD, you need a little liquid courage from time to time.'

'*Mami*, trust me, half of the people at that place are either high or happy after lunch. It's hard work!' Rabecca protested when she saw the expression on Farusja's face.

'Great, I was just interviewed by a company full of drunkards and druggies,' Farusja shook her head.

Rabecca ignored her barb, sipping her spiked orange juice gleefully.

'Well August says it was Dante. She say's that the two of you were a bit wrapped up in each others arms on the stairs. And that you seemed to be enjoying every moment of it,' teased Rabecca.

Farusja blushed deeply, and tried to steady her breathing. 'Damn it Becca, you can't be serious! No wonder she looked at me like that when she passed us on the stairs! Oh well, who cares? There's no way I am working at a place where they treat you like you're worth shit at the first interview.'

Rabecca clicked her tongue warningly. 'Ag rubbish, Kobus treats everyone like a second-class citizen. It's nothing personal. But I'll bet Dante spotted you from miles away. Dumeno's smile can stop traffic and he knows how to use it!'

'I didn't know it was him, Becca!'

'That's why I told you to do your research, but *iwe wali tumpa*, you're still making those moves from varsity!'

Farusja smiled. Rabecca was one of her oldest friends and together they had thrown bricks and shouted slogans with the youth party, The Zambian Freedom Fighters, at the University of Zambia. It seemed like a life-time ago when they had met at university, and immediately became fast friends. The only thing that had come between them was Farusja's expulsion from the university after the student riots, which Rabecca had narrowly missed by being ill on the day. Eventually Rabecca had joined the influx of Zambian students who transferred to the University of Namibia after closure upon closure and strike upon strike had lengthened her four-year degree into a seven-year degree. When she finally completed her degree in marketing, she decided to settle down in Namibia. When Farusja had been expelled, her mother had shaken her head, more irritated than annoyed, pressing the keys of the family business firmly into her daughters hands.

'Oh oh oh *mutima wandi*,' her mother had shaken her head. 'If I had only known you would grow up to be like your father. You'll have to work to make up for the money you wasted. God forbid I'm too old to sit here and struggle with you like I did your father!'

She had only planned to manage the family's saloon for two years, but when her mother had her first stroke, it had turned into five. She fought a constant battle between dealing with the problems that came with taking care of their extended family; who held out their hands unashamedly despite her circumstances, taking care of her ailing mother and trying to make sure that the business did not fall around her head due to the lax attitude of the workers employed there.

The second stroke had not spared her mother and the funeral had been bleak. Farusja had wasted no time in packing her life into a small suitcase, wanting to get as far away from Africa, from Zambia, as she possibly could. To join the millions of people that looked for a better life elsewhere; away from the extreme poverty, away from the numerous funerals that now occurred more often than the weddings. It had broken her heart to liquidate her mother's business, but she had figured that it would have gone bankrupt if she had put one of her relatives in charge of it. They had cursed her and ranted at her, and called her a westernised bitch. Her spell in London had stretched to five years, until at the age of 32, Africa called her home.

'Those days we had something to fight for Becca. We had a cause, we had that right. Who knew we would find ourselves smashing buildings and starting fires?'

Rabecca shook her head. 'Did you hear about Gregory? Your Gregory?'

Farusja smiled, the condensation from the glass of orange juice in her hand slowly forming droplets that claimed and smothered her fingers. The education she received at the University of Zambia was a completely different education to the one that she had enrolled for. Despite being registered to study a degree in graphic design, she found herself literally intertwined with a political science student, Gregory Banda. He was an intense young man who, with a full head of thick hair and a beret perched precariously on one side, protested the government's corruption, condemned the countries skilled workers who fled overseas, and shouted for the complete breakdown of the economic system in any way he could. She had found his passion for a cause refreshing, and had been swept away in it, organising peaceful protests and creating petitions to push into parliament. 'What about my Gregory?'

'The idiot was arrested back home. He always talked too much and now he's considered a traitor to the state.'

'I admired his passion,' she sighed. 'There are times I just want to go home Becca, to help our people.'

'*Iwe* you really are crazy,' Rabecca swore frustrated. 'Your home is right here with me. Do you want to inherit your mother's problems?'

'They're the only family I have Becca. Who's going to take care of them?'

'God gave them two hands and two legs – they can take care of themselves! You are still too much of a child to pay for the bills of five other families because that is what will happen! *Mami*, you really should have stayed with the *Muzungu's* up there! But it's settled, you will now stay here with me for a while, until we decide what to do with you next.'

Lunch finally came and went in companionable silence. Rabecca paid for the meal, ignoring Farusja's protests, and quickly drove Farusja back to her block of conjoined townhouses in the Windhoek suburb of Pioneerspark. The houses were all arranged in a grouping of twenty, protected by a wall enclosure. Each house was attached to the next one, and the cluster offered much needed security and the community of people that she craved for. Although Rabecca's neighbours were right next door, the way in which the townhouses had been designed made each exclusively private.

Rabecca unceremoniously threw Farusja out of the car with the house keys. '*Mami*, I am late!' she shrieked. 'And my report, how will I ever finish?'

Farusja shook her head, laughing as she watched Rabecca attempt to speed away in her old Volkswagen beetle.

The call from August finally came at 16h30 that afternoon, informing Farusja that her application had been successful, and that she was expected to report to Mr Jaco Viereen promptly at 08h00 the following morning.

CHAPTER 5

Tuesday, 17 April

Dante drummed the top of his car with his fingertips, irritated. With all the work that needed to be done at HD Advertising and at DI Storage, it seemed he would not be getting any rest this month. He had cancelled dinner last night with Roberta, and instead had headed to DI. He had stopped work just in time to see the early morning sun rise gently off the storage units. He then sped off to HD to answer Roberta's urgent call before his staff had even arrived at work. In quieter days he used to have the luxury to sit and watch as the rays of the sun lit up the empire that was his. But now he was just far too busy. DI Storage was open 24 hours a day, which unfortunately meant that the public thought they answered enquiries 24 hours a day. He had been accosted by an old german-speaking woman on his way out this morning, which had irritated him even further. He did not like doing staff jobs.

'*Guten Morgen!* What is it that you do here young man?' she walked with a spring in her step, and winked at him as she had walked up to the gate, her little yellow Peugeot parked on the curb.

'If you need storage space we have it. Whether you want to store a few household items, industrial equipment or even a small car, we give you the space. You can access your storage container any time you want to.'

'*Ach so.* Is it safe?'

'Ultimately it's at your own risk. But we do have a full security team patrolling the premises and have security cameras all over the park.'

He had left her in a flurry of pamphlets and information brochures. During the years he had been in business, the most action DI had seen was a group of thieves that had tried to break into the business park; security had quickly taken care of them. Housed in the northern industrial area of Windhoek, each storage unit had been built, depending on their size, in fours back to back. The bigger storage areas stood alone like parking garages, and were easily accessible to big cars or trucks. Dante had made a fortune within those walls.

He parked in his allocated parking space at HD and had just exited his car when the receptionist, August, drove up in her little black Toyota Tazz. He had stumbled across her morning routine by accident one morning, and once she realised that he was watching her, she had slowed down the entire show, making sure that each move she made was more pronounced than the previous.

The last time he had seen her routine, her bag had somehow fallen from her shoulders and emptied its contents onto the ground. Dante had watched as she had made a show of picking up every item slowly, her bum wiggling seductively in the air. This morning it was her shoes. He leaned on his car leisurely, a wide smile on his face, watching as her legs stretched out of the car door, barefoot. Her hands and head followed, and the grin on his face widened as she slowly tied a pair of red stiletto heels around her slim ankles, her hands tracing the length of her legs back up to her thighs which were hidden by the car. He sighed wistfully as she completed her show and sashayed into the office, her bum seductively moving in the tiny black skirt. He would have taken her to dinner and dessert a long time ago, but Roberta's jealousy and possessiveness held no bounds, and there had been too many scenes with her to relish any more. Rule number 1, *Kifo*, which meant death in Swahili: *don't play with the staff*. Roberta had attempted to learn Swahili in preparation for a visit to Kenya, but had failed miserably, and funnily enough the only word that stayed with her was one of doom. So she had used it to proclaim anything off limits or dangerous. Of course this rule wasn't applicable to his own staff at Dante International Storage. Although DI's staff component was much smaller, Dante allowed himself a fair amount of fun during and after office hours.

He glanced at his car to make sure it was closed, the smell of his newly upholstered leather seats still pleasant in his nostrils. One of the few Bentley GT Coupe's in Windhoek, it was a car that demanded respect, and he deserved it, he thought smugly.

Farusja looked critically at the building she would be spending the next six months in, and despite the feelings of fear and nervousness welling up inside her, she grudgingly admitted that it looked like a great place to work.

Rabecca had driven them to HD Advertising half an hour early, parking her small beetle in one of the spaces directly in front of the office, and had rushed off to finish her report that was due at eight. On giving Farusja strict instructions on where to go and who to ask for, she had scurried into the building as fast as her stubby legs could carry her.

Farusja exhaled deeply. She opted to sit in the car and stare at the building for a while longer, nervously watching the people walk past her chattering in the cool morning air. She glanced at her watch, knowing that she would be late if she sat outside any longer. She self-consciously checked her appearance mentally; her hair was pulled back tightly, and yes, that old, yet still graceful black three-piece suit that she had worn yesterday for her interview still hugged her snugly. She wished she'd had a chance to buy new clothes, but lack of time coupled with a lack of budget had not allowed this privilege. She had resisted Rabecca's attempts to strong-arm her into any clothing choices and had sent up a silent prayer, grateful that her best friend's clothes were all too big for her.

'You cannot wear the same thing you wore yesterday!' Rabecca had shouted at her in the early hours of that morning, throwing her own clothes around.

'Becca what can I do? I'll change my shirt, or I can wear jeans.'

'Jeans? Jeans? Are you mad?' exclaimed Rabecca, looking as though she might faint at the mere suggestion. 'Why didn't you tell me that you had no suitable clothes yesterday? We could've run during lunch to get you some trousers or a nice skirt!'

'I hardly thought I would be expected to start work the day after my interview. Especially since it was such a bad interview! Aren't they supposed to at least give you a week, or ask you when you can start?'

Rabecca ignored her, riffling through Farusja's cupboard. 'These are all silly summer clothes. They are not professional at all! *Eish mwaiche*, I really hope no one notices!'

'I'll wipe everything down, it will look good as new.'

Rabecca had almost cried, and sat down holding her head heavily in her hands. 'I really hope no one notices, *mami*, and even that is pushing it …'

Farusja now wished she had told her friend about her clothes situation yesterday. She watched as a black Toyota Tazz slid to a stop and parked next to her. It was that secretary, August. Farusja watched out of the corner of her eyes as August touched up her make-up in the mirror, then pulled a pair of red heels out of her bag and, turning to her right, opened the door and gracefully lifted one leg and then the other out of the car. Farusja exhaled slowly. The rest of the employees walking into the building in front of her were also the shine of perfection. Not a woman went past without the matte sheen of make-up lining her face and a crisply ironed shirt, and the men were just as resplendent in shiny suits and multi-coloured ties.

Farusja felt sick to her stomach. She would buy a new suit as soon as she was able to, but at least she had great London shoes. She tapped her feet, glanced at her black stiletto heels and grinned. Her shoes made her feel slightly more confident. She loved her high heels; they made all the difference in her small frame and lengthened her legs. She brought herself back to the present with a start as the door of the Toyota slammed shut next to her.

Farusja exhaled slowly, and grinding her teeth, opened the car door and stepped out, pressing the locking mechanism a bit harder that she normally would. Despite the graceful heels wrapped around her ankles, her feet felt too heavy to lift, the weight on her shoulders growing heavier with every step she took.

Dante was just about to move away from his car when he saw his badly-dressed freshie, as he now silently called her, walk up to stop at the curb ten paces in front of his car and tug nervously at her suit. He had not seen her drive in; she must have come in with Rabecca Mulenga. He remembered her very well.

He loved to personally oversee every interview at HD Advertising. He did it at the annoyance of Roberta and the long suffering HR Manager, Kobus, but he always believed that the mettle of the people they worked with was important. Putting a candidate in a tight formal suit in front of a panel of five judges and watching them attempt to bumble and lie their way through an hour of formal questions was not the style he wanted to promote at HD. The dress code that was enforced was formal, even stylish, but that was part of a cover of a human being. What Dante was mostly interested in was their spirit.

He had asked Kobus to keep her waiting for over an hour to see if she would crack under the pressure, then to give her no interview whatsoever, just a psychological test to see what she was made of.

Kobus had shaken his head at him. 'I'm surprised you even have employees, with what you put these poor people through. You'll damage them forever the way you're treating them. Interviews can be traumatic experiences for the weak.'

Dante had dismissed his words with a wave of his hand. 'If they are weak they shouldn't be working here.'

'Half of the administration at this organisation is weak, Dumeno. Would you have me fire them all?'

'That's because you let Erlichmann oversee their interviews. If I had chosen all our staff, we would be running a great establishment.'

'God forbid you actually let me do my job Dumeno.'

'What are you talking about anyway? All lies. I can remember that you did quite well at your interview.'

'That's because I didn't put up with your shit Dumeno.'

'So let's see how well she can put up with yours,' Dante had grinned at him.

Kobus had come to him with a nodding report. He had been surprised; she looked so small and fragile, but he could see her resolve in the way she kept her composure and did not hesitate to tell him how great she would be for the job. She had not even looked shocked when he had dismissed her with a wave of his hand. Most of the people Kobus had interviewed like that never came back, even when they were offered the job. He had suggested they give her the position and see how she coped within six months – HD Advertising could be a very unforgiving place.

Dante had personally overseen her application because of another reason, her eyes. They had captivated him. When he had caught her on the stairs and her hands had grabbed the lapels of his jacket, she had glanced up at him briefly, the surprise and shock in her eyes was not enough to hide their beauty. They seemed to change with the light, becoming almost luminous. After staring into her eyes for what seemed an eternity he had finally let her go, making a show of checking that she was steady on the stairs; he realised he needed to leave the pool he was staring into before he drowned himself. He had advised Kobus to offer her the job.

The only thing that bothered him was her clothes, which looked years old and like they had seen the inside of a dry cleaner too many times. Had she not been wearing those same clothes yesterday? He shook his head in disdain. *She does have nice shoes though.* He watched her as she stood on the curb, his eyes sliding around the small ribbon that fastened the top of the shoe to her ankles.

Well, I want to see more of her, he shrugged to himself. For a moment all thoughts of Roberta and *Kifo* far from his mind.

He checked again to see that he had locked his car doors and then started strolling over to where Farusja was standing. He caught up to her just as she began to walk into the building; and touched her shoulder, exerting slight pressure which made her stop in mid-stride.

Farusja froze as she felt a hand squeeze her shoulder gently. She whirled around, her eyes flashing, startled as she stared into the dark and amused eyes of the man she had just come to work for.

'Miss Mumba,' he smiled briefly as he greeted her. He felt a chill as her eyes met his and stopped the frown that was beginning to show on his face. *What colour are they?* He was sure they were brown, but yesterday on the stairs he had not been able to tell.

Farusja gazed at him nervously, wondering how he had remembered her name and wishing that she was wearing better clothes. He was impeccably dressed, in a cream suit with a crispy white shirt and a single silver chain lying against his neck. She sighed inwardly, *I look like an old vegetable next to him.*

'Mr Dumeno,' she nodded back, eyeing him, feeling so insecure that she silently dared him to attack her appearance.

Now what? She had nothing to say to this man, an important partner at HD Advertising. She did not want to be here anymore; she had not yet started her new job and she already felt like she had lost a few points. She had thought that at this juncture in her life she would have no need for insecurities. She would be doing what she loved and that money would have ceased to be an issue. But the reality was, as Rebecca had pointed out enough times, that Farusja had to work. She simply did not have enough resources to allow her the privilege of being unemployed any longer.

Farusja wrestled with herself. She was speechless. Not only was she embarrassed about having stumbled into Dante Dumeno's arms yesterday, but now her nerves had gotten the best of her. They stood there, staring at each other.

Dante gazed at his badly-dressed freshie. The tension in her body was so great that he actually felt it sparkle between them. He gave her a dazzling smile. 'Don't you know where to go? Or are you just admiring the building?'

Farusja, her mind now emptied of all thoughts except the truth, stared at the silver chain which lay against the grooves made by the bones in his neck. It shimmered slightly.

'Good morning to you, Mr Dumeno,' she murmured, her knuckles curling tightly around the handles of her bag, remembering too late that they had already exchanged pleasantries.

'Here, let me guide you to the right place,' Dante smirked. He relished the effect he was having on her. He took her elbow and led her through the doors of the building, steering her towards the staircase as he flashed a smile at August.

'August, I am sure you remember Miss Mumba from yesterday? She's working under Jaco. Be nice to her,' Dante grinned at the secretary, not letting Farusja go.

He prodded her to move up the perilous staircase, his hand applying pressure on the small of her back.

Farusja stepped stiffly, trying to stem the angry flush that was warming her face. She wanted to start and move at her own pace, but here she was being prodded and pushed to where she should go, and by no one other than the womanising Dante Dumeno. That woman August would now have a lot more to say! Farusja angrily pursed her lips as she was pushed up the final stair; ripples beginning to graze the surface.

'Hey hey, whoa pretty lady!'

Farusja started, feeling the hand in the small of her back tighten to hold her weight as she tilted back. The boy stood relaxed at the top of the stairs, his stance and manner nonchalant. He nestled two large books in his hands which he held up to his chest. He was dressed in jeans and a polo shirt, and on top of his head perched cockily to one side was a black cap with a gold letter 'R' adorning the front. White sneakers peaked out from the bottom of his blue, low slung jeans. He could not have been much more than twenty, and had the most devious smile she had ever seen. She liked him immediately.

'Whoa there pretty lady,' he repeated as he grinned at her, his white teeth flashing. 'You look angry as hell, tripping up these stairs like an ice queen, almost throwing the brother down the stairs. Is this your first day? You'll be alright though, you're very pretty. D there behind you, he likes them pretty.'

Farusja stared at him, her mouth opening slightly. She shut it abruptly. *Who was this boy?* She could feel Dante's displeasure behind her as they both reached the top stair and she watched as his hands motioned angrily at the boy.

'What have I told you, again and again, and yet you don't listen?'

'Just telling these ladies the truth, bra,' the boy shrugged. 'They deserve fair warning.'

The three of them were standing at the top of the staircase and were in plain view of the open cubicles and the boardroom on the top floor. Farusja moved discreetly to the side so that she was not standing between them, and gasped in surprise. They both had the same intense dark eyes, which were now clashing with each other silently, and the same stubborn set to their mouths which held no room for concessions. *Are they brothers?* Her exclamation came out more loudly than she intended and both sets of dark eyes swivelled to stare at her.

She cleared her throat awkwardly. 'Something stuck in my throat.'

'Take the lady to Jaco. Or help her out on his behalf, the way you're in everyone's business you should be able to manage it,' Dante said gruffly.

'You need to learn to relax man, it's only eight. You want to make a lady work on her first day?' Jerome laughed out loud, as he extended his arm to Farusja, motioning her to take it. 'Let's go, pretty lady.'

Farusja casually placed her hand on his forearm, making a point not to look at Dante. She could sense rather than see his dark eyes still staring at her.

'She's in good hands. What you worried about?' Jerome placed his other hand over hers and tugged at her to move.

'Good day to you, Miss Mumba,' Dante sighed noisily.

'And do me a favour, Miss Mumba. We pride ourselves on the great image we present to our clients. Try to look presentable next time I see you.'

Dante locked eyes with her before he turned on his heel and walked away from them towards the boardroom.

Farusja watched him and felt her face burn first in embarrassment and then in anger. She screamed silently at his receding back but managed to calmly turn to Jerome. He had an apologetic look on his face and was rubbing her hand vigorously.

'My brother. He can be damn unsympathetic some times,' he said quietly to her. 'Don't mind him. Just used to a certain way you know? Doesn't let anyone tell him what's what.'

'He's your brother?' Farusja asked. 'And you work here, with him?'

'Yeah, pretty lady,' Jerome grinned at her. 'I am the grunt around here, doing everything for everybody. You'd think being the boss' brother would command me my respect. Anyways, let's take you to your new home.'

Dante strode across to the doors of the boardroom; frowning when he saw it empty. Roberta had called him for an early morning meeting and when he came late he never heard the last of it. He moved away from the door and strode to her office. He nodded briefly to the choruses of 'good mornings' that met him, and pushed open her door. It smelt of freshly brewed coffee and freshly baked bread. Roberta was waiting for him with a teasing smile on her bright red lips.

Dante looked at the mahogany desk which housed the bare minimum of resources. All that covered the desk was a set of black telephones, a stationery holder, two laptops, and this morning, Roberta Erlichmann. She was leaning against her desk, the cup in her hand trembling slightly with anticipation. She looked up at him and smiled a seductive smile that stretched across her face with hidden meaning. Nothing Roberta did was by coincidence. She was wearing his favourite today. A red tube dress that settled just below her knees, and hugged every inch of her body. Her bare shoulders were covered in a matching red shrug, and her red stiletto shoes gleamed dully in the sunlight coming from the double glass windows.

Without turning around, Dante used his foot to gently close the door behind him. They heard the satisfying click as the door locked. He went to stand in front of her, close enough so that the tips of her knees brushed his thighs. He took his car keys out of his pocket, and leaned around her to place them on the table.

He gazed at her, keeping his stance in front of her. 'Nice dress.'

'I knew you would like it. It has your name written all over it,' the smile spread itself slowly over her face, 'and under it.'

Dante leaned forward and brushed his lips against her neck.

Roberta's left hand covered his and drew it up to the top of her ribs, just below her left breast. 'I ordered breakfast but it took so long to arrive and then when it did it was horrible,' Roberta squeezed his fingers lightly. 'So I ordered you.'

Dante shook his head, tightening his grip on her. He was glad that her office did not have glass walls. 'I am a busy man Erlichmann. Maybe I don't have time for this.'

Roberta smiled her lazy smile, and curved her free right hand around his neck. 'I heard from Kobus that the new girl is a pretty little thing. Was that your doing?'

Dante smiled. 'Jealous already, Robbie?'

Roberta pulled his head towards hers, her lips centimetres from his. 'I have no reason to be jealous of anybody. As I've always said, play all you like but don't play with my staff.'

'*Kifo*,' breathed Dante. He increased the pressure of his hand on her, staring at the ruby red of her lips. Placing his hands on the outside of her thighs, he caressed the thick material, slowly raising it higher.

'Is this what you want? Right here, in the office?' he asked gruffly as he, in one move, wrapped his arms around her chest and lifted her off the table, setting her down on the floor gently, feet first.

Dante's dark eyes stared into her green ones as he grasped the hem on the bottom of her dress, pulling and folding it up over her stomach and over her head, revealing a red lace brassiere and matching panties. He reached behind her, pulling a pair of scissors from the stationary holder on the table.

'Oh Dante, they're new,' Roberta mewed softly as he reached down and cut her panties off on both sides of her hips, doing the same with her brassiere.

Dante lowered his lips to hers, whispering at the side of her mouth. 'I think it's about time we consummated our relationship.'

'How many more times do we have to consummate things, Dumeno?'

'How many more times do you want to?' Dante shrugged his jacket off, his tie, shirt and trousers adding to the crumpled pile of forgotten clothes on the floor. He wrapped his arms around her, crushing his naked body against hers.

'As many times as it takes Dante,' she sighed pleasurably as he kissed the side of her neck. 'As many times as it takes.'

CHAPTER 6

$\mathcal{F}$arusja stared around as Jerome gave her a brief tour. The workspace was open plan, with the exception of three offices and the boardroom; the employees were arranged in cubicles. She knew that Rabecca and other administrative staff shared the offices downstairs, but this had been a blur yesterday when she had come for her interview.

Jerome's words became more dramatic and with every new area he took her to his hands took on more flair. He was almost a carbon copy of his brother; but lacked the seriousness and arrogance that Dante carried. Instead Jerome had a lazy, playful air. He moved seemingly without a care in the world. He counteracted the atmosphere in the office, and Farusja decided that she would spend as much time as she could around the happy vibe that surrounded Jerome.

They came to a stop in front of one of the three offices that were cordoned off.

'This is yours,' he winked. 'As you can see there is not much office space at HD, so you get to rub heads with the Creative Director.'

'I'm not sure whether I should be scared or not,' Farusja murmured, smiling faintly.

'Oh no,' Jerome laughed out loud as he pushed open the door. 'I am sure you will find Jaco very interesting.'

'*Hei*, you must be my new follower!' a voice boomed out at her as Jerome pushed open the door.

Farusja jumped, knocking her shoulder on the half-open door and dropping her handbag. Picking it up hurriedly, she straightened herself and lifted her eyes to look at who she assumed was the Creative Director. She felt relaxed around him immediately, he reminded her of the gigantic brown teddy bear she'd had when she was twelve.

He did not look a day over thirty, but was well-rounded and his face and head were drowned in a fully grown beard and head of hair. He was dressed casually in blue jeans and a brown shirt that stretched over his immense gut, straining at the seams, and she could not help but raise an eyebrow at his casual attire. He looked as though he would be more suited to working outdoors than in an office. Especially this image-conscious office.

She exhaled as she looked around the small space that she was to share with the bear in front her. There were two tables, two chairs and two computers. The rest of the office was covered in stacks of paper, which littered the floor and windowsills. One of the tables was angled to face the door, while the other sat against the opposite wall. The table facing the door was bare, and the other was a collision of designs, brochures, memos, various fast-food wrappers, more stacks of papers and a number of coffee mugs. The smell of tobacco in the room was faint. The highlight of the room was a huge ugly fish mounted on the back wall of the office above the table away from the door. Its mouth was open in what she considered a grimace, the death throes of an animal deprived of air. The teeth were tiny and sharp, and she had a feeling that the fish looked more menacing in death than it had in life.

'Come in, Come in! Jaco Viereen. Just call me Jaco, everyone around here does.'

He stood up, gingerly skirting around the papers on the floor, and held a big hand out to her. She expected it to be warm, even soft, the hand of a pencil pusher, a man who had never done a day's work in his life; so she was not prepared for the rough calluses and blisters that scratched lines in her own hand.

'Don't be fooled by his nice guy act, pretty lady,' Jerome shook his head. 'I'll leave you to it.' He winked at Farusja, then turned on his heel and went back into the depths of the building.

Jaco released her hand and gave her a crooked smile. 'How are things so far? *Miskien moet ons vir jou induction gee ... ag fok, ek het geen tyd nie!*'

Jaco frowned at her contemplatively, his mind momentarily elsewhere.

Farusja looked at him wide-eyed. 'Huh? Excuse me?'

Jaco stared back at her, shaking his head absently. '*Jy praat nie Afrikaans nie*? You don't speak Afrikaans, *eesh* try to learn some of the languages, it will make things easier.'

Farusja stood her ground. 'I've only been in the country two weeks.'

Jaco laughed heartily as he laid his hand on her shoulder. Farusja swallowed and had a moment of panic because his hand enveloped her entire shoulder.

'Your name is Farusja, can I call you that?' he asked and continued without waiting for her response. 'Whatever preconceptions you had about coming to work here, you need to *gooi* them out of the window now. *Jy moet gooi*! You're going to work your hours. It's going to be a usual eight to five job, but man, mind the language. *Fok.*'

He peered down at her, his blue gaze piercing her own. 'Some things might shock you!'

Farusja looked back up at him giving him a smile. 'Enough has already! Is that your fish?'

'She's a beauty eh? She's my angel fish. My *boeti* and I caught her last year.'

Farusja stared at the fish, already making plans to get it off the wall.

Jaco lifted his hand from her shoulder. 'Now, most people on their first day just catch a tan. But you my friend, will not be able to go into the sun.'

Farusja stood there staring at him, straining to understand what he had just said to her. *Nothing follows procedure in this place*, she thought, *if it's not one of the partners, it's this*. As soon as she got a moment to herself, she was going to sms Rebecca and find out what she had gotten herself into.

Jaco turned back and rummaged through the pile of papers on his desk, muttering quietly to himself. When he was unsuccessful, he started searching through the piles on the floor. He finally exclaimed in delight and pulled several files from the stack to the right of his paper-covered desk, brandishing them like a sword.

'Ag, Farusja, you really should learn some Afrikaans,' he pushed the files into her hands. 'Expressing myself in English. *Eish* man.'

'You should learn my language too,' Farusja smiled brightly.

Jaco looked at her, his eyes widening in surprise. '*Fok* man, I'll be careful of you!'

Farusja shrugged. 'I'm hoping the empty desk is mine?'

'*Ya*, have a seat. Let me brief you quickly.'

Farusja sat behind her desk, and Jaco pulled his chair in front of it, taking the files back from her and placing them on her desk in front of them.

'I'm not sure how much they have told you?' he began.

'Absolutely nothing,' answered Farusja.

'Ok, well we are currently busy with a major, major AIDs tender thingy. We did the presentation to the client yesterday, and should have an answer *gou gou*. Now, what this means for you is that we've all been working flat-out on preparing the presentation, and we've all but chopped our other client's campaigns.'

'So,' he dramatically indicated to the files in front of them, 'you start with a fun game I like to call Catch-Up.'

He opened the first file. Farusja quickly read the label on it *Visser Car Hire*.

'This is a new car hire company, we need to design a logo. I correct – *You* need to design a logo. In this file, as you can see, are logo's of their opposition. This here,' he pointed, 'is the ugly thingy that they've been using to date. Feel free to design in whatever programme you are comfortable with – we've got Photoshop, In-design and Illustrator on your machine. As long we can easily convert the successful logo to a vector. Don't want no raster logo – obviously. *Dit sal nie werk nie.*'

"Seems fairly straight forward,' said Farusja, taking the file and flipping through it. 'When's the deadline?'

'Yesterday,' smiled Jaco.

'I see you favour PC's,' said Farusja, looking at the machine on her desk.

'*Ya*, problem is there's no mac support in this country. If a mac has a problem, it needs to be sent to Cape Town.'

'No issue,' Farusja was confident. 'Haven't worked on a PC for years, but it should all come back to me.'

'*Eish*, great! I've got a meeting with Roberta now about the whole AIDs *ding* – it's taking up so much of my *foking* time. Settle in, get started. I'll be back in an hour or so to see your ideas, and then we can start on the next project.'

He stood to leave, and then turned, looking at her in sympathy. 'By the way, the aircon *is gebreek*, it's broken – they are coming today to fix it – so just bear with the heat.'

Farusja smiled as his receding back left their office, and ignoring *Visser Car Hire*, took another minute to survey her surroundings speculatively, wondering how she could get the office a bit more organised and infuse some of her own personality into the space.

Her desk was a rectangle, big enough to house the PC and to allow her adequate work space. She could see the years of use on it, but it was sturdy all the same. The carpet looked like it had originally been a deep maroon, but had now faded to a light shade of brown. The walls were brightly white-washed, and a small cupboard sat next to Jaco's desk, nestled delicately among the stacks of paper around it. She swivelled herself back to face the door; she would have to rearrange the furniture in this office soon, she hated directly facing the door, it spoiled the flow of energy in the room.

She leaned forward and turned on the PC, releasing a deep breath. The cleaning and re-organisation of the office, especially the removal of that ugly fish, would have to wait.

Jaco was right about the heat. It wasn't even nine in the morning, and she was already feeling sweaty. She unbuttoned her jacket, revealing the tiny black spaghetti stringed top. She knew that she would not have any unsolicited visits from anyone in the next hour. She chuckled as she thought of Mr Dumeno seeing her now. The spaghetti top was just as old, and even more worn, than her suit.

She laughed loudly, tossing the jacket behind her onto the backrest of the chair. She swivelled around on her chair gleefully a few times. Now, onto *Visser Car Hire*. She had just looked down to the file again, when a voice startled her.

'Looks like you're having fun.'

Farusja stopped abruptly, her heart thudding uncomfortably to the floor as she recognised the owner of the voice. She guiltily straightened herself up in the chair, looking up to face the door. She flung her head back self-consciously and made her movements deliberate and slow. Dante, Mr Dumeno, was lounging in the doorway, regarding her with what looked like amusement.

'Mr Dumeno,' she smiled warily back at him. She had not even spent ten minutes in her new office. *Why is he here? Did he see me swinging about like a ten year old?*

She was so embarrassed and cringed inwardly. Today was obviously not going to be her day. Farusja clenched her teeth, forcing her embarrassment away and compelling her eyes to travel up the length of his chest and settle on his face. Him in his bloody beautiful Lauren suit. *Is he here to give me more grief about mine?* She began to stand up, sitting back down rigidly when he waved a hand at her to keep her seat. She watched as he looked around the room speculatively and sauntered in. He stood at the edge of her desk and gazed down on her.

What is he doing? Does he get this familiar with all his new recruits? Is this a test? His cologne wafted around her and filled the room, there was something else too, something musky, he smelt of ... Farusja shook her head slightly and dragged her gaze from him, looking down at the faint coffee stains on the table, ignoring the creamy suit that was advancing.

'Where is Jaco? I've been looking for him everywhere and he refuses to pick up his phone.'

'He said he was going to a meeting – with Roberta, I think,' Farusja replied. 'Do you want to leave him a message?'

Dante made a sound between exasperation and frustration. 'No, you'll have to help me instead. I'm looking for the pdf of a job we did last month for the Hospitality Corporation. It should be on the server. You'll be able to access it from your machine.'

Farusja made no move to comply with his wishes.

'Well?' he asked, eyebrows raised.

Farusja stared at him, then looked at the PC reclining in front of her. 'I'm waiting for the computer to turn itself on, Mr Dumeno.'

'What, all by itself?'

Farusja bit her lip. This day was getting better and better. She would have to bring a camera to work to immortalise some of these moments.

Dante sighed inwardly and walked to stand behind Farusja. The PC was now on, the delightful standard blue windows background staring at them.

'Ok, just go into windows explorer,' he instructed.

Farusja panicked quietly. *Windows explorer. Where the hell do I find that? All these years on macs!* She searched the desktop items in vain.

'It's not that complicated, just push Windows-E,' Dante was impatient. The day was promising to be busy and despite Roberta's naughty red underwear earlier, he was feeling incredibly restless. But he did not want to be the boss took out his frustration on staff, especially this particularly interesting one, so he willed himself to slow down and relax.

'I'm used to macs,' Farusja mumbled, her eyes racing around the keyboard looking for the keys. 'I need some time, Mr Dumeno.'

'Farusja Mumba *that* I don't have. Give me some space,' he leaned over her, and showed her the short-cut keys. Windows Explorer opened up, and he motioned to files he wanted copied. He dug into the pockets of his suit, hauling out a memory stick and handing it to her. She plugged it into the front of her hard-drive, praying that he could not see her shaking hands. His breath on her neck felt warm and made her tingle in the strangest places.

She gratefully handed him the stick when the copy was complete, and he moved around the desk to stand in front of her again.

'Thank you. I hope all is in your comfort, Miss Mumba?' he said quietly, his eyes fixed on hers.

Farusja looked up at him and nodded, vainly trying to read the expression on his face, and wishing she had not taken off her jacket, knowing very well that the top she was wearing was sizes too small for her, but to pull her jacket over the exposed crests of her breasts would be an act of defensive insecurity.

'You need new clothes. Not only do these not sit well on you, but they are so old,' he looked down at her, dragging out his last words, his eyes examining her critically. 'Image is everything here. It's part of what runs my business, if you hadn't noticed.'

Farusja's eyes flashed and she stood up abruptly, her eyes now level with his.

'Point taken, sir,' she smiled at him coolly. 'I gathered as much from this morning's conversation. No disrespect intended, sir, but from what I have experienced this organisation does not follow the general rules that every other company does. So I would like to say that I understand that the focus is on my image, rather than on the quality of my work, or any of my achievements.' She paused, her smile growing wider. 'I'll do all I can to help out this great company.'

Dante kept his expression neutral, and lifted an eyebrow at the minx being revealed in front of him. His eyes traced the outline of her cheeks, the outline of her lips. They seemed more full and rounded, slightly pink and seeming to form a permanent pout. The shirt she was wearing looked like it belonged to a twelve-year old, another old creation. *Does this woman have no new clothes?*

Dante flicked his gaze downward to the skin exposed under her neck and ever so subtly flicked his eyes back up to her face again, a slow smile beginning to tug at the corners of his mouth. Her small perky breasts not enclosed in a bra, were pushing against the lycra fabric and he felt a slow throbbing begin in his nether regions as he saw her nipples take shape and strain against their covering. He knew why *Kifo* was in place. Playing with staff was tantamount to leading to issues of sexual harassment. Although the effects of that paled in comparison to Roberta's jealousy and outbursts. But things were different with this one. He couldn't help himself. He wanted those strange eyes of hers to watch him as he sucked on her. What a challenge she would be. He did not have many challenges these days. Most of the women he met were just so predictable.

'Here is some money,' he said, taking his wallet out of his pocket and removing several N$200 bills. He leant down, not taking his gaze off her, and put the money on the table. 'Take the afternoon off and go buy yourself some clothes. I expect to see a change in your attire by tomorrow.'

Farusja watched with mouth open as the devil, dressed in cream, in one fluid movement exited her office, leaving a faintly electric air behind. She moved slowly, her limbs feeling heavy, her mind numb.

What just happened? Farusja was bewildered. She moved around her table and stopped as she reached the door, standing on the threshold and peering out; wanting to make sure that he was gone. She shook her head slightly and closed the door halfway, holding the door jamb in her hand. What type of company had Rabecca introduced her to? What was that all about? Farusja shook her head harder and returned to her desk, putting on her jacket. Oh *mami*, she sighed to herself, drama seemed to follow her everywhere she went, and she was barely an hour into her first day. She stared at the bills lying so casually on her table, trying not to think of the numerous things that were wrong with what she was doing and reached out, collecting them in one hand. She did need new clothes, they would just have to take the money out of her first paycheque.

Dante's lips curved faintly in a smile as he strode back towards his office. He had liked what had happened seconds ago, he had liked it very much. His phone rang, and he stopped dead in his tracks, frowning, staring at the number flashing on the screen. It was Roberta, again.

'What do you need Robbie, more dessert?'

'Come to my office, now,' was all Roberta Erlichmann said, but the way she said it raised the hair on the back of his neck.

As he entered the room, goosebumps raised themselves along the length of both his arms. She was standing rigidly against the side of her desk, the chair that was in front of her had been awkwardly cast askew. The tips of her fingers rested lightly on a newspaper on the table.

'Have you read the paper today? It just came in,' she looked at him anxiously. 'And there's a detective waiting for you downstairs.'

Dante opened his mouth to reply and then stopped. The words frozen on his lips. He glanced at the newspaper lying on the table in front her.

'She was one of yours,' Roberta breathed out noisily. 'What the hell is going on?'

Dante felt cold as he moved towards her, staring down at the newspaper. He snatched it up, the headlines blurring as he skimmed through the story.

'Ask August to find out who it is,' Dante said quietly. 'Ask her to call Hienry to find out were the hell he is. He was supposed to call me earlier. And get August to send the detective to the boardroom now.'

'Do you think this is what Naks was warning us about yesterday? The rumours he'd heard?' Roberta asked anxiously, her voice bordering on shrill. 'What're we going to do?'

'We didn't do anything wrong, Robbie.'

Dante chose to ignore the look of anxiety on her face as he picked up the newspaper, turned and walked out of her office. His eyes scanned the article again as he made his way to the boardroom. A woman had been strangled in the early hours of Sunday morning. Her shoes and clothes indicated that she had been out partying, dancing or fishing at the numerous watering holes that littered the city. She had not been identified yet, but police had found an electronic key-card in her purse that belonged to DI Storage. Whether or not the suspect worked at the company was still being investigated. Dante frowned as he sank into a seat at the table. He did not have a large staff component. DI employed a total of ten people, five of those were security guards, of the remaining five, only four were female. That meant the murdered woman was either his secretary, finance officer, marketing officer or cleaner. It made him sick to his stomach. He'd left DI this morning before his day staff had arrived, so he didn't even know who was missing.

His emotions were in turmoil. He could not believe the story. Someone had killed one of his girls. He scowled as he tossed the paper aside, his thoughts whirling sluggishly. He hoped it was not one of the girls he had known intimately. He needed to get Hienry on this, but first he had to deal with the detective.

He had just pulled his phone out of his pocket intending to call Hienry, when the door opened, admitting a smiling man. He was tall and dark, almost swarthy, and he sauntered into the boardroom with the calm, self-possessed air of a man used to being in authority. A visibly deceptive twinkle in his eye, and the wide-toothed smile of a hunter.

'Miles Mkazi,' he intoned, the smile never leaving his face. 'Detective Miles Mkazi.'

'I got your name the first time, Miles,' Dante said wryly as he stood to shake hands with the policeman, examining the identification that was thrust in front of him. 'Are you not supposed to be sitting behind a desk drinking tea, delegating and signing documents? Since when did detectives make house calls?' Dante motioned towards the chair at the end of the table, waiting for the detective to sit before he took on the seat opposite him.

'Unfortunately, the police force has now become an institution of the standing that if you want something done properly, you have to do it yourself. I don't trust my subordinates not to be swayed by your position long enough to be objective.' The detective drew back his badge abruptly, placing it in his trouser pocket with a fluid smile.

'No one in your department is on my payroll, detective,' Dante beamed at him, but his eyes were hard. 'I cannot help the fact that most of your higher ranking inspectors enjoy a good party.'

'No, that can't be helped I'm afraid,' Miles paused. 'I guess you know why I'm here?'

Dante glanced at him. 'Would you like something to drink? Water, juice?'

'I think we've more important things to discuss than to sit around having drinks.'

Dante shrugged. He headed for the refrigerator in the left end corner of the room and took a bottle of water out of it.

'In your line of work I thought drinking all sorts of things would be an entry requirement.'

The detective laughed. It might have been a cheery sound if there had not been such an edge to it. 'I think we've had enough of the pleasantries. I'm assuming you already know the news?'

Dante nodded, opening the bottle of water as he sat back in his chair. 'Yes I saw it in the paper this morning. Who was it? The article didn't say.'

Miles pulled a small black notebook out of his pocket, a black ballpoint pen following it. Despite being on duty, he was wearing plain clothes. His black dress shirt was carefully pressed and ironed, the top button closed. His black trousers followed the same stead, their pleats thrown in crisp relief by the way the iron had cautiously pressed against them.

'Her name was Frieda Lyme, twenty-five years old, no children, single. But,' Miles raised his eyes sharply, shooting a look at Dante, 'you already know this.'

Dante went cold. Frieda had been his secretary for the last two years. How could she go off and get herself murdered? Dante returned Miles' gaze steadily, his eyes locking with the policeman's.

'Actually I didn't know. I'd have saved you the trouble of coming into my office if you'd contacted me first.'

'When she didn't arrive at work this morning, did you bother to find out where she was?'

'Our hours at DI are flexible, if someone needs to come in late, we work around it,' Dante said pleasantly. 'We'd assumed she was still coming in.'

Miles looked at him speculatively, and glanced at his watch. 'Hmmm, it's ten o'clock now. Two hours late is acceptable?'

Dante clenched his teeth. 'Well, now that we've established she's dead, she won't be coming in again, will she?'

'What was she? Your personal secretary?' Miles asked blithely. 'I heard that you make it a habit to know your female staff intimately.'

The detective leaned back in the black recliner, making a steeple out of his hands, looking thoughtful. 'Your reputation with the ladies precedes you. In fact, who knows what might happen to a lady who refuses your generosity?'

Dante kept the expression on his face pleasant, but his eyes were hard. 'Do you have something you want to say, detective?'

Miles Mkazi smiled again, the curve of his mouth widening. 'Let's get one thing clear, Mr Dumeno, I'm not one of your many friends at the police station.'

'Yes, I noticed,' Dante was blunt as he lifted the water bottle to his lips. 'I'll send you an invitation to the company's next dinner party. Don't come here with floating accusations Detective … Miles,' Dante paused, adding his name as an afterthought, 'instead of chasing real criminals.'

'I think you have me confused with someone else, Mr Dumeno.'

Dante leaned back in his chair. 'Before we carry on sniffing each others shit, tell me what happened to Frieda.'

Miles released the steeple he had made out of his fingers and sighed theatrically. 'There were signs of a struggle, which were not very effective due to the amount of alcohol in her system. She was strangled early Sunday morning, rather violently.' Miles shifted in his seat. 'We found her in the bushes a few metres from the club she was at, Magix. Did you know Frieda intimately?'

Miles leaned forward, staring at Dante.

Dante shook his head, reigning in his desire to smash his fist into the detectives sneering face. 'I did not, detective.'

'If you cannot recall, maybe a picture will remind you,' Miles rapidly reached into his pocket and before Dante could react had placed a close-up of Frieda's dead face in his vision. Dante felt revulsion well-up inside him.

'She tried to fight. It's amazing how self-preservation instincts kick in when we feel threatened. Those scratches on her face and neck, do you see them? She was trying to remove his hands from her neck. He had them very deep in too, see those tiny disc shaped bruises? His fingertips.'

Dante, stilled, dragged his eyes away from the death in front of him. His hands trembling slightly in spite of himself.

'She was my secretary and I was not intimate with her,' he said quietly, lifting the bottle to his lips and downing the rest of the water. 'This has sounded like an interrogation from the beginning, detective. Charge me with something or stop wasting my time.'

'We have to cover all of our bases, Mr Dumeno,' Miles said. 'We even have to look into our friends from time to time.'

Dante smiled back as pleasantly as he could manage. 'Is there anything else?'

'We'll let you know when there is,' Miles stated as he rose from his seat.

Dante ignored the barbed wire in the detectives tone, and stood with him. 'I look forward to being of assistance.'

'Yes,' Miles said dryly. 'I'm sure you do.'

Dante smiled until the detectives receding back was blocked by the closing door of the boardroom, his smile descending immediately into a deep scowl. He raised his eyes angrily as the door was pushed forwards moments later.

Roberta hurried in, a worried look on her face. 'What did he…?'

'Did Hienry call you?' Dante interrupted her sharply, collapsing back into the black seat directly beneath him.

Roberta shook her head. 'Didn't you notice Frieda missing when you went in to work this morning? Prior warning of this impending disaster would have been nice!'

'I was here before 8 this morning. Need I remind you that you summoned me for your breakfast?'

Roberta blushed, realising that she was to blame in their late warning.

'Did August find anything?' Dante asked. 'Did she have problems at home? Did she have money problems? Was she a prostitute? Did she take drugs?'

Roberta sighed loudly. 'This is not your problem Dante. She was just your secretary – people die every day.'

'But they do not die at my bloody company!' he scowled as he pushed himself up off the seat and reached out to grab the folder she was carrying. He flipped through it, tossing it on the seat across from him. 'Is this all the information August could give you?'

Roberta glared at him. 'Yes, that's everything. What did the detective want?'

'He accused me of killing her. What the hell do you think he wanted?'

'And I am sure you handled it, right?' she retorted, as she walked around to the seat in front of him, picking up the folder he had thrown. 'I need not remind you what we both have at stake here, this has to go back to human resources. Why on earth we have files of your employees at HD, I have no idea!'

'Did you call Hienry?' Dante interrupted her again, impatient.

'Hienry this, Hienry that. You call that bulldog of a bodyguard of yours if you like. What a joke, you think you're so important. A fucking African man with a fucking French bodyguard! But I'll be damned if you let all our hard work go to waste because you fucked your damn secretary!'

Dante smirked at her, crossing his arms. 'You're just filled with compassion aren't you, Roberta? While you are feeling such great concern, would you ask August to call her family and offer condolences. Send flowers. I want a condolence advert in every newspaper by tomorrow morning, and tell the family we'll pay for the memorial service.'

Roberta Erlichmann was tense. She picked angrily at the olives on her plate, opting to have an early dinner alone at Oshizizi, fuming quietly. She needed to think, and she did not need one of her chattering friends fogging her brain. She knew she should feel nothing but elated, but she didn't. Everything with the tender had gone as planned yesterday, and she had it on good authority that the job was practically in-the-bag. But somehow she just could not shake the uneasiness that came with the murder of Frieda.

From the conversation Dante had with Miles, it seemed as though Dante was the only suspect. This would make life very, very difficult for them both. The situation was going to turn into an ugly, stinking mess, she could feel it and she could smell it. She scowled, picking again at the olives on the plate in front of her angrily.

Any bad publicity for DI Storage meant bad publicity for HD Advertising – her and Dante were so entwined. With all the struggles she had to contend with in establishing her business and getting her life on track, one dead girl was the last thing she needed. What really made her angry was the fact that Dante had been sleeping with Frieda. At first she hadn't been jealous of the tall girl with the arrogant airs. But when Frieda had started waltzing in and out of both businesses and Dante's home, Roberta had told Dante to put a stop to it. He had laughed at her, telling her not to worry, but had finally ended the relationship when he had found Frieda sitting behind his desk at DI Storage. For some reason he had still kept her on as his secretary. Roberta did not know whether it was something to be admired that all Dante's ex-floozies adored him even more after he ended things with them, and Frieda had been no exception.

It was only a matter of time before this side of the story broke publically, and then that smug detective will be dripping down their backs like a bad sweat. And although Dante appeared unfazed, even he couldn't be so arrogant to believe that he had all of the police force sleeping in his pocket.

She almost jumped out of her skin when her phone rang, startling the waitress that had been clearing away her dirty dishes. She stared at the caller identification tag. It was her mother, again.

'And then *Meme*?' she asked quietly as she picked up the call.

'Roberta? Where are you? Your father is back in town,' her mother sounded exasperated.

'I'm busy,' replied Roberta smoothly.

'What are you talking about, its 8 o'clock at night! Aren't you at home? What are you doing out so late?'

Roberta rolled her eyes. 'Actually, we're quite busy at the office. Tell Heinz if he wants to see me, he can call August and make an appointment.'

'He's your father! Why do you insist on calling him by his first name? What have I said to you? An appointment? For your father? *Aweh*!'

Roberta sighed in exasperation. She did not want to fight with her mother over this again. She had spent a good part of her childhood doing just that. When she was younger, she had never understood why she did not have a father like the other girls and why she had looked so different – why her hair was blond and brown and curly and long, and why her skin was the colour of chocolate milk. Her mother had not explained anything to her until she was almost fifteen years old, and by that time her self esteem had taken such a hit that she still struggled with who she was. She felt no attachment to her German father. When he came down to Namibia to top up their bank accounts and view his property, he always attempted to spend time with his bastard African daughter. She had grown older and less receptive to him as time had gone by, and soon she had only begun to demand the monthly maintenance cheques and had quietly released him of all his other fatherly duties by simply not being available at the right time. Her father had not resisted and the money had kept coming in. Eventually her father had been reduced to nothing but a series of numbers in her bank account. It suited her just fine.

CHAPTER 7

Friday, 27 April

Michael Katjihingua vomited loudly into his sink, his chest heaving as a mess of chicken and chips from today's lunch spewed from his mouth. He wiped his mouth slowly, his eyes bleary as he stumbled against the sink, a beer bottle in one hand and his body feeling as light as a feather. He had started drinking this evening when he had knocked off work; it had all been in preparation for the celebration party at the country club tonight.

What started as one drink to take the edge off, had turned into four and on top of that he had added a few lines of his magic dust. He had been moving so fast for the last while that everything was still a blur. The food he had eaten must have been bad, because in all his years of taking a few lines or drinking, he had never vomited. That was for amateurs; and he was a veteran. He put the bottle to his lips, sloshing the beer around his mouth to get rid of the sour taste of his vomit and, not wanting to waste good beer, he let it trickle down his throat. He knew he had to keep the high going, he did not want to cause a spectacle at the launch party tonight by coming down; and besides, he did not like the feeling. He lurched away from the sink, smiling as he thought of the girl he was going to bed tonight. He had met her at work the other day. A soft doe-eyed curvy little thing. Michael's face contorted as he ran back to the sink, his stomach heaving again. The lasts bits of his lunch trailed from his lips. He had less than an hour to get ready for tonight. He had to pull himself together quickly. He needed more beer.

He looked around, disgusted. Everyone was dressed up in their finest clothes. The women had painted their faces, all those bright colours made them look like parrots, and they did not stop talking. He ground his teeth restlessly. He was angry at this elaborate display of excess. He needed to cut these people down to size and remind them of how expendable they really were, how naïve. It was easy to get into their lives and destroy them. Just as his life had been destroyed. The women revolted him, all those tight dresses that showed off every part of their bodies; he could see everything, the curve of their hips, the shape of their bosoms – it left nothing to the imagination. Some even had the indecency to go around bare-shouldered. The men were just as bad, indecent in body and mind, chasing after these mindless and promiscuous women like it was the only thing they lived for. He breathed deeply. He had to act soon. He could feel the shake starting in his fingers again. Once the shakes began he had very little time left to do things right and the glow of joy that had surrounded him after Frieda was starting to fade. He had to free his next one from this life of excess tonight.

Farusja smoothed her dress over her thighs, exhaling quietly. She laughed self-consciously, an ecstatic smile creeping onto her face, sobering up suddenly as she remembered the social event of the evening. The party was in celebration of wining the AIDs tender. Last week the newspapers announced that HD Advertising had been awarded the initial five-year contract.

The past two weeks at HD had gone smoothly for her. She had bought sufficient smart clothes to keep her corporate image-enforcers happy, she had worked on fun and inspiring projects with Jaco; even Roberta Erlichmann had nodded at her in approval once. Farusja was beginning to feel that HD wasn't really such a bad place to be working at.

Except for Dante. Despite her improved wardrobe, Dante always seemed to be around. He frequently bumped into her in the passages, or came into her office demanding her to copy silly files, or print-out ridiculous memos as though she was his secretary. But he was her boss, so she had no choice but to grin and bear it.

She sneered at her reflection in the mirror. Just thinking of him made her blood boil. *The man sees us whenever he wishes, pushing his way into our offices unannounced hoping his arrogance makes a lasting impression in our lives.* She sighed in exasperation; it hadn't taken her long to realise that most of the women employed at HD Advertising were beautiful, sexy and talented, whether they were 25 or 49. It seemed that he had personally been in charge of their recruitment. She snorted. She would not be another trophy for Dante, that was for sure.

'Are you ready *mami*?' Rabecca said as she came up into Farusja's room. With all the company events and dinners that HD Advertising had over the years, Rabecca made a habit of buying a few new dresses every month, and tonight her wide frame was clothed in a black off-the-shoulder ensemble that swept the floor, a pearl necklace and earrings adding to her elegance.

Farusja nodded as she turned away from the mirror, smiling as she viewed her new room, and the numerous shoes and accessories now strewn over the bed and dresser. Stepping gingerly over the mess, she made her way over to Rabecca, handing her a small black evening handbag.

Rabecca took the bag from her, snapping closed the compact case she had opened to touch up her make-up. 'You look fabulous, I look fabulous!'

Farusja sighed. 'Let's get this over with.'

Jerome laughed uproariously as he watched them step out of the black beetle, taking the keys from Rabecca in a flourish, laughing even harder at the defiant look in her eyes.

'You're not serious Rabecca! Still driving this old Volkswagen? They must pay you more than they pay me! Can't you see the type of cars that are parked around here?'

He turned to Farusja, still laughing. 'Hey pretty lady, looking good mama, but you can't be serious about rolling with Rabecca? She's too loud, too aggressive. She'll make you commit social suicide!'

Rabecca bared her teeth at him mockingly, snapping her tongue against her mouth and making a clicking sound. '*Mwaiche iwe*, don't bring your insolence here. I am ten years older than you, regardless of who your brother is!'

Farusja stared at Jerome, her head cocked to one side, a smile spreading itself across her face. 'You're the regular jack of all trades, aren't you?'

He shrugged, jangling the car keys in his hand. 'You learn a lot of things when you fade into the background. After a while, people don't even see you. The colour of your skin makes you invisible and people forget,' he winked at her. 'They forget whose brother you are, and after a while you begin to see things, you begin to hear things you're not supposed to hear.'

He stopped short and gave her a little nudge, motioning her towards the entrance, his face creased in a smile. 'But then again, pretty lady, tonight is your night to party, and I,' he winked at her again, 'am just your valet.'

Rabecca shook her head at him, motioning Farusja to join her on the red carpet that had been laid out on the driveway and beckoned cheekily towards the gilded doors of the country club. She grabbed Farusja's arm and intertwined it with hers, leading her inside.

'Why does he treat his brother like maintenance staff?' she murmured to Rabecca as invited guests and employees of HD Advertising swept past them.

Rabecca shrugged her wide shoulders. 'The boy works as a valet, a sweeper, a handyman, and now he's doing odd jobs in human resources. Maybe they don't want people to start crying corruption, this is an international organisation you know. If it were me I'd have given the boy an office a long time ago.'

'Nepotism shouldn't be considered normality, Becca.'

Rabecca laughed loudly. 'Who's talking about nepotism? I call it taking care of my own! There's nothing nepotistic about that! Why not bring your family into something you worked so hard to achieve? And Dante has more reason than most!

Apparently his mom was just a cleaner in some rich persons house when he was young. If there's no family money, obviously you give your brother a job. They call it a family business in some places, but in Africa they call it corruption and nepotism? Rubbish!'

'The dynamics of a family business and a corporate enterprise are not the same Becca!'

'Sure they are! And besides, we take care of our own here, it is expected in our society!'

'And what about the cries of corruption, greed and the promising future of dictatorships that nepotism leads to?'

Rabecca swept them into the foyer, pausing to admire the newly erected chandeliers above them. 'If you haven't noticed the world we live in *mami*, everyone is it in for themselves. I have no desire to be any different.'

'So, his mom was a cleaner?' Farusja was battling to process this information. It put Mr Dumeno in a completely different light.

'Yeah, and she'd hoped that Dante would aspire to be a gardener! But she died when he was young.'

'And he looks after his brother?'

'Him and his sister. Jerome and Cherise are twins. He's looked after them ever since their mom died. Well, that's what they say, anyway. We don't see much of the sister, she's in Cape Town studying – engineering, can you believe it!'

'You're well-informed,' Farusja said dryly.

'I am well-gossiped!' Rabecca trilled. 'Let's go party!'

Farusja quickened her pace to keep up. Some male she had met recently at work suggested that they could resume getting to know each other better tonight. She smiled inwardly; secretly delighted that she was not off the dating market yet. She grinned to herself, as she presented their invitation to the maitre'd in the lobby. His name was Michael.

Rabecca steered them towards the ladies toilets, following a group of chattering women who were already on their way there.

Farusja had actually met Michael on her first day while sitting in the kitchen and drinking coffee during her lunch hour. He had presented himself across her table and said hello, flashing a set of marvellous white teeth. She had not yet made any friends, so had grudgingly allowed him to sit and shine his teeth at her.

Men worried her, but looking at those teeth had made her retract her kitty claws just a little bit. There had been only two kinds of men in her life so far: the really nice guys that would do anything at the drop of a hat, who catered to her every whim.

The second type were the men who thought of her as an excellent accompanying side-dish to the main course they already had, and unfortunately she was often the last one to find out.

In her long quests to find a companion, she had sampled, tasted and discarded various dishes, from the luscious jungles of her home country, to the white west and the chocolate creaminess of the Caribbean, but it had just been the same type of man packed up in a different wrapping. But how she had loved those wrappings! Chester, one of her good friends whom she had left behind in the snow and sunshine that was London, was a passionate man who intertwined the beats of his life with music and love. He had hinted that maybe it was something in Farusja that attracted these types of men to her, that her attraction to them was due to something empty or left wanting in her own life. She always cut him short, hating it when he was right. She remembered her conversations with Chester in startling relief when Michael had flashed his gleaming white teeth at her, but she had shrugged away the apprehension she felt, looking instead at what she was seeing in front of her.

He was strikingly handsome. His eyes were dark brown, almost black. He had smiled crookedly at her, his lips curving at the corners. He had exuded so much energy, and oozed charm; she had thought he had been almost restless, and the apprehension had come back, but in the end she had chalked it up to exuberance. She could see that he was getting soft around the edges, probably the result of too many weekends nursing bottle after bottle of beer, and enjoying the *kapana* meat that was the crux of Namibian society. His tales of night life in this tiny city had intrigued her.

Farusja was dragged back to reality as Rabecca pulled at her arm, leading her into the hustle and bustle that was the ladies room. Farusja felt herself rejecting the familiarity of chit-chatting with a bunch of women about silly things in the small space and pulled away from Rabecca.

'But *mami*,' Rabecca protested. 'Don't you want to …?'

'Find me by the food,' Farusja said hastily and taking one last look at her face, left the sanctuary of the bathroom. She closed the door on the twittering ladies and the smell of perfume floating in clouds of face powder. She strode across the tiled floors, taking a right turn once she reached the lobby and advanced into the hall. A wisp of fear enveloped her as she wondered how she could avoid sticking out without her friend by her side. She kept her eyes open for Michael, looking forward to seeing someone familiar.

The hall was enormous. Jewelled chandeliers hung from the ceiling to complement the warm soft glow of the bubble lights strung around the room. A stage had been erected in the front of the hall where a variety of musicians were playing, with a small dance floor surrounding the stage. There was a buffet table directly to the right enclosed within a cascade of heavy damask curtains, and just outside this a bar had been erected against the wall.

'Farusja!'

Farusja turned, stopping midstride on her way to the buffet table, her smile freezing as she saw Michael Katjihingua. She recoiled instinctively as her eyes settled on him. All previous anticipation gone in an instant. The clean charm that he had carried on the day they had met had disappeared. His eyes were now bloodshot and a little bit too bright. She could feel his restlessness a mile away although he was impeccably dressed in a grey tuxedo.

Michael reached her, flashing his white teeth, his eyes staring at her, bright and unfocused. It was all she could do to not cringe as he laid his hand on her shoulder, making an exaggerated motion of staring into her face.

'I never thought I'd say this so soon,' he smiled at her. 'But you're beautiful tonight.'

Farusja smiled politely, turning slightly to remove his hand from her shoulder. She crinkled her nose. Whatever perfume or cologne he was wearing had been layered on thick, but the smell he had been trying to disguise was still permeating the air around him. He smelled like something rotting. He smelled of vomit. She was disgusted at herself for even thinking him worthy of her time.

'Thank you,' she continued her polite smile, darting quick glances around the hall for Rabecca, wondering how this miraculously disgusting transformation of Michael had taken place in so short a time.

'So, this is our first date then?'

Farusja detected the slight slur in his words and her revulsion for him grew.

'I don't remember ever being asked,' she said stiffly, shrugging his persistent hand off her shoulder again.

He laughed, and despite herself Farusja grudgingly admitted that it was still a handsome sound between them. 'I expected some resistance.'

Farusja felt cold fingers caress her back, the chill running the whole length of her spine. She felt disgusted at his touch, and coughed lightly, putting her right hand to her chest while the other covered her nose and mouth. She was not going to put up with this disgusting and unwelcome attention.

'Are you okay, sweetie?'

Her teeth clenched at his nerve of familiarity. She did not want him around her, and she did not want his stench sliding off her skin either.

'My throat is dry Michael. Would you get us some drinks from the bar?' she smiled at him, lowering her eyelashes demurely.

Farusja watched as he turned away from her, the swagger in his step almost charming from afar.

She looked around for an escape and realised that the crowd had started to move towards the buffet table. As she had not eaten anything all afternoon, she turned on her heel and rapidly made her way towards the food, hiding herself in the curtain that surrounded the table.

Dante appreciated beauty. He especially appreciated the ladies on his arms tonight and how sensual they looked in their evening gowns, and how incredible they would both look with them off. Windhoek was a small city and it was getting harder and harder to find women who had not said marriage vows yet or whom he had not already slept with. He would need to fly out of town for his amusements soon.

Normally he would revel in a night such as tonight, but lately he'd begun to feel bored and restless. It was always the country club, he sighed, the board always out-voted him on that one. He was bored of the food and tired of the conversations that he already knew by heart. He tried to get into the moment, and smiled seductively at the women on his arms, his dates for the evening. It would have been better if he could remember their names. They were dressed like all the other women he had ever invited to these functions – in as little as possible, no matter how cold it became. He smiled. They were just so predictable, but the good thing was that there would be even less to peel off their bodies later.

Dante had been one of the first on the dance floor, but now it was time he mingled with his guests. He started moving around the hall, stopping at the tables to meet and greet the people. He nodded as Kobus walked up to him.

'It's still early,' Kobus said, smiling at the two women at Dante's side. 'We have another hour before we start with the speeches.'

'Is Michael behaving himself?'

Kobus shrugged. 'With all this alcohol before the speeches start, you're still only worried about Michael? What about the rest of the staff?'

'Michael is a drunk and a user. He's the only one I don't trust, especially after his very public meltdown at our last dinner. He's redundant, he'll be on his way out very soon. We no longer need the support of his parents any more, not like we used to in the old days.'

'Well, who the hell gives the guests a party before the business of the night has been concluded? He seemed to be alright. I saw him by the bar just now, he hasn't lost the plot…yet.'

Dante nodded. 'Keep an eye on him.'

He was just about to make his way to the bar when out of the corner of his right eye he caught a slight movement that stood out in his peripheral vision. Turning slightly, he caught a glimpse of white silk disappearing behind the damask rose curtains surrounding the buffet table. He knew that figure.

He quickly scanned the faces around him, and a smile tugged at his mouth as he spied his marketing manager, Tony Kapunda. He motioned him over, disentangling himself from the women on his arms. 'Take over for me Tony.'

'Mr Dumeno?'

'These women need an escort. Don't make me ask you twice.'

'But my wife?'

'Don't worry, I'll find some young men to escort her as well.'

He left Tony stammering and impatiently greeted his other colleagues and business associates as he made his way to the buffet table.

Parting the curtains, he stepped through with a determined look on his face. He took one look at her and he wanted her, much more than before. It was a complete transformation. She was tall as his shoulder. Her black shiny hair swept her shoulders softly, complementing the slender lines of her neck. She had generous curves, but it was clear that she knew this and was making the most of them. Her off-the-shoulder white silk dress clung to her like a second skin, brushing the floor gently. Her skin shimmered under the lights and he could already imagine how soft it would feel under his fingers. She was in the middle of stuffing *hors-d'oeuvres* into her mouth, and had partitioned off a piece of the table which she seemed to dominate by the sheer force of her presence.

Farusja admitted to herself that she was hiding. She was hiding from Michael, hiding from the party and everyone else for that matter. She had received a message from Rabecca a few minutes earlier that had asked her where she was, and judging from the number of angry symbols that accompanied the message, she had decided to hide out for a few minutes longer; seeing Rabecca angry was not a pretty sight.

Farusja almost choked when she saw Dante step through the curtains, her hand leaving the tray she had been demolishing, quickly placing the back of her left hand against her throat, the barbeque sauce still clinging to her fingers. Startled, she attempted to maintain some form of dignity and discretely wiped her hand on the table cloth.

They stared at each other for a moment. Farusja wondered desperately if there was somewhere she could go to escape him. Was there anyone else at the table that he needed to talk to? She did not need tongues wagging, especially not here in front of the entire organisation.

Her heart hammered against her chest as she watched him stride towards her. *I wish he would stop looking at me*, she groaned inwardly as he moved towards her, *he might be arrogant, but he is all they say he is – impeccably dressed and devilishly handsome*. He reached her, and rested his fingers lightly on the buffet table next to them.

'Mr Dumeno,' she cleared her throat, clasping her hands nervously.

'You clean up well, Miss Mumba,' he continued smiling at her, his dark eyes roving her body.

Farusja felt her hands go clammy, and she focused on that damn silver chain that was resting against his neck, feeling like his eyes could see right through the flimsy material covering her body.

'So do you Mr Dumeno,' and she meant it.

He had changed into a completely black, patterned suit set with a contrasting blue hue, which set off the tones in his skin and hair. But then again, when was Dante Dumeno ever not perfectly dressed? She smiled inwardly, catching herself before it reached her face.

'Farusja,' Dante let her name slide off his tongue, caressing it, 'what an unusual but beautiful name.'

An unusual but beautiful name, Farusja mimicked him silently, sarcastically. *Arrogant fool,* she grimaced, *what does he want?* She ground her teeth more in frustration than anger as she recognised the look in his eyes. She had seen it on so many other men. Dante Dumeno just did it with more style. She had not been working for a month yet ... and she already had two men that wanted her to fill their beds tonight. She did not know whether she should be flattered or appalled.

'What does it mean?' Dante lifted his fingers off the table and, reaching out, brushed an imaginary piece of fluff off her bare shoulder. His fingers lingered on her skin for a few moments longer than necessary. 'It's hardly anywhere near a Zambian name. Do you even have an African name?'

She cringed inwardly, summoning as much strength as she could not to draw away from his touch, angry that she felt so vulnerable.

'Well, your name is hardly anywhere near being African, or Namibian for that matter Mr Dumeno, and neither is your brother's.'

He regarded her quietly, his fingers feathery light and back on the buffet table. 'Even though that was not phrased as a question, I'll answer it for you. But I believe I asked you first.'

'Farusja Amra was a journalist who advocated for women's rights all over Africa. She died in Somalia, where she was stoned for protecting a woman accused of adultery after she was raped,' she replied quietly. 'The woman she was trying to save proclaimed Farusja the bringer of strength, insight and new hope to women like her, before she was also stoned.'

'I've never heard of her.'

'It was never newsworthy, how ironic. A journalist's death not to be newsworthy. Outcry over her death flared-up and in a week was silenced. She was one of my parent's closest friends.'

'That's a big name to live up to.'

Farusja gave him a wry look. 'It's your turn, Mr Dumeno.'

Dante grinned, his smile curving slowly. 'Nothing so magnificent I'm afraid. We were named after my parent's favourite American sitcom on NBC. My parents knew they would never be able to go to the place where the show was filmed, so they brought a little bit of it to their home.'

'Well, that's a bit unsettling. Have you ever bothered to find out what it means?'

'Yes, of course. Even though they named us in what seemed to be a completely random fashion, our names hold. Mine means enduring and steadfast. Besides being named for one of the great poets of all time, and his famous character.'

Farusja could not stop the laugh that escaped her. 'So now you're alluding to yourself as Dante in *Dante's Inferno*? Have you gone through the seven levels of hell and purgatory to get to where you are now? Did you lose a woman because of your infidelity?'

'That's three more questions than you have answered. It's your turn.'

Farusja looked at him speculatively, ignoring what he had said. 'Even so, but so much importance is attached to our names, how could they name you after a character in a TV show?'

'Well Miss Mumba, it seems that you're having trouble living up to your important name, otherwise you would not be here … working for me,' he smiled at her, and gesturing a drinks waiter towards them, plucked two glass stems from the tray, offering her one. He raised it in an open toast between them, putting the glass to his lips, his eyes unreadable above the rim.

Farusja took the glass from him, letting the smirk show on her face, trying to quench the emotion rising up inside of her. *Why do I put up with him? Who cares who he is?* She did not need him or his job. He had insulted her, and was now making assumptions about her and her name! She did not need to be nice to him! Her eyes flashed as she raised her chin defiantly, raising the glass in a toast.

'We all have certain things we have to live up to,' she paused. 'Mr Dumeno. And it is not always a name. I am sure you have first-hand experience of that.'

Dante narrowed his eyes at her, noting the defiance in her posture, the angry look in her eyes.

Apparently, she's immune to my charms. The last time I met one of these was when I was fifteen. He smirked as he cocked his head at her. 'I hear you are doing well at work. Even Roberta seems impressed. Are you enjoying it?'

'It was what I expected,' she admitted grudgingly.

Feistier than I thought. Dante narrowed his eyes at her, a predatory look on his face. He liked a challenge. 'I apologise for my behaviour when you started at HD, it's just that I pride myself on appearance, and I would like my business to reflect that.'

She smiled back at him politely, not leaning towards an acceptance or a decline of his offer of an apology, it was so obviously insincere. 'You're the boss.'

She lifted her shoulders slightly and permitted herself to give him a small smile, and raising her glass again in a mocking toast between them, she downed her drink in one gulp, setting it firmly down on the buffet table with a tiny bang, ignoring the slight cough of the buffet waiter nearby.

'Come and dance with me,' he leaned past her to place his glass next to hers, and reaching out closed his fingers around her wrist, watching her expression turn slightly alarmed. He smiled and pulled on her wrist gently. 'Don't you want to get to know who you're working for? '

'I know who I'm working for Mr Dumeno,' she said through clenched teeth. 'But my last dance was in high school. I don't dance.'

She tugged her wrist away from him, and turned her side to him, facing the buffet table. She hoped he did not notice the way her hands were shaking, the way she had to rest them on the table in order to still them.

It was then that she felt, rather than heard, an intense silence surround them. She looked around and noticed that the other guests around the table had been watching their exchange. Farusja stiffened, her body rigid and tense. She realised she had overstepped an invisible line which was never crossed. She waited for him to boot her out of the party, out of the office and out of town. She should never have run away from Rabecca in the first place.

Dante stared at her, noticing her rigid posture, and the way her fingertips lightly touched the top of the table, coiled.

'As you wish Farusja,' he smiled, though the smile did not reach his eyes.

'Thank you, Mr Dumeno,' she did not bother to turn to look at him, instead she stared at the wide silver caterer of meat stew in front of her. It began to make her faintly nauseous.

Well, she thought airily, staring at the globules of fat swimming in the stew, *if all the dinner parties of HD are going to serve this disgusting concoction, it's a good thing I'm going to be fired anyway.*

She tensed as there was a slight commotion at the entrance to the buffet table and almost breathed an audible sigh of relief as she felt the attention shift from her and Dante. The curtains parted after a bit of a struggle and Michael stepped through them, his face covered in a slight sheen of sweat and holding two drinks in his hands.

'Ag Farusja!' he grunted. 'I'd have been back sooner but everyone was at the bar.' He paused, his gaze alternating between her and Dante. 'Ah Dante, a good evening as always.'

Dante smiled pleasantly at him, allowing the distraction, maliciously dismissing Michael as any form of competitor. 'How is Riita?' he asked quietly.

Michael shook his head, his hands curled around the glasses he was holding. 'She's always asking when you are coming over to the house again.'

'Your mother is very persistent.'

'Yes, yes,' Michael paused, still clutching the glasses. 'I was just going to invite Farusja over to the house so that she could see how the other half live since she's new to the country …'

'Oh, you two know each other?' Dante continued quietly, his eyes swivelling to rest on Farusja.

Farusja bristled at the veiled insinuation behind his words; she had not asked for any of this attention; she could not tell who repulsed her more at the moment: the black snake with its tongue caressing her neck, or the handsome drunk with an expensive perfume that covered the rotting of vomit inside him. She took two deep mental breaths, steadying herself. She did not want to know what was going on here; this was the type of drama she had worked to stay away from.

Michael glanced from Dante to Farusja, the expression on his face twisting despite his smile.

'We met in the kitchen by chance. We were intending to get better acquainted this evening,' he paused for emphasis. 'I brought your drink Farusja.' He trailed to a stop, eyeing her and holding out the glass, almost thrusting it in her face.

She had half turned, resting her right hand on the table and almost leaning onto it, stubbornly looking at the two of them and refusing to rise to the bait. She did not say a word. She did not take the drink from Michael's hand either.

Dante watched her, noticing the lines her neck made with her little chin lifted in the air. He almost laughed out loud as he watched the little pout materialise on those full lips. He could feel the stubbornness radiating off her, and her anger. She was going to be so much fun to play with, but he wondered how she had let trash like Michael latch onto her like this. He had had enough.

'Michael, I was discussing something with Miss Mumba. Please leave us alone, at least for the time being,' he drawled, turning his full attention to the woman in front of him.

Farusja watched Michael from the corner of her eye. She could feel the resentment barely held in check by the handsome smile still plastered on his face. His eyes settled on her, the drink still thrust in front of her, and she felt a chill at the hard brightness she spied in them; wondering what consequences she would suffer for this. He withdrew the drink slowly, clutching both glasses at his sides.

'Of course,' he smiled at Dante. 'What should I tell my mother?'

'I'll let her know,' Dante said shortly, not even turning to look at him.

Michael turned around and walked through the thick curtains, the drinks still in his hands, his body rigid. Farusja glanced at Dante, her heart beginning to beat against her chest at the way he was looking at her. She grimaced. The layer of disgust towards Michael receded as he walked away. The repercussions that would follow from her rejection of Michael did not bother her, that she could deal with. It was Dante that she was worried about.

'Come and dance with me Miss Mumba, everybody's watching us,' he said quietly, his voice barely above a whisper, the words only meant for her ears.

Farusja couldn't handle any more emotion tonight, and barely managed to shake her head at him before turning away from him and resuming the demolition of the *hors-d'oeuvres* in front of her for lack of anything else to do. She froze as she felt his hand close over her wrist again, gentle but firm.

'That's enough Miss Mumba,' he said loudly. 'It will not do to have you too fat to sit at your desk.'

Farusja's face burnt at the sniggers around the table, and for the second time that night she almost choked, drawing on all her reserves to keep from bolting. She moved unresisting as Dante led her away from the table, through the curtains and across the hall onto the dance floor. He swept her around in a wide arc before pulling her up to him, his other hand resting lightly on her waist.

Farusja's mind was in turmoil as she tried to still her trembling body. *What must I do,* she thought desperately, *all these people are looking at us!* She put one hand on his shoulder and swore inwardly as she felt it shaking independently, despite all of the strengthening thoughts she sent to it. He maintained a respectful distance from her but kept his hand firmly on her waist and Farusja found the proximity of his body disturbing. It was that scent around him ... that musky, masculine scent ...

she breathed in deeply, focusing on the silver chain that she could see a hint of in between the top button of his black shirt.

'See Miss Mumba,' Dante murmured, 'it's not so bad. There was no need to cause such a commotion.'

Farusja's hand tightened on his shoulder, her anger flaring up again as she watched the surprised faces of the other guests fly past her as they swung around them.

'I'm an unwilling participant,' she said stiffly. 'I told you that I don't dance, Mr Dumeno.'

'Dante,' he said quietly.

Farusja stopped. His hand had moved up her back as he had spun her around, decreasing the space between them. His lips had grazed her earlobe and when he said his name, it was whispered directly into her ear.

'I'm afraid this dance is over, sir,' she said shakily, disentangling herself from him as calmly and naturally as she could despite the circumstances. She knew all eyes were on them, but this was not doing her any favours with any of the other employees or with herself; she could feel it.

'Are your really?' Dante asked, a smirk on the corner of his mouth. 'An unwilling participant I mean? All of a sudden too.'

He raised an eyebrow at her and let his hands fall to his sides.

'I came with Michael and need to get back to him,' Farusja lied and smiled coolly at him. 'Thank you for your time.'

Dante's eyes hardened as he bowed slightly, turned on his heel and moved back into the crowd.

CHAPTER 8

*F*arusja yawned as she walked slowly out of the country club, past people in the throes of a party in full swing. Dante Dumeno had disappeared over an hour ago, leaving his fuming partner to handle almost two hundred people alone. She smirked, *I say good riddance to bad rubbish, no matter how sexy the guy is, he is just as arrogant outside the office as he is inside it.* After all the drama of the evening, she decided to leave after the speeches had been made and when the real fun finally started.

Rabecca wanted to stay on to party with her friends, and begrudgingly allowed Farusja to leave on her own, giving her a long lecture about how she would kill her social life if she insisted on a solitary existence and giving her the directions to the house four times until she was sure Farusja could repeat them word for word.

Farusja reached the valet booth, brushing her hair out of her face as the wind picked up around her. A chill had cooled down the air, and she wished she had brought a scarf with her.

A country club staff member was the only person in the valet booth. 'Can I help you madam?'

'I need my car keys, do you know were they are? What happened to Jerome?'

The man shrugged, his over-sized uniform shrugging with him as he took Farusja's key number. 'They left me in charge, but I can't leave to get the car for you or there'll be no one here.'

'Just point me in the general direction.'

Farusja strode away from driveway curving around the entrance to the country club, her dress swishing from side to side as she moved towards the parking lot. She was completely drained with the evening's events, all she needed was a hot shower and the remains of Rabecca's ravaged ice-cream drawer in the fridge.

Dante stood leaning against his car, shaking his feet impatiently at the cold. The desert air, although hot and angry during the day, became a mistress at night, cooling the skin and caressing places it had never been. He had not become used to this air despite having lived here all his life. He had suffered through too many winter nights, shivering against a long bony back, trying to keep warm amidst the cloying sweet smell of alcohol, the heavy hand hovering above his head, the competition to gain warmth amongst his siblings and the distant rumble of his mother's tears. The cold spread icy fingers up his back that reeked of the past. He hated it. He shivered involuntary.

He had needed some time to compose himself before he went back into the party, and so here he was standing in the parking lot trying to deal with the anger he felt at the loss of control he had earlier. He had to admit it to himself, he had chased her. He never chased women; he had worked too damn hard for too damn long to have to invest time in running after them. So he sat back and watched one after the other come to him, beseeching him with their eyes to make them the latest flavour of the month. He smirked. The women who came to him could not afford pride, they left that at home. They knew what they wanted: the recognition, the money, he could smell it a mile off, and after keeping up the pretence for a while, their true colours bled through the very pores of their skin.

Farusja gritted her teeth; she had spent almost ten minutes walking around the parking lot, her feet were aching in her heels, and it was so cold. She finally found the car, it was nestled between a white minibus and a grey Bentley. Farusja stopped cold, her heart starting to beat faster than usual. She stared at Dante Dumeno, leaning against the Bentley. The beat in her heart turned into rumbles of thunder. She took her time and acted as though she had not noticed him, her movements even more slowed, she walked towards the front boot of Rabecca's car, her posture casual but her insides reduced to putty. She watched his eyes raise themselves to hers, the look on his face mirroring the shock she felt.

'Mr Dumeno,' she nodded curtly.

'Farusja Mumba,' he drawled. 'Leaving the party already? Not having fun with Michael anymore?'

Farusja laughed despite herself, trying to stem the sour taste of bile rising in her throat. 'I was never with Michael, Mr Dumeno, and yes, I'm leaving.'

Dante shrugged his shoulders. 'You truly aren't the life of any party, so get out of here. You can't dance. You refuse to have a normal conversation. What can you do Farusja Mumba?' The smirk on his face was all too visible.

Farusja stared at him in shock. 'What? I refuse to dance with you, then you force me to dance with you and expect me to accept that gracefully? So someone doesn't do what you want them to do and you make up your mind about them? I shouldn't even be having this conversation with you anyway, Mr Dumeno. Is this how you treat all new employees?' As she spoke, she moved in front of him, the anger radiating from her.

Dante narrowed his eyes, knowing she was right, hating himself for wanting her. Magical things happen in deserts, and tonight it laid its bare cool arm lightly on his shoulder. He watched as the moonlight weaved its way across her skin, caressing it softly and laying its white shadows in the crevices of her collarbones, making them little hollows filled with silver moonlight. Her eyes, those eyes, watched him, their colour and shade changing again in the magical light. Without thinking, he closed the distance between them, his fingers reaching out to touch her bare shoulder, lightly brushing her skin, wanting to touch the silver filling the hollows of her collarbones.

Farusja jerked away from him, falling back in her haste to get away from him, the rumbling in her chest faster, the breath leaving her body in short gasps, her eyes wide with shock. She stared at the hand that was grasping her arm, preventing her from falling, suspending her in air. She could see the strength he was exerting to prevent her fifty-five kilogramme frame from hitting the ground.

Dante, his fingers digging into her arm, pulled her upright slowly, only withdrawing his hand when she was standing on her feet again. He licked his suddenly dry lips, still feeling her skin under his fingers, feeling the moonlight slipping away from him, the desert was taking back what was hers.

'I keep catching you. We have to stop meeting like this, what'll happen when I'm not around the next time?'

Farusja pulled herself away from his gaze and moved around the boot of Rabecca's car, squeezing herself between the beetle and the mini-bus. She glared in consternation as the space grew smaller, cursing the haphazard way in which the cars were parked. She mentally banged her head against the car's roof, she would have to go around the other side of the car, which meant going right back to the lion that was Dante Dumeno. She exhaled deeply, gathering her dress in her hands, hoping that he would not be there when she turned around, hoping that she was having a really bad waking dream.

Farusja gasped, dropping the car keys. He had followed her into the small space and had closed the distance between them. He stared down at her in amusement. 'Come on Farusja Mumba, let's go and have a good time.'

Farusja exhaled, he was so close she could see pores in his skin. 'Mr Dumeno, I do not respect your ethics with regards to the women in your employ.' She hoped he could not hear the tremble in her voice. 'Please move, you are in my way. I'll be reporting you to the union or employment tribunal for sexual harassment first thing on Monday morning.' She stood firmly, wondering how she was going to bend herself under the car to look for the keys.

Dante sighed, rather theatrically, loud enough for her to hear. 'You still don't know who I am in this town, do you?' He shook his head slowly, a smile spreading itself across his face. 'I am the union baby, I am the tribunal, I am the courts and I am the police. You want me, trust me, you want me.'

Farusja flinched as she heard the edge that peppered his voice with those last three words, and could feel the air changing around them, becoming frantic, more frenzied and more alive.

'And I want you,' he continued making the air around them even more electric. 'Why are you making this more difficult and complicated than it is? Whatever pride you pretend to have, let it go. Let me paint a picture for you: new girl, new town, knows nobody; first good contact is a drug addict that wants to get her into bed.'

'And you don't?' Farusja interrupted sarcastically.

Dante smiled at her, watching her luminous eyes, watching the anger fill them, the moonlight changing their colour again. He dropped to his knees suddenly, his head ducking under the two cars. He straightened up and laid his hand flat, palm facing up in front of her, the keys to Rebecca's car nestled merrily in the middle of his palm.

Farusja looked up into his dark eyes, suddenly feeling very cold and very scared. Goosebumps rose all over her shoulders and arms with a tingle. She wished she had a jacket to cover her naked shoulders. She gave into the insecurity that a woman feels when her choice of dress attracts unwanted attention. Feeling that she should have worn something else instead, that maybe her show of skin was what had caused such inappropriate behaviour to be displayed. If it was not one thing it was always another, she grimaced, there were no small choices left to her anymore.

Every decision she had made in the last few months had been a life-changing one, and like clockwork another piece of drama had come her way. Her eyes lowered to her fingers, trying not to think about what he had said. She was shaking; whether from the cold air around them or the coldness she felt inside her, and so she did not hear him step closer to her. She started in alarm as she lifted her eyes to his dark ones staring down at her less than a pace away from hers. She stood inhaling the scent coming from him, it was intoxicating. The wind ceased its screaming and despite herself, anticipation began to slowly tingle through her body, infusing it with warmth. The coldness began to ebb away.

Dante shrugged his jacket off; the black leather a direct contrast to the black patterned suit he was wearing. Reaching around her, he laid it over her shoulders, and holding onto the lapels of his jacket, tried to fit it around her shoulders as best as he could. 'You're cold,' he whispered, 'take my jacket.'

Dante, still holding onto his jacket, could not resist those pink lips trembling and pouting below him. He slowly pulled her closer to him, bringing his mouth close to hers, his breath tickling her chin.

She closed her eyes involuntary, fighting the emotions inside her, the hot and cold trying so desperately not to mix, sighing when his lips caressed hers gently, savouring his taste and trembling at the way tiny sharp spasms of pleasure were lighting their way through her.

'Let me go, Mr Dumeno,' she whispered breathlessly as she raised her hands to his chest, unsteadily, trying in vain to push him away. The moment her hands touched his chest his mouth covered hers; hot, humid and hungry. His tongue took possession, stroking her, and removing the last remains of the coldness inside her.

Farusja felt her body surrender, and with a small sigh she opened up to him, curving her arms around his neck, moulding her body to his. She could feel the desert wind return to sparkle between them.

His lips not leaving hers, Dante trailed his hands down the length of her torso, letting one hand rest on her waist and fastening the other right under the curve of her behind and the swell at the top of her thighs. Leaving her mouth, he swept her up into his arms, squeezing them both between the cars to the front of Rabecca's car, settling her gently on it's hood. His lips lit a trail of fire down her neck, his jacket fell off her shoulders as his hands caressed her bare skin.

'Dante,' she whispered. The warmth inside her had turned to fire.

'Yes baby,' he said huskily; his hands in her hair, caressing the long, silky strands. Farusja closed her eyes as he kissed her forehead, kissed the shiny hair covering her head and came back down to her lips. Goosebumps raised themselves all over her skin. She barely felt it when the zipper on the side of her dress made its way down to her waist, and when her black strapless bra followed. His hands were burning long forgotten fires across her bare breasts and skin. She had forgotten what it felt like to be alive like this.

'Where are the keys?'

'You've got them.'

'Check your bag!'

Keys? Farusja half-opened her eyes, disorientated for a second. She heard the tap-tap of shoes and the voices before she saw them. It was a group of people from the party, laughing and joking with each other and, even worse, making their way towards them. Farusja's eyes flung wide-open in panic, meeting Dante's black ones at the same time. Without hesitation, he wrapped his arms around her tightly and pulled her as quickly as he could off Rabecca's car, pushing her around into one of the other parking bays, then holding her close. As they crouched there in silence, they listened as the voices came closer and stopped at the small minibus. They stayed immobile, and both breathed a sigh of relief as the bus was started and drove out of the parking lot.

Farusja, now washed cold, stared at the chest of the man holding her, her hands clutching protectively at the top of her dress, covering her nakedness. This was the life she was trying to build, and if she allowed Dante Dumeno into it, she would forever establish her place in the food chain in this small city, and it would not be pretty. Making her decision, she placed both hands flat against his chest and pushed against him, struggled against him, almost falling in her haste to get away.

Dante caught her halfway, and after settling her feet on the ground, rose with her until they were both standing upright. He watched as she stomped around, looking for her underwear, finding it, and unashamedly fastening it back on, her dress following until she was respectable again.

'Farusja.'

'No! Mr Dumeno,' Farusja shrieked at him, her chest heaving with the effort of smoothing down her dress frantically. 'You leave me alone! Leave. Me. Alone! How dare you?'

Dante glared at her, the look on his face thunderous. 'Don't act so righteous. You're acting like I did this all by myself.'

Farusja glared back at him, the anger building inside her, livid at her body for betraying her. 'I am the one who stands to lose everything here, so please spare me the bullshit!' She picked the car keys off the top of Rabecca's car, and went to unlock the door.

'Farusja Mumba.'

She ignored him, and unlocked the car door, her hands shaking as she turned the key in the ignition and backed out of the parking bay, driving away as fast as she could. Dante watched her go, and picking up his leather jacket from where it had fallen to the ground, strode back towards the entrance of the country club, smashing the rear end of his Bentley with his fist as he passed it.

Farusja closed the door slowly behind her; her anger had ebbed during the drive home. She could still see his eyes, those beautiful dark eyes … she shivered; delayed paths of previous tingling sensations running up and down her spine. She smoothed her hands across the material covering her legs, trying to get rid of what he had made her feel, as if the silk could somehow wipe away all that had happened.

Well done darling, this is as great as a time as ever to start looking for a new job, move town, or kill your boss and make it look like an accident, she sighed, *so what, we're attracted to each other …* she touched her lips faintly, remembering the way his lips had caressed hers.

With most of the men she had been with the first kiss had never been perfect; it was always full of teeth, too much tongue, too little lip, hard, hungry, but his …

Farusja touched her lips again. She could still smell and taste the faint odour of smoked fish on his breath … shaking her head violently, she reached down to her ankles and pulled off the dress that had caused so much trouble. Yanking it over her head violently she got up and threw it away from her, watching it crumple, its spirit crushed at her rejection of it. She stood unsteadily, still in her black stiletto shoes, wearing the black underwear that she had bought specifically for the occasion.

What would happen to her now? The fear returned, and with it the sour taste that accompanied it. Leaving a trail of accessories in her wake, she ran past the living room and straight into the shower, opening the tap to its full strength and sighing as the water soothed her. Standing under the running water, she could still feel him growing hot and hard against her stomach, he had felt so huge; she had wanted to wrap her hands around him and guide him into her.

She exhaled, despite the water her nipples were taut again and the ache between her legs grew fierce and insistent. She quickly closed the hot tap and shrieked as a spray of cold water cascaded over her, effectively ruling out any other thought of Dante.

The shaking in his hands had stopped; he was okay for now. Until it started again. He was releasing them from the bondage of this ugly life. He loved to watch as their rescued souls escaped from their gaping mouths, tongues flapping like the wings of a bird rising in flight. He was happy. This hell on earth that created illusions of happiness and of peace, and ended up crushing them by bringing people to their knees in death and suffering had ended for her. He blinked as his vision blurred, the ecstasy he felt destabilising him. This hell had taken so much from him, it was up to him to put things right, and maintain the balance. He had never come remotely close to experiencing the good of this world, but now, now ... He circled the tiny room aimlessly, his head was hot, feverish, and yet there was no pain, only the euphoria of bliss.

He had to do it, he had no choice. If he did not they would be caught in the deceit that had been spun around them and would fall, doomed to live as slaves. He was changing that; he was the one who would save them and crush the source of the evil that held them captive.

He had freed another one today, wrapping his hands lovingly around her neck to gently urge her to leave. This was what he was meant to do, and he did it so lovingly; not even their fathers, not even their families, would treat them as lovingly as he would. The one today had not been as desperate as Frieda, but she had been on the list all the same. She was now in a better, safer place, and the shaking had stopped. Thank God, the shaking had stopped.

He had waited for her in the parking lot of the country club, sitting in his car after HD's campaign launch dinner. He had been too afraid that she would reject him if he walked right up to her, so he had opted to follow her to her home instead, planning to surprise her.

He had not expected her to have any welcome planned for him; after all she did not know he was coming, what he was going to do with her. When he forced his way into her house, she was even more drunk than when he had seen her earlier. All the paint on her face had been smudged and it looked like dirt on a canvas. He could not help but scare her, and instead of taking his time ... his steps grew frenzied, sweat beginning to bead and form on his forehead and nose. He had not been prepared for that, for a fight. He had just wanted to be welcomed. It had been too much for him, he had hit her. What type of a man hit a woman? Would his mother and sister have approved? He could not remove the pain he had caused when he had hit her, but he hoped that when he released her it would make up for it. The dizziness came again, blinding him with euphoria. He had not meant for it to be this way at all; but it would more than satisfy him until the next kill.

CHAPTER 9

Saturday, 28 April

*F*unnily enough, his office at DI Storage was where he could get the peace and quiet he needed. Even on weekends there was no silence at home.

Dante sighed as he recalled the meeting of the morning, with one of the makers behind *Single Quarters 061*, the proposed name for a brand of clothing named after one of the informal settlements. The clothing label would be what the fashion industry termed as street wear; customised graffiti sprayed shirts, baggy jeans, caps, sneakers, bags … Dante sighed. He had thought this would have been an original idea but lately all he seemed to be getting where reworked versions of already existing ideas. When he had looked at the initial designs that would be sprayed on the clothes it had been no more interesting than the designs displayed in most hip-hop-street-wear-stores around town. It was a waste of his time, but it was all in the name of HD Advertising's corporate social responsibility activities. Every year they donated some of their profits to a promising new entrepreneur, but so far, this years promising entrepreneur had not yet been found.

The owner of the idea, a young man who called himself by a number of abbreviations which Dante always had to look at before he could say them, had come into his office wearing his designs. Dante had smiled faintly as he noticed the jeans hanging halfway down the boys behind, and the hat pulled low and perched at an angle on his head. His graffiti designs stated who he was, from the hat on his head, to his baggy white t-shirt, jeans and shoes. He reminded him of Naks.

It had been a long day … despite the advice he had given the boy, he had wanted to keep running the show his own way, and the meeting had ended on a sour note.

After the meeting Dante had escorted the boy out and closed his office door. He had stripped down to his white t-shirt and boxer shorts and had made himself comfortable in his chair.

Dante tapped his fingers slowly on the single, solitary file in the middle of his desk, his fingers lingering a little longer than usual every time they made contact with the smooth finish of the paper that made up all the personnel files.

He stared at the luminous eyes looking up at him from the photo stapled to Farusja's file. They were slightly narrowed, perhaps squinting at the glare of the flash when the photograph was taken, and stared at him with a slightly amused and bewildered look, as though she had been surprised by the photographer. Despite this, the light emanating from her eyes was not disguised. He frowned; the sexual energy she aroused in him was amazing, the first moment his fingers had made contact with her skin he had wanted to get her into bed, he had no other use for her ... but now ... a lusty smile curved around his mouth. Now he wanted to possess her completely, to own her body and mind, not only for what he could get out of her physically, but just for the sheer challenge of it, the challenge of making her give in to what they both already knew.

Dante smiled slowly, his fingers coming to a rest on top of her photo. It had only been one night and as corny as it sounded, he could not stop thinking about her; so he had approached the problem of her stubbornness like he approached each and every one of his business problems; with extreme prejudice. He had never had to do this with a woman, but he had not known how to react last night when she refused him. It had made him angry and doubt his charms. He glared at the photo looking up at him, he could not believe that she insisted on not wanting him, he was the most eligible bachelor in town! Did she know how many mothers had offered up their daughters to him, begging – no beseeching – him to take them in as his wife, in exchange for nothing but his name?

Dante sighed, rubbing his eyes tiredly. He was also going to have her watched. After last night, he found himself consumed with jealousy. Not because he felt anything for her, he told himself, but because he wanted her to be his and his alone. No other man would be allowed to sully his goods before he did. After he was finished with her that was another story and her business.

As of now she became his, he wanted her to run to someone, and from his foray into her past the only person she knew here was Rabecca, her parents were both dead and she had no other relatives living in Namibia, she would run straight to him. He had a plan, and although he was having second thoughts about it, he was too proud to retract his decision. He never retracted his decisions. He was not surprised that she already thought him an unethical bastard. She would soon find out just how unethical he could really be!

He raised himself from his chair, taking one last look at the picture on his desk. He paced the length of his office and walked to the bathroom. Hienry would be coming to see him soon.

Dante had made sure that the office had been renovated to include his own personal bathroom, made complete with shower and amenities. He loved it; his bathroom at DI more than made up for sharing a bathroom at HD, but he had hardly had the space to make it perfect. He sighed heavily. How he longed for a quiet evening at home! He had revelled in it once – the private parties, dinner engagements, social functions, every weekend there was something. Now he found himself tiring of it all. More and more he found himself wanting to round up a few of his close friends and family to go down south to the city of Cape Town, or north to the beaches of Nairobi, just to relax, to talk … about anything other than business, anything other than alcohol and parties, anything other than the small talk destined to get another woman into his bed. But he struggled against this desire; he needed to keep up his bad boy image.

He stood in the middle of the carpeted floor and stripped down, surveying himself in the mirror, thinking about the predictability of the evening ahead of him. Roberta had already dropped off his evening clothes, and would be waiting to be picked up as they set off for yet another boring social engagement. He did a half turn in front of the mirror, looking at himself critically and liking what he saw. As he stood looking at his side profile he did a little hip shake, twisting his hips left to right, watching his penis dance from side to side. He gave a satisfied smile. What girl would not want some of this?

After the shower, Dante dressed in his formal attire, feeling refreshed. His phone rang, startling him.

'Usually not even a locked gate can stop you.'

He had initially employed Hienry to quietly oversee that his accountant was doing her job; you could never be sure who was stealing from you these days. This was not all Hienry did for Dante, and in close circles he was referred to as the bodyguard. Dante knew that if anyone found out about Hienry's other services, he would be liable for gross misconduct.

'It hasn't old friend, I just didn't want to startle you.'

Dante looked up and saw Hienry standing in the doorway of his office. He was hardly surprised any more at the way Hienry moved through locked doors. 'Still moving around like a ghost Hienry?'

Hienry moved into the room, settling his huge bulk into one of the armchairs in the office. 'Getting up to your old little tricks again Dumeno?'

They had met during one of Dante's adventures to Paris. Hienry had been working for a small Paris accounts firm, his wife had just left him and he was miserable. He had been drowning his sorrows that day and had forgotten that drinking did not go hand-in-hand with driving. By the time he had been arrested for drunken driving and had smashed into Dante's hired car, the men had become fast friends. And that friendship had proved invaluable. Hienry had packed up his misery in Paris and moved to the desert of Namibia to work with Dante.

Dante got up to pour them each a drink. 'You Frenchmen are all the same. Or are you just in a league of your own Hienry?'

Hienry laughed with gusto, accepting the drink and re-settling his large bulk into the other armchair that looked like it could accommodate him. 'So who is the latest woman in your life?'

Dante gave a non-committal shrug. 'No woman.'

'No woman!' Hienry roared, almost spluttering him in scotch. 'That's a first!'

'Well, she's not mine. Yet.'

'Ahh,' Hienry smacked his lips. 'Sounds more like you now, eh? What's the problem this time? I'm not cleaning more of your mess Dumeno.'

'She's not cooperating.'

Hienry laughed loudly, his stomach shaking with him. 'Now that is a first, and you just cannot handle it can you Dumeno? Is it, how you say, eating you up, old friend? I'm almost afraid to ask why you are telling me this.'

Dante pursued his lips, staring at his friend. 'I want her followed. Find out things about her, something that would make it easier ...'

'For you to get into her bed?' Hienry interrupted, clicking his tongue against the roof of her mouth. 'You are always playing with fire my friend.'

'Just to it. As long as she doesn't know, who will it hurt? Anyway what's on your mind, old friend?'

Hienry's face became grave as he leaned forward and placed his glass on Dante's desk. He picked up the black case he had come in with, pulling out a sheaf of papers, and throwing them onto Dante's desk with a thud. 'We have a problem.'

Dante picked up the folder, scanning it as fast as he could. 'What the hell is this, Hienry?'

Hienry picked up his glass again, and swallowed the rest of his drink in one gulp, sticking the glass out, nudging Dante for another. 'What's it look like? That Italian ice-cream of yours is up to something.'

'You know she hates it when you call her that.'

Hienry rolled his eyes. 'Okay, Orabella Ricci, CEO of Hunter – that creamy Italian ice-cream with the dark blue eyes. She's up to something.'

Dante narrowed his eyes as he continued reading, the look on his face incredulous. 'What the hell is Ricci on about?'

'Is this how you treat me now, dry mouthed?' Hienry grumbled, forcing himself out of the seat to pour his own drink. 'This social responsibility program you guys have going, stop it. Hunter was one of them and look at what Ricci is doing to you now.'

'She had, still has, a great idea. All natural fragrances and oils sell in our markets, Orabella Ricci made us a lot of money in managing her brand.'

Hienry snorted. 'Ya, and apparently according to that file, you gave her a lot of money in and out of the bedroom.'

'You knew that Hienry. I was just helping her out of tight spots.'

'Not the way she's painting the picture. And you didn't say you gave her so much money!'

'It was all my own money.'

'Still not the way she's painting the picture.'

'Roberta will back me up. She knew exactly what was going on,' Dante threw the file back on the table, annoyed.

'Roberta will love to crush the obvious challenge to her position that comes in an ivory hue with long, flowing black hair. She knows full well what you two were up to, and she probably hated every minute of it.'

'Orabella got married three months ago, I haven't heard or seen her since. She's not even answering my calls. And I am a major shareholder!'

'Maybe this is why she was avoiding you. This file has all your financial payments to Orabella; dates, bank transfers, the amounts, including the dinner dates you had.'

'What do you think she's up to?' Dante asked.

He never regretted meeting Hienry that day, and over the years as the two men began learning more about each other, Hienry's skills in other areas became apparent. He never divulged many details of what he had done or what activities he had been involved in, and would only drop a hint to Dante here and there about what he could do if the organisation needed him to. Dante was satisfied to work in comfort around the principle of plausible deniability. As far as he was concerned, Hienry was on no paper trail connected to DI Storage or HD Advertising. He was paid out of Dante's own pocket. So when his friend would lay information of a confidential and explosive nature in front of him, Dante never asked where it had come from, never asked how he had managed to acquire it. He often suspected that Hienry's entire past had been fabricated to hide a truth more sinister and definitely more devious, but so far Dante had no reason or cause to question him on this.

'I don't know what it is for yet, my friend,' Hienry shook his head slowly while Dante continued thumbing through the folder.

'The only people that had access to this information are Orabella and I.'

Hienry shrugged his big shoulders, picking up his glass again thoughtfully. 'Why did you give her such large amounts?'

Dante ignored the question. 'Do you think it's Orabella doing this? I don't believe it. I want to know why!'

'Don't act the innocent Dumeno, it does not suit you. How do you think I get my information?'

'What are we going to do about it?'

'What am I going to do about this you mean?' Hienry picked up his briefcase and pulled out a number of photographs, which he pushed across the table to Dante.

'This makes it the second one that's gone off in the last month. It happened an hour ago. We have lost the garden shed, luckily no one was in it.'

Dante looked at the pictures of the leftover debris from the small structure that used to be in his back garden, and the small resulting crater that the bomb had made on detonation. 'All we have been is lucky. Last time it was the doghouses, with the dogs still in them,' he said quietly. 'Who the fuck would blow up a dog?'

'My father would,' Hienry muttered.

'How are we missing this Hienry?' Dante tapped his fingers on the top of the table lightly.

'I do not want to lie to you my friend, it is difficult to trace something that is no longer there but we will sift through the remains and see what we can find out.'

Dante shrugged his shoulders, the rigidness of his shoulders betraying him. 'How are they getting onto my property?'

Hienry shook his head. 'We obviously have a security breach. I'm working on it.'

They both stared at the table quietly for a while, until Hienry sighed, getting up. 'Ah good friend,' he said quietly. 'I'll visit you again soon; we will tighten security around the house again, yes? I'm sure you aren't too busy for this?'

Dante nodded, pushing the pictures towards Hienry, who put them back into his briefcase. 'I'm never too busy to deal with bombs exploding on my property Hienry.'

'God forbid you let me do my job Dumeno.'

CHAPTER 10

Sunday, 29 April

*T*he laundry had piled up to epic proportions during the last week, so Rabecca and Farusja spent the whole Sunday morning trying to make a dent in it. In the late afternoon, Rabecca fancied herself a hairdresser and decided to tackle Farusja's hair.

Farusja sighed, twisting herself uncomfortably on the cushion she was sitting on.

'Sit still, *iwe* Farusja!' They were sitting in Rabecca's small backyard, with a view that was one hundred percent dirt and rock.

Rabecca shouted frustratingly at her, Farusja's hair tangled in her fingers. 'How do you expect me to do your hair?'

'I'm tired Becca!'

'But we've just started *iwe mwaiche*! Your mother was so right about you!'

Farusja laughed and made an effort to keep her body in one position, worried about what her hair would look like once Rabecca had finished. She could vividly recall the times her mother had sat outside on the veranda in their Lusaka hometown, her head nestled in her mothers *chitenge*, which somehow always smelled vaguely of pounded groundnuts and fish. A small smile played across Farusja's face as she remembered how that smell had permeated her worst and best memories of her mother.

An African woman's hair grows not in singlet's or waves, but in tight, kinky, stormy curls. And on Farusja's head those curls had a mind of their own, going whichever way the wind would take them. The struggle would then begin: her twisting and turning in her mother's grasp, her mother holding her head firmly between her knees, the smell of groundnuts wafting around her face, her mother's fingers tugging and twisting her hair into plaits that would circle into a crown around her head.

Farusja had decided to relax her hair during her university days, which meant she had chemically treated, primped and pressed her hair, changing the structural integrity of each and every hair follicle, straightening out every single curly strand, until it was now just a shadow of its former unruliness. This was seen by only some as the solution to the black woman's kinky hair, and as much as Farusja had loved the curly afro of her teens, she never had any problem with having a straight hairstyle. With the hair on her head as controversial as the battle between the races, she had been through every argument about staying true and sticking to her African roots by keeping her hair natural, but at the end of the day she had refused to let her hair define who she was, and she had glared back at the snobby educated, dreadlocked and nappy haired women that had been arrogant enough to call her rootless. Before her mother had died, Farusja had wanted to shave her head bald, just for the sheer fun of it, but she had always had to contend with her mother. 'I grew that hair on your head every day of your life!' her mother would shout at her. '*Mwaiche*! If you even decide to cut that hair without my permission, you will feel your father's belt in my hands!'

Rabecca stared at the top of Farusja's head; worried. She loved Farusja like she would love her own sister, and she was concerned about her the same way. It had taken the whole weekend to pry what had happened on Friday night out of Farusja. They were close, they had always been close, and Farusja had never hidden anything from her, let alone kept secrets. She could feel the anger emanating from her best friend as she paced the house. Rabecca felt guilty because she had not been there to extract her from the situation; and not only that, but she had pushed Farusja into the job at HD. She had been too blinded by the joy of having her best friend live with her after so many years that she had forgotten the extreme predatory nature of the men at HD. Dumeno was a notorious womaniser – practically every woman in Windhoek claimed to have had some sort of encounter with him. She had not even considered that Dante would be attracted to Farusja, let alone that drug addict Michael.

Rabecca shivered in revulsion, the number of times she had come across Michael during one of his drug binges was too horrifying to repeat, even to August. His days of sober brilliance were slowly becoming fewer and farther in between and the inside information was that his days at HD were numbered. And both of these assholes were after her friend. She sighed, she needed to do something about it, but what could she do?

'I'm fine Becca,' Farusja said loudly. 'Why did you stop?'

'Are you sure you don't want to quit?'

Farusja snorted. 'It's just hair Becca, what are you talking about?'

'I meant the job.'

'You can't be serious, I'm not letting Dumeno or Michael run me out of town. Let them try.'

Rabecca sighed. What was even scarier was the relentlessness with which Farusja refused to admit defeat. If she had been the one tangling with those two men she would have packed up her little box of belongings at work and left quietly. No use in stirring the pot when the food was already burned, and still burning. Farusja twisted again, her seat beginning to feel uncomfortable. 'Sooo, how come you haven't fallen prey to Mr Dumeno?'

Rabecca laughed heartily. 'I am too round to be his type! When I tell you image is everything at HD, I mean it. All those skinny bitches eating carrots for lunch, Dumeno does not like real women.'

'So you're calling me a skinny bitch Becca?' Farusja asked, swatting at the mosquitoes biting her knees.

Rabecca rolled her eyes. 'Yeah I am, but the difference is you're an intelligent skinny bitch, and that's what I am very, very, afraid of.'

Farusja sighed heavily. 'Well this skinny bitch is not going to take any crap lying down.' She turned to look at Rabecca, and they both instantly burst out laughing at the pun in her words.

Rabecca sobered up instantly. 'I am serious *mami*.'

'So am I.'

Miles Mkazi swore in frustration. On evenings like this it felt like he was the only one who was trying to uphold the law in this city. He hated it and he hated whoever had killed Frieda because it gave him more paperwork to take care of. The clerk in the constables department at the police station did not seem to realise that she actually had a job to do, and despite spittle flying in her face from Miles' outbursts about the quality of her work, her endless list of personal phone calls and manicures took precedence over the work he asked her to do, his emails often sent back unanswered. The amazing thing was that he was the one laughed at by his colleagues and told to clean up his act.

Miles frowned, his entire face twisting in concentration. It was Sunday night, and he was not being paid overtime; but the case was leaving a burning hole in his chest. The pictures of Frieda Lyme littered his desk, close-up shots of the bruises around her neck and under and around her jaw. Her brown eyes stared back at him, with dead horror. He had nothing. They had found nothing on Frieda that gave any clues as to who had killed her; nothing. It was as if her body had been cleaned thoroughly after she had been strangled. Her struggles against her killer had been ineffective; her blood-alcohol level had taken care of that. Miles sighed again, riffling through the photographs. The forensics team had not even found a stray fibre that they could safely say was the killers, and never mind where her body had been dumped. In an area full of human debris of all kinds, there was no way they would find anything that would pinpoint the killer. Sifting and analysing all the trash they had found around her body would take weeks, if not months, and even then it was a fools chance.

And that guy … Miles thought as he squinted at the shape of the bruises around the late Frieda's neck. Dante Dumeno. He had gone to see him not knowing what to expect. The man had not disappointed him and the visit had not seemed to faze Dumeno at all. He had paid Dumeno a visit on a whim, he was rarely wrong about his whims, they always led him to a potential suspect or a potential lead, but Dumeno had surpassed even his wildest expectations. If anyone in the department had found out that he had gone to talk with Dante Dumeno he would be seeing the inside of an office for a very long time. As long as Dumeno continued to support local police efforts in monetary form, he was untouchable. Miles had expected a call from his commanding officer the minute he had left the premises of HD Advertising, and had been surprised to arrive back at his desk and hear no mention of his visit. It had shown him the character of the man, and begrudgingly Miles had to admit to himself that he was impressed.

And what if Dante himself was the killer? Miles frowned thoughtfully. His exploits around town and especially with women, were no secret to anyone. So if he was the killer, what would his motive be? To prevent the drama that occurred after he dumped her? Just for the thrill of having her body and then their life in his hands?

Miles sighed, shaking his head. He knew he was grasping at straws, but this case seemed to have been closed the minute it had opened, and he needed to go on every whim, lead or piece of straw that floated his way.

CHAPTER 11

Monday, 30 April

*F*arusja was nervous when she went to work on Monday. She had spent the night tossing and turning. Not only was she scheduled for a major briefing session regarding the winning of the tender, but it would be the first time she would see Dante again since being naked with him in the parking lot. She had dressed slowly this morning, watching with ever rising nausea as the clock ticked towards eight.

On Friday, before the party, Jaco had already pulled them into a brainstorming session. Farusja with her new found friend Sidney Kimani had worked on a few different design concepts for the first batch of awareness adverts. She and Sidney had frequently been paired-off on working on designs together in the past two weeks and had become fast friends.

Sidney was a tall regal woman, whose braids hung down her back in a complicated maze of design. She had come from Kenya and there was little the Namibian sun had done to change her clear complexion. She was also a freshie, having started work at HD only three months before.

Farusja exhaled noisily. The adverts were to appear in every magazine and newspaper in the country and needed to be nothing short of amazing. Luckily the meeting was only at 12h00, which gave her more time to perfect her design ideas.

It was a cool morning, but the tension in her was thick as she walked into the office. She did not know what to feel, or how to even begin avoiding Dante Dumeno. She was two weeks new and she had already filled out being naked with a male boss on her CV. The humiliation was absolute and the realisation that someone at work might find out was terrifying. She hoped that Dante would be professional enough to forget the whole incident and leave her alone.

'Morning Jaco,' her insides quailed but the smile she plastered on her face was perfect.

'Ah, Farusja,' Jaco was in a flurry of activity, grabbing print-outs and design concepts from Farusja's desk. 'Dante has moved the meeting up by four hours! We are needed in the boardroom now!'

'What?' Farusja said aghast. 'He can't do that!'

'Unfortunately he *mos* can, and he has,' said Jaco through clenched teeth. 'Okay *fokus*! We know this, we went over this on Friday, breathe! Help me collect what we've got. I'm going to quickly find Sidney and get her ready! *Fok* man!'

Farusja put her hand to her mouth, straining to contain to the anger building up inside. She was seething. *The bastard. The unethical bastard.* Dante Dumeno knew exactly what he was doing, and his first punch had been to destabilise her. So much for him being professional about things, and she could feel that this was just the beginning.

Farusja, Sidney and Jaco entered the boardroom together. Roberta and Dante were already present, sitting together at one end of the room, their heads together and smiles on their faces, talking quietly. The marketing team, both Michael and Tony; Michael studiously avoiding her gaze; were sitting to Roberta's left, and they were also joined by one of the junior finance executives that Rabecca had introduced her to at one point. The table unanimously raised their eyes as the three of them entered, the smile on Dante's face enigmatic. Farusja exhaled, and could not help but meet Dante's eyes across the room. He smiled back at her innocently.

'Sorry to reschedule the meeting at such short notice,' drawled Dante. 'But nevertheless, thank you for being here.'

Roberta stood. 'Okay, quick recap of the brief people, then the design team can show us what they have. What we're going to do is take a look at each concept, accept or reject it, and work on the best of the few. This is not a democracy; if either Dante or I don't like it, out it goes.'

Farusja sat staring at the folders in front of her. She wondered if she should have rather called in sick. She could feel those dark eyes on her, but she would not give him the satisfaction of rising to the bait.

Jaco took the floor. 'As you all know, we've had very little time to work on this pitch. The deadlines from the client are horrific, but because this job is going to be our biggest breadwinner, my team is working round the clock to live up to the international standards of HD. The guidelines provided, as you all know, was Transform the current HIV/AIDS campaign.'

'Each of my designers have come up with a campaign idea, both of which, in my opinion, are brilliant. But you'll have to decide which one to go for. Farusja, you first.'

Farusja slowly scrapped her chair backwards, stood up and moved towards the pin board which graced the left wall. On the outside she was calm, the shine of perfection, but her hands shook slightly with the force of emotion that tore through her insides. She pinned some print-outs to the board, taking a deep breath.

'So much campaigning to date has already been done with the ABC methodology; abstaining, faithfulness to one partner and condom use,' she started.

'We do not have time for things we already know. Get to the point Miss Mumba. Show us what you have,' said Dante, his gaze locking onto hers, the smile no longer on his face.

Farusja flushed, but kept her composure. 'Apologies. Our brainstorming has yielded the use of a completely different concept. The message of ABC is old, if not redundant in today's society. Why not focus on love relationships instead? Why don't we redefine monogamous relationships and make them of relevance and importance again in today's society? It will be like free relationship advice with added messages on how to protect yourself. No one has looked at it from this angle, and trust me, people are dying to have any form of guidance in their relationships, other than movies and books.'

She then proceeded to show them various sketches that she had come up with, drawing strength from the encouraging smile on Jaco's face.

'Enough, Miss Mumba,' Dante cut her off. 'I know the team did not have enough time to do a good job, but this is too amateur for HD. We need cutting edge designs that bring the message across but also stimulate peoples ability to take action. What you have shown does none of this, it's all second rate. Jaco, did you not look through what Miss Mumba was going to present before she wasted our time?'

Roberta narrowed her eyes at Dante, worried, not listening as Jaco explained the concept in detail. She looked up at Farusja who was still standing. She did not need intuition to know that the woman was angry. She could see it in the way the folders were twisted in her grasp, by her rigid stance. What was Dante playing at now? Did it have something to do with this girl? Dante was acting up, and when Dante acted up, problems followed.

'Alright Jaco, I'll take that explanation as sufficient for now, but this gets no vote from me. I am tempted to say that this pitch is too important and Miss Mumba has only been with us for what, two weeks? Maybe she still needs some training. In the meantime I suggest you take over.'

Roberta did not like what was happening. The other employees sitting on the table were looking everywhere except at the exchange taking place. They were all used to Dante expressing his disapproval at what he did not like, but this time he was taking it too far.

Roberta stood, wanting to end the display. 'Farusja, you are dismissed. Take this time to brainstorm around the concept a bit more. Sidney, you're next up. Let's not waste any more time.'

Farusja looked around the faces in the room, her eyes settling on Dante. He looked pointedly at her, the smile back on his face. Without another word she gathered her folders and stalked out of the room, the anger inside her finally boiling over.

She went back to her office seething, contemplating whether she should pack her bags and hop on the first flight out of Namibia. An hour later, Jaco and Sidney returned in a flurry of reassurances and dismissals of what had happened in the meeting. Farusja was grateful when they left her to stew in a humiliated silence.

The latest cargo came with an Angolan girl of dubious intent. 'Where's my money?' she looked at him, the gum snapping in her mouth.

Michael looked at her, from the big hoop earrings, the tank top hugging her torso and the tiny shorts that clung to her every curve. He already knew how she had managed to move it across the border. He asked her anyway.

The gum snapped louder in her mouth and she looked straight at him, her body relaxed but coiled with the tension of their illegalities.

'Why you need them?' she said back to him, her eyes never leaving his face.

Michael laughed, watching as she raised her hands to her hips. 'You're a cheeky one this week, eh?'

The girl continued snapping her gum at him, her jaw now moving in double time, betraying the anxiety she felt. He watched her steal a glance at the blue Range Rover idling outside the small house which he had hired for the day. The driver in the front seat swivelled his head around so hard that Michael sniggered at the whiplash the man would suffer later. 'That your boyfriend? Is that car his?'

'Listen, I just need my money,' she spread her hands wide away from her body, her jaw still moving. 'You gonna give it to me or what?'

Michael sighed theatrically. Reaching into his pocket he pulled out a stack of N$200 bills which he handed to her. 'You can count it, if you like.'

'You wanna turn around and give me some privacy?'

'You left your privacy at home when you decided to bring this across,' Michael smiled at her. He smiled wider as she proceeded to stuff as much cash as she could into her bra, smoothing the notes around her breasts and then forced the rest into her miniature shorts, staring at him as he watched her, the look on her face snide. Then he watched her pert little bottom swing out of the house and out of his view, closing the door behind her. He had no fear of being recognised, blackmailed or shot for that matter, *that* person had taken care of that. *That* person who had come to be known as *satana, der teufel, Diablo*. People were known to have disappeared, changing their names, appearance and city rather than confess to this *Diablo* how they had crossed *him*. The ones that did not disappeared eventually anyway.

But he, Michael, was one of the lucky ones. He was essential to *his* plan, and if anything he would disappear first if he saw signs of not being needed anymore.

Michael stared at the black canvas bags on the table in front of him that she had left in exchange, his whole being rejecting the bag. He hated these trips, sure they were vital to his work but they never got any easier and the more he made them, the sloppier he became. He had been told to be brash, arrogant even, but loud enough so that he could be noticed; noticed, recognised and dismissed, which allowed him the leeway to do what he really had to do.

That face, he shuddered, cold shivers racing up and down his spine, *he* had told him, had trained him, had persuaded him that what he was doing was right, and would make him a lot of money. The money had convinced him along with a little firecracker of a word called revenge. With this bag he would make his eighth trip in two months to DI Storage, since he had been approached by *him*. During those two months it had been planning, more planning, and setting the stage for what was going to happen next. He had been excited, even aroused at times by the work he was doing but he was no fool; he covered his tracks and himself just as well as *he* did. He had watched too many movies not to know that the fall guy was always the hired help.

He remembered the day he had come into contact with *him*. It had been a non-eventful Saturday, which he had spent as he usually did, sleeping until twelve o'clock and watching television in his boxers, not bothering to shower or change, when the intercom buzzed. She had been brief, even nonchalant, asking him to let her in, promising to explain why she was showing up unannounced on a Saturday afternoon. He had depressed the button to open the gate resentfully. The electric gate had slid open, and when he opened the front door of his suburban, three bedroomed house to rant and rave at her for disturbing his peace, but the words had died in his throat. He grimaced as he remembered the smile she had thrown his way. Casually coming into the house as if he had already invited her, *him* following slowly at her heels, those eyes boring and burning into his. He knew he would never refuse *him* anything. That was when everything had begun.

He shook his head as though to clear the memory, he did not want to think of such memories at the moment, he had work to do, and he only had an hour to do it. His gaze moved over the three canvas bags in front of him, inspecting them critically. They were of adequate size and strength, he did not need anything stronger or more versatile, and these would do fine.

He was running out of time. He had disappeared from work at 12h00 today, claiming an appointment with a fictitious doctor to allow him to get the cargo. It had been a simple matter of waiting for the girl, and now it was 13h00. It had taken her a whole hour to get here, and he had to rush to deposit the bags at home before he left for work again. It was ideal that his house afforded him the privacy he needed, from the high walls to the dark blinds that could be pulled down on the prying eyes of the houses that stood above him on the hills, he would not be disturbed and was sure that no one could get into the house without his knowledge. The only problem with the design of the house was the garage, from which he needed to work. In order to reach it he had to walk outside to the right side of the house and open the garage, at which point he was in full view of whoever was watching. The people of Windhoek were noisy busybodies, always on the lookout for fresh fuel to feed the gossip fires; he had to look as natural and as normal as possible at all hours of the day.

Farusja frowned. It was late afternoon when Kobus summoned her. Heart thumping, she went into his office, her eyes drawn immediately to the painting above his desk.

'Farusja, sit,' he said, barely looking up from his paperwork. 'Our people have done a bit of investigating into your past. There's this issue of a criminal record which you failed to disclose to us. Rioting and arson at The University of Zambia? Didn't you think that this would come back to haunt you?'

Farusja made an attempt to interrupt, but Kobus didn't let her. 'We want to keep you but we cannot have a potential political dissident on our hands without any insurance, I am sure you understand. As from today you are under probation for the rest of the year. Jaco will monitor your work closely, you will make no move without his go-ahead. You will at all times be accompanied by him or by Sidney to any meeting or function HD needs you to be present at. That will be all.'

'Do I not get to state my case?'

Kobus looked back down at the papers on his desk. 'You have no standing to do so. I said that will be all.'

Farusja turned on her heel as her chest heaved in anger. All because of a riot during her university days? Or because she wouldn't open her legs for Dante?

Once most of the HD staff had left for the day, Farusja put her head in her hands, rubbing her temples tiredly. She was grateful that tomorrow was a public holiday and that Rabecca had gone off with friends for the evening and left her car at Farusja's disposal. She did not want her best friend to see her in this state. Unfortunately Sidney knocked on the door, peering in as she opened it.

'He is after you, am I right?' she had said quietly, closing the door behind her once she had made sure that Jaco was not in.

Farusja just looked at her, not affirming or denying it.

Sidney shook her head. 'You cannot play with that man, my dear. He is dangerous.'

'I am not!' Farusja whispered furiously at her. 'He's the one who is chasing me!'

'All I am saying,' Sidney laid her hands flat on Farusja's table, 'is that he is dangerous. You can't get involved with him. I have only been here three months and the stories I'm hearing about how notorious he is with the women, *eish*.'

'I am not getting entangled with him! You make it sound as if I'm considering it!'

'All I am saying,' Sidney repeated, 'is look at the guy. He's not a guy you just pass up a chance to be with.'

Farusja smirked at her, fuming, getting up from her chair to pace the small office. 'He's a bastard that's what he is. An unethical bastard!'

'He is also a man looking at you,' Sidney sniffed in her direction, avoiding the hand that almost hit her. 'You've not been with one in what, two years? Four?'

Farusja smiled ruefully at her. 'I will not be the girl that screws the boss then gets a promotion.'

Sidney came around to her, putting her arms around her shoulders. 'I have a solution for you,' she whispered. 'Keep your legs closed and keep away from him!'

Farusja felt that working at HD was a lot more than she had bargained for. She had seen Michael twice this morning, and both times he had treated her courteously and avoided her like the plague. Farusja had refused to let it faze her, but it had made her feel like a woman marked.

She wondered what else Dante Dumeno had done without her knowledge. She had felt watched since Saturday, but she couldn't be too sure. She was now the most popular woman at HD Advertising.

She also knew that it was not going to stop unless she did something. She only had two options; she could stand up and face the monster that had become Dante Dumeno overnight or she could simply sleep with him. Farusja sprang up from her desk, she knew what she had to do.

Farusja stood in front of the gate. While the sunset kissed the sky around her, she took a moment to admire the houses around her. The city was rapidly expanding, and as a result the African bush was being pushed back square metre by square metre, new suburbs constantly being created. One such place was where Dante Dumeno's house stood. Being a mountainous and hilly area, Farusja found herself staring up at the short incline of the driveway, which curved to the left and lead up to the house. The gate was electrified and from where she stood, all she could see was the communications intercom system.

Farusja stared at the incline in consternation. She hated driving up hills, so did Rebecca's car. The Volkswagen beetle was an old and much loved vehicle, but she groaned every time she was put through her paces, and this hill would be a huge challenge for the minute vehicle. But she did not want to leave the car outside where it would be a target for thieves. Farusja stood with her hands on her hips, undecided about what she should do. The intercom above her head buzzed.

'Miss Mumba, what do you think you are doing?' Dante's voice floated down at her, even without seeing him, Farusja could hear the smirk in his tone.

She started; looking around self-consciously. She could not see any cameras, where were they hidden? She bit her lip contemplatively; she still not know why she was here, and she knew she was doing exactly what he had done to her – chasing him. She had gone home after work just long enough to drop off her folders and new laptop, and without thinking it through had jumped into the beetle and driven to Dante's house.

When she had started working at HD Advertising, Becca had shown her this house; it had been her own star map for Farusja to show her just how decadent and detached the rich in Namibia were. She was glad she had remembered the directions. The intercom to her left buzzed again, and she smoothed down her hair haughtily, angry and nervous that her train of thought was being interrupted.

'I asked you what you thought you were doing Miss Mumba,' Dante's voice, sounding faintly annoyed came through the tiny intercom system.

She smiled. 'Trying to get your attention Mr Dumeno.'

A grunt came from the intercom. 'What do you want Mumba? Why are you here?'

'Let me in, Dante.'

There was silence, and with a faint sigh, the gate begun to slide back on its hinges. Farusja walked back to the car, clenched her teeth and put it in gear. She accelerated heavily before letting go of the clutch and encouraging the beetle up the slope. The driveway, paved with interlocks, led her directly to two garages nestled side by side. There were no cars parked in front of either them; so she parked in between the two, knowing that she would be making a hasty exit anyway.

What now? She walked up the short path leading to the front door. She could see no one, no gardeners nor any other house helpers. She was surprised by the size of the house; she had expected a three-storey monolith that defied the space it was built in or the people who lived in it. She was surprised. It was a two-storey house painted a cheery green. There was not much space in the front of the house that she could see and the path led straight to the door; she assumed the garden was behind the house.

She trudged up to the front door, feeling heavier the closer she got. As she raised her hand to knock, the door swung open. Her eyes locked with Dante's immediately.

He stood with his hands in his pockets, looking down at her with an amused expression on his face. 'What brings you to my home?'

Farusja's mouth twisting at the corners. 'Is it not enough that I came to you?'

His eyebrows rose at her and he stepped aside, sweeping his hand away from his body, a bemused expression on his face. 'Would you like to come in?'

She swept past him, stopping in the foyer.

'Well, you came all the way here, so I don't see why you're stopping here,' Dante said dryly as he moved past her, going deeper into the house.

Farusja sighed, and followed him. She stopped in surprise. The décor of the house was warmer than she had thought it would be. It was an open-plan house, there were no long corridors, every room led off to a different area of the house. The furniture was in deep shades of brown with bright splashes of colour in the form of cushions and paintings that adorned the house and walls. From the sitting room she spied a separate dining room and the kitchen; she thought she saw glass doors leading off the kitchen to the back before Dante's chest blocked her view.

'Drink?' he questioned her, one eyebrow raised. 'Are you going to sit?'

Farusja bristled, her skin prickling angrily, she was starting to wonder again why she was here. 'No, I do not want anything Mr Dumeno,' she said through clenched teeth. 'But yes, I'll sit.'

Dante shrugged his shoulders and motioned around the sitting room.

Farusja moved past him, plopping herself down on a brown couch. There was a small coffee table to her right covered in magazines, and as she looked around she saw the pattern repeated across the room. She counted four ottomans, two couches including the one she was sitting in and two beautifully carved, antique high backed chairs. On the wall to her right was a mounted widescreen television, the only evidence of an entertainment system.

'Why are you here Miss Mumba?'

Farusja sighed and dragged her eyes back to him. He had seated himself on the couch across her, one jeaned leg crossed over the other. His brown toes peeked at her, while his eyes regarded her coolly, no hint of what he thought visible in them.

'You know why I am here,' she paused, 'Dante.'

She grimaced as she saw a small smile play across his mouth; she had not wanted to give him any satisfaction with regards to her status with him, but she now saw that by using his first name she had already lost the first fight. She scowled. 'You play a dirty game.'

Farusja laid her hands on lightly on her knees, breathing deeply to prevent herself from screaming in anger. He was not going to make this easy was he? She grimaced, *well I want my life back and two can play this game.*

'Miss Mumba,' Dante sighed. He moved off the couch in one fluid motion and stood looking down at her. 'You have no business here. My employees are not invited to my house, ever. Do I make myself clear? You are trespassing.'

Farusja gaped up at him her mouth opened wide. 'Trespassing?' she spluttered angrily. 'You let me in!'

'Maybe in the next few minutes that will slip my mind.'

'Ah, you're a class act Dumeno,' Farusja said quietly, her head shaking from side to side. 'You've crossed the line almost ten times already – and that's just in one day. How many women have you played this game with?' Farusja stood up facing him, sneering into those dark eyes.

Dante exhaled as he watched her eyes change again. *Is it really the light? Or something else? How do her eyes change like that?*

He turned away from her, moving back to sit on the couch, his composure regained.

'Actually, I've never needed to play before,' he said slowly, his eyes raised to hers. 'You are the first opposition I've received in a very, very long time.'

'What?' Farusja seethed, her voice coming out in a hiss.

'Well, to put it frankly, Mumba,' Dante's voice was indifferent, 'you are the first woman ever to say *no* to me. I've been battling with how to deal with this.'

Farusja swallowed hard. She could not let this man get her angry. When she got angry she threw things and punched cushions, she would not be accused of aggravated assault.

'You've tied my hands and reduced me to nothing but a grunt at HD,' she said quietly. 'I want it to stop. I want everything that ever happened between us to be forgotten. I want you to leave me alone to do my job.'

Dante ignored her as he stood up, leaving her sitting, turning on the lights in the foyer, in the sitting room and kitchen. He walked back to her lazily, resuming his place on the couch opposite her.

She paused. 'Now, Mr Dumeno.'

Dante smiled. Despite himself, he felt admiration for his *badly dressed freshie.* She had, he looked down at her groin area, big balls. 'And let's say hypothetically I did all that you are asking of me, what would be in it for me?'

'Listen Dumeno,' Farusjas eyes flashed at him. Getting up she almost kicked the ottoman out of her way, and stood inches from him, dying to tear him apart. 'Just leave me alone! I don't want you. I never did! You are making me detest you.'

'Detest,' he mused, interrupting her, scratching the back of his head. 'Strong word Mumba. Why are you here anyway? You could have just as easily made an appointment at the office but yet you walk straight into my house, and alone too. Have you not been warned about me? About how dangerous I am?'

Farusja made a strangled sound in her throat, her hands clenched at her side.

'I own people in this town Farusja,' he said quietly, his eyes on his fingers as he picked at his nails. 'There is not one person you can run to for help that does not have their fingers dipped in my pocket. But if you were with me, you would not even have to work for a while. I'd look after you, while you're with me that is. And when you do go back to work we can negotiate a better,' Dante paused, his dark eyes suddenly raised to hers, 'a better package.'

Farusja sat back down with a thump, her body numb. She remembered Sidney's words and wondered again how she could hammer some sense into the man sitting in front of her.

'For how long?' she said tiredly, rubbing her hand across her eyes.

'Let's not put a timeframe on pleasure Mumba,' Dante drawled.

'Then Mr Dumeno,' she said softly. 'I refuse your offer. You must be very lonely if you have to resort to such methods to get someone into your bed. It's quite pitiful really.'

Dante sat looking up at her, trying to stop the stubbornness that was rising inside him. He knew she had every reason to be angry at him, he knew she was right, but he refused to lose, he hated losing ... Dante growled to himself. He wanted this minx, he would just have to find another way to get to her.

He stood up and moved to the ottoman that was angled slightly to her right, smiling. At one point he had thought she was going to hurl it at him, and he did not know what had stopped her. He would have liked to tussle with her, angry as she was. He watched her as she glanced at him warily, wondering why he had come so close to her. He inhaled, trying to catch her scent; her eyes had changed, they no longer flashed fire at him and had become soft and luminous again. They were breathtakingly beautiful. Bedroom eyes, he thought to himself.

'Why don't we...' he stopped, and raised his head as though smelling the air.

At that moment the sound of crashing, tinkling glass filled the room. Without another word Dante grabbed hold of her arm tightly, propelled her to her feet and from the room, half running, almost lifting her off the floor in his haste to get out of the sitting room.

Farusja, bewildered, took a look at his face, and felt alarm well up inside her. 'What's happening?' she gasped, her heart beating a tattoo against her chest.

Dante dragged her from the living room into the dining room, then into what looked like a study.

'Up the stairs,' he commanded her as he left her at the bottom of the staircase leading to the second floor. 'Now! Go!'

Farusja stood still puzzled, now scared. 'What? What's was going on?'

Dante growled and grabbed her around the waist, pulling her up the staircase, depositing her on the second floor while he dashed to a door on his left. Farusja had no time to register her surroundings before Dante ran back to her, lifted her boldly around the waist and deposited her into the room whose door she had seen. It closed firmly behind her with a click.

Dante ran back to the staircase, almost vaulting down the steps. Reaching the bottom he paused, grabbing a heavy fake stone tablet from the desk and started to walk towards the kitchen, his body tense and alert.

'Everything is okay old friend,' he heard Hienry's voice call out to him.

Dante sighed, placing the ornament on one of the ottomans as he walked into the kitchen. The tiled floor was littered with broken glass and chips of stone. The glass doors that led out to the backyard of the house had been smashed. He looked around the kitchen, spotting the culprits almost immediately. The bricks had crashed into the table tops, other than that nothing else had been broken.

Hienry was standing outside the broken doors, glancing around speculatively.

'Well, you sure took your time,' Dante retorted. 'Where have you been? I thought your men were watching those screens and patrolling the house twenty-four-seven?'

'This is what I have been telling you!' Hienry yelled at him. 'How do you think those bombs got on your property? Eh? How? We have people watching this house every day, every hour!'

He motioned with his hands to the broken doors in front of him angrily. 'And we still don't know who's coming in, who's going out. We don't know!'

Dante frowned, staring at the shattered glass around him.

'There is more,' Hienry said quietly. 'That ugly car parked out front.'

Dante turned away and strode through the foyer and out of the now open door; coming to a stop in front of the garage. The Volkswagen was wrecked, the windows were smashed, the glass making an ugly pattern around and inside the car. The exterior was dented and scratched and the interior still had smoke coming out of it from a fire that had very recently been put out. There were two men milling around the car; there was a big black utility box next to them and they systematically took tools out of the bag to aid them in their task of taking the car apart. They stopped and nodded as they saw him, and continued their work, right now in the process of removing the doors.

Dante's jaw clenched as he swore under his breath. 'Damn it!'

'Yes, we thought the exact same thing when we saw it,' Hienry said coming up behind him.

'Did you not see who did this?' Dante said quietly, his teeth clenched so tightly his jaw started to ache.

'Now this,' Hienry moved past him and stood two paces away from the wreckage that was Rabecca's car, nodding to his men. 'This is something else.'

He kicked at the glass that was littered in front of the garage. 'This little baby was wired before it came in the gate.'

Dante stared at his friend, uncomprehending. 'What?'

'This car,' Hienry repeated patiently, rubbing his stomach, 'was wired before it came through your gate.'

'What are you saying Hienry?' Dante snapped at him. 'First you did not see who smashed my doors, now you did not see who wrecked Farusja's car? What am I paying you guys for?' He was angry, his voice raised as he shouted more at the men who were working around the wrecked car than at Hienry.

'I told you we have a security issue!' Hienry turning away from the car turned to face Dante, snapping back at him. 'And you did not listen!'

'Fix it then! Fire everyone and get new help!'

'Argh!' Hienry dismissed him angrily with a wave of his hand. 'That's even more dangerous! Where is the girl?'

'Girl?' Dante frowned.

'The owner of this car!' Hienry growled angrily. 'You took her upstairs!'

Dante turned on his heels, sending his friend a scathing look as he strode angrily back inside.

CHAPTER 12

*F*arusja fell on her behind hard, her mind reeling. *What is going on?* She had heard glass breaking and it had scared her. Him rushing her upstairs and into a room which she was sure had locked the minute the door closed behind her had not helped either.

She hoped this was not another one of his stunts. She looked around curiously, it had been dark when she was pushed in, but the lights had gone on automatically when the door closed. It was the size of a guestroom, and was pleasantly warm. The floor was covered in a black carpet and there were two beds separated by a side table. Farusja got up, rubbing her behind as she ventured into the room, passing a fridge and deep freezer. She peeked in, wondering why these appliances would be upstairs. They were both filled with provisions, from water and juice to instant chicken nuggets and frozen vegetables.

She frowned; stacked against the walls next to the beds were boxes filled with long lasting canned and dried foods. Farusja went through three small boxes before giving up on the other ten littered around the room. There was also a simple two plate stove and a bathroom, complete with a shower and toilet.

'Okay,' Farusja said out loud, her hands on her hips, looking around her. This seemed to be some sort of bunker or panic room. Either Dante Dumeno had some very bad enemies, or was preparing for a natural or civil disaster that the rest of them did not know about. She turned to the door as she heard a sound and walked towards it, putting her ear to it. She could hear pounding; she put her hands on either side of her head on the door. There was a small electronic keypad where the door handle should have been, it looked as though one needed a code to get out of the room. She banged on the door in frustration, and jumped back in surprise as the pounding from outside grew to a low growling sound, ending suddenly with a little *phut*! Thick black smoke started seeping under the door slowly.

Farusja watched it swirl around her feet in surprise, taking two steps back, willing herself to stay calm. But she shrieked as the door was forced open, curly black tendrils of smoke wisped around her, thick in the enclosed space, obscuring her vision. She choked as it assaulted her nostrils and throat. This was not smoke from a fire, it smelled of a crude mixture of chemicals. Hands grabbed her and dragged her back out of the room, rubbing her back as she took deep breaths, choking and trying to clear the air in her lungs.

'Mumba,' Dante's voice was quiet in her ear.

She stared at the closet doors that swung back on themselves behind her as she was dragged out of the room. She was suddenly in a rather big bedroom. The room she had been in had been built into the bedroom but camouflaged to look like a closet. Before she could process the information, she felt herself pushed down onto the bed in the room, and gratefully accepted the glass of water that was thrust into her hand, gulping it down in a hurry, leaving half of it on the black pencil dress she was wearing.

'Are you okay Mumba?' Dante said again, his hands on her shoulders.

Farusja looked up into his dark eyes, the expression on his face was one of anger, and she watched as a muscle in his jaw began its slow twitching.

'What is going on?' her voice came out more shrilly than she intended it to.

Dante sat down beside her, taking her hands in his.

'What a bad host I've been,' he smiled at her, warmly. 'That closet I pushed you into only opens from the inside and you needed a code. There is no way you could have opened it, the walls and door are reinforced it's difficult to even get a mobile signal in there. We needed to use other means to open it.' His face grew serious. 'I'd appreciate if this remained between you and I.'

Farusja waved her hand at him. 'Whatever Dumeno. I'd prefer to remember nothing of this visit the way things are going.'

She had only just noticed that the smoke had dispersed as quickly as it had appeared and that there were two men wandering in and out of the room she had just vacated. She put her hands to her head shaking it slightly; she had no idea what had just happened.

'What is going on here?' she turned to Dante who was still sitting next to her.

'We had a little security problem,' Dante said quietly, 'but it's taken care of.'

Farusja rubbed her chest vigorously, still tasting the smoke in her throat.

'Farusja ...'

Farusja went rigid, unable to explain the butterflies that suddenly exploded in dance in her stomach at the sound of the change in his voice. 'Your car ...'

Dante did not have the time to finish. Farusja reared off the bed and ran down the staircase, and through the house, almost skidding in the kitchen to avoid the shattered glass, out through the foyer, through the door and outside. She stopped dead, her mouth open in shock as she looked at the wreckage that was Rabecca's car.

'Oh she's going to kill me,' she whispered. 'Oh my goodness …' She stood numbly as she felt hands close over the tops of her arms.

'I'm sorry Farusja,' Dante's voice seemed to come from far away. 'Unfortunately it was me they were after.'

Farusja blocked his voice out and stood staring at the smoked out blackened interior of Rabecca's car, the slashed wheels and the broken windows. Even the doors were now removed. The car was but a shell of its former self. She felt anger well up inside her. None of this would have happened if it had not been for the chain of events that had led her to this house in the first place!

She shrugged Dante's hands off her shoulders, turning around to face him, her face set in stone. 'You bastard,' she said quietly. 'You did this on purpose, didn't you? '

'I wouldn't stoop so low Mumba,' his voice was hard. 'My house was damaged too.'

'And so what if it was?' Farusja put a hand to her chest in an effort to slow down the beating of her heart, her voice choked.

'Don't you think it's enough?' she said softly almost to herself, turning back to look at the car. 'This is not even my car! It's Rebecca's! What the fuck did I ever do to you?'

'I didn't do this Farusja,' Dante put his hand on her arm.

'Get away,' Farusja flinched away from him and moved towards the car, walking carefully to avoid the broken glass.

Dante watched her, his eyes dark, his face expressionless.

'You bastard!' he heard Hienry exclaim in Farusja's voice theatrically behind him, a chuckle in his throat. 'Ah Dumeno, you've really done it this time.'

Dante's mouth set in a thin line, anger drawn all over his face. He saw Hienry's bulk out of the corner of his eye, not turning to acknowledge him. 'If you had done your job I would not be in this mess.'

'So that is the girl you're seeing now,' Hienry mused speculatively. 'She is magnificent, good stock. Ah, if she does not find you in good taste Dumeno, which I can see she does not, I trust you know where to send her?'

Dante glanced at his friend. 'That is the last thing I'd do.'

Hienry laughed with gusto as he took a swig from the bottle he was holding in his hand, wiping his lips appreciatively.

'With all this going on, when did you have time to raid my cellar?' Dante said sarcastically, turning away from Hienry to watch the prone figure of Farusja who was still gazing at the car.

'Ah friend,' Hienry sighed. 'I'm not suggesting anything, all speculation.' He burped, loudly. 'But that car was wired to explode as I said, before it came through those gates. Maybe you should be careful about who you keep as company.'

Dante stiffened immediately, turning his head to Hienry sharply. 'What?'

'You heard me,' Hienry's voice went quiet, all traces of his accent gone. 'Either that girl is being used or she is part of it. If you look at the bigger picture ...' Hienry paused, taking another swig from the bottle, 'she might not be who she seems to be. Things are just too convenient.'

'You're not suggesting that Farusja might be involved?'

Hienry spluttered, wine dribbling down his chin. 'Oh no, such beauty could never be at fault!'

Dante's lips thinned. 'She's too innocent, too naïve. She could never even think up such ...'

'Yes, of course! Sharpen up those wits again Dumeno.' Hienry said dryly. 'Eh, Madam!' Hienry called out at Farusja, leaving Dante's side and, reaching her, caught her by the wrist, halting her progress forward.

'Let me go!' she yanked away from him angrily. 'You people! I want the rest of my friend's car and I want to get off this property now!' She stood facing Hienry, her chest heaving, her face twisted in anger.

'Ah Madam,' Hienry said quietly, 'I'm very sorry about what happened, but I insist you don't go any closer, it may still be dangerous.' He spread his arms wide. 'We do not know if there is anything else explosive inside.'

Farusja's eyes widened.

'We will compensate you adequately, Madam,' Hienry continued quietly. 'But right now you need to step aside so that I can do my job. You're in danger. I know you do not want to be here now, but go inside, have some tea and relax for a minute. We will take care of everything.'

'My purse,' Farusja felt numb, 'was in there. Rabecca will kill me ... all her stuff.'

'Don't worry my Madam,' Hienry continued softly. 'It will all be taken care of. All I want now is to see you relaxed. Here, look Joseph will show you around inside. Write a list of everything that was in the car, yes? Leave it in the living room, I'll find it. You go into the kitchen have some tea, switch on the time waster and watch a movie.'

'I want to go home,' Farusja mumbled.

'Madam, there was a bomb in your car,' Hienry told her sternly. 'You have been driving with a bomb in your car, for how long we don't know. You must trust me when I tell you it is not safe for you to go anywhere but back indoors. And we need to replace all your things. Now please, give us some time, yes?'

Farusja nodded, turning quietly and walking back towards the house, followed by Dante's security detail.

Dante stood watching the exchange between Hienry and Farusja, feeling an enormous amount of jealousy at the way Hienry had calmed her down and had her doing exactly what he wanted her to in that short space of time. He wished he had that sort of effect on her.

Hienry stood looking at the wreckage, then turned away and walked back to where Dante was standing beside the house.

'How did you?' Dante started asking him gruffly.

'Ah my friend, you're not French so you would not understand,' Hienry swaggered, then placed the still fairly full bottle on the pavement in front of him, straightening up immediately, all traces of his gaiety gone. 'Let's get to work.'

Dante nodded. The stars had slowly started winking their way into the night sky, it was going to be a very long night.

CHAPTER 13

Roberta sat on her balcony, her fingers stroking the condensation on the glass of white wine in front of her. Despite her conversations with Naks she was still worried about Dante, especially in light of the recent events involving that girl. He was starting to use HD as his personal playground again, and she did not like it one bit. It had all come to a head when she had found out what he had done to her. He did have the grounds to discipline her, she had lied on her application, but he was going too far. He was being personal about it. She did not really care what happened to Farusja, she hated all the girls that Dante had an attraction to, and she hated this Mumba girl even more because Dante seemed to have a genuine interest in her. It was too bad that she was currently one of HD's best designers.

Roberta knew that she needed to do something to bring him back; she just did not know what. She wanted the Dante who did not care about anything other than money, his businesses and watching her and Naks' back; and most especially, the part of him that cared about her.

Roberta did not mind who Dante fucked, but she most certainly had a problem if he happened to fall in love. He was not capable of it, none of them were, she told herself, and that's why the three of them made such a good team and she had to keep the team together.

Roberta snatched her phone up, rapidly dialling Naks number. She listened to it ring for a while before she stabbed the button ending the call. She would have loved to have Naks with her, but it looked like she was going to have to do this by herself. She would pack a bag and remind Dante of who he was and who he could still be if he kept his head in the game. She would be damned if she let some small good for nothing doe-eyed girl get between them. First Frieda's murder and now a bleeding romance, Roberta pursed her lips in disdain. She was sure the murder at DI Storage had something to do with the multitude of women Dante had slept with, she did not believe in coincidences. Roberta stood, making up her mind. This was all going to end now, if it was the last thing she did. Although public holidays during the week usually riled her, especially since tomorrow was only a Tuesday, but it would give her and Dante more than enough time to catch up on things in the Jacuzzi, even better that it was just a stone's throw from his bed.

Farusja thought she should feel mad, angry, maybe a little disgruntled, but Hienry had promised to take care of everything that had been lost in the car which made the entire ordeal just a little easier. She did not know how she was going to tell Rabecca. She was very relieved that Rabecca would be out for the night. Now her future in Namibia was set, she had no choice but to stay here and pay Rabecca back every cent she owed for the car. Farusja was not angry anymore, it took too much energy. All she felt was the burden of what was happening to her, and it had turned into a horribly empty feeling in the pit of her stomach.

She watched as the so-called Joseph walked around her, turning on a random channel on the television. He held out a pen and paper to her. She stared at him. He was an average, nondescript looking man. His hair was closely cropped to his head and his eyes were wide and bright. The black overalls he was wearing were covered with dirt and grease and he looked at her questioningly as he laid the stationery in front of her on the table.

'The list,' he said quietly. 'You will have to find some food in the kitchen yourself. Mr Dumeno does not have a woman who helps.'

Farusja glared at his back, angry and annoyed all over again. She snatched the pen and paper from the table, but could not remember anything except the pine tree air freshener that had been sitting on the dashboard. She looked up as footsteps sounded, and Dante came into view, the look on his face grave.

'I'd make you something to eat but I need to leave the house for an hour or two. Please stay, you'll be safe here.'

Farusja did not look at him, her eyes remaining fixed on the paper in front of her.

'Farusja.'

'What?' she replied shortly, not moving her head.

'I said I'm leaving. There's food,' Dante said impatiently, the frustration thick in his voice.

'I heard you the first time,' Farusja interrupted brusquely.

Dante pressed his lips together, knowing that he had no grounds to berate her. He turned on his heel and left without response. Farusja turned her head slightly, exhaling slowly.

Once he'd left, Farusja rummaged in Dante's kitchen, the contents of his cupboards surprising her. The image that Dante portrayed in the office was not the image that was being displayed around the house. She could not find junk food anywhere; it was all brown bread, detox teas and low fat cheese. She made herself a large sandwich, putting ham, cheese, salami and tomatoes on it; and armed with a mug of herbal tea spread herself out on the couch, watching TV. The sandwich lay in her stomach like a rock and she fell asleep.

She awoke with a start. The house was dark and quiet except for the low hum of voices on the television. She raised herself up slowly, wondering what she should do. It was obvious that Dante was not home yet, where the hell was he? Just thinking about him made her blood begin to boil again.

'Farusja,' Dante said quietly.

Farusja jumped, shrieking as the room flooded with light. 'Are you just skulking around in the dark?' she yelled at him, raising herself from the couch, her eyes glaring up into his. He looked tired and there were faint circles under his eyes, but she refused to have pity on him. 'I want to go home!'

'I wanted to … to, you know, to …' Dante's voice, a bit strained, came out slowly.

'Apologise?' Farusja offered sarcastically.

'Yes!' Dante breathed out in relief. 'I did not blow up your car Farusja. I'm not that kind of person.'

'And yet you have bent me to your will all day? And by the way, it's not my car, it's Becca's. So you actually owe her an apology,' Farusja crossed her arms across her breasts, her anger rising with each word she spoke.

Dante looked at her and breathed in deeply. 'Yes, I acted like a bastard today. But, hey you shouldn't be driving other people's cars without their permission. And besides, you're a criminal.'

'And so you discredit me in front of my colleagues? What else are you doing to me that I don't know about? And it's none of your business whose car I drive! And I'm not a criminal! Who didn't have a bit of action in university?'

'Well, yes Farusja, but…'

'And you tell me in no uncertain terms that if I do not sleep with you, I'll not get very far in the company or in this city?'

'I never said that,' Dante's eyes turned dark, he looked down at her.

'Oh, really? Would you have done all this to me if I was already in your bed? And now,' Farusja continued angrily. 'I have to spend all my hard-earned savings to buy a car that would not have been destroyed if you had never sent any of these events into motion. And after everything you have said and done to me, I'm to accept that you had nothing to do with it because you don't stoop to such methods?'

'I know how this looks, that you don't believe me.'

'Oh, really?' Farusja's voice rose shrilly, piercing the air between them, crackling with rage. 'You have played the dirtiest game Dumeno, and you expect me to just forgive everything and believe what you say?'

Dante scratched the top of his head, his eyes expressionless and unreadable. 'Well …'

Farusja noticed the grime stains on the back of his hands, and the black stains on his jeans.

'I'm sorry Farusja,' he spoke quietly. 'I'll set things right.'

'You've some nerve Dumeno, after all you've put me through. So it takes an explosion to stop you?' Then she added quietly, 'How can you be so callus?'

Dante looked down at her and knew that if she had a bit more testosterone in her, if she were more his height and had a penis, he would probably have punched her by now. He quenched the stubbornness rising in him, swallowing hard.

'Farusja Mumba,' he said through clenched teeth. 'I said I'd make things right but you have to listen to me now.'

Farusja set her mouth in a stubborn line, her arms still crossed over her breasts. 'I don't need to listen to anything you say Dumeno, as far as I'm concerned you can …'

'The bomb in the car,' Dante said, interrupting her, 'was put in the car before you came onto my premises. Do you understand?'

Farusja looked at him for a moment, bewildered.

'We don't know when it was put in the car,' Dante tentatively reached forward and placed his hands on her arms, holding them gently. 'You've both been driving around with it for god knows how long and it only detonated when it was in my yard.'

Farusja's arms dropped limply to her sides, her eyes looked up at him, curiously blank.

'I don't understand,' she mumbled.

'Yes, you do Farusja. Before I met you, I was already having these little surprises sent to my door, but now they're using you.'

'Ah, what the hell Dante,' she whispered as her body sagged. He moved forward, catching her in his arms, the eyes looking up at him had changed colour again, now they were as dark as his and as expressionless.

Dante gripped her upper arms more tightly, his voice gruff. 'I need to have someone with you at all times. At your house. Everywhere.'

Farusja felt weak, her entire body refused to obey her, Dante's voice came to her from far away and she felt as if she were struggling to breath and hear through a veil of dirty sluggish water. Now someone was using her as bait to get to Dante?

'Someone's trying to kill me?' she heard her voice ask as if from a great distance.

She saw Dante move his lips and then the water settled over her, covering her from the world and bestowing a beautiful and welcome kiss of darkness across her face.

Farusja opened her eyes tentatively, her mind clear. She struggled upright, looking around her blearily. She was no longer in the sitting room but lying on a bed in a room she hadn't seen before. *Where am I?*

It was a clean, sparse room, with a large double bed set in the middle. It had minimal furniture; a wardrobe, table and chair set all carved out of wood, and tiny side tables on both sides of the bed, one supporting a lamp and the other a phone line and alarm clock.

'You're awake.'

Farusja's heart accelerated, as she watched Dante come into the room, dropping a backpack on the floor. He sat down on the edge of the bed and peered into her face, scrutinising her.

'You had some sort of attack,' he cocked his head to the side. 'It wasn't even a fainting spell; you just slid into nothingness.'

'I don't have attacks,' Farusja grumbled, running a hand through her hair.

'No,' Dante looked at her speculatively, 'it wasn't. It was as if things just got too much for you and you shut down.'

Farusja glared at him, sitting up abruptly. 'I want to go home now Dante.'

'First you call me Dante, and then you call me Dumeno, stop sending me mixed messages.'

Then he sighed, rising from the bed, he stood looking down at her for a moment.

'It's not safe,' he said quietly, his eyes meeting hers. 'I'd feel better if you slept in my house tonight. At least until I send one of Hienry's men to make a thorough search of your house.'

He saw clearly that she was about to protest, so he continued quickly. 'What happened to you today was my responsibility, allow me to make a little of it right.'

'Put me in a hotel then,' she said gruffly.

'I have six men sleeping on my grounds today, including me and Hienry. It's the safest place in town right now,' Dante's eyes bored into hers. 'Humour me tonight, and on Wednesday we can go back to work and back to being enemies. Dinner, ten minutes.' He turned around and headed towards the door. 'Oh, and I took the liberty of packing some stuff for you.'

Farusja watched as he disappeared, leaving a faintly electric air behind him. Despite herself, the seeds of unease had been planted and she was starting to think it might be safest to sleep at Dante's house for one night.

She sighed and reached for the backpack Dante had brought, dumping the contents on the duvet. She did not know what to feel knowing that he had gone through her wardrobe; her clothes, her underwear.

Her face burned as she riffled through the contents of the backpack. He had packed two outfits for her, both jeans and t-shirts, each complete with their own matching pair of bra and panties. *How did he find these?* Even she could not find the matching sets in the chaos that was her underwear drawer. She shivered, a tingle of pleasure racing up her spine despite herself, the thought of wearing the underwear his hands had touched gave her a thrill. There was a small package wrapped in plastic, and as she unravelled it, the keys to the house and two new purses fell out. She fingered the purses, opening them, they were full of the paraphernalia that she had written on the list.

Farusja sighed, and pushed herself off the bed. There was a shower somewhere in this house. She would wash all that she was doing away in the shower, and then join her handsome offender for dinner.

The lighting was quiet and soft; if her house had been broken into she would have had her lights blazing. The glass doors leaving the kitchen had been completely knocked out and replaced by sheets of hard plastic, and of the glass on the floor there was no trace.

'Where is everyone else?' she asked timidly, her eyes on the food in front of her. She had made her way to the kitchen after her shower, stopping short as she had come across Dante bent over a chopping board. He had shooed her away to the dining room, telling her he had already finished preparing the food.

Farusja now moved the food around her plate, her body and mind tired; she had no appetite tonight after all that had happened, a nice warm bed would be okay with her right now, but the food looked so delicious … she sighed wistfully at the mixed vegetable stir-fry and chicken colouring her plate, it smelled so good.

'You don't have to eat if you don't want to Farusja,' Dante's quiet voice came across to her. 'It's been a long day.'

Farusja looked up at him gratefully, her eyes tired. 'It looks and smells amazing.'

'You need to sleep,' his dark eyes bored into hers searchingly. 'Go back to your room and don't worry, it's safe. Hienry's here, and so are the others.'

Farusja pushed her plate away from her slightly, resting her fork on its side. 'So, Jerome is your brother?'

'Yes,' answered Dante. 'He drives me mad most the time, but he's a good kid.'

'I heard he has a twin?'

Dante raised his eyebrows. 'Not only do I hire drug addicts and criminals but seems I've hired gossipers as well. Yes, she's studying in Cape Town, misses her brother like crazy but she failed and was held back a year.'

Farusja stifled a yawn.

'Am I boring you?'

Farusja yawned again, her mouth opening wide. 'I'm just so exhausted.'

'Need some help getting to your room?' Dante grinned wryly.

Farusja's skin tingled, alarm bells running up and down her spine.

'That's okay,' she said quickly. 'Thank you.' Pushing her chair back she raised herself out of it, and pushed it back into place under the table.

'Well, goodnight then.' she said awkwardly, watching him as he put down his knife and fork.

'Goodnight.' His voice was quiet, his eyes still boring into hers. 'Oh and by the way, I forgot your pyjamas, so I put something out for you. It's on the couch.'

Dante went back to eating, his eyes on his plate.

Farusja did not move for a moment. She was having trouble reconciling the two images she had of Dante in her mind, one image was hardnosed and callus, and the other was this quiet, cooking man, who was serving her dinner in his home, and taking care of her. She shook her head slightly. She was so confused that she did not know what to think. Was he like this just because he really felt remorse and guilt over what had happened or was this just part of his new plan?

CHAPTER 14

Dante watched Roberta sashay into the living room. He had been in his study when Hienry had warned him that he was sending Roberta up to the house. Before he could protest, Hienry had already hung up the phone, the last thing Dante had heard was him chuckling to himself in the background, with a fading line that sounded something like, 'That woman comes in all the time, what do you want me to do? I'm not your gatekeeper! But let me know how it goes, eh?'

Sometimes he really had to wonder if Hienry were on his side. He of all people knew what would happen if Roberta found him with an employee of HD in the house. He wandered into the living room to wait for her.

Roberta carried an overnight bag in her hand. She was wearing a skimpy see-through white summer dress, the end of it barely skimming her knees. She had let her hair down, it was curly and full, the blond shimmers in it caught the light. He tried not to think of running his hands through it, and instead eyed the overnight bag warily. This was not a good time, not a good time at all.

'Robbie, what's on your mind?' his voice came out strained, the tension in it easy to hear.

Roberta smiled at him, depositing her bag on the chair closest to her, moving to sit next to him on the couch, crossing her long legs to cover Dante's jeaned ones. Dante looked down at the bare legs covering his; trying very hard not to slide his hand up her thigh.

'Hi Dante.'

'Hi Robbie,' Dante breathed out heavily. 'I thought you were busy with Naks this evening?'

Roberta shifted, her dress sliding even further up her legs. 'He wasn't picking up, so I came to keep you company.'

Her eyes were mischievous, and the curve to her mouth betrayed her words. 'I'm worried about you baby. With the murder and what's been happening at the office – it's so much to take on.'

'I'm fine Robbie. I thought our motto was do or die?'

Roberta sighed, pursuing her lips. 'And what about the murder? Aren't you even the littlest bit worried that it will happen again?'

'The woman was in the wrong place at the wrong time, it had no bearing on my business.'

Roberta flicked back her hair, getting irritated. Her plan was to seduce Dante but she was becoming more frustrated by the minute. 'Really Dumeno? Really? Do you think this will just blow over? Do you know what the papers have been saying?'

'Yeah,' Dante grinned at her, 'all they have managed to do is hash up both our fucked-up lives, and if you ask me, I think it not only gave us some publicity, but showed us as the underdogs that rose to power. People like those kinds of stories.'

Roberta stared at him in disbelief. 'You can't be serious.'

'I'm very serious Robbie,' Dante said quietly, finally giving in to temptation, and resting his right hand on the bare leg crossed over his. 'I won't get distracted from my, our, businesses. We've worked too hard to let such distractions cause damage, and besides I think the press statements we released took care of the problem.'

Roberta smirked. 'You mean took their attention off your crazy little affair with Frieda?'

Dante slowly slid his hand up her leg to where her dress ended, resting it at the top of her thigh.

'Jealous Robbie?' he asked huskily. 'Why don't we take this upstairs and see just how jealous you are?'

Roberta smiled, and pulled his hand further up her thigh, until his fingers were touching the edge of her lace underwear. 'I'm never jealous of your fuck exploits, Dante. As long as you keep them out of HD. And talking about that, tell me about this silly child you're running after – one of my staff I do believe. You're crossing the line. Have you forgotten *Kifo*?'

To Roberta's surprise, he withdrew his hand from her, sliding it all the way back up to her knee. 'Well, I'll have to see, she's in the guestroom right now.'

Roberta narrowed her eyes at him. 'You cannot be serious!'

She did not finish the sentence but got up abruptly, taking long strides towards the guestroom.

Dante followed her as she pushed open the door, his eyebrows raised, peeking into the room over her shoulder.

'What is she doing here?' Roberta's voice was calm, but Dante heard the veiled anger behind the words.

Farusja was lying there, holding the blankets up to her neck, looking back at him in alarm.

'Who Robbie?' he said casually, leaning against the doorframe.

Roberta's lips twisted, her hands on her hips, anger seething from every pore of her body.

'You're playing Dante, again. What the fuck?' she turned back to Farusja. 'You're our employee. What the fuck are you doing here?'

'I don't know what you're talking about,' Dante interrupted, cocking an eyebrow at Farusja. 'Hey, you there, are you comfortable?'

Farusja nodded mutely, her body frozen in place, her mind whirling in circles.

'Good,' Dante nodded, ignoring Roberta by his side. 'Do you need anything?'

Farusja shook her head again, unable to make a sound, her stomach somewhere near her feet.

'Good, goodnight.'

Dante pulled Roberta, protesting vehemently out of the room, and shut the door firmly behind him.

Roberta wrenched away from him, almost shouting at him in her anger. 'What is that girl doing here Dante?'

'I thought you'd be asking why she wasn't in *my* bed,' he raised his eyebrows at her, an amused smile on his face.

Roberta breathed out noisily, exhaling in anger, her face turning impassive, her mouth in a twist. 'This is what I'm talking about, you keep breaking the rules! You never learn!'

'You act like this doesn't happen. Like you don't join me sometimes,' Dante chuckled mirthlessly as he moved back towards the sitting room, turning his back on her. 'We agreed to no jealousies Robbie.'

Roberta followed him, still breathing noisily, still angry. 'No Dante, we agreed you would keep your hands off HD staff. That's what we bloody agreed!'

Dante perched himself on the edge of the couch, staring up at her. 'Come on Robbie. Why are you acting up? You do this even more than I do.'

Roberta huffed quietly, her hands on her hips. 'I do not play with the hired help. You of all people should know that. I stick to our rule.'

'Ah, but I love playing with the hired help,' Dante smiled. 'Are you going to stay?'

Roberta smirked at him, reaching over the couch in front of her to pick up her bag. 'I don't associate with the help Dante, and neither should you. Stop fucking everything you see.'

'So does that mean you don't want to test-run the new girl with me?' Dante asked, watching as she threw him a poisonous look and slung her overnight bag over her arm and strode towards the door, flinching as it slammed loudly behind her. He knew he was going to pay for this.

He lifted himself off the couch, and went to the guestroom. He knocked lightly on the door, and opened it slightly when he heard no sound.

'Farusja? I'm coming in,' he moved into the room. She was still sitting as they had left her, gripping a pillow in both hands, a stricken look on her face.

'Are you alright?' he said quietly, moving to stand at the foot of the bed, his arms hanging loosely at his sides.

Farusja nodded, a strangled sound emerging from her throat. 'Ms Erlichmann, she saw me here ...'

'Yes,' Dante moved forward, perching himself on the edge of the bed. 'She did.'

Farusja groaned, her head dropping onto the pillow that she held. Dante looked at her lowered head, her face buried in the pillow. Her hair covered her head in a dense forest of split ends, shininess and long wayward strands. Dante reached his hand out to smooth her hair down, stopping abruptly as he realised what he was doing.

'I'll fix it,' he drew his hand back away from her, lifting himself off the bed. 'Get some rest.'

Farusja looked up to see his retreating back leaving the room, and flipped herself sideways onto the bed, covering her face with the pillow, her insides curling in shame. She was so embarrassed; this was another thing she would never live down.

Farusja woke up with her heart racing. It had been one of those dreams again, the ones were the lines of fact and fiction were blurred, the ones that always woke her up terrified and screaming inside. She put her hand to her chest, trying to still her heart, gasping for air. She groped around, reaching out to turn on her night light, and she found air. Disorientated for a moment she felt panic, where was she? She looked around at the dim silhouettes of the room lighted by the moonlight streaming through the windows, calming down as she realised she was in Dante's house.

Milk, Farusja thought as she threw back the covers and stepped onto the floor with her bare feet, padding slowly towards the door, trying to breathe in deeply and evenly. The pounding in her chest had slowed, and she opened the door and stepped out into the hallway, peeking around warily. The house was dark, illuminated only by the scant moonlight that peeked through the clouds. Farusja sighed in exasperation, she did not know where any of the light switches where and she did not plan on stumbling around in the dark. She was wearing the pyjamas that Dante had put out for her earlier – a t-shirt of his. Although ironed and laundered, she could still smell him on the fabric.

Farusja stood in the dark for a moment, staring in the direction she had remembered the fridge in. She did not see the light that was burning in the study, did not hear the faint footfalls coming into the kitchen from the sitting room, and gasped in surprise as bright light burnt her eyes.

'Hungry?'

Farusja whirled around, squeaking in fear at the way he had startled her.

'It's late. You couldn't sleep?' Dante stood in front of her, scratching the short kinky hair on his head, yawning.

Farusja stared at him, taking in the white vest and grey sleep shorts. His feet were bare like hers and the floor was pleasantly warm.

'Yes to both,' she murmured. 'You're still awake?'

Dante nodded ruefully. 'Sleep does not come easy at the moment.' He walked towards the fridge, pulling its door open contemplatively.

'What's the matter?' he asked, his head still buried in the fridge, his voice muffled.

'Nothing. What are you talking about?'

'Then why do you look close to tears?' Dante pulled two containers out of the fridge and turned to her, his eyes scrutinising her face.

'I wasn't …'

'Come on Mumba,' Dante turned away from her, going towards the microwave. 'I do listen to people. Well, now and then, when it suits me.'

He grinned as he heated the food.

'It was nothing,' she answered as she headed for the refrigerator, closing it with a carton of milk in hand.

Dante shrugged, his eyes watching the food revolving on the glass plate in the microwave. 'Suit yourself.'

'It's beautiful isn't it?' Farusja, her neck craned, stared at the lights twinkling above her that were steadily pouring themselves onto the dark night sky.

Dante had led her upstairs again, through his bedroom and out to his private balcony. There was a small table and two barstools on the balcony, which ran almost half the length of the room, curving at both ends to form an oval. Here they sat, eating in view of the stars. Behind them lay Dante's domain, which encompassed the entire upper floor.

'Yes,' Dante said, staring at the stretch of her neck. 'It is.'

Farusja flushed, sensing his eyes on her, suddenly aware that she was only wearing his t-shirt. The air was warm, but goosebumps begun to scurry their way across her skin.

'You are,' Dante said, his voice flat. 'You can't take a compliment, can you?'

Farusja stared down at her food, muttering a reply. 'So what happened to Rabecca's car again?'

'Someone put a bomb in it.'

'Why couldn't they just catch you at work or something? They should have put it in your office.'

Dante smirked at her. 'You're a bundle of laughs, aren't you?'

'I'm just saying,' Farusja put down her fork and pointed at him. 'It's so easy to kill you, all they need to do is attach it to a subject you can hardly refuse.'

Dante's eyes narrowed at her, his face impassive. 'Someone like you?'

Farusja looked at him, her eyes locked on his, their gaze unflinching. Without another word, she picked up her fork and continued eating. 'Every time you open your mouth you remind me why I despise you so much.'

'Every time you open your mouth I want to cover it with mine.'

'I'm sure,' Farusja muttered sourly, throwing down her fork. It clattered onto her plate, the noise like a shot in the night air.

Dante reached over the table, picked up the fork and speared a piece of chicken. He held it in front of her face.

'Come on, eat,' he butted at her lips with it. 'We can go back to hating each other later.'

'I'm not hungry anymore.'

Farusja stood up abruptly, crying out as her foot became entwined with the stool she was sitting on, and she fell to the balcony floor. Dante moved quickly, but was unable to stop the cavalcade of arms and legs.

'You need to stop running,' she heard Dante say quietly as his arms settled on hers and pulled her in a sitting position on the floor of the balcony. 'Are you hurt?'

Farusja shook her head mutely and self-consciously pulled the shirt down to cover her bare thighs.

He sighed, and sat down next to her, facing the opposite direction. 'I may not be the best person to say this, but you run from everything. What happened between us in the parking lot – you ran and left me there, you couldn't even deal with that. When we hired you, I didn't peg you as the type who would leave things unfinished. Stop,' he lifted his hand slowly and placed it tentatively on her bare knee, 'running.'

'That should not have happened,' Farusja whispered.

'But it did,' Dante said quietly. 'Are you just going to pretend it never happened? Is that what you do, just sweep things under the rug and hope they go away?'

Farusja stared at him. Tears, unbidden sprang to her eyes, her thoughts wavering and bursting between them. Yes, she was running, she was always running, but it was no business of his, he did not need to know that. She yanked his hand off her knee and sprang up, fleeing from the balcony through his bedroom.

'Ah, come on Mumba.'

She moved faster on hearing his voice, almost running down the staircase, grasping the iron railing as she descended into the dark. She wanted to get out, away from this man, away from this house. She headed for the dim lights in the kitchen, her arms and hands spread out in front of her feeling for any obstructions, her eyes wet with tears. When she reached the counter in the middle of the kitchen, the floor was no longer warm, and the kitchen no longer offered the comfort she craved.

'Farusja.'

She choked back tears as his hands closed over her arms, holding her firmly from behind. He turned her around.

'Stop it,' he spoke quietly.

Farusja shook her head, sobbing quietly. 'Let me go, I'm not running.'

He let go of her arms and placed his hands in the small of her back, pulling her towards him.

'Stop,' he repeated as he pulled her closer and moving forward, brushed the tears off her cheeks with his lips. Her body became still, the air between them expectant and waiting. Moving his head he brushed away the tears on the other side of her face, his lips caressing her skin gently, moving down past her nose, covering her mouth with his.

Farusja's breath released in a pleasurable sigh; his lips were warm but insistent, demanding, and she tried in vain to stifle a moan as the heat begin to spread from her toes and bloom fiercely between her legs.

His hands moved further down her back, and pushing the material of the shirt she was wearing out of the way, he grasped the swell of her buttocks at the top of her thighs, his mouth hard against her neck as she arched her back in response, moulding their bodies together. Dante grunted, his erection between them, he guided her to the counter, bumping into the chairs as he lifted her and placed her sitting on the edge. He lifted his head and looked at her. Her eyes gazed up at him, completely luminous, her lips were parted, pink and swollen, her chest heaving; he could see her nipples straining through the flimsy cotton shirt that was now haphazardly gathered at her waist. He bent his mouth to her, covering her completely, grunting as she arched her back and cried out in pleasure. His hands scrabbled under the t-shirt, finding the hem of the underwear she was wearing he tugged it down, pulling it out from under her buttocks, yanking it down to dangle at her ankles.

Farusja sighed in pleasure as the ache between her legs became more insistent. She pulled the t-shirt up and over her head, casting it aside, doing the same with his. He kissed her, passion flaring at the sight of her bare breasts, biting her neck as his hand moved up the inside of her thigh. He pulled his shorts down, pulling her to him with his other hand, his breathing ragged.

'Baby,' he grunted, 'move forward.'

Farusja slid forward, her bare flesh rubbing against the counter, she half turned to push the fruit bowl on the counter away from her side and screamed, startling them both cold, her body twisting towards the now broken doors covered with plastic, her legs hitting Dante squarely in the chest.

'There's someone outside,' she whispered, her eyes staring at the plastic covered doors.

Dante followed her gaze, squinting, seeing no one there. He bent down and pulled his shorts up, all signs of his arousal gone, his body scared cold by Farusja's scream.

'There's no one there,' he said quietly as he reached past her and grabbed the shirt off the counter, dropping it in her lap.

'I saw someone,' she twisted back towards him, her eyes defensive, her legs hanging from the edge of the counter. 'I saw something!' She said again loudly as she took in the sceptic look on his face.

Dante looked at her, already feeling the stirring begin again in his loins. 'There's a lot of security on my grounds tonight Farusja, if someone was out there …'

He stopped as a knock sounded on the kitchen window behind Farusja. A frown creased his forehead and he raised his hand to still her as he walked towards the window. The sheepish face of one of Hienry's Smiths looked up at him, clearly visible in the early morning light, crouching under the window looking like a deer caught in headlights.

Was it already dawn? Dante wondered, gazing at the lightening of the sky.

'I'm sorry boss,' the man muttered, his eyes making a point in not meeting Dante's, 'I saw a light in the kitchen, I did not know it was you.'

Dante looked down at him through the window, his expression wry. He could not even remember which Smith this one was.

'Could not be helped could it?' he replied quietly.

Farusja listened to this exchange in silence, her back towards them. She gazed at her bare thighs, the puddle her underwear formed on the floor in front of her, and the shirt lying in her lap and sighed, a long drawn out sigh. She pulled the shirt over her head slowly, the smell of him emanating off her, reminding her of just how much she wanted him. Her skin still tingled where he had touched her; she placed her hand to her lips, feeling the imprint of his lips on hers, and slowly pushed herself off the counter. She bent forward, picking her underwear off the floor, one hand clutched protectively to her chest.

'Farusja,' Dante said, his voice low, he turned away from the window, away from Smith, coming towards her.

She held her hand up, stopping him where he was, her body rigid, tense, cold, tired.

'No more words,' she whispered, fingering the cotton material of her underwear gently in her hands. 'No more Dante. I can't. Just no more.'

She walked away from him towards her room, opening the door and closing it behind her. She dropped her underwear to the floor and ran to the bed, wrapping the blankets around herself, hugging the pillows to her chest, letting the tears run unchecked down her cheeks.

CHAPTER 15

Tuesday, 1 May

*F*arusja finally passed into a deep troubled sleep as the sun rose on Tuesday morning, exhausted, her eyes swollen from crying, only waking up after lunch. She wanted to leave without seeing Dante, without talking to him.

She crept out of bed, trying to make the least noise possible. She dunked into the bathroom, her main aim to wash his smell off her. She stumbled out ten minutes later, pulling on a pair of well-matched underwear that Dante had picked out for her, flushing hot as she put it on, covering it hastily with jeans and a shirt. While she brushed her hair with her fingers, she contemplated how she could sneak out of the house unseen. She was startled by a knock on the door.

He had not waited, had not asked if she was fully dressed, but had walked in almost impatiently, stopping two paces into the room.

'There is a taxi waiting for you,' he announced, his face expressionless and his eyes dark.

Farusja stilled, waiting for him to continue, glancing at him appraisingly. He was wearing a grey tracksuit, the top long-sleeved with a hood, the bottom some fancy mixture of polyester and cotton, his hands tucked into the pockets.

'The rest of the contents you remembered from the car are in your flat, I'll have someone watching you. This time to keep you safe.'

He then turned and left the room; leaving her staring after him.

She arrived back at her house to find the fat guy, Hienry she thought he was called, waiting for her, and a brand new, very shiny and very red Volkswagen beetle puttering on the doorstep. She exited the taxi, dumbstruck, her jaw hanging open.

Hienry waddled over to her, placing his arm around her shoulders. 'Ah madam,' he peered into her face, scrutinising her. 'We have replaced all that was lost. If your friend does not like the colour, we can have it repainted, eh?'

Farusja shook her head, almost drooling. 'It's perfect,' she choked out. 'But can I accept this? Becca's car was so old. This is so new! I don't know …'

'Madam,' Hienry said quietly. 'First of all it is not your choice; this was never your car to accept. I'll tell you a truth, you will accept this gift and you will let go of the misplaced pride in your head. A great wrong was done to you and your friend on Mr Dumeno's property.' He let the sentence hang, staring at the car in front of him. 'Let him repay you both as he sees fit. No strings attached. You will accept it and that's all.'

Farusja was dumbstruck, speechless. Hienry guffawed heartily at the expression on her face, his hands holding onto his stomach.

'Only the best Madam,' he winked. 'We take care of you in only the best way. We will be watching you. *Bon courage.*'

He trotted over to the taxi she had just vacated, which had been idling at the curb, and left.

Rabecca arrived in the evening. Despite her post-alcohol lethargy she noticed the car and proceeded to drag the story out of Farusja. After getting the entire story from her, Rabecca quietly picked up the new car keys sitting on the table.

'*Mami,*' she said quietly, fingering the keys. 'I want you to be very careful with Dumeno, and you need to watch your back with Roberta Erlichmann. She will not let you take the man she loves. Now that I have inadequately warned you in a terribly insufficient manner, let's take our new car for a spin. I don't even know how to thank Dumeno for this.'

Roberta raised her drink, staring at the clear liquid of her martini before tossing the entire drink to the back of her throat, placing the empty glass on the table in front of her. She smirked wryly at the man laughing at her across the table. Naks sat back in his chair, looking at her speculatively.

He raised his glass to her with a wide grin. 'You need to relax, sweetie.'

Roberta looked at him and sighed, signalling the waiter to get her another drink.

'He's completely out of control Naks, and it's getting worse. He's causing scenes at work. You should have seen him yesterday at HD. He took our best designer, one of the better concepts, and tore it down, just because … because why? I don't know.'

Naks stared at her over the top of his glass, the cognac swirling around slowly.

'After all this time you still love the brother, I kept telling you, you will not get anything more from that one. But really, do you expect anything less with the things that are going on? Look, his secretary just got murdered, and he had something with her.' The grin faded from Naks face, and he set the glass down on the table top between them. 'That's enough to mess anyone up.'

Roberta looked up at him, her heart pounding faster than she would have liked. 'A detective came to see him just after the murder. They think he did it. Is this what those rumours you heard were all about?'

Naks shrugged. 'I didn't think it would be something like this sweetie, but yeah I heard something big would go down. Is D coping?'

'I don't know, he doesn't show anything. He seems fine.'

Naks shook his head. 'You know D better than that girl.'

'I wish I did. I'm feel as though I'm losing him Naks,' Roberta looked almost vulnerable, 'and I don't know what to do.'

Naks had not changed over the years that they had all been friends; from that first day when she had gone to their house and sat in drug induced stupors day after day. Although the trio had been separated due to their business interests, with Roberta and Dante spending more time together, Roberta had always thought that Naks would become the lonely odd one out, and that was why she insisted on meeting him every week, no matter what was going on.

'You know I like to fuck you, Robbie,' Naks sighed. 'But if its love you want, Dante and I are the wrong places to look.'

'Thanks Naks,' Roberta snorted.

'You can't keep driving yourself crazy over him, you know he's his own man. He'll never settle down.'

'I'm not so sure about that anymore.' She related the story of what had happened between Dante and Farusja on Monday, and the steps Dante had forced the company to take against her. And how she had found her in his house. Roberta watched as Naks' face changed. She did not know what to make of his expression.

Naks whistled. 'So my brother is getting serious?'

'It's the first time he's acted like this,' Roberta laughed mirthlessly. 'And also, he's not supposed to play with the staff. It's our death rule. When did you last see him?'

'It's been a while.'

'Talk to him Naks, before he makes a fool of himself.'

Naks raised his eyebrows at the urgency in her tone, his whole lean face rising with his brows. 'You mean before he makes a fool of you.'

'It's not like that Naks.'

'Then what is it?' Naks raised the glass to his lips. 'Every time Robbie, every time I'm bailing you out of D's emotional jails. You've been on his tail since the first day he rolled a joint for you, the first time I met you. D loves you girl,' Naks sighed. 'But he doesn't love you like *that*. How many times have I told you?'

Roberta signalled the waiter, who promptly delivered another martini to the table. 'You're not even fighting in my corner Naks.'

'You don't need the man,' Naks reached forward, his multitude of chains sliding in-between the two of them, he juggled his drink in his right hand as he reached for her left hand with his, wrapping his fingers around hers. 'You're hot sweetie. You could have any man in this town, but you keep going after what you can't get. That's always been exactly the type of girl you've been, always chasing things that seem impossible.' Naks moved his fingers to her arm, caressing the inside of her elbow.

Roberta smiled, placing her right hand over his. 'Shall we call it a night?'

'Girl, that makes it twice this week, you really must be sad,' Naks shook his head. 'We should put a stop to this, you fucking the both of us. This is the most messed up three way friendship I've ever been in.'

CHAPTER 16

Wednesday, 2 May

*F*arusja and Rebecca were early for work on Wednesday morning, despite Farusja's lack of sleep. After they had returned last night from test driving the new car, Farusja lay in bed, watched by god-knew-who. She had stayed up most of the night watching the clock, wondering what she would say when she saw him again, and trying not to admit to herself that she was waiting for Dante to call, to come, to do anything. But he had not. She had even put her phone right next to her head just in case it rang while she was sleeping, but it had not.

They snuck around the building in the morning shadows, hoping to avoid both Dante and Roberta. Farusja slipped quietly into her office, intent on hiding behind the sanctity of her desk.

She had just turned on her computer, when Roberta Erlichmann strode into the room. Farusja tensed, rising to her feet, standing, her heart fluttering within her rib cage like a trapped bird. She plastered an impassive look on her face. Roberta Erlichmann was, as always, the picture of perfection and the dream of every woman and, quite possibly, all men. She was wearing a deep black, long skirt suit that shimmered blue as she moved. Her hair and skin were accentuated by the colour, and she had topped off the entire outfit with bright, red, angry, lipstick; the same colour as her shoes and the thin belt that fitted snugly around her waist.

Roberta was angry. She needed to reassert her authority. Dante was hers, they were one person, and no one was going to change that. Her mouth was twisted in an ugly grimace. She had been with Dante from the beginning and this woman, this doe-eyed woman, presented the biggest threat she had ever had. She was so unlike the other women Dante had played with, the ones they both knew would last a week. For the first time Roberta had to grudgingly admit that she was contending with some very serious competition.

Roberta moved up to Farusja's desk and looked at her up and down, not even masking her contempt.

'You must be so naive,' she purred quietly. 'I'd leave town if I were you, we don't take kindly to women who sleep with their bosses to gain status here. You're just a passing fancy for a bored man. Stop chasing him.' She smiled at Farusja with a measure of distasteful sympathy.

Farusja stared at her, the corners of her mouth raised slightly. 'I like this town ma'am, I think I'll stay.'

Roberta pursued her lips and stabbed one long red fingernail in Farusja's direction. 'Do you really think I'll let you stay here? Know your place in this food chain, you're my employee. I'll let you go if you do not tow the line and start to behave.'

Farusja's skin prickled, her head beginning to ache as she tried to quell her temper. 'I have rights even as your employee, and as far as I'm concerned I can file not only charges of sexual harassment against Mr Dumeno but other charges against other people as well.'

She almost did not see the hand coming at her, and she froze as the long lacquered nails stopped centimetres from her face.

'Do not play with the big girls,' Roberta hissed at her, trailing the tips of the nails of her right hand across Farusja's cheek, 'we don't play nice.'

She dug the nails into Farusja's skin, hard enough to hurt, but not hard enough to draw blood.

Farusja exhaled sharply, keeping her face calm and impassive, deepening her breathing as anger boiled up inside her. Did these people all have no morals?

'I'll not leave this town Miss Erlichmann, and I like my job at HD.'

'There is nothing for you here, go back to the hole you crawled out of.'

'Yes,' Farusja said, 'people keep on insinuating that.'

Roberta withdrew her nails and put her hands on her hips, cocking her head at Farusja, her blond curls bouncing. 'No wonder Dante is attracted to you.'

Farusja flushed, remembering how he had lifted her onto the table and pulled off her underwear. 'No, Mr Dumeno does not feel that way about me. My friend's car had exploded, he was helping me.'

'Really? Those big innocent eyes, stupid pouty lips, they make you look vulnerable, weak. Dante loves weak women, it brings out the protectiveness in him.'

'I'm not weak, ma'am,' Farusja faltered, her composure failing.

'Yes you are,' Roberta smiled, a long curve that ended before it began. 'It's pathetic. So weak that within a month of working here you're already in the CEO's bed, sleeping in his house. If I were a man, you probably would make your way into my bed too, wouldn't you?'

Farusja's lips quivered, the weight in her heart heavy and constricting, although she knew that these words were meant to hurt her, to scare her away, she saw the awful truth in them. Not only did she run from her problems, she was too weak to say no, to recognise the right and wrong way to conduct herself, and too weak to keep her emotions in check and know her place.

Roberta smiled cruelly at her and without another word, turned on her heel and left the office. Farusja sank back down in her chair, numb, trying to keep her tears at bay. She would have to resign, she had no other choice. She could not keep up with the emotional roller-coaster ride HD was taking her on.

Dante looked speculatively at Roberta as she sat across him in her boardroom. 'What exactly are you saying Robbie?'

'Do I sound like a broken record? That girl you're fucking, she came to my office and insulted me, verbally abused me. I want her gone, this is immediate grounds for dismissal.' Roberta sat with her legs crossed, her back straight and her face a mask of shock and anger.

Dante winced as the words spilled angrily from her mouth. 'I'm not fucking anybody Robbie, just in case you were asking,'

'Oh please, you're always fucking somebody Dumeno, and that girl was at your house. Since when do you keep women at your house for harmless sleepovers?'

Dante eased himself away from the table, standing up, remembering the way Farusja had felt that night, warm and soft. 'I did not sleep with that woman Robbie. Her car exploded on my property I had to help her out. Come on, you've never been this jealous before.'

'And what was her car doing on your property in the first place?'

Dante shook his head. 'I don't understand your question Robbie.'

Roberta made a frustrated noise. 'I don't know what game you're playing with her, but it's dangerous. She's the one that asked me for the appointment! You know I never interfere with your flavours of the month, but this one works here, at my company. She invaded my space and she has crossed the line.' Roberta's mouth was set in a hard line, her lipstick looking like a slash of red on her face.

'Miss Mumba's personality doesn't seem to be all that aggressive.'

'You wouldn't know, you're pushed so far up her ass you can't see straight,' Roberta shook her head slowly. 'That girl is trouble Dumeno.'

'And you've made your mind up by spending all of three minutes with her?'

Roberta smirked at him, crossing her legs over each other again. 'Sort it out Dante. I'd have fired her immediately but I know what a soft spot you have for her. God knows what you see in that girl, she even has a criminal record. I wonder if she's even doing her work right or if Jaco is covering for her.'

Dante sighed. 'Fine Robbie, I'll take care of it.'

Roberta stood up, facing him across the table. 'If you don't let her go, Dante,' she said quietly. 'I'll do it myself. This was not in our agreement. We made a promise.'

Dante stared at her as she straightened herself up, watching the muscles in her face twitch. 'I do love you Robbie,' he said quietly. 'I'll never leave your side.'

Roberta stood, looking undecided. She set her mouth in a hard line again. 'Just fix it Dante, so that we can all get back to our lives.' She turned and left the boardroom, leaving Dante to stare after her.

'Good morning Mr Dumeno.'

Dante focused on the tall black woman in front of him, her braids weaving a complicated design around her head and down her back. She had just exited Farusja's office and closed the door behind her subtly, standing in front of it. She held herself gracefully, her eyes never wavering from his, her lips not quite forming a smile but offering polite recognition.

'Good morning,' he smiled at her.

She did not move from his path, instead shuffled the papers in her hands quickly. 'Good morning sir.'

Dante glanced at her, placing his hands in his pockets. 'What's your name again?'

She hesitated for a fraction of a second before she said rather grudgingly. 'It's Sidney Kimani, sir.'

'Ah Sidney,' Dante regarded her with a smile on his face. 'I'm looking for Farusja Mumba.'

Wordlessly she stepped away from the door, still clutching the papers.

'Thank you,' Dante said graciously, watching her turn and walk away from him. He watched her buttocks as they swung from side to side inside her skirt, the dark ebony of the skin of her thighs visible through the little slit at the back of her skirt. He would love to find out if that colour spread evenly across her body. He turned towards Farusja's door. He knocked lightly and then pushed the door open.

Farusja was staring down at the coffee and tea stains ringed around her desk, mentally planning her resignation. She would leave as soon as soon as the month was up, in 12 days to be precise. There was a knock on the door and as she looked up, Dante strolled in, looking absolutely divine in a charcoal grey suit with a fitted white shirt.

'Mumba?' he stated quietly, looking down at her. 'The last thing I expected was for my partner to complain about you. What's all this about?'

He moved into the office and closed the door behind him.

Farusja swallowed and stood up. All her attempts to hide this morning were failing dismally.

She remembered the new car she had found idling at their doorstep, remembered the way he had touched her that night, how she had waited for him to do something, to do anything, how she was still waiting for him to call her.

'Do you have an appointment with Jaco? You do know that he's not in yet?' she asked him mildly, standing up to face him across her desk.

'Are you serious?'

'I don't see what else you could be doing here, Mr Dumeno.'

'You and my partner had an altercation, I want to know what it was about; she's now accusing you of harassment,' he said rigidly.

He moved forward, went around the desk, sitting on the extra chair she kept on her side of the desk, looking up at her pointedly as he waited for her to sit.

Farusja could not help but take a step back, almost falling into her chair, tumbling into it ungracefully. She sighed angrily to herself. Why did she have to act like a klutz around this man all the time?

Dante narrowed his eyes at her, his eyes emotionless and questioning. He was in his element, he was in control. He knew it and so did she.

She swallowed hard, and gazed blindly at her desk, everything that had happened between them seemed erased, the coffee stains had new meaning.

'Yes,' she admitted, inhaling the husky scent emanating from him. 'I did have an exchange with Miss Erlichmann, but I did not harass her, we both know that. I did not do any of the stuff she may have accused me of doing either. She told me to leave town, I said I was staying.'

Farusja shrugged her shoulders, still gazing at the stains on the table. Then she looked up at him, meeting his eyes, which were looking back at her openly.

You did not call me, sure I had better things to do with my time and it's not like I was waiting for you to call; but you did not call me.

'She's calling for you to be disciplined or fired.'

Farusja sighed. 'Surely you know her far better than I do, and I'd think in this short time you might have a small inclination to what my personality is like. Do you really think that woman has my best interests at heart?'

'Do not ever speak of her in that way again, do you understand? Roberta has been with me way longer than anyone else ever has,' Dante's voice was quiet.

Farusja raised her hands in surrender, mocking him. 'Well that's how it happened, but don't worry, I won't be inadvertently causing drama in HD anymore. I'll hand in my resignation to Kobus before the end of the day. This job is not my only lifeline.'

'Resign?' Dante scoffed at her. 'HD is a great place right now, and we're going regional with the winning of the tender. Besides, where would you go?'

'I don't see why you would care Mr Dumeno,' she said shortly.

'I care,' he said just as shortly, glaring at her.

'Probably back to Zambia. I have people there.'

He fell silent, and just looked at her. He liked to look at her. Her eyes seemed to play tricks on him again, the way they changed every time the light moved; he had realised it was not the light but her body signalling a change in mood. Her hair was down, and brushed her shoulders lightly, her liquid eyes were now calm, and regarded him just as steadily as he was looking back at her. He had not even wanted to call her last night, he had wanted to drive over to the little flat and finish what they had started. He had wanted to see her naked and lying under him, drenched in sweat. Instead the years of habit, pride and insecurity about what she expected of him had kicked in and he had stubbornly stayed away. And now he was about to lose her.

Dante pulled his eyes away from hers and quenched the emotion rising in him. They waited on each other in silence for a while, Farusja watching Dante, and him staring at the tips of his fingers. The silence stretched, and they both shuffled restlessly.

'You ran away from me, again,' he finally said quietly, still not looking at her.

Farusja swallowed and stared at a point on the wall behind him. 'Leave it Dante. There's nothing left to be said.'

'What about what happened between us?' he raised his eyes to hers and held them. 'Is there nothing to be said about that?'

Farusja gritted her teeth, trying to stop from flinging herself at him. 'There is nothing left to be said Dante.' She pulled her eyes away from his, aware of what effect they had on her.

'Indeed.'

Farusja squirmed, thoughts pouring from her mind and body and to her mouth which she kept stubbornly shut. 'Look Dante.'

'I thought there was nothing left to be said?' he countered quietly.

'Well, there isn't. I just want to make a few things clear with regards to the situation we have here,' she inhaled audibly, as the words came out in a rush, 'and I have to get back to finishing these designs.'

'Indeed?'

Farusja clenched her teeth, and saw herself squeezing his neck until he passed out. 'Indeed,' she repeated through clenched teeth. 'Since I came to work for you, you have been nothing but arrogant, rude and you have not taken my no for an answer.'

'Farusja,' Dante interrupted.

'No, let me finish! I'm nothing but a game to you, a target who you just happen to be attracted to.' She inhaled sharply. 'Yes, something did happen between us, but to you it's just another case of being bored and finding a toy to play with. For me, this is my life and because of you I find myself in the terrible position of having to move again!' She trailed to a stop, standing up abruptly, looking down at him as he looked up at her.

Dante watched her, the corners of his mouth twitching. He watched the way her eyes flashed at him and the way her skin glowed with exertion, she was absolutely delectable when worked up. He kicked himself mentally, and realised that she had fallen silent and was looking down at him, silent and angry.

'You look nice today,' he smiled at her as he leaned back in the chair and surveyed her casually.

'Huh?' Farusja's jaw dropped and she stared at him confused.

'You look nice today,' he grinned at her mischievously. 'Although I believe I have seen this suit before. Should I buy you a new one?'

'Thanks, but no,' she grunted, her anger draining from her, leaving her feeling lightheaded and confused. She looked at him puzzled, as he continued to smile at her.

'So what happens to us? You cannot still be denying that you want me?'

'There's no us, Dante! Don't you get it?' Farusja's temper began to rise again, her hands clenched into fists tightly. The man had switched personalities in seconds. She looked at him disgustedly; the man she had stayed with on Monday night was a completely different species from the one she was with now! 'You just keep insisting on ruining my chances at a new life don't you? Please get the hell out of my office.'

He smiled sensually at her, and to her consternation, stood up, a pace away from her, immediately crowding and filling the room. Her throat went dry as the husky scent emanating off his skin assailed her nostrils, filling her head with his smell. She took a step back, meeting the chair behind her.

'Not too brave now are we, Miss Mumba,' he said softly, his eyes slowly tearing her apart. 'You want me and I want you. Why don't you just let me fuck you once or twice and we can get on with our lives. You will get a great deal out of it, unless of course you want more …' he drawled, leaving the sentence unfinished.

'Dante, I don't want any more trouble,' Farusja's whispered. He reached out, and grasping her chin held it firmly in the palm of his hand, keeping her staring at him.

'You're trouble Farusja,' he said ruthlessly. 'And this game we're playing is no longer exciting. It's getting old.' He spat out at her angrily.

Farusja slapped his hand away, her eyes flashing at him, her hands raised up palms facing him, ordering him to keep away from her. 'Get out.'

'Do you really want me to go?' he said softly and reaching out folded his hands over hers, lowering them, holding onto her. 'I could easily stay here, being the boss.'

He tugged at her hands gently, pulling her to him. 'But I want you to say it,' he murmured huskily. 'I want you, Farusja Mumba.'

He leaned forward slightly, peering into her face, and then let go of her hands. 'I want you to tell me that you want me to go.'

Farusja concentrated on the silver chain lying against his skin, the ache was already there, fierce and insistent. She wanted him, and she wanted him now.

'I want,' she started.

Dante leaned forward and reached behind her, his hands in the small of her back and pulling her to him. His breath tickled her skin softly, his hands gentle as he bent down and lifted her off the floor and onto the desk. He pushed the knee length skirt she was wearing up past her thighs, running his hands up her legs, almost laughing to himself as he dragged her panties under her buttocks and past her thighs to hang at her ankles, just like he had done before.

Farusja opened her eyes, her breathing shallow, disorientated as her shaking ceased, leaving her warm and sated. She took in the walls of her office, her eyes resting on the designs she had been working on, the cabinet door open with the papers spilling out, her arms wrapped tightly around the man in front of her, him inside her. She gasped; the realisation of what she was doing hit her like cold water. She tore her hands away from him. Raising her hands to move them apart, her palms against his chest, feeling the wet warmth of him run down her leg as he came out of her and onto the skin of her thigh.

He looked down at her, confused. His skin covered with a sheen of sweat, his eyes dark and lusty.

They faced each other in silence, their breathing heavy, ragged.

Dante, still looking at her, reached down and pulled up his boxer shorts, followed by his trousers.

Farusja got off the table slowly, no longer able to contain the tears. She reached down to pull up her underwear, her hands shaking as she smeared his essence up back her leg, collecting it in her underwear. His smell was pervasive between them as she smoothed her skirt down longer than necessary, unable to look at him. They were right about her, she was weak. She had tried so hard, she had tried so hard. A sob escaped her and she wiped the tears off her cheeks angrily. She was so afraid. Afraid of what to do and what to feel and how to feel it, she was so afraid of being right when she was so completely wrong. She choked back the tears, her body still throbbing with the yearning to have more of him. She wanted him, but she knew she could never have him in the way she wanted him.

'It's time for you to leave, Mr Dumeno,' she whispered, her voice hoarse.

The expression in his eyes was unreadable as he stood there staring at her, his composure regained. 'I'm tired of leaving Farusja.'

'No, Dante, no!' she cried at him. 'Just leave, please. You got what you wanted, so please just leave.'

'You wanted it too,' he said quietly, his arms hanging limply at his side.

'I know,' she sobbed. 'I know! And do you think that makes it any better?'

He moved to come up to her, stepping back as she flinched away from him.

'I'm done. Take this as my resignation,' she said her voice hardly above a whisper.

'You can't.'

Farusja stared up at him, shaking her head from side to side. 'You can't stop me.'

Dante expelled his breath noisily, the sound coming out ragged between them.

'Don't go,' he said quietly. He clenched his teeth; he could feel his pulse banging against his head, and whether it was from the heady feeling he had got from being inside her or from the prospect of never seeing her again, he did not know.

She looked so thoroughly defeated, her right hand clenching the table behind her tightly, as if by letting go she would release her tenuous hold on reality.

'I won't bother you again,' he said quietly, hesitating, the air stilling and chilling between them.

She raised her tear stained eyes to his, they swam in her face like liquid chocolate. 'I want you to bother me again,' she whispered. 'And that's why I have to leave.'

'Farusja Mumba,' Dante whispered, and moving up to her he gathered her up in his arms, hugging her tightly against him, his chin resting on the top of her head. 'Why can't you just let us be?'

Because your jealous partner will make my life a living hell if I stay. The words were at the tip of her tongue, but she did not allow them to leave.

119

'Because it will never work Dante,' Farusja sniffled into his shirt, luxuriating in the feel of his muscles underneath the suit, unashamedly rubbing her cheek against him. 'All this is so wrong.'

Dante, placing his hands on her shoulders, pushed her away from him, holding her at arm length, his grip on her shoulders tight.

'Make a decision!' his voice was harsh. 'Enough with this bloody indecisiveness, what will it be? Do I make you that miserable?'

He continued, his eyes searching hers for a denial. There was none. With one last look at her, he let his hands drop from her shoulders, walking away from her towards the closed door, dragging it open and closing it behind him again quietly, closing his eyes momentarily as he leaned against it.

'She's my friend.'

His eyes flew open, settling on the tall beauty he had met a few minutes ago. *What's her name again*? *Ah, Sidney*. There were no papers in her hand this time; she stood squarely to his right, a pace away from him, watching him with hooded eyes, her hands folding in front of her.

'She's my friend,' she repeated quietly. 'Please.'

Dante felt something inside him break, the pain as physical as it was mental. It was all he could do to stand staring at her as the force of emotion pulsed inside him, almost bringing him to his knees. He could not speak, and hurried away from her, from this woman standing with a plea in her eyes, and away from himself.

Sidney watched him go and, sighing heavily, pushed the door to Farusja's office open, closing it behind her.

'Oh my sista,' she whispered, rushing towards her, she wrapped her arms around Farusja's bent form. 'He's gone, he's gone okay? Here, sit, sit.' Putting her arms around her friend's shoulders, she raised her up until she was standing on her feet, pushing her into the chair behind the desk.

'I couldn't stand anymore, legs were weak,' Farusja smiled thinly at her, collapsing into the chair.

'He's gone,' Sidney's voice was muffled as she rummaged through the bottom of the filing cabinet where Farusja kept her bottles of mineral water. She screwed the cap off one and handed it to her, forcing her to drink.

Farusja sighed in relief as the cool water coursed down her throat, its soothing wetness helping her relax.

'Are you better now?'

Farusja nodded, pressing her hands to her temples and then placing the heels of her hands against her eyes, rubbing them vigorously. She knew they had already begun to swell up from the tears. She covered her hands with her face as Sidney scrutinised her. 'I'm okay, I'm fine, you can leave.'

Sidney reached forward and pulled Farusja's hands from her face, peering into her eyes, taking in her flushed expression, the brightness in her eyes, and the musky smell around her. Her eyes opened wide, comprehension dawning in them.

'You had sex with him,' she laughed quietly. 'You had sex with him just now, you're practically still dripping him.'

Farusja flinched, as if accused. 'Yeah, so what?'

'*Ai* my dear, are you crazy?' Sidney moved over to collapse in the chair to the left of the desk that Dante had pulled over. 'What now? From the way you look it was good, was it? Maybe we should have nailed your legs closed. What now?'

Farusja shrugged, not wanting to speak, too tired, her mind whirling in circles.

'Well, even though this stinks, no, reeks, because you've got to admit this is just shit,' Sidney said pointedly at her, waiting for her approval, going on only as she saw the small nod Farusja made. 'It's done? He's not coming back?'

Farusja looked up at her, her heart fluttering wildly in her chest.

'That's the problem,' she paused, her voice quiet. 'I'm always wishing he would.'

Dante decided that he was not going to stay at HD this morning. He needed space. He needed to get out. He paused right on the top of the spiral stairway, trying not to think of what had just happened, trying to still his breathing. He was never one to be a slave to his emotions; he did not even know what the words meant!

He laughed shakily to himself; the force of those three words said to him by Sidney had had an effect on him. An effect he could not control, and one he did not like.

He continued down the stairs, the thought of what it felt like to be inside her still lingering with him, making him go hard again. He wanted her, again and again and again. He wanted those eyes to watch him pleasure her. He wanted to grab fistfuls of her hair and kiss the entire length of her body. He stopped, his breathing ragged again. He stared at the stairs in front of him, lost in thought. He regretted not making his first time with her better than a worn out office desk and hastily rearranged clothes. He regretted not taking the time to explore the body he had been lusting after for so long. Now he would never be able to do it, never be able to see those eyes change again. It was like the teaser trailer before the movie.

He sighed, continuing his descent down the stairs, and walked outside towards his car. His phone rang. He answered it without even looked at the screen, he knew it was Roberta.

'What the hell are you playing at Dante? Where the hell are you now? Have you sorted it or are you still trying to ruin us?' she hissed over the line.

'I've been busy. I took care of that problem of yours, she's going to resign today. She should be heading to Kobus as we speak. Is that not what you asked me to do?' he said tiredly, placing his hands flat on the car as he reached it, staring at the silver under his fingers.

Roberta was silent for a moment. 'She's going to resign? Just like that?'

'Yes Robbie, just like that. She will no longer be here come the end of the month,' he replied, lifting his hands off the car and running them across his scalp, scratching at the tight curls on his head.

'Dante Dumeno! Tell me you're not planning to employ her!' Roberta asked rigidly as she held the phone tightly to her ear, listening for his denial. It had just dawned on her that if Dante had been quick to give her what she wanted, there must be an ulterior motive lurking somewhere in the shadows. Dante never did anything without it playing his way.

'Why would you care about her future Robbie?' asked Dante. 'I'm allowed to play aren't I, as long as it's not with your staff. This was always our agreement.'

'Are you crazy? With all the stuff that's been going on?' Roberta's voice was shrill. 'I didn't know that this girls tits made you stupid too?'

'Acting the jealous type again Robbie? It does not suit you.'

'Dante we have been together so long! How can you accuse me of such trivialities?' she snapped back at him, grasping at straws. 'You know I care about you, and that girl is poison not only to our peace of mind, but to our businesses as well!'

'Our peace of mind Robbie?'

'You know what I mean,' she said quietly, so angry she felt like her chest would burst from the force of the emotion.

'Let's continue this another day. Roberta Erlichmann! Not now! I'm tired, I'm stressed and I have to spend some time at Dante International before it closes from neglect!'

The phone line went dead and Roberta stared angrily at the device in her hand. This was not the Dante she knew. Her eyes narrowed down to slits and her face hardened.

Farusja's resignation letter arrived as promised that afternoon. Because she had been employed for less than a month, no notice period was required and she threatened to vacate her desk by the end of the day. With the new tender, this put them back one designer, and the post had remained vacant for months before Farusja had filled it. Now that she had gotten what she had wanted, Roberta tossed the offending letter aside, and wondered if she had made a very grave mistake.

Farusja packed her few personal belongings in a small box, clenching her teeth to prevent herself from feeling anything. She would not give anyone else in the office the satisfaction of knowing she loved her job. When she had told Jaco and Sidney, Jaco had nodded knowingly, a sad look on his face. 'I could see that there might be some intense issues,' he had said hastily. 'But reconsider Farusja, *fok* man! Where will I find someone as good as you?'

Farusja had smiled at his subtlety, grateful for it. Sidney had made much more noise, threatening to report the whole matter to labour court. But Farusja was staunch in her decision, she had never been more sure of anything in her entire life. She needed some space and time to clear her head of Dante and think about her future. She certainly did not need more talon like-nails threatening to scar her face. Farusja shivered involuntarily. As tough as she was, Roberta Erlichmann scared her. The best thing was to put as much space between herself and the two of them as possible. Then they could go on with their own sordid sex lives.

Farusja took one last look around her office. She bent her head, the tips of her fingers clenching the box of her few measly belongings that had littered her office. She hated to admit it, but she would miss the devil in his cream Lauren suit. But she also knew that there was no future with him. She grabbed her stuff and headed outside, thankful that at this time everyone else was going home, and so no one spared her a cursory glance. Half of them did not even know she was leaving, but she still breathed a sigh of relief as she spied Rabecca waving at her from her new shiny red Volkswagen. Farusja smiled. She wondered what story Rabecca had concocted to explain away the new car to her colleagues; she could not wait to hear it.

'*Mami*, I'm sorry to have introduced you to these crazy people. And I'm sorry you've resigned. But we'll find you another job, perhaps with one of the rival companies. Yes! That'll piss Roberta off.' Rabecca tried to comfort her friend.

Farusja blinked at her, reclining on the couch, swirling around the wine in the glass in her hand. It had been a really long, long Wednesday.

She had been threatened by one boss, had sex with another one, and then resigned, all in one day. She was surprised she was still standing.

'Thanks, but no thanks,' Farusja answered. 'I need to get out of this city, out of this country. As far away as possible from Dante Dumeno.'

'Since when did he become such a big deal? Since when did Roberta get threatened by another woman?'

Farusja looked up at her friend. 'Let's not dwell on that right now Becca, but just so you know, I have no idea. But what I do know is that there is another bottle waiting in the fridge and it has our names on it.'

'Farusja Mumba!' Rabecca shouted at her, sweat had beaded across her face, her expression more worried than angry, stopping her frantic walk around the sitting room to stand in front of her friend, hands on her hips. 'There is something you are not telling me!'

Farusja stared at the now empty glass in her hand. 'I slept with him Becca.'

Rabecca's mouth dropped open. 'What? When! What?'

'What would you like first; the what or the when?' Farusja asked her, still looking at her empty glass.

'Does it matter?' Rabecca shrieked.

'What, well I'm attracted to him, I have been for a long time,' Farusja said quietly. 'As for when it was this morning, in my office, and nearly on Monday night.'

'In the office? Our office? What do you mean nearly on Monday night?'

'There was one thing I didn't tell you, after that whole incident with your car, I slept in his house, we kind of had dinner, we almost had sex, and Roberta Erlichmann kind of saw me there …'

Rabecca backed away from her and fell onto the couch, fanning her face as if she were feverish, gasping for air like a fish. '*Eish,* no wonder Roberta is using you for target practice.'

'She threatened me this morning, those talons she calls nails almost ripped my cheek open.'

'Oh *mami,*' Rabecca whispered, sounding out of breath. 'You're right. I think we should take that bottle out of the fridge and celebrate your resignation; and then we can go and buy more bottles later so that we can try to forget. But I have to ask, was he good?'

Farusja nodded, bursting out into laughter.

'*Eish* then we have a serious problem.'

'Tell me about it.'

CHAPTER 17

Thursday, 3 May

*D*ante was angry. He had not expected Farusja to carry out her decision. Kobus had called him, telling him that she had handed in her letter and had cleared her office and it had made him even angrier. Because he did not want to lose her, and more importantly because he was afraid that she would never want to see him again. He did not want Farusja to leave the country with nothing but the memory of a cheap fuck in an office with him. And that's why he was here, parked in front of her driveway in the morning. He could not, would not, let her go. Not yet.

Farusja was making herself a cup of tea and wondering what to do with her life in general, when she raised her eyes to lay her teabag in the small flower pot on the kitchen windowsill. Her hand froze in mid air as she stared out of the window, staring at Dante who was reclining on his Bentley in front of Becca's townhouse. She dropped the teabag and grabbed her phone, dialling Rabecca's number without taking her eyes off Dante.

Rabecca whispered as if Dante could hear her over the line. 'He's at the house?'

Farusja stared at Dante, her breathing shallow. 'Yes Becca, I'm looking at him now.'

'What does he want?' Rabecca asked. 'I thought he said he would leave you alone? And how did he get in?'

'Gates don't stop them,' Farusja murmured, her eyes glued on Dante. It was good seeing him again, it made her feel happy and funny inside all at once.

'What the hell does he want?'

'He wants me,' Farusja said softly.

'Farusja Mumba! Do not go anywhere with that man! I'm ...'

Farusja cut the phone call, interrupting her and saying a hurried goodbye to Rabecca.

She opened the door, walking to stand in front of him, her breathing shallow. He looked amazing as always, today he was wearing a white vest with blue skinny jeans.

She stopped a pace away from him, staring up into those dark, almond-shaped eyes.

'Farusja,' he stared down at her. Her hair was tousled and fell softly about her shoulders; he breathed raggedly, trying to ignore the heat.

'Dante,' she smiled back at him, staring up at him. 'Why are you here?'

'To take you away,' Dante reached out and took her hand, raising it to his lips, his dark eyes unfathomable over her wrist. 'And since you no longer work at HD, let's try this again. Come with me.'

Farusja murmured. 'Do you think I'd go anywhere with such a weak apology Mr Dumeno?'

'You're the one who chased me away remember? Come.'

Farusja stared out at the mountainous scenery, clad in a large white terrycloth robe, her feet bare. The silence, all but the sounds of the nature around her was peaceful. The moment she had slid into the Bentley, Dante had taken the car out of town, only stopping long enough to get them something to drink while filing up the car. It had been like driving in air on wheels, she had watched in silence as he had driven them to something called Ongsbruk Lodge. They had been met with champagne and hot face towels after parking in the tarred parking lot, and then had been driven up to the lodge twenty kilometres into the dense bush in an off terrain tour vehicle. The lodge was a five star resort, each luxury bungalow had a balcony that opened up to a view of the mountains around. Farusja ignored the king-sized bed reclining in the middle of the room, and turned on the Jacuzzi.

Dante joined her on the balcony, handing her a flute of champagne.

'This is where I come to relax,' he said quietly, pointing out a giraffe in the bush outside, smiling at her exclamation of delight.

'You must come here often then,' she murmured, straining her eyes to look for more animals.

Dante slid his arm around her waist, hugging her to him. 'I took the liberty of getting a few things for you, enough for three days.'

Farusja turned to him, not resisting his hand. 'That sounds familiar. Are we going to pretend that this is normal Mr Dumeno? I can buy my own underwear thank you very much.'

'It's Dante. Are we still enemies?' Dante's hand left her waist and he turned to stand in front of her pulling her to him, his hands on her shoulders, tilting her face backwards to stare into her eyes.

Farusja stared back up at him, her face flushing warm. 'You're my boss.'

'I was your boss, remember?'

'Either way your partner will kill me, literally.'

'Again? I thought you had resigned?' Dante teased.

Farusja exhaled slowly. 'This is going to put me at the bottom of the food chain in town.'

'If you had not been so quick to leave HD, I'd have offered you a position at the top.'

'Don't insult me Dumeno,' Farusja smirked at him, her hands still by her sides.

Dante grinned at her. 'They have some sort of game viewing thing planned for us, then dinner. We have five minutes to get ready.'

Farusja sighed in satisfaction for the third time today. The late afternoon game drive had led to sundowners on the top of a hill and then back to the main restaurant for more drinks and the start of a four-course meal. Dinner was served on a balcony overlooking the mountains, the setting sun creating a kaleidoscope of colour and beauty in the early evening sky.

'So,' Dante raised his glass to her, his eyes twinkling at her over the rim of the glass.

'So,' Farusja murmured, mirroring his movements. She cut to the chase. 'Well this is interesting, isn't it?'

'Very,' Dante drawled. 'You've got three days to get to know me better.'

'Three days?' Farusja spluttered, opening her eyes wide. 'I can't stay here for three days!'

'With me you can,' Dante said quietly, amused as he saw her flushed expression. 'I said I'd set things right, and this is part of it.'

Farusja stared at him. 'You said you would leave me alone.'

'I like your eyes. Everything that happened between us was because of your eyes,' Dante said quietly, exhaling as he watched them change again. 'I tried to leave you alone, but the damn navigator in the car is always sending me back to your place.'

Farusja shook her head slowly, a laugh on her face. 'Who are you? One minute you're this quiet, thoughtful family man and the next you're a brutal asshole.'

Dante sighed, nodding as one of the waiters refilled his glass. 'When you're in the business I'm in, you need to wear more than two faces.'

'Which face am I getting?' Farusja said softly, her eyes connecting with his. He looked at her for a moment, the slow smile beginning on his face.

'What do you plan to do with yourself now?' he asked instead, his eyes twinkling. 'Come back to HD. You're our best designer.'

Farusja smiled at his change of subject, and decided to do the same. 'You love your companies I take it, you're willing to do anything to have the best, to be the best. But you also have terrible enemies, who are trying to kill you. Trying to kill me.'

Dante did not say anything, but resumed his demolition of the game steak in front of him.

'You want to know what I think?' she said quietly. 'I think you're scared. You don't like this person you've become, but you can't change because it's become the personality of DI, and of HD. And yet you love family, you're a health junkie and an undercover romantic, but you can't be any of those things can you? Not without losing so much.'

'You've got the wrong guy.'

Farusja smiled triumphantly. 'I don't think so Mr Dante Dumeno. I see right through you.'

Dante cleared his throat, pushing his chair back as he stood up. 'You talk too much,' he said gruffly, 'and you owe me a dance.'

Farusja laughed as he moved around the table and held out his hand to her, motioning her to stand up. 'I do not dance Mr Dumeno, and there's no music.'

Dante growled low in his throat, tugging at her until she stood up and followed him to the far side of the balcony away from the tables. He pulled her close to him, one hand in the small of her back, the other slowly caressing the length of her back; he started moving to an imaginary tune.

'Way too close Mr Dumeno,' Farusja said softly, staring at the brown skin of his neck, and feeling his muscles hard against her. She slowly twined her hands around his neck, lifting her face to look up into his dark eyes. His breath tickled the top of her head as he laughed softly, pulling her even closer.

'You owe me,' he whispered into her ear. 'You gave me nothing but attitude the last time.'

'All you earned was attitude last time,' she whispered back, laughing and shrieking as he tightened his arms around her and lifted her off the floor.

Farusja stood in the middle of their bungalow, watching Dante as he accepted more champagne and a tray of food from a waiter at the door. She marvelled that he was still hungry after all the food they had just eaten. Farusja inhaled shakily, she was not giving herself enough time to process what was happening, but she was loving every minute of it, and her stomach fluttered with anticipation of what would happen next. She watched as Dante came into her field of vision and looked up at his eyes, the flutter turning into rumbles of flashing heat and thunder in her body.

'Are you waiting for me?' Dante moved his hands up to her shoulders, pulling at the spaghetti straps that held up the yellow summer dress she was wearing.

'Such a silly dress,' he said softly, tugging at the strings so that they came undone. He flicked them off her shoulders. He pushed the dress down and off her body, his hands on her skin, tracing her contours and watching the dress crumple at her feet, her black underwear following the dress. Her eyes were staring at him, and were changing again, the light in them bright.

Farusja exhaled slowly, her chest heaving with the effort of standing naked in front of him. 'Are you going to keep a lady waiting?' she said softly, reaching out to touch his shirt briefly.

Dante bent down and in one swift move lifted her into his arms, moving towards the Jacuzzi; he slid her into the warm bubbling water feet first, ignoring her protestations as he gently pushed her into the water until it was up to her neck.

'Mr Dumeno!'

'Dante.'

Farusja sighed, sinking into the warm water, it bubbled around her, frothy, inviting and warm.

'I just don't care anymore,' she murmured, submerging her head under water briefly. She raised herself up again, the bubble bath sleek and shiny on her skin, and found herself breaking water right next to him, his naked skin brushing hers in a very familiar fashion. Farusja swallowed as she had a vision of his smooth, hard body, carefully moulded in all the right places, and soon hot tingles were coursing through her body.

'Hey,' Dante said softly, his hands trailing around her bare waist underwater, 'getting warmer?' He moved closer to her, the water shifting between them. Reaching out his right hand he slowly caressed the space between her neck and collarbone. Dante exhaled as he watched her eyes change again, and felt the tension rise and settle like a cloud over them. He trailed his hand down her neck, past her breasts, his eyes drinking in her rising swells and perfect roundness, her skin glistening with the heat that was shimmering off her body.

Farusja kept still, watching him pleasurably with her eyes half-closed as his hands explored her naked body, watching him as he gazed down at her.

'You're beautiful,' he whispered hoarsely, his eyes drawn to her lips, 'absolutely perfect.' His lips on hers were warm and gentle, his hands still exploring the rest of her body, causing her to moan softly, growing more hot and insistent as she responded to him. She moaned his name into his mouth, her eyes closed in ecstasy as she crushed her body against his, her arms curling around his neck instinctively. His mouth left hers and trailed a line of kisses down her neck, nibbling at her skin gently. Farusja's head dropped back against the side of the Jacuzzi as wave after wave of pleasure enveloped her, her body felt so light, and the ache for him was so unbearable. She gasped as his lips trailed down and across her breasts, his head disappearing under the water, finding and spreading the fire between her legs.

Dante opened his eyes, yawning widely. He raised himself on his elbows, staring down at what was the silk and cream of Farusja's body, her hair was flung over his arm, and her chest rose slowly with her breathing. Her back was pressed against him, the white bedspread tucked under her armpits and barely covering the top of her breasts, the look and feel of her already beginning to stir his blood. Sex with her in the Jacuzzi had been amazing; after she had moaned and screamed for him to find protection and come inside her, he had finally let himself ago, and it had been even better than he had thought it would be. He ran his hands across her bare back, watching her contours move with her breathing, feeling her heartbeat against the palm of his hand underneath her skin. He leaned forward, moving her hair gently away from her neck, caressing her skin, kissing her neck. She stirred against him, her eyes still closed as a shy smile stretched itself across her face.

'Dante,' she murmured, and turning over she nestled herself into his chest, sighing as his arms wrapped themselves around her tightly.

'Farusja,' he laughed softly at her, his hands beginning their slow descent down to play between her legs. 'Did I not say I could make you very, very, happy?'

Farusja moaned quietly against his chest. 'No you did not, and I still need a bit more convincing.' Her hands moving up to grasp his arms as his fingers found her.

'Well it's a good thing you resigned then,' Dante breathed against her mouth, his lips hot against hers. 'You're not leaving this bungalow until I say so, Farusja Mumba.'

Farusja teased her mouth around his. 'You play dirty Dumeno, what on earth am I going to do here for three days?'

'The name is Dante,' he crushed his mouth against hers. 'Well fuck me for three days and we'll find out.'

CHAPTER 18

Sunday, 6 May

Detective Miles Mkazi stared at the freezer in front of him. Two weeks ago he had one death on his hands and today he had another one. He did not like where this case was going. She had left the world crammed in her own freezer, another girl strangled to death. Miles rubbed his eyes tiredly. No evidence on who had killed Frieda Lyme had been forthcoming. The people around the club who were questioned had been just as drunk as she had been; the security guards and bouncers claimed ignorance, and none of her friends had any knowledge of a new boyfriend or a new man she had come to befriend on an intimate level. The fact that Frieda had been a serial dater and frequently had a new man on her arm did nothing to help matters either.

The debris that had been found around her body had yielded nothing. There had been no skin, no fibres under her nails. It was as if the killer had come up from behind her and strangled her without touching her, and now this one … This had blown apart the earlier suspicions that he had of Dante Dumeno having an affair with Frieda. Till this day, he was still waiting for a call from his superiors to tell him he was fired for going after Dumeno, but it seemed he had misjudged the man. Whatever act the man was putting on there was more behind him than people realised, but even so he would not be swayed by the man's character, he was still a suspect.

Miles stared into the empty freezer, as if he could gauge who the killer had been from the crystals of ice sparkling on the freezers now empty insides.

Miles leaned forward, keeping his body well away from any part of the freezer. The body had been taken away less than an hour ago and he already felt the case getting cold again, except for one small detail which brought him back to his original thoughts. The freezer had been found in the house of an Erica Nangula, the marketing officer at DI Storage. Things were becoming very interesting indeed. Erica had been on a night out, had been elegantly dressed, and her blood alcohol level had not been as high as Frieda's. She had been dead in her own freezer for a week.

Erica was still wearing her evening dress when they had found her in the freezer. Her high heeled shoes clung to her feet covered with sparkling ice crystals, and her dress stood frozen stiffly as though it had been starched. There was no sign of forced entry; she had even placed her bag on the table in the sitting room. She had been surprised in the kitchen and she had put up a fight. The items that had been on the kitchen counters had been scattered all over the floor, cups, plates, cutlery and food lay everywhere.

When her daughter did not arrive for a long-planned family engagement on Saturday afternoon, her mother had tried to call her. She had attributed her lack of response to either a party or another engagement and had not given in to her instinctive motherly worry that night, but on Sunday – today – when Erica did not return her calls, Anna Nangula had gone straight to her daughters flat and had immediately known that something was terribly wrong.

Miles could not even imagine what it had felt like have found her only daughter lying dead in her freezer. He said nothing but sat on the late Erica's couch and held her mother's hand. He finally escorted the heart-broken woman into the hands of another police officer who took her home.

Some fingerprint or clue must be somewhere, he was sure of it. Miles frowned. It could not be a coincidence; someone was killing the girls at DI Storage. First the secretary, and now the marketing officer, but why? And they were all being strangled. What was the significance of it all? He would have to speak to Dumeno. The rest of the staff at the company would have to be protected, but Dumeno was still his prime suspect. As much as he loathed saying it, with the second death everyone on the force would start paying attention.

'So, are we back to being enemies,' Farusja exhaled as she watched them slide to a stop before Rebecca's small flat. The euphoria of her three days of talking, eating, game viewing, sex and more talking had not waned, even as they had slowly driven back to Windhoek, the prospects of both of their lives was more stressful than comforting.

'Only if you want to be,' Dante smiled at her, raising his hand to caress her cheek. 'But it is so much more fun being more than that. Did you have a good time?'

Farusja laughed self-consciously, covering his hands with hers. 'I did Mr Dumeno.'

'Dante damn it,' he growled, shaking her chin gently. 'I'll be coming to get you again, Farusja Mumba.'

Farusja leaned forward, kissing him. 'Don't hold your breath Dante, I have things to do.' She tried to laugh but failed as Dante effectively shut her up by covering her mouth with his.

CHAPTER 19

Monday, 7 May

*T*he news broke at midday. The police had made an effort to keep it quiet, not only to avoid public panic but to carry on conducting their investigation for a few days unhampered by public concerns, but the flow of information within the department had its own flaws and the loose lips of an officer told members of his family who in turn had told their friends. By Sunday night, three quarters of the city knew, and by the middle of Monday, the everyone in Namibia knew that a serial killer was preying on women from DI Storage.

After the news was verified, it had been broadcast on the hour by the radio stations throughout the country, and now it was on television. Detective Miles Mkazi was angry, his foot a staccato tap against the desk in front of him.

'Detective Mkazi, I'll throw you out of my office if you continue that stupid noise.'

'My apologies commander,' Detective Miles said quietly, arresting his shoe in mid air.

'It has been almost three weeks detective. You have no evidence and no leads, except a new body lying there in the morgue and one already buried. If these murders are going to go serial, we have no choice but to make a public statement.'

'Commander Mbunga, all respect to you, but let the story remain what it is, a rumour,' Miles spoke earnestly, convincingly. 'If we advertise this we will scare away whoever is killing these girls, they will become more careful and it will make our job harder.'

The commander shook his head, the medals pinned on his too small uniform shaking with him. His fat hands were laid flat on the desk in front of him, the tips pointed at Miles. 'We have spent too much time on this case, we cannot have the public start saying we're incompetent.'

But we are. Miles stared angrily at the black sweaty face staring back at him angrily. He always thought his commander was just too lazy to be in the police force. His office was amazingly comfortable; the huge desk, the television, the big couch, and there was not a paper in sight; it amazed him every time. 'Commander, all I'm saying is hold off on the press conference, give us time to get something on this guy! Right now we have nothing to report!'

'We have a duty to the public, you should know that detective,' Commander Mbunga said sternly. 'Do I really need to keep calling you here to ask you why you are not doing your job?'

Miles kept the expression on his face neutral, his insides boiling with anger; he was the last person to be lectured about not doing his job. 'My respectful apologies commander, I'm strongly insisting that we don't make more of a mess of it than it already is.'

The commander clicked his tongue against the top of his mouth. 'How many times must I repeat myself? The statement is going out as soon as our PR is finished with it, sort the fall out with your team and carry on the investigation, now go. I have other things to do!'

Miles stood up slowly. 'The killer will know everything we're doing commander, is this really wise?'

'Do I need to repeat myself Detective Mkazi?'

Miles decided to push his luck. 'If I may ask one thing before I leave, I'd like permission to search DI Storage.'

Commander Mbunga stared at him, his eyes bulging out of the fleshy folds that made up his face. 'Mr Dante Dumeno has been our generous patron for almost ten years,' he hissed at Miles. 'To even suggest that he must be treated like a criminal.' He shook his head, the look on his face thunderous. 'Detective my patience is wearing thin. If you do not solve this case, I'll make sure someone pays for it. And you don't want that someone to be you.'

Back in his office, Miles was just in time to watch another news broadcast, his anger directed at the only person he knew to direct it to, the news broadcaster. Her face portrayed the right mix of compassion, outrage and fear. Compassion for the victims of the serial killer, outrage because the police had kept the information from the public, and fear for the women of the town, especially those at Dante International Storage. Miles watched her lips, his anger boiling over as she listed the incompetence's of the police department and warning women to take safety precautions. He did not care what his superiors said, they would have to talk to the staff at DI, starting with Dante Dumeno.

'We're going to get him boss.'

Miles looked at the deputy sitting across from him. He was tall, almost reaching the two metre mark, which made him seem clumsy and, despite being in his late twenties, almost adolescent at the same time. His black face, with its wide generous mouth and protruding eyes gave people the impression that he was more open and honest than his fellow officers. This made him a favourite partner when suspects needed to be interrogated or a member of the public needed to be informed of bad news; he always played the good cop. He had therefore been exposed to a lot more than other colleagues in the department.

The single murder of Frieda Lyme had gone noticed, just filed with the growing number of unsolved crimes in the country. But now Erica Nangula had also been found strangled. *This is what it takes for the department to sit up and take notice.* Miles recalled how his superiors had finally called him in and asked him to organise the crime investigation unit to tackle the case. He had no illusions about the department. They did combat crime; but they did it at their own speed. Miles had known the only reason that a unit had been organised was because the case would be blown wide open soon and the police would need to save face.

And that day was today.

And so here they were, Philip and himself. The other task force members conspicuous in their absence. It seemed inadequate. They had even been assigned one of the new conference rooms that were usually only available for visiting dignitaries or people of rank at the police department.

Miles had brought in a large pin board and had put up the details of the two victims, and the last gruesome photos that would ever be taken of them; their deaths.

'Have we found out what these girls had in common yet? Did the latest autopsy reveal anything?'

'Not yet boss. None of the girls had been violated in any way. There was little if no trace of any foreign substances on their bodies, the only samples we recovered were from their surroundings. The interesting thing about the both of them was that besides them being colleagues, their murders seemed to be very intimate. Look at these photographs,' Philip pulled one of the photographs over to scrutinise. 'Despite the violence of their deaths, it seems he tried to arrange them in a peaceful way.'

'So he's not only a killer, but he also feels remorse over what he's doing?'

'Either that, or he feels like he's playing a part in providing them with the peace they did not have in life?'

Miles nodded, riffling through the stack of photographs that he had not yet pinned on the board. 'So our killer might be a priest? Or a spiritual healer? This just gets better and better. What more do we have?'

'He might just be the ordinary guy next door. In general we have two strangulations, both manual, no ligatures involved,' Philip raised a photograph closer to his eyes, as though he could see something different from looking at it from at a different angle. 'The perpetrator put the last victim in the freezer and accosted her in her home, but not the first. I assume he did not have the time he needed with Frieda?' He put the photograph back down onto the long conference table.

'Frieda Lyme's lifestyle was not predictable so maybe she could not be surprised, but she did struggle, and there is not even a shred of evidence of the killer on her. How did he manage that? Even if he is covering himself from head to toe in plastic, there should still be evidence of whatever fabric or material he's wearing under their fingernails or on their bodies,' Philip stared at the photos, oblivious of Miles. 'The only pattern is the strangulations and the fact they are colleagues. Either it is Dumeno killing them off one by one to keep them quiet about his messy affairs with them, or it is just some random crazy person that has taken a liking to the girls at DI Storage.'

'But the only obvious loose woman among the two was Frieda. As far we know Erica had no relations with Dumeno,' Philip glanced at him, and Miles smiled inwardly as he saw the inner battle raging within the man-boy in front of him.

Phillip cleared his throat. 'Yes Frieda was the only,' he paused, 'woman who had many men, but we don't yet know that for sure. We have not rummaged sufficiently enough into these two girls pasts.'

'And why the freezer?' Miles interjected, his eyes bright but his face unsmiling. 'Frieda was just dumped out there. And he took the time to arrange Erica in her deep freezer?'

Philip shrugged. 'All I can think of was what I said earlier, he did not have the time he wanted to have with Frieda.'

Miles stared hard at his deputy, grasping his meaning but loathe to explore it. 'Is there any possibility that we can get into DI without anyone knowing it?'

'That would be illegal boss,' Philip stared at him.

'Find out, but find out discreetly.'

'Boss …'

'It's been almost a month deputy. With nothing! There are times we need to work above the law!'

'But Dumeno is protected boss, if word gets out to Commander Mbunga that we touched him ...'

'I'll take the fall deputy.'

Phillip shook his head. 'I advise against it boss. And what about the women of DI Storage? There are only two left; the cleaner and the finance officer. What do we do about them?'

Miles tapped his fingers on the table in front of him, seeing Dante Dumeno in his mind's eye. He had been given the go-ahead to use whatever resources and do whatever was necessary to catch this killer, but Dante Dumeno was still off limits. Miles glanced at Philip briefly. 'Police protection. In other words, God help them.'

Dante listened to the news in stunned silence. He had arrived at work in pleasant spirits, refreshed and elated from his weekend with Farusja. Erica had been on a week's annual leave. It was only today, when she was due back and did not arrive, that the temporary secretary, Ndeshi, tried to contact her, and for the next hour had reported that her cell phone was on voicemail. And again, they had made the mistake of not thinking too much into it as Dante always encouraged flexibility around the hours in his company.

It was mid-morning when the broadcast hit the streets of Windhoek. Dante could mentally feel fear pervade his company. Erica had been found, strangled. Dante felt goosebumps begin their slow ascent up his arms. His girls were being killed, but why? Who would want to kill them? Did he have any new enemies? He would have to get hold of Hienry; he would know how to find who was doing this.

Dante stared at the radio on the desk, and at the phone that had just started ringing. He shouted at Ndeshi to hold all the calls.

All that was left of the women at DI now were the finance officer, cleaner and Ndeshi. After the broadcasts, he doubted whether anyone would ever want to work at DI Storage at all. Should he close the company for a while?

A knock sounded on his door and he sighed at the meeting he would now have to face with his staff, again. The memorial he would have to assist in organising, again. He drew a ragged breath, contemplating the meaning of it all. His girls – Farusja, Robbie. He would need to double their protection. He decided to give all female staff at DI compassionate leave until this was all over. He was also going to summon Detective Mkazi and demand results.

First Orabella was planning to sell him out and now this? The financial statements would not look good at the end of this financial year.

But most importantly, right now, he needed to phone the two important women in his life. He needed to warn one of them. And he needed to let the other one go. For her own protection. Just for now.

Before he could pick up the phone, it started vibrating, very few people had this number. 'What do you need?'

'What do you mean what do I need?' Jerome's angry voice came down the line. 'You're the one lining up bodies. I'm coming over.'

Dante cursed loudly. 'Stay where you are.'

Jerome laughed, his laugh small over the noise around him. 'You can't be serious bra, you think I'm okay sitting by the sidelines when you're in trouble?'

'Don't get involved!'

'Whatever, you think I didn't pick up anything living with you? I am heading to the house until we get to the bottom of this bra, I can also watch your back you know.'

Dante yelled angrily at his brother as the phone was cut in his ear. He knew he was wasting his time in arguing with Jerome; who was just as hard-headed and as stubborn as he was.

Dante stared at his phone, breathing in deeply, he did not want to call her, after the amazing weekend he had just spent with her … Dante ground his teeth, quelling the emotion inside him. He had to do it, he had no choice. He did not want to see her wind up dead. He listened as her voice came down the line; this would probably hurt him far more than it did her.

'Dante?' Farusja said quietly. 'Are you okay? I just heard …'

'That's not your concern,' he said quietly. 'Listen Mumba, this thing between us … we had a great weekend.'

'Yes,' Farusja said slowly over the line, he could hear the caution in her voice. 'What are you getting at?'

Dante steeled himself. 'I got what I wanted. I don't think there's any point in continuing whatever this is. I have more important things to deal with right now, as the radio told you.'

'Are you serious? You're saying this to me over the phone?'

'Yes,' Dante said harshly. 'What did you think this would turn out to be? A relationship? Get your head out of the sand Mumba. It was just sex, that's all it was.'

'You are a coward and a bastard Dumeno,' she said quietly. 'You're such a fucking bastard, and funny thing was I was actually starting to think you were human.'

'Look, go back to Zambia. There's nothing for you in Namibia anymore,' he said shortly. 'Do not come to HD, or DI. I don't want you anymore.'

'I resigned you bastard. I won't come near your freaking businesses if I were under threat of death!' she hissed angrily at him down the line. 'Add my name of your list of enemies!'

Dante closed his eyes momentarily as she hung up. *It had to be done.* He got up angrily and threw the phone across the room. *It just had to be done.*

Roberta stood with her phone clutched rigidly in her hand, staring out of the windows of her office that overlooked the parking lot. Dante had only just called her with the news and it was almost noon, too late for any damage control to be done with the media or with the police. Their lives would be blown wide-open, and their businesses will suffer. She knew it and it scared the hell out of her. She would have to bring the board together as soon as possible. She turned as a knock sounded on her office door and August's concerned face peered back at her. Her eyes were wide and Roberta could not help but notice the apprehensive look in them.

'Ma'am? I have calls for you, can I put them through?'

'From who August?'

August's lip faltered, trembling slightly. 'Is it true? The women at Mr Dumeno's?' she stopped abruptly as she saw the look on Roberta's face. 'I'm sorry Ma'am, I ...'

'I do not indulge in idle gossip August. Who is calling?'

August swallowed visibly. 'Everybody. The board, the patrons, the clients.'

'Direct all calls to me, and bring me some coffee.'

'Yes ma'am,' August backed out of the room as fast as she had come in.

Roberta inhaled slowly; why on earth would someone target the women at DI Storage? What had Dante done? For the first time in her life she did not know what to do and she could not even begin to imagine how they would get out of this mess.

She was so pretty. She would be his real beginning after the heartache and pain of the other girls disappointing ends. He would make her end spectacular; she deserved that much since she had been such an object of so much affection. He loved her for it, and he would make sure she died well for it. She would be his beginning; again. She would be his ultimate revenge, for his mother and for his sister. He saw them both in his dreams every night, both of them walking towards him, the burnt ash of their flesh falling off their charred bodies as the fire consumed them, their arms stretched out towards him. They always walked to him; he was so close to them that he could see their hair disappear in little tongues of flame as it burned off their heads, and he could smell the flesh burning off their bones. He could never get close to them; they always crumbled to ash before he could touch them, but he could speak to them.

As their lips burned off in the fire, their words formed out of smoke drifted towards him. He looked forward to talking to them every night, and in time he got used to their burning faces and empty eye sockets. He could never help them; he could never help them when they were alive and now that they were dead he could not even touch them, but he could hear them and he would do what they asked. They had all thought an apology would be enough, that they could sit there with grief on their faces and that eventually in time the pain would go away. But it had not, not for him. It remained burning inside him, each and every waking hour of the day, eating him up from the inside, until he had nothing left but what felt like a bloody stump where his heart was supposed to be. And now they went on with their lives as if nothing had happened, as if he was not in pain. Over the years he had grown to hate them, to hate their indifference to his suffering, their riches and their arrogance. He had made a promise to his mother, to his sister, every last one of them would die for what they had done to his family. The two dead girls had given him some relief before his great finale; his mother and sister would be so proud of him.

CHAPTER 20

*O*rabella Ricci stared at the wall in front of her, huddled on her own living room floor, her hands hanging loosely at her sides. The walls around her echoed back her pain miserably, offering no comfort, dispelling all illusions of being safe in one's own home. She rubbed her ankles, trying to infuse some warmth into them, then moved to her arms, rubbing them almost frantically. She could no longer process what was going on around her; it had been days, weeks, months since it had begun, and her life turned into a nightmare cycle of abuse and fear. She was scared. She tensed as she heard the door scrape open, she did not bother looking up. She knew it was *him*.

She touched her numb fingers to her bottom lip, now swollen to twice its size.

'You're keeping me a prisoner in my own home. Why are you doing this?' she whispered, her voice hoarse.

She lifted her eyes to *him* as *he* came to crouch in her vision. 'How long do you intend to keep me here?'

She shivered as *he* stared at her. *His* eyes had changed during the time she had known *him*, and she had known *him* a long time. 'How can you make me do this? Are you heartless?'

He smiled at her, and the slash across *his* mouth combined with those dead eyes was terrifying. Orabella touched her lip again, nervously. *He* had hit her not more than an hour ago. *He* came and went as *he* pleased in her house, and as far as she could deduce, it had just been for the fun of seeing her cower in front of *him*, vulnerable, unprotected, not in control. Thankfully, *he* left her alone at night, and she had cried in relief knowing that *he* would never force her to share *his* bed. She hoped Dante would forgive her for what she had been forced to do. She wished she could get a message through to him, but it was impossible.

She watched *him* raise *himself* back onto *his* feet, still staring at her. She had tried to get *him* to talk, but *he* refused. 'When are you going to let me go?'

He turned his dead eyes on her. 'When I kill you.'

Orabella's blood ran cold, tendrils of fear dragging their way across her back. She regretted ever coming to Namibia in the first place.

She had come from Italy on a two week holiday, invited by her uncle who owned an Italian restaurant in the capital. She had fallen so in love with the place that she had never looked back. After long hours of working in the pizzeria, she had heard about the program HD Advertising and DI Storage had for start-up businesses and she had decided to try her luck. Her grandmother, a cook by nature and a cultivator of every plant under the sun was a natural herbalist and botanist; she had raised Orabella. Orabella recalled long trips into the lush Italian countryside, where her grandmother would not hesitate to point out the various herbs and perfumed flowers and their uses. With this knowledge embedded in her from an early age, she had never bought a bottle of perfume, a jar of face cream or a bar of soap; everything she had made with her own hands, using her knowledge of plants and herbs as a base. This is what she had taken to HD Advertising that day, and that was the day she had met Dante.

Her association with Dante had been sexy and intense. They recognised each other for what they were; in business together, and a few trips in and out of each other's beds never changed that. Their association had brought a lot of things to the two of them; satisfaction, financial leverage, mutual realised ambition. But now that all seemed to be a crutch, one which had led them fatally to this moment in time, and left them paying for all their indiscretions.

Orabella choked back a sob, as she watched *him* leave the house. She was allowed free rein of the house, nowhere else. She was being watched every hour of the day and night, and it did little to ease the fear in her heart. Such was her fear that she had let herself go; she had lost so much weight her bones shone through her once healthy skin, her hair was ragged and dirty, her clothes … she could not remember when she had last changed them and she did not even bother turning up or down the temperature in the house anymore, be it hot or cold. And she was married; Orabella let the tears run unchecked down her face, holding her knees to her chest, rocking herself slowly. She was married to a monster.

'Forgive me Dante,' she whispered to herself, rocking herself slowly. 'Please forgive me.'

Dante sat in the reception of DI Storage, manning the phones. He could have had someone assigned from HD to do it, but he did not have the stomach to see someone else get killed. After he had met with the staff, the women had been happy enough to keep away. He felt sorry for Catherine Mbuende, their finance officer and the last remaining woman of his professional staff. He could not imagine what she must be feeling knowing that both of her friends had been killed. At the meeting, although she had not said anything, her eyes had been red rimmed and swollen. Dante would not have faulted her if she had burst into tears right then and there. The security guards had all been stoic in the meeting, and all of them decided that they would remain.

At this point in time that was all he could do. He had been on the rampage in the morning, wanting to rush into an audience with that Detective Mkazi, but had decided against it. He wanted to be distanced as much as possible on a personal level from this mess. Let the business absorb most of the damage. He had more than enough money and investments stashed away.

The intercom buzzed and he depressed the button, waiting for his visitor expectantly.

Naks sauntered in through the door, looking unconcerned and unruffled. Today he was wearing his favourite low slung black pants, a baggy white shirt, and the dark sunglasses ever present. The wry smile on his face belied the seriousness of the situation.

'Not like you to give up so easily Dumeno,' Naks dropped the six-pack he was carrying on the reception counter, and pulled up a chair. 'What happened to them girls?'

'You know full well what happened to them girls,' Dumeno reached forward and pulled the beer towards him, ripping open the six-pack and opening a can.

'I meant the remaining ones,' Naks reached out to accept the can that Dante was handing to him. 'I'm not so cold-hearted.'

'I'd disagree,' Dante smirked at his friend. 'What brings you here, man?'

'For one the murders. What the hell is going on? And then there's Robbie, that chick is freaking out in so many ways.'

'You were with her on the weekend?'

'You know her ass only comes to me when you are not on it,' Naks adjusted himself, slinging a leg over the arm of the chair. 'That ass was sweet too.'

'Robbie is at her best when she's depressed and desperate,' Dumeno shrugged. 'You catch her at those times and you're guaranteed a good time.'

'Is she safe?'

'Yeah, I've put a guard on her.'

'And the other one?'

Dante glanced at his friend, pursuing his lips. 'Robbie told you?'

'She told me a lot.'

'The other one is safe too,' Dante sighed as the cold liquid trickled down his throat. The great thing about Naks was that he always seemed to anticipate what was needed at the right moment.

'Robbie won't stand for it man.'

'She's a big girl acting like a child,' Dante opened another can, handing another one out to Naks.

'So what the hell is happening here man?' Naks swirled the can around the small reception area. 'Who's your enemy this time?'

Dante shrugged, frowning. 'I don't know anymore than you do. Weren't you the one that had inside information about this?'

'Well, it was just rumours at that time. I had no idea it would lead to this. And that French dude? Can't he find out? The guy is hard, fat as he is, *eish*, he's hard,' Naks shook his head.

'Yeah, he's on it.'

'And the other girl?' Naks looked at his friend from the top of his beer.

'She's gone.'

*H*ienry sagged into his friend's couch, grumbling, pretending to feign interest in the soccer match on television. The soccer was at least serving as a slight distraction to Dante. He had brought Jerome to the house who was now clattering about in the kitchen.

Dante glanced at Hienry briefly, his mind a whirlwind of thoughts. As his overall head of security, Hienry had imposed security checks at all the entry ways into the storage facility. The police department had mentioned that a special unit had been assigned to the case and it was accorded a top priority status, but DI had not had any official visits during the day.

Dante snorted. He was sure that the detective or constable whatever he was, would beat a straight path to his door pretty soon, and he knew that this visit would not be as friendly as the last one had been.

'I have nothing,' Hienry grudgingly admitted, looking at his friend from under his brows.

Dante continued watching television, making a sound between a groan and a painful moan as his team missed another goal.

'Do you hear me?' Hienry roared, almost lifting himself off the couch. 'I have nothing!'

'I heard you the first time,' Dante said quietly, his eyes not leaving the screen.

Hienry scowled. 'Do you want to hear if I have nothing on the first issue or what nothing I have on the second issue?'

'Suit yourself.'

The scowl on Hienry's face deepened. 'So far it's only been two girls, both strangled. It was done cleanly. He may have hit one on the head to keep her quiet but not hard enough for her to actually pass out. He wanted them awake while he killed them.'

'Sick bastard. But we know all this already.'

'We think he was on friendly terms with Frieda Lyme. The last one surprised him; she was not as easy.'

'That's my marketing officer you're talking about there,' Dante said dryly.

'Was your marketing officer. The man is a ghost, he leaves no scent or track. I have my men out but so far they have had as much success as the police.'

Dante sighed as his team missed a goal opportunity. 'And what of the girls' friends?'

'Nothing there Dumeno. Frieda was with a different guy every week, during the weekend almost every day, but you know this already. I wish I had met her, maybe...' Hienry sighed wistfully. 'The other girl had the same boring routine week after week, that's why it was so easier for him to get hold of her. What a way to leave the world, eh? The killer is not finished Dumeno, so you'd better start preparing for more damages.'

'We have another memorial service this weekend,' Dante scowled. 'You'd think we were in the business of funerals. Someone is killing my girls Hienry, I want him found.'

Hienry reached towards the table in the middle of the room to grab a beer. 'Hienry do this, Hienry do that,' he grumbled. 'You know how much I'm doing already?'

'So what is the second bit of nothing you don't seem to have?'

'Ah,' Hienry's eyes lit up, 'our friend Orabella now works from home, she does not step into the office anymore. All our efforts to contact your little chocolate éclair have failed. We cannot get her by phone, we cannot speak to her directly. I cannot catch her at home. Whoever is protecting this woman is very good at what they do.'

'What about her husband?'

Hienry scoffed, laughing dryly. 'What husband?'

Dante sat up, and for the first time since the match had started, looked at his friend.

'Ah, that got your attention you bastard, eh?' Hienry chuckled. 'You know as well as I do that no one has ever seen that man. Those stories of her going to Italy to get married and the three month long honeymoon, rubbish! That woman is not married!'

'But the certificates? And the pictures of the two of them together?'

Hienry waved his hand in the air, dismissing the claims. 'I've informed you better than that my friend. All those things can be faked.'

'So then who is the man in the pictures?'

'That could be anybody – an actor, an escort. They are very well paid these days.'

'And the file on me?'

'It seems to be finished,' Hienry said quietly. 'But she's still sitting on it.'

'Why?'

Hienry shrugged, his wide shoulders lifting his entire torso. 'Do I know everything? I don't have a clue. Now, about that girl whose car blew up ...'

Dante's threw the remote control onto the table and stretched his body out on the couch. 'What the hell Hienry? You really don't want me to watch my game do you?'

'She is a suspect, whether you like it or not.'

'She is not a suspect.'

'Just because she has a pretty face and a plump backside does not mean she is without blame.'

'She is without blame.'

'Who are we talking about? Farusja Mumba?' Jerome interrupted the conversation as he came from the kitchen, holding a large wooden spoon in one hand. 'That girl is hot!'

Dante looked at him. 'She's older than you, leave her alone.'

Jerome winked at his brother, the blue jeans and white t-shirt peppered with flour. 'That girl is good stock, don't mess her up for someone else.'

'There is no one else for her, but me,' Dante said pointedly.

Jerome stared at him. 'You really like her, don't you?'

Dante turned back to Hienry, ignoring Jerome. 'She is not a suspect. Besides, I've sent her out of the country.'

Hienry sighed, his voice taking on a harder and more serious tone. 'How? Are you sure she even left? Dante, the evidence is there my friend. These little surprises you have been getting? They are all planted with the utmost care by someone who knows not only who you are with but who also knows the outlines and confines of this house. The bomb was in her car.'

'And so? And she's only been in my house once, and she had ample opportunity!'

'What if everything she told you was a lie, just to get into your house, into your bed and then,' Hienry made the sound of an explosion, 'she hits you where it hurts the most!'

Dante smirked at him. 'She's had the space and time to do that, and she did not.'

'Maybe she's biding her time.'

'Yo, wait a minute, you guys think Farusja is the one leaving those bombs around the house?' Jerome stared at them incredulously. 'That chick is one hell of a graphic designer but I doubt she can hot-wire a car, let alone create a bomb.'

'You can get anything online Jerry,' Hienry twisted his mouth.

'Nah it ain't Farusja, I bet on my life on that!' Jerome shook his head vehemently. 'You really want to go and arrest the first girl my brother actually has feelings for?'

Dante got up, exasperation showing on his face. He did not want to talk about Farusja, did not want to hear her name. It hurt too much. He craved her body, he wanted to see those eyes of hers again; he had not had enough of her. He had even taken to looking at the picture on her personnel file, just to have a glimpse of her. He envied the guy who Hienry had set to follow her and protect her. He thought back to the phone call to her that morning, the hurt in her voice.

He pushed his emotions aside. 'It's not her. If I know anything Hienry, if I could trust anyone besides you and Roberta and my family it would be my instinct, and it is not her.'

He stopped abruptly as his phone beeped. He pulled it out of his pocket, and stared blindly at the message that followed. 'It's the detective, and he's outside.'

Hienry stood up, motioning for Jerome to follow him. 'I'm supposed to be informed by those stupid men outside. What the hell do we pay them for, damn fools? This is our cue to leave, tell me what he says.'

Not waiting for an answer, Hienry moved quickly towards the back door leading out from the kitchen, disappearing from view.

Jerome lingered a moment longer. 'Wish I could do more to help, bra.'

Dante nodded at him, simultaneously patting him on the back and pushing him to follow Hienry. He frowned after his brothers receding back; it annoyed him that the detective had come to his house, and not only that but that he had come after hours. What on earth was he playing at? The message had said he was outside and would very much appreciate a meeting with him. Dante frowned; he did not like people dictating to him, and right now most especially this guy. But saying no would only postpone the meeting for another day and increase the detective's suspicion. He growled, angry, and strode towards the front door, opening it just as the detective was about to knock.

Dante raised his eyebrows as he saw the white polyester tracksuit that the detective was wearing.

'I thought the police spend all day taking the day off? Why are you bothering me at home detective?' Dante asked dryly as he shook Miles hand and allowed him into his sitting room.

'We may be above the law Mr Dumeno, but we're still human,' Miles said, the look in his eyes belying the smile on his mouth.

Dante motioned him towards the seat across from the television. 'If you don't mind detective Mkazi, I have work to do that will not be done on its own, and so we shall be on unequal footing here. What can I do for you this evening?'

Miles lowered himself into the chair, looking around Dante's sitting room unashamedly. 'Maybe those girls at work refused you?'

Dante stared back at the detective, unfazed. 'What are you getting at?'

'You're the only suspect in this investigation Dumeno,' Miles continued. 'And the girls are all coming from one place, your company. You lied. You were intimate with Frieda Lyme.'

'Who was not detective?'

'Erica Nangula? You were intimate with both of them.'

'Then obviously there was no refusal from them,' Dante stared at the detective across the desk. 'I have been intimate with most of the women in my organisations Detective Miles.'

'So it's just a coincidence that some of the women you have been intimate with start dying? Strangulation is a way of demonstrating power Dumeno. It allows a male to dominate a female mentally, physically and emotionally; and ultimately hold someone's life in their hands. Was sleeping with them not enough?'

'Are you accusing me of something detective?' Dante said quietly. 'Because if you are, maybe we should do this the right way and have my lawyers present. I have entertained your lack of procedure thus far and allowed you into my home. But my patience is wearing thin.'

Miles laughed, a hearty sound that filled the air of the room with a brittle edge. 'It is a sad day when the police are dictated to by civilians who have more money than they know what to do with.'

Dante leaned back in his chair. 'Get to the point Mkazi, I should have called your superiors long ago.'

The laughter disappeared just as suddenly as it had appeared. 'I think you killed those women Dumeno. You have taken advantage of your privileged position with the police and you're using your organisations as your playground to do whatever you like.'

'Killing my women would be bad for my business Mkazi,' Dante said dryly to the detective. 'As it stands now I'm losing money, I have clients closing accounts with DI Storage, I'm concerned about my bottom dollar detective. I hardly even have time to kill anyone, let alone kill anyone that would have a negative impact on the organisation which I built by my own sweat. The women make my organisation the epitome of feminine success. If I killed anybody it would be the men,' Dante twisted his lips dryly, his stare at the detective impassive.

'Killers do strange things Dumeno.'

'Come back when you have some evidence Mkazi, or with a search warrant,' Dante paused, 'if your superiors allow it. In the meantime, leave my premises.'

The smile returned to the detectives face as he stood up slowly, all his movements exaggerated. 'I'll be coming back with that search warrant then.'

Dante nodded and stood up, watching the detective as he got up and made his way towards the door. Dante followed him quietly, leaning past him to open the front door.

'I'll catch you Dumeno.'

Dante looked at him as he crossed the threshold. 'Always a pleasure detective. Try not to fabricate any more lies on your way down my driveway. My men will let you out.'

Dante did not wait for him to answer but closed the door and returned to the sitting room, not surprised to see Hienry reclining in the chair that the detective had just vacated.

'Okay, even that I did not know.'

Dante threw him a nasty look. 'Eavesdropping again Hienry? Are you bugging the house again?'

'It is my job. I know everything that happens around you Dumeno, but that I did not know.'

Dante shrugged.

'You were making love to the other dead girl? How did I not know this?' Hienry looked at him in disbelief. 'You pick well my friend, because I saw the pictures of that girl and she was,' Hienry smacked his lips, touching his thumb and index finger to them.

'Stop it Hienry.'

'So what, you thought no one would find out? You think it can just be swept under the carpet? When was the last time you saw her?'

Dante exhaled noisily. 'It was before the launch dinner at HD, a week before. I might have also picked up Catherine after that ...'

Hienry gaped at him. ' Ah you surely are a class act Dumeno. And what do you think will happen once the news gets out? Was Catherine not the finance girl?'

'Yes, she still is my finance girl.'

'That's left to be seen, as long as she does not get herself killed,' Hienry grumbled.

'I did not kill my girls Hienry.'

'Tell that to the bloody public; tell that to the bloody police when they kick down your door,' Hienry continued grumbled. 'And again I have to pull you out of yet another bloody mess.'

Miles Mkazi pretended not to see the man walking next to him as he strolled down Dante Dumeno's driveway, and instead looked around as unobtrusively as he could at the neighbour's houses and what little he could see of Dumeno's house. Philip had done an excellent job in unearthing the victims past lives and activities. They would never have known that both girls had been with Dumeno if it had not been for his dogged persistence, but that still did not prove anything. Miles knew he needed to obtain a search warrant, and the only way to do it was to get information that would damn Dante Dumeno to his superiors.

Even Dante sleeping with both girls before they died would not be enough. As Dumeno himself said he had slept with half of the women in both his organisations, and all of them had been willing participants. Miles ground his teeth in frustration; he could even mention a few female police officers that Dante had slept with. If he was the killer, Miles could see the obstacles he faced in trying to bring Dumeno into the station for questioning. But there was one thing Dumeno had been right about; he did not strike Miles as being more concerned about anything other than his profit margin. He had watched Dumeno for the past couple of weeks and despite the women beating a path to his door, his first love always seemed to remain his work. But the man had motive; the women were coming from his company and no matter how weak the motive was, he was the last person to be close to both victims before they died. Miles did not believe in coincidence, he did not believe in coincidences one bit.

CHAPTER 22

Tuesday, 8 May

M ichael parked his car at the gate, his body tense. He wiped his damp palms on the knees of his jeans, beads of perspiration forming on his upper lip despite the cool air. Although he never had any trouble whenever he came up here, the excitement and nervousness of each trip he made to DI Storage had begun to wear him down. And now that the killings had started it was getting even more difficult to keep making the trips.

In the beginning he had been overzealous and had gone to the park frequently, off-loading new stock and organising his storage area. When the guards had stopped joking with him, and had begun to search his car more thoroughly, becoming suspicious of his visits, Michael had pulled back. He lessened his visits to once a week, never staying long enough to arouse more suspicion. He exhaled with relief as the guards waved him through now, not even bothering to check his Audi's boot, not even bothering to look in through the windows.

Idiots, he thought smugly, *you can get away with anything in this town if you know how to play the game.* He was surprised that he had not been searched or stopped with a killer on the loose. Did Dante know how lax the security guards were? He would definitely mention it the next time he was at HD Advertising, just to give Dante a chance to fire his old security detail and hire new ones, which would work well for the job he had to do.

The park was quiet, although there were some clients at their storage containers. Double parking, he made a show of being unhurried, taking his time. The worst thing about his trips was the fact that he actually had to do some work in the mornings, and that girl was supposed to be watching him today.

Michael twisted his lips distastefully. He tolerated her because he had to. The day she had walked, no, waltzed into his house bringing the devil with her he had never forgiven her. Now she acted as though she was in control of everything. Like she was *his* favourite. It was more than enough having to see her at HD Advertising every day. He hated her.

Farusja woke, dragging her body from her bed. She was exhausted. She had finally fallen asleep after the emotions raging inside her had been spent, and with her eyes almost swollen shut from crying. She could not say she had not been warned about Dante, but after such a great weekend, it made the realisation of what he had said harder to bear. She had known who he was before she had allowed him into her heart, her mind, her body, and she had no one to blame but herself. But it still hurt like hell.

It must be mid-day, she thought, scrunching up her eyes and allowing the light in slowly. She had to get out of the house. She had to get away from herself for a while. *Run, run,* she muttered.

What made matters worse was that Rabecca had left for the coast, taking a week's leave, so she had no idea what had happened. Farusja had decided that she was not going to call her best friend and spoil her vacation. God knew they all needed a break from the constant drama.

Farusja expelled her breath strongly; she would go to the gym. A gruelling workout would push that bloody womaniser out of her mind.

Farusja frowned, her eyes squinting up at the windscreen mirror, Dante hadn't taken the guard off her tail, that was certain. He'd been watching her for about ten days. Every time she had stepped out of the house, out of the office, he was there, she knew he was. She could feel the hair rise on the back of her neck. She had tried on countless occasions to get rid of him, sneaking out the back doors when she was still at HD, even letting Rabecca drive home alone and jumping into a taxi, but she had not managed to shake him. That was when she and Rabecca had found out that they both had their own individual tails. After the events of yesterday, Farusja had assumed that Dante would call off her follower. Apparently not. She could not help but feel relieved at her privilege of having a bodyguard. She briefly wondered how many more of Dante's women had their own personal bodyguards. She snorted, angry that she was now in the category of women that were called *his*, and ignoring the feeling of jealousy that welled up inside her. She grabbed her backpack from the seat next to her as she made her way into the gym.

There was rarely anyone at the gym during working hours, and that was just the way she liked it. She sighed, running her hands through her wet hair. Her muscles had turned to putty after the fifteen minutes she spent in the steam room; the hot steam had made its way deep into her pores, relaxing her to such an extent that she had lost track of time. The advent of a headache from the heat finally forcing her to leave.

Farusja yawned, wrapping the towel more tightly around her body, stepping away from the bank of showers, wiping the water out of her eyes. She stopped, her head cocked, listening. Since when had the women's changing rooms been so silent? The ladies showers were quiet too; she could hear no other movement in the spa dock. A shiver ran down her spine involuntarily, goosebumps raising the surface of her skin; she was alone, and suddenly she was scared. Farusja hurried towards the bank of lockers, moving faster than normal.

'Ah, Farusja.'

She gasped audibly, almost dropping the towel around her body, her pulse racing. She turned around slowly towards the door, knowing who it was, and almost afraid to look. Michael Katjihingua stood looking at her.

'You're not supposed to be here Michael, this is the ladies dressing room,' she said sharply to him, her body tense. 'What are you doing here? Leave now.'

He looked at her, smiling, his eyes roving her body. 'Ah Farusja. If you were paying more attention you would have known that some hysterical lady called in a rodent infestation just ten minutes ago, and everyone is waiting outside. I'm surprised no one told you, but not to worry, amazing me volunteered to save the day.'

Farusja scowled at him. 'There are no rodents in here.'

'Exactly, I needed a few moments alone with you. Since you resigned, it's been so difficult to get hold of you. I imagined you would have been a better fuck for Dumeno and that he would have promoted you already. But I guess things didn't work out, huh?'

Farusja's body started to shiver. 'Get out Michael. Now.'

He laughed, shaking his head, stepping two paces into the changing room. Two paces closer to her. 'You know I really did like you.'

Farusja stood her ground, holding her towel tightly. She was vulnerable in this situation, but she was not going to run out and make a scene because of this junkie in front of her. Had he followed her to the gym? How long had he been following her? Was he the one who was killing the girls? He was no longer the Michael Katjihingua she had first met in the cafeteria at HD Advertising. This was somebody else. He was colder, still arrogant but with an intensity that was petrifying.

Farusja gripped the towel tighter, her fingers so tense they had begun to hurt. Her heart beat a tattoo against her chest as her body coiled up in preparation, every muscle clenched. She breathed deeply, calming herself. 'I don't have time to play your stupid games.'

'Yeah, keeping your legs open is hard work,' he sighed dramatically. 'That man spoiled us Farusja, you know we would have been good together.' His voice became harsh again as he suddenly reared up, his face a mask of anger. 'You know, we can still be good together!'

Farusja, keeping her eyes on him, backtracked with her mind through the shower stalls and locker room, wracking her brain for something she could use as a weapon.

'How did you know I was here?' she said, trying to keep him off the subject of them. 'Did you follow me here?'

He smiled, taking another step towards her. 'That is none of your business, although we could make it ours.'

Farusja clenched her teeth. 'Out Michael. Now.'

He took another step towards her, his hands hanging loosely at his sides, a faint sheen of perspiration on his face. 'Come on Farusja.' The charming smile she remembered so well plastered itself over his face. 'Just you and me.'

Farusja stood her ground as he took another step towards her, now less than three paces away, her heels and toes digging into the floor, bracing herself to knee him in the groin if he touched her. If she could just get past him, she could make a run for it.

'Michael,' she said coldly, her voice even, 'if you don't leave now I'll have you fired. I might have resigned from HD but I'm still fucking Dante and the only reason I have not called him or the bodyguard he appointed for me right now is because I think you're a decent guy. Don't make me change my mind.'

He raised his hands, taking a step back. 'First of all you cannot have me fired, my parents are HD Advertising's bloody patrons.' Then he winked and the lewd glint in his eye did not escape her, and despite herself Farusja felt a twinge of shame. 'See you around. Maybe the next time we meet, you will be more inclined towards me, towards us.'

He turned and, without another word, headed for the men's shower and locker rooms.

Farusja flew into action, her fingers scrabbling to find the combination to her locker, pulling out her backpack that contained her clothes and shoes. She only dared to breathe when she had safely locked herself in one of the toilet stalls, her chest heaving. Who was that man really? Was he the one? She shivered as a chill crept up her spine. Eliminating any other thought as she quickly pulled on her clothes.

Michael sauntered out of the men's changing rooms lazily, nodding to the crowd of women who had gathered with worried faces waiting expectantly outside the women's changing rooms. They were all so stupid, even the gym staff were stupid; how could they let a strange man into the women's changing room? Even if he was solving a problem; they should have known better. Today he had done the last bit of work that was required of him at DI Storage and then the fireworks would really start. All his hard work was about to pay off in a very big way. He wondered which country he would visit first with all the money that he would be getting.

He had not expected to spot Farusja driving past him today. He had followed her, he needed to speak to her.

He had done all *he* had asked him to do. *He* could not find fault with him, no one could, not even that bitch he was working with. He had covered his tracks well and had made sure that he was not expendable like she was. He had knowledge about DI Storage that none of his other colleagues had, he had worked hard to get it, slept with those now dead women, and with men, in order to get what he needed.

The bitch was completely and utterly expendable, he had known it the moment *he* had outlined *his* plan to him. That girl he could kill, he felt no remorse for her, she deserved it, but as for Farusja ...

Michael sighed, the sound contrasting the twisted grin on his face. Yes it was a shame, he thought, looking around watchfully as he slipped into his car. She was so pretty; her skin would bruise horribly.

CHAPTER 23

*O*rabella had lost all track of time, but she worked slowly and steadily, her fingers numb with cold. Her voice was hoarse, she had shouted, and screamed and yelled to no avail. The walls had echoed her voice mockingly, as if waiting to see what her next move would be. Earlier that day she had tried to escape. She had feigned illness and when the one guarding the front door, a big burly man who looked more like a pit bull than anything else, found her lying semi-conscious on the floor. He had bent over her. As he peered unconcernedly into her face; she had driven the edge of her vanity mirror into his eyes, yelling as she stabbed him repeatedly. She had not looked back, ignoring his high pitched screams, ignoring the blood that gushed out onto her. She ran, her clothes flapping behind her, reaching for the open doorway with outstretched arms, tears streaming down her face. She had stumbled across the threshold, shouting for help, screaming for help, and hobbled her way down towards the main gate, her eyes seared by the bright sunlight after being confined indoors for so long.

The dogs had come for her. There had been dogs patrolling her house and she had not even known it, had not even sensed their presence. Time had slowed for her at that moment, and she had watched the silent deadly form of the Dobermanns, teeth bared, came quietly, their eyes fixed on her. She felt the warm river of urine ran down her leg, the scream frozen in her throat as the dogs leaped for her. She had fainted as the first set of fangs closed over her arm.

She had woken up here, locked in the bathroom of her own house, lying in clothes stained with her own urine. She had looked longingly at the bath, but dared not let one of them find her naked, and so she had hastily changed clothes using the ones in the dirty laundry basket and wiped herself clean, her eyes on the door. Her arm stung mercilessly, but had been bandaged and cleaned thoroughly; she knew now that any object that could be used as a weapon would already be dismantled or removed from the house. *He* had already done so in the beginning but now she dared not waste an opportunity again. She started working on the metal bars that held her shower curtain and towels, fashioning a weapon. *He* had come to the door earlier; she had sensed *him* and had immediately stilled her movements. *He* had whispered quietly, *his* voice a rasp against the door, a mar on the cleanliness of her universe. If she tried to escape again, *he* would not kill her, *he* would let the dogs do it.

Orabella shivered uncontrollably. She knew it was only a matter of time.

Hienry's instinct troubled him, and the more it did the more angry he became. He had too many problems on his hands without having to worry about who was killing girls at DI Storage. He had been so sure that it was that girl who had been at Dante's house that was causing all the trouble with the little surprises, but now…

He grimaced to himself. The man who was tailing her was not only providing information to Dante about her security but also supplying Hienry with details of who she talked to and her routine on a daily basis. It had all proved fruitless, either the girl was as innocent as Dante claimed her to be, or she was an excellent con artist, and then there was this other thing … He held two surveillance tapes in his hands, his anger blooming. He trusted the men he employed as security for Dante's house, and now he was the one who looked like a fool.

In light of recent events, he had started going over the security detail for Dante's house with a fine tooth comb. The cameras, both hidden and in view, the trip alarms in the dim recesses of the grounds, the security alarm itself and the human detail that was patrolling the house at least three times a day. The whole operation was running smoothly, nothing had been out of place. Until he had started watching the security tapes. As old fashioned as he was, he had used VHS surveillance tapes for Dante's house and grounds, they had agreed that they did not need anything more technologically advanced.

He remembered it from his school days; there were only a limited number of times that you could record over a VHS tape before the video became grainy, but more importantly, there was this fuzz of white noise that appeared between recordings. This is what Hienry had been looking at for the past twenty-four hours, and it troubled him even more than anything else that he had learnt today. Someone was getting to the tapes, someone was recording over security footage, someone was tampering with evidence, and that someone was in his camp. The traitor was his. He had sat in front of the television screen for over an hour, refusing to believe it, refusing to believe that such a sloppy and obvious job had been done by one of his men, knowing that the simplicity and stupidity of it all was what had made the traitor get away with it. The fact that one of his men was actually trying to blindside him was astounding. He had sat a few minutes longer, his anger turning to seething fury. He had an inkling as to who it was but needed to conduct his own internal investigation first. God help the man when he caught him, because there would be no mercy for him left on earth.

CHAPTER 24

Wednesday, 9 May

'Robbie, I need you to do me a favour,' Dante looked at her seriously from across the table.

Roberta's instincts twitched. So this is why Dante had invited her to lunch at his house. Sushi, followed by strawberries and bloody champagne. All because he wanted something from her. Couldn't he just want her for a change?

Roberta Erlichmann frowned, anger written all over her face. 'What is it?'

'Orabella Ricci,' Dante replied. He could see the changing mood in Roberta's face, so he stood and walked over to her side of the table, refilling her champagne glass for her. 'You know how close she's been to us, I think she's in trouble.'

'Why me?' Roberta snapped. 'I'm not your lackey Dante. Didn't you hire that disgusting Hienry to do things like this? Or even better send your precious new fuck instead.'

The last thing Roberta wanted to do was chase around Dante's women, especially fucking Orabella Ricci.

'There is no one else in my life right now, Robbie,' Dante grasped her hand and pulled her up, pushing the chair behind her out of her way, looking straight into her eyes. 'You asked me to get rid of her, and I did. There's only you again. It's always only been you.'

Dante cupped her face in his hands, staring down into her eyes, his gaze straying to her lips. 'Please Robbie,' he had whispered huskily, the intimacy of his hands on her face closing the distance between them. 'Please.'

He lowered his lips to hers and kissed her gently, his tongue firmly in his mouth, his hands leaving her face and caressing the top of her arms lightly. 'Come on Robbie.'

He breathed against her lips, his hands had already found her naked breasts under the black silk shirt she was wearing, squeezing her insistently.

Roberta sighed, surrendering herself to the pleasure of being with him again. He knew exactly which buttons to push to get her excited, and she wrapped her arms around his neck, arching her back in response to his lips kissing her neck. 'You're such a slut Dante.'

'You would know,' he laughed softly as he left her neck to unzip her skirt, pulling it down her legs.

'And what about our ex-graphic designer?' Roberta murmured as her top came off..

'I honestly have no idea why you keep talking Roberta Erlichmann.'

Lying on the balcony floor, they had climaxed quickly and noiselessly, his mouth gentle between her legs. A few minutes after they had collapsed, he had taken her again. They now lay naked, staring up at the blue sky, each not looking at the other, but Dante's fingers lightly ran the length of her body, caressing her skin.

'Will you do it for me?' he had asked her again, his voice quiet, his eyes still fixed on the sky.

She had nodded, her eyes closed, too tired and complacent to argue. He had then got up and standing above her naked and shining with sweat, held out his hand to her. She took his hand and sighed as he lifted her off the floor, bringing her close to him, his naked arms twining around her naked body. 'Thank you Robbie.'

Roberta spent the rest of the afternoon trying to track down Mrs Ricci. The calls she made had been in vain. She was not allowed to speak to Orabella, she could not even get past the gatekeeper of a secretary. She had been told that all her calls and messages would be answered in time, and a message would be passed on to Mrs Ricci. Roberta loathed the word failure and so here she was, only hours after climaxing with Dante on his balcony floor, parked in front of Orabella Ricci's house. Now, sitting in one of the company cars with the driver looking quizzically at her through the mirror, she was growing angrier by the minute. Dante used sex to get his way. The beautiful after-sex-glow was fading rapidly, it pissed her off.

She nodded at the driver who opened the door for her, and she stepped out, walking towards the gates. She pressed the doorbell.

She looked at Orabella Ricci's house, frowning at the red brick that constituted the structure. Unlike most of the houses in this suburb of Windhoek, Orabella's house was not on a slope, so as she stared at the gate her gaze travelled down the driveway and straight to the front door. The sun was starting to descend for the day, and she did not want to find herself here after dark.

Orabella jumped, startled as she heard the doorbell ring. She half crawled, half stumbled across the living room floor, ignoring the pain in her ankles and wrists. She cried out in frustration as she was jerked back, the thick shackle around her ankle holding taut as it tugged her back to her position in the middle of the floor.

Help, she thought desperately, tugging at the chains. She had thought she would be safe in the bathroom, away from *him*, but *he* had not left her alone. *His* new torture for her was sitting within reach of freedom, almost tasting it, and not being able to do anything about it. She swallowed hard and opening her mouth, screamed as loud as she could.

Roberta sighed, disgruntled at no one answering the doorbell, and was about to turn away from the gate when she heard a sound. Was that a scream? She turned back to the house. She had heard something. She was sure it came from Orabella's house.

'Can I help you Madam?'

Roberta jumped as the biggest man she had ever seen emerged and stood, blocking the house from view. Roberta knew instinctively that if she even tried to push the gate open he would not hesitate to break her fingers.

'Yes you can,' she snarled at him. 'Where's Orabella Ricci? I've been trying to get hold of that bitch all day and so have millions other people. Her evasiveness is costing a lot of us a ton of money!'

The man's small eyes stared at her viciously, quickly darting from the driver in the car back to her. 'I'm sorry madam, but she has given us strict orders. Please leave her a message.'

'Bullshit!' Roberta sneered at him. 'Open the gate, and let me talk to her myself!'

'I'm afraid I can't do that madam,' the man stared steadily at her. Roberta felt a chill run down her back, but stared back at him defiantly.

'Aren't you going to at least let me into the grounds or what?' Roberta stabbed her finger at him. 'You're going to let a lady stand outside like this speaking to you through the bars of a gate?'

'I cannot madam. Mrs Ricci insisted on it, you see it's the dogs.'

As if on some hidden cue, two large Dobermanns came padding silently down the driveway and up to the man. They stood next to him, the look in their eyes even more menacing than his.

Roberta stood frozen for a moment, staring at the dogs. *What the fuck is going on here?* She was frightened. And that scream? Had that been a scream? Had it been Orabella?

She exhaled, her breath choppily flowing down her nose. 'Tell her Dante Dumeno needs to speak to her. It's urgent,' she said to the man, the breeziness of her voice masking her fear, 'understand? He'll be waiting. And do not fuck that message up.'

She flounced back into the car without another word and settled inside breathing noisily, trying to still her trembling limbs.

'Are you okay Miss Erlichmann?' her driver looked concernedly at her through his mirror.

'Fine, fine,' she muttered, shivering as she looked around at the darkness beginning to kiss the sky around them. 'But something's going on over there, and I don't want to be the one to find out what.'

Orabella sobbed helplessly, her head ringing. Would she ever get out of here alive?

Before she could force another scream out of her lungs one of the guards had rushed up and hit her so hard she had fallen to the side, her head crashing to the floor.

'Dante,' her voice sounded broken over the phone.

'Robbie, what's wrong?' Dante, alarmed, pushed away the financial statements of DI Storage that were scattered across the kitchen table, and focused on Roberta's voice. It took a lot for Robbie to get scared, but when she did he became extremely nervous too.

'You were right,' Roberta whispered over the line. 'Something is wrong with Orabella. You can't get near her. Not even into the yard. Something really terrible is going on over there. I can't go back. I can't. I even heard screaming Dante, I think it was her! You have to do something. Call the police. I'm not going there again!'

'Robbie, calm down, listen I'm coming to get you okay? Stay at home!' Dante felt goosebumps begin their frenzied way up his arms. He was nervous, about Orabella, and Robbie …

'No, Dante,' she whispered. 'I'm with Naks. I need to get away from this craziness tonight. Please be careful.'

Dante stared at the phone lying beside him, chills running down his spine. He knew Naks would probably pump her full of her favourite drug to help her forget, but he didn't care. As long as she was safe. Could it be that Orabella was being held against her will in her own home?

He had wanted to avoid visiting Orabella so as to not add more fuel to the rumour fires, but now it seemed as though he had no choice. He had not yet told Hienry what plan he had put into action to find out what was happening to Orabella. Hienry had enough to worry about at the moment.

Dante raised his head to the noise of a scuffle at the kitchen door, and watched in surprise as Hienry came through the now repaired glass doors, dragging one of the security guards by the collar of his jacket. Another man followed him, a long black whip hanging loosely from his right hand.

'Hienry?' he questioned, rising from the bar stool at the kitchen counter. Dante stared at his friend; he had never seen him so grim or look so old.

Hienry did not say anything but pushed the man he had been dragging to the floor of the kitchen. The man was unremarkable; he looked like another one of Hienry's branded Smiths. He was of medium-build, medium-height, had closely cropped black kinky hair and the same blank look of total loyalty on his face that all Hienry's subordinates had. The only difference was that this one was breathing heavily, his coat was covered in dirt and large moons of sweat embraced his underarms and collar. He fell down hard, his eyes on the floor.

'Hienry?' Dante repeated his eyes narrowed at his friend. 'What's going on?'

Hienry wiped a hand across his forehead.

'He is the one,' he growled, his voice coming out in a hiss.

'Which one?' Dante asked quietly, staring at the man on the floor.

'The one who has been leaving us the little presents.'

Dante could not stop the look of shock that crossed his face. This man had worked at his house, in his security detail for the past six months. He had even been assigned to follow Farusja in the first instance when he had wanted to prove to her that … Dante suddenly lunged forward and grabbed the man by his collar, and pulling him up smashed him head first into a kitchen cabinet. The man crumpled up, still conscious, grunts issuing from his mouth as he touched his head where it had opened up, the blood flowing freely down his face onto his jacket.

'You tried to kill me, you tried to kill Farusja!' Dante growled, his anger un-sated. He laid his hands on the traitor again, this time smashing him through the glass cabinet that housed the wine glasses.

'Easy Dumeno,' Hienry said tiredly as he moved forward and grabbed Dante by his shoulders. 'You really want the police coming? Here? Now?'

Dante shook him off angrily, his eyes never leaving the traitors face.

'His name is Munda Chawame. He has been in my employ for half a year,' Hienry stared at the man lying on the ground, his arms covering his head in a defensive gesture.

Dante whirled around, his face twisted in his rage. 'I'd not have hired you if I did not think you knew what the fuck you were doing!' he snarled at Hienry.

'I do,' Hienry returned quietly. 'It is shameful. Yes, I admit it, but I have kept you safe for so long Dumeno, so you say something like that again and you can find another chief of security.'

Dante grunted at him, and still angry he turned away from his friend, staring at the man cowering on the floor in front of him.

'I have already found out what he knows,' Hienry walked over to the man, looking down at him, ignoring the pleas for mercy, and the cries he made as he cowered away from him, his eyes wide open in terror.

'And?'

'And he says Diablo told him to do it. Satan, the devil, that's who told him to do it,' Hienry said quietly.

'What?' Dante barked at him. 'So you hired not only a killer, but a lunatic as well?'

'All my men are killers Dumeno,' Hienry threw him a hard look. 'He said Diablo told him to do it. Do you know who Diablo is? Have I not taught you anything?'

Dante stilled, his anger dissipating. 'What are you talking about?'

Hienry sighed. 'Do you live in a bubble old friend? Diablo is the stage name; they say he is a man so evil he has no soul, no fire behind his eyes. He takes perverse pleasure in killing, and he thinks he's doing his victims a favour by releasing them from this cruel world.'

'Another killer just trying to make their darkness look like fools gold,' Dante scoffed. 'Stupid fanatics. When did you start believing such nonsense?'

'I wish it were all shadows my friend,' Hienry sighed again. 'But I know when I'm being lied to, and this man was telling the truth, or he believes it so much that to him it has become truth. He tells me Diablo hired him to plant those bombs around the house and in that girl's car. This man has been recording over the security tapes almost daily.' Hienry paused, and looked up at Dante, his eyes grave.

'Diablo is feared Dumeno, I have heard of this, this,' Hienry paused again, 'this legend. It has been whispered for years, but now more than ever. He is not an ordinary underworld criminal, people are afraid of this ghost; he has always been a ghost.'

Dante looked at his friend sharply, his eyes narrowed. 'This legend has been circulating for years? And it has come to roost in my backyard?' Dante laughed, the cynical sound shattering on the broken glass in the room. 'Hienry are you serious? And why now? What would that someone, if he really exists, want with me?'

Hienry shrugged, his eyes drawn back to the man on the floor. 'They say it all started with a personal tragedy, that Diablo decided to rid the world of its evil because of the evil that had been done to him.'

'So why was this guy never caught?'

'He was a ghost Dumeno, the killings stopped for over three years and the files grew old, the bodies they could not find decomposed and disappeared.'

'And now he's back?' Dante looked at Hienry sceptically. 'In my backyard? So he destroys me because I did evil to him? Makes no sense!'

Hienry sighed. 'That is all I know Dumeno. I still think it is dangerous for you here. I'll move you and Jerome as soon as I can arrange some safer accommodation.'

'I'm not running Hienry; especially from a ghost,' Dante scoffed. 'You know who I am. What good will come of me turning tail and running away at the slightest whisper?'

Hienry paused, his eyes fixed on his friend. 'They're also saying that this Diablo is behind the killings at DI Storage.'

Dante stared at him, his gaze moving between the man on the floor and his friends face. 'Who's they?'

'The whispers, the rumours, the wind. People are scared old friend, no one is talking,' Hienry nodded, his eyes still on the man crumpled up between them, ignoring the moans and cries still issuing from his mouth.

'And what do we do with him?' Dante gestured towards the man still cowering on the floor.

'I'm not sure Dumeno,' Hienry looked down at the man thoughtfully. 'He says we should kill him because he will be killed anyway. He was not supposed to leave alive.'

Dante raised his eyebrows, staring back at Hienry, indifferent.

CHAPTER 25

Thursday, 10 May

Miles was not sure that it meant anything, but they had come across a very small lead. At this point in time he had no choice but to follow every tidbit that came his way. He had heard some rumours about one of their informants, a Mandume Carstens, who had started to deal with one of the big dealers in town. Mandume was a small-time thief, a smuggler of all kinds of goods and information across the border. He was staring at him now, as he was herded across to his table by one of the undercover detectives on the force.

Mandume was one of the best and dirtiest informants in the business. Miles crinkled his nose as a mess of long raggedy dreadlocks, dirty jeans and a well worn black shirt fell into the seat in front of him. He could not place the smell but it was a cloying mixture of food, weed, beer and god only knew what else. The man was tall and wiry. His long frame, now slouched opposite Miles, was emphasised by the oversized clothes he was wearing. His small brown eyes squinted at Miles, and the thick dreadlocks hung around his black face were limp and greasy.

'I did nothing sah,' he mumbled. 'I just do as you asked me, but when you come to the business and mess me up like this, people start talking, want to know what is going on, see?'

'I can't let you walk Carstens, not this time,' Miles folded his hands across the top of the table, fixing his informant with a glaring stare. 'You know how it's like now with the girls' killings. People have seen you enter the station, you wanna leave here and live? Answer my questions.'

Mandume looked at him, surly, his mouth twisted in a grimace. 'I did what you asked sah, I did it. Why you treat me like this?'

'Who is strangling those girls Carstens?' Miles snarled at him, banging his hands on the table.

Mandume jumped back in his chair, startled awake.

'I don't know,' he mumbled. 'I don't know. I just do what you ask. You ask Mandume who's doing chickens? I tell you. Ask Mandume whose running cars. I tell you.

Now you ask Mandume who's killing girls?' Mandume made an incredulous sound in the back of his throat. 'I don't know sah, I don't know!'

Miles withdrew his hands from the table, not missing the quick nod he got from his deputy. Among his many talents, Phillip was a learned psychologist – he knew when people were lying.

'Then get out,' he spat at Mandume. 'Get lost. I don't want to see you anymore.'

Mandume stared at him, his face a mask of horror. 'You can't no do this to me, sah! If people they see me now coming out of this place, they will know what I do!' he cried, his hands reaching out to grab the table. 'I'll be killed sah. Please arrest me. Make me a criminal!'

Miles shrugged, standing up. 'I told you when you stop giving me what I want, I'll stop protecting you. Now get out.'

Mandume started blubbering, the snot coming out of his nose before the tears did. 'Please sah, I tell you what I know, please!'

His whole body shook in fear. 'I don't want no die,' he sniffed. 'Okay, I tell you, I tell you!'

Miles laid the tips of his hands on the end of the table, staring down at Mandume. 'Start talking.'

'I no know who comes to collect, man or woman, I no know. But I think its woman 'cause it's all about cleaning materials, body plastic suits to keep away spills and stuff. See?'

'When did this start?'

'A month ago, when the kills started, sah,' Mandume mumbled, wiping the snot from his nose with his hand and wiping it on his jeans.

'How do they contact you?'

'The post box in town, I get a paper with orders. I make order and I leave goods at the post office.'

Miles growled at him, his chest heaving in anger. 'And you never asked why all the secrecy? You never asked yourself why someone would need all these cleaning materials and supplies?'

'People have cleaning business,' Mandume shrugged. 'I no ask questions when money is delivered!'

'Who owns the post office box?'

'Monthly rental from post office,' Mandume mumbled, his eyes on the floor.

'How did the buyer get hold of you?'

'Stories are passed around,' he mumbled. 'I no know, I no remember.'

Miles stood up slowly. 'How many plastic body suits and cleaning material sets did you supply?'

Mandume cringed in his chair, becoming small. 'I no know sah. I no know it was about the girls!' he cried. 'I no know!'

'How many Carstens?'

'Fifty,' Mandume whispered. 'I sold them fifty sah.'

Miles stared at Mandume, murder in his eyes. He suddenly and violently turned around and threw the chair he had been sitting on across the room, watching it bounce off the wall in defeat.

'Lock him in the cells overnight!' he bellowed at the plainclothes detective who had brought Mandume in. 'Give him a few bruises to make the point!'

'Thank you sah,' Mandume cried. 'Thank you so much sah!'

Both Miles and Phillip watched quietly as Mandume was dragged out of the room, Miles kicked at the table leg again for good measure.

'There's no definite connection boss,' Philip said quietly.

'It started the same time as the murders.'

'So?' Phillip shrugged, 'that means nothing. All of it means nothing, as he said. It could just be a cleaning company.'

'And all the secrecy?'

'Maybe someone is embarrassed to be starting a cleaning company?' Phillip mused. 'The connection is tenuous and coincidental at best.'

Miles shook his head disquieted. 'If it isn't, this means there are 48 women left to be killed.'

'Has Dante Dumeno slept with that many?' Phillip shook his head. 'You really think it will get to 48 more bodies?'

Miles snorted. 'Just ask Lydia downstairs, even she has photos of her and Dumeno enjoying a night out! 48 is probably a small number to Dumeno!' he shouted angrily. 'Two dead girls Philip. Two girls, and we have nothing!'

'When do you think Mandume will leak the information?'

'A week, maybe two, but by then he will be long gone,' Miles sighed angrily. 'And then the newspapers will start again, causing havoc!'

Philip sighed, turning fully to face his superior. 'On a lighter note, I tried to see Roberta Erlichmann as you instructed.'

Phillip related the information to Miles. After he had declared who he was and what he wanted to the secretary, he had to wait for over an hour for Roberta Erlichmann. She had approached him with suspicion, her face a closed invitation to converse as he had introduced himself and told her who he was. She had not divulged any information but had sharply told him that he was looking in the wrong place, and if anything Orabella Ricci should be the one to have her head on the butchers block, not her and definitely not Dante. With this news and the view of Ms Erlichmann's back, Philip had headed over to Hunters headquarters where he had gleaned that Orabella had not come to work for the past month as she had recently found herself engaged and wedded, and had informed everyone that she was taking an extended honeymoon. He had inquired as to whether he could speak to Orabella or her husband, and had been brusquely told that they only communicated using the telephone or email, and that Orabella had not even informed her staff as to when they could expect her back.

With no one to reprimand her, the chubby secretary at Hunter had been only too happy to confide in a tall, easy going handsome stranger. She had drawn Philip closer to her with a discreet wave of her hand and whispered conspiratorially that it was rumoured that Mrs Ricci was preparing something explosive against Dante Dumeno, and that was why she had taken the time off. Apparently her new husband did not like the fact that Dante and Orabella had been so close, and the moment she married all the meetings and business lunches with Dante had stopped.

Miles stared at his deputy, grudging admiration growing in him. Philip did not need to be heavy handed or throw his weight around like he had to; he had the greatest weapon of all by his side, charm. He had charmed the secretary and took her to lunch. During which he had acquired Orabella's home address, and the personal email address that she used to communicate with the staff. She was apparently still on her honeymoon, and had now been gone for the past three months. Philip had then decided to make this next stop Orabella's house.

He had barely pulled up to the gate when a burly security guard had loomed over him and informed him that Mrs Ricci was not at home. Try as he might his charm was lost on a member of the same sex and his attempts to be heavy handed with the security guard had wasted his time.

Miles grimaced, painfully aware of the impending talk of failure for their task team that was going around the police department. Whatever it was that had happened between Dante Dumeno and Orabella Ricci had been enough to put a large dent in their personal and business relationship; maybe Mrs Ricci knew Dante was connected to the killings and had withdrawn herself?

Miles swore in frustration, knowing that he was grasping at air.

'We need proof,' he grimaced. 'We need solid proof – of anything! How is getting that search warrant coming along?'

Philip shrugged his shoulders. 'You're not going to get a warrant to search Dumeno's private property or his business premises, boss. I was told I might lose my job if I pushed for it again.'

Miles grunted. He now actually wished that more girls would die so that the politics and corruption in the police force could finally be brought to justice.

'I got a reply sir; I can trace the IP address now.'

Miles eyes snapped back to his deputy, and without a moment's hesitation, almost vaulted over the desk separating them, coming to a stop behind Philip who was perched in front of a computer screen. They had sent an email to Orabella Ricci using the email address Philip had extracted from the chubby secretary. Their message had been brief, and Miles had decided that approaching Orabella with the truth would be a better way to get any results for the investigation. In an attempt to cover up the truth, people usually made all sorts of mistakes, releasing more information than they should.

Miles now knew that he had underestimated Orabella Ricci. The reply was brief; the incoming message had only one sender, Orabella Ricci. It read. 'Dante Dumeno has not honoured his integrity in conducting business with Hunter or the rest of the business community, the dossier I'm compiling will reveal all the evidence you will need to keep Dante Dumeno locked away for a very long time.'

Miles eyes narrowed, the bile beginning to rise in the back of his throat. Despite the ineptitude of his police force, the one thing that terrified him was civilians taking the law into their own hands; he exhaled noisily. The situation was going to get very ugly, very soon.

Dante's hand hovered above the metal gate. He had spent almost the entire day trying to get hold of Orabella. He had wandered around Hunters offices, stalked Orabella's personal assistant and made a general nuisance of himself until security had been called and, apologising to him profusely, they had almost ashamedly escorted him off the property.

After exhausting all other the possibilities, he decided to drive by her house. He did not believe that she was on an extended honeymoon. Orabella loved Hunter, she had built it lovingly with her own two hands, and she had loved the intricacies and problems that had to be dealt with on a daily basis; it was her life. She would not have left staff to run her company for three whole months.

As Dante pulled up on the curb outside her house he knew immediately that something was amiss. The house was all wrong; something was terribly wrong. Orabella would never have allowed the grass that crept up and through her cobblestoned drive, the autumn leaves falling from the trees would have been disposed of a long time ago. Even on the rare times that she went on holiday Orabella managed to keep a tight rein on her property. She loved to be in control, she relished it, and something like wild growing grass was not going to stop her from bending it to her will, with or without her presence.

Dante frowned, ignoring the approaching build of a man. Swiftly he unlatched the gate and stepped onto the cobbled path, striding quickly to the front door.

'Wait!' the man barked at him, and without preamble put a halt to his progress, his entire hand closing over the top of Dante's shoulder.

'Let me go,' Dante raised his eyes to the biggest man he had ever seen. 'Do you know who I am?'

The man looked immovable, dressed in black, his tiny dark eyes stared down at Dante with nothing, no curiosity, no menace, nothing. 'Mrs Ricci is not in, sir.'

Rendered immobile, Dante could only stare up at the hulk in front of him. The black shirt and trousers were nondescript. 'Do you know who I am? Let me go or I'll have the police here.'

The man turned them both around so that they were facing the gate, his tiny eyes still looking at expressionlessly at Dante. 'She does not want anyone on her property sir, and she is on her honeymoon.'

Dante snorted; the sound was harsh. 'She is no more on her honeymoon than I'm on mine. Take your hands off me.'

'I cannot let you by, sir.'

'I'm calling the police.'

'Will this do?' the man reached into his back pocket and pulled out a slim black phone. He held his palm out to Dante, handing the phone to him.

Dante took the phone from the man's palm, dialling the emergency number without taking his eyes off him.

'State your emergency,' a woman's bored voice answered. 'Tony can't you bulldogs take care of Mrs Ricci's property by yourselves? I'm supposed to go on my tea break in ten minutes.'

'Is that Dolores?' the man, his hand still on Dante's shoulder, held his palm out, waiting for Dante to hand back the telephone. 'Sorry Dolores, I dialled your number by mistake, no there is no problem here, there's no need to send an officer. Yes we're handling everything just fine. Yes please send the plainclothes later.' He cancelled the call and placed the phone back into his pocket. 'You can communicate with her via email if you like sir. They will not give you the address immediately at the office, but I'm sure they will make an exception for you.'

'I was thrown out of their offices.'

'Maybe they did not know who you were, sir?'

Dante squinted up at the man, expecting to see some expression; of sarcasm or victory, but there was nothing in the man's eyes, not even the snide look that would accompany such a comment. He shook his shoulder out of the man's grasp.

'I'm sorry sir, but I cannot allow anyone on Mrs Ricci's property without her express permission. Maybe you can speak to her and ask her? You would need to bring the email proof.'

Dante grunted, dusting off his clothes self-consciously. He did not know what game Orabella was playing but it seemed as if she did not want him around either. He had not seen her for so long; maybe the Orabella he knew no longer existed. He grimaced. He had two businesses to run and was having girls from his company murdered, the last thing he should be doing was chasing a woman who did not want to see or be with him.

He nodded and heading for his Bentley. This would be the last time he tried to track down Orabella Ricci.

CHAPTER 26

Friday, 11 May

arusja stared blearily out of the kitchen window, at the grey wall of brick outlining Rabecca's yard, a mug of tea swirling in her hand. It had been two days since Dante had called her, humiliating and embarrassing her, but even more than that, hurting her. The pain ate at her every day. She had not made any definite plans yet, and had been content to just sit around and mope for a while, but she couldn't sit around forever. Her first instinct had been to tuck in her tail and run back home; both Dante and Roberta has said it so harshly, and she was afraid that if she tried to get another job in Windhoek, they would make her life a living hell.

She had not wanted any drama, but it had come in great waves with Dante and his organisations. She sighed, placing her hand on her mouth as she felt the tea threatening to come up. She missed him and hated him, all at the same time. She turned away from the sink, sighing loudly to herself, mentally getting ready for another long day. She almost dropped the mug as the doorbell rang. Frowning, she went to the door. It was seven thirty in the morning; no one came to the house this early. She gazed through the peephole, frowning and unlatching the locks, she opened the door. Hienry stood staring at her, shifting his bulk from one foot to the other, a man not used to the rigours of exercise.

Farusja opened her mouth to berate him and stopped when she saw the look on his face.

'What is it Hienry?' she asked alarmed, stepping up to him and putting her hand up to touch him, her hand stopping within centimetres of his face.

He sighed, and took her hand, pulling her out of the house. 'It is good you didn't leave. Come with me.'

'Hienry?' Farusja, now frightened, pulled on his hand, arresting their movements.

Hienry sighed. 'You must come with me, Farusja.'

Farusja snatched her hand out of his, stepping back into the house, shaking her head from side to side, shouting. 'No, no, no!'

She had not seen the man slip behind her until she bumped into him and his hands closed over her shoulders gently but firmly, stopping her from moving. She turned, looking at him in consternation, tears starting to run down her face. 'No, no, no, go away!'

It was Joseph, the man in Dante's security detail that had given her the pen and paper in Dante's house the day the beetle had been blown up.

'You must come,' Hienry emphasised quietly.

Farusja trembled despite herself, allowing him to move her towards the car, vaguely registering the house being locked behind her.

'He is not critical,' Hienry said quietly as he placed his arms around her and led her into the car. 'He is going to be just fine.'

Farusja stared down at Dante's face, her heart in her throat. He looked pale, if it was possible for a black man to look pale. She swallowed hard, gazing at his inert form, willing his eyes to open. Hienry had driven to the hospital in Dante's Bentley, he told her that Dante had been attacked and shortly thereafter that had been arrested. Her mind whirling, she had ridden the elevator up to his floor at the medi-clinic, not seeing anything around her.

Hienry had spoken to her quietly in the elevator, his voice seeming to meld into the background voices and questions in her head. 'He was shot this morning at the house. The shooter was one of my men, the same man who set the bombs in your friend's car.'

Farusja had exhaled noisily, her heart hammering against her ribs.

'The same man who has been setting bombs around Dante's house, the same man who broke the glass door of the kitchen when you were last there,' Hienry had paused, sighing in the silence. 'We had him locked up in the garage. We had him handcuffed.'

Hienry exhaled tiredly, watching the elevator doors open slowly. 'There was an axe in the garage, he used it to escape.'

Farusja had shivered as he had placed his hand on her back and propelled her forward.

'The axe was not strong enough to smash the cuffs so he dislocated his wrist. Then he cut off his left foot to remove the cuffs on his ankles. He opened the door from inside and killed my man on guard with one stroke of the axe, took his gun and came in the house. We were in the process of moving. Dante was the only other person there.'

'He was arrested this morning,' Hienry had continued quietly as he led her down the corridor to Dante's room. 'They found him here at the hospital and stationed a guard at the door. No one is being allowed into his room except for family, and I consider you family to him,' Hienry paused again. 'Jerome should be here soon. This morning, if you have not heard the news yet, DI Storage has been implicated in gun smuggling. Guns were found on the property.'

Farusja had watched and listened numbly as the guard had frisked her for weapons, her throat and mouth dry.

'You can comfort him, yes?' Hienry asked quietly, coming up to her on the side of the bed.

'Is he going to be alright?'

Hienry nodded. 'The bullet barely grazed his upper thigh, but he was yelling and cursing so loudly that I asked the nurse to knock him out. When he wakes up handcuffed he will be angrier than usual.'

Farusja looked down at Dante's prone form, refusing to look at the handcuffs on each hand; both exclusively connected to the steels bars on either side.

She watched his chest rise and fall quietly with his breathing. 'What happened to the man who did this?'

'We killed him,' Hienry answered quietly.

Farusja sat frozen, listening to the news on the radio, her mind numb. She had come down to the cafeteria after spending a few minutes in Dante's room, hoping to find out more about what was happening at DI Storage.

She had bought sludgy cafeteria coffee and now stared numbly at the cup in front of her, still shocked by the news. Guns had been found on DI Storage grounds, and the CEO and board had been arrested and confined to house arrest. The story was sensational; the murders of the girls had been linked to the gun smuggling, saying that they were killed to silence them.

Farusja gulped down the bitter coffee, the heat stinging her throat. Even though Hienry had told her what scrutiny both companies would be facing, there was a part of her that did not want to believe him, that had ignored the silver handcuffs that encircled Dante's wrists. Farusja gulped down another sip of the coffee, hoping the sludge would clear the cobwebs cluttering her mind and numb her reactions. What was going on? She thought, when had all this happened? Had it not just been a week? She shivered as fear started to crawl its way up her spine. She knew Dante was innocent; she had no doubts about that, so who hated him so much to destroy everything he had worked for? Dante was sure to have a list of enemies; she had only just the other day asked him to add her name to the list...

She groaned as she got up, hurrying away from the offending radio, the fear refusing to let her go.

Hienry stood in front of the client storage block at DI, surveying the damage. He ignored the yellow tape and looked with interest at the guns being piled up into the van in front of him. Uniformed police officers swarmed around but he ignored the dirty looks from them. He had prided himself on his covert skills, revelled in his merits, and these had meant nothing for the past few weeks when he had failed his friend three times, yes, three times.

Hienry sighed and turned away from the van. He could see the black canvas bags being brought up from the entrance of one of the storage boxes.

Hienry raked his fingers through what was left of his hair. It had all happened under his nose. *How could he not have known?*

This was his domain, his territory. He had men all over DI Storage. He sighed, staring at the policemen moving past him. With all his training, with all his years of experience, it had come down to this moment, and he had failed.

His face was grim as he walked across the paved ground, heading straight for the man who was in charge. He was a tall, dark man, his face shiny in the mid-morning sun, half-moons of sweat already stood out underneath his armpits, staining his smart police uniform. He stood before the entrance to the biggest storage space that DI Storage offered, shouting orders to the two uniformed officers that were inside.

Hienry stopped in front of him. 'I'm going in.'

Dark eyes met his, the resentment fully etched on the man's face. 'That's why we can never do our job,' he spat in his direction, an ugly smile on his face. 'People like you, who don't know how to do yours, messing up our work, whatever it is that you do.'

Ignoring him, Hienry carefully stepped into the most expensive storage space to rent out at DI. It was an area of 150 square feet. The goods that had been placed in the storage space had been moved outside, the padlock broken. There was a large hole in the middle of the floor. From where he was standing it looked as though some form of chemical had eaten away as much as it could of the concrete foundation. Past the foundation, a deeper hole had been dug into the earth, the length and width almost covering the sides of the storage area. The two policemen working in the hole had to literally jump down into the space.

'It took hard work.'

A voice spoke close to his ear. He turned; a second man was looking at him contemplatively. He was also tall, dark, but had a swarthy and sharp complexion. Hienry raked his brain for all the information Dante had given him about the detective. He had no doubts that Miles Mkazi was sharp, especially so because of the laid-back appearance that the man portrayed.

Miles looked at Hienry and sent him a sympathetic smile, answering his questioning glance. 'It took a lot of work to do what has been done here. You would have to chip away at the concrete bit by bit in order to get through the foundation.' He popped a matchstick in his mouth, his eyes watching the men digging into the dirt to reveal more black canvas bags, his jaw moving slowly. 'Or in this case, melt it away with acid; and with the level of security here every day?'

'Who's renting this space?' Hienry questioned quietly.

'No one. We have Orabella Ricci to thank for getting to the bottom of this whole mess. It will just be a matter of time before Dumeno confesses guilty to all charges against him. I cannot wait to put that bastard away,' he paused, casting a sidelong glance at Hienry. 'You're the one they said would come? A foreigner?'

Hienry nodded his eyes at the hole in the floor.

'My name is Miles, Detective Miles Mkazi,' he waited, and then sighed as Hienry volunteered no information. 'I see. I shall have to be dealing with a ghost. Please don't interfere,' Miles paused again, his jaw moving slowly around the matchstick, 'too much.'

'I'm going in there.'

'By all means Mr Ghost,' Miles spat out the matchstick on the paved floor, 'just do not hide anything from me. It would not be professional.'

CHAPTER 27

The noise around her was unbelievable. If she had known what would happen at DI Storage today she would not have bothered to get out of bed.

Hienry had phoned and quietly informed her that DI was in trouble, Dante had been shot, but was okay and that by all means she should keep away from him until he could find out what was going on.

The sirens came first, shrill and piercing the early morning air; but she had paid them no attention. She knew that HD would be under the same scrutiny as DI Storage, simply because of Dante's affiliation with the organisation. She had been on her way out, wanting to get to the hospital, and had almost got to the boardroom when the phone calls to her mobile started. August's voice was shrill, the panic hurrying down the phone to her. 'The police are here, Miss Erlichmann, and they are preventing anyone from entering or leaving the building.'

Roberta turned sharply, her heels screeching across the tiled floor. She ran back to her office, her heels tapping the floor in a staccato burst of sound, flying past bewildered colleagues. They had come so quickly and she was not prepared. She knew Orabella Ricci was somehow behind this, that bitch! Her phone rang again, Roberta answered it without a word. 'They are asking for you Miss Erlichmann. They say they have a search warrant. They have surrounded the office.'

'August, tell everyone to remain calm, and to gather in the foyer. The police might have the right to search our premises, but they cannot hold us here.'

'They will not wait for you ma'am,' August's voice was trembling. 'They have already started …'

Roberta, moving to stand at the office door and raising her voice as loud as she could, called the nervous staff on the second floor to gather around her.

'As you can all see we have a situation, the police are here. Take your stuff, go downstairs; leave when they finally open the doors. It is a routine search, don't worry.'

With everything that had happened at DI Storage during the past week no one argued, but just simply scurried away from her without another word, pulling open their drawers and snatching out a paraphernalia of handbags, books and gym bags.

Roberta ignored them, and turning on her heel headed to her office, closing the door behind her. She grabbed the overnight bag she kept under her desk, throwing items randomly into it, wondering what files she could take before everything was messed up. She froze as the door to her office flew open. John Oduraa, a tall imposing man, did not bother to greet her but strode in, the air following and surrounding him an angry red. His hair was streaked white with age, and his weather-beaten face had taken on a leathery look. This man from Ghana was formidable, as both she and Dante had found out. Roberta had tensed up, but her hands dropped in relief that it had not been the police. She wondered how Oduraa had gotten past the commotion downstairs, had he been in the building all the time? She knew what this man was capable of and they had crossed swords on more than one occasion, but somehow he and Dante had got on very well; and that was why he had chosen to be a full board member of DI Storage and a silent one at HD Advertising.

John did not waste time on preliminaries, and stared hard at her, his eyes glancing briefly at the overnight bag on her desk.

'As I'm sure you already know DI Storage has been overrun with the police, and so has HD from what I'm seeing.'

Roberta nodded, her eyes never leaving his face.

He tossed a small folder onto the desk between them. 'This is the reason why. The police are outside so take it quickly!'

Roberta stared fearfully at the clear plastic folder in front of her then almost tentatively snatched it off the table, her eyes devouring it greedily. It was Orabella Ricci; she knew no one else who would have even stooped to such depths. Roberta's fingers went numb as the words leaped off the paper, sweat beading her forehead as chills ran down her spine.

Orabella Ricci had prepared a statement in which she accused Dante Dumeno of blackmailing her and Hunter in order to assist him with moving guns across the border. Hunter, in desperate need of financing had agreed, and the payments had begun.

It had all been meticulously recorded, every amount Dante had ever given Orabella; the personal loans, the dinner dates, it had all been detailed to look like payments to keep Orabella quiet and to keep the guns flowing into the country.

Roberta exhaled sharply as the folder dropped from her fingers. She knew the amounts without even looking at the folder, and she knew that Orabella had receipts. Roberta knew, because she had personally watched over the money Dante had given to Orabella. He told her every time he did it, and she had argued with him every time.

'It's not true,' she whispered to John. 'None of it is true.'

'Regardless of whether it is true or not Roberta,' John said harshly. 'Dumeno's impishness has placed us in a very awkward position; I have the other board members of DI sending me their resignation letters from their mobile phones. Mobile phones!'

'What are they saying?'

'I can only account for three,' John said shortly. He paused, expelling a deep breath. 'How is he?'

'He's in hospital, he was shot. It's a flesh wound,' Roberta's shoulders collapsed again, she focussed on breathing deep and even, trying to calm herself.

'You had better try and get all you can out now,' he turned his back to her, speaking over his shoulder as he strode towards the door. 'They'll be coming to take as much as they can.'

'John, what are you going to do?'

'Try to keep both companies afloat. I do care for this company too you know, Roberta.'

She stared at his receding back as the door shut behind him. Where would she go? Who could she turn to? Her upper lip curled in decision as her mind was made up.

Roberta stared at the gate in front of her. She had managed to get away from HD eventually. She had found out from Hienry that most of the police officers were digging up DI Storage. With Dante implicated wholeheartedly by Orabella, all the police were looking for was another stash of guns hidden by Dante, or any information that could aid them in their investigation. After turning HD Advertising into carnage, the police had finally left the building, and Roberta had gratefully closed the door behind them.

And here she was, once again outside Orabella Ricci's house, and once again she felt uneasy. This time she had driven alone, and her car idled in front of the house as she leaned against it, restless and afraid. Both gates to the house were ajar.

Where were the dogs? She thought wildly as she took a step forwards. The house was silent and the windows closed.

Roberta frowned, clenching her teeth as she suddenly catapulted herself forward through the small gate, up the stone steps and looked around warily, ready to run at the slightest hint of any four legged creature.

Roberta sniffed against her fear as she picked her way to the door, goosebumps rising in a dance on her arms. She continually turned around to check that the gate was still unlocked and that the Dobermanns were nowhere in sight. Where was her pepper spray when she needed it? She skirted around the grass that had grown wildly between the cracks, and the leaves and seed pods that had gathered in piles at the foot of the trees where they had fallen; the brown patches resplendent on the grass lawn showed signs of neglect and absence.

Roberta shivered as she reached the door, wishing she had brought her bodyguard with her, her whole body crying out to leave the house with its terrifying garden and run back to the relative safety of her car. Roberta reached for the doorbell, her hand suspended and trembling in mid-air as she surveyed the scene in front of her. The iron grill door was slightly open, and she could see that the heavy wooden door was swung inward. Roberta knew she was a tough woman, she prided herself on how easily she could get out of sticky situations, but this was different; something here was terribly, terribly wrong.

'Orabella?' Roberta cleared her throat as her voice came out squeaky and warbled, fear choking every syllable. Breathing deeply and muttering what a fool she was, she swung the grill door open slowly and took a step over the threshold, pushing the wooden door forward into the house.

'Orabella?' Roberta squeaked as she stepped into the house and gagged; her throat and nose closing involuntarily as a smell assailed her nostrils. It was a sweet, murky, cloying smell that clung to her nose and throat every time she inhaled. Roberta coughed, her eyes streaming with tears as she stumbled outside. She fell to her knees on the browning grass, gulping huge amounts of air, trying to release herself from the smell that now clung to her.

Roberta could not stop the tears that dripped onto the grass as dry heaves racked her body, letting loose the dry vomit of air; the smell that had most terrified her was the smell of urine, the smell that was a prelude to a majority of terrible things that could befall human beings who had been rendered incapable of taking care of themselves. As the last dry heave racked her body, she stood up. She was scared. Something bad had happened here. She could feel it. She could smell it.

Roberta swallowed tightly, her body rigid, looking around at the deserted house. She had to go inside, and then she had to tell Hienry and Dante what she had found. That fat bastard Hienry, goodness she hated him, he would know what to do; and so would Dante. Roberta pressed her hand against her mouth, stopping the flow of tears that threatened to overwhelm her, and slowly dusting herself off, she walked towards the house again.

A few minutes later she ran out, screaming uncontrollably, almost tripping over her feet in her haste to get away from the cursed building. She ran to her car, fear propelling her forward, and pressing her foot down on the accelerator drove away as fast as she could. She did not see the man with the dark eyes standing quietly behind the driveway wall, watching her. She did not see both gates close behind her, and she did not see the Dobermann that silently padded up and down the pavement, inhaling and remembering her scent.

Dante strained angrily against the handcuffs, sweat pouring down his forehead. Every muscle in his body hurt, and pain that felt like fire had wrapped itself around his thigh; he was angry. He blearily woke out of the medicine induced stupor he had been forced into and watched his nurse move around the room slowly under hooded eyes.

'Where am I?' he croaked at her, it felt as though he had swallowed a bucketful of sand. She looked up at him. She was a pretty little thing, all big brown eyes and a mouth which he knew would wrap around him snugly. She continued looking at him, and he watched as pity moulded her face into a sympathetic mask that turned him cold.

'Mr Dumeno,' she whispered, 'you are under arrest. I'm not allowed to speak to you,. There are policemen outside. Your company – did you really do what they say you did?'

They were interrupted by a knock on the door.

'Ah Mr Dumeno, you're awake I see. Now I can charge you formally,' Detective Miles Mkazi strode cheerfully into the room, stopping one pace away from Dante's bed and looking down at him in barely concealed victory. 'Remember I said I was going to get you for something Dumeno. And I have to say, as horrible as it may sound, this is better than two murdered girls.'

Dante struggled upright, anger written all over his face, his rage building as the handcuffs forced him to stay in a semi-sitting position. 'And what exactly are you charging me with?'

'Smuggling weapons into the country, for starters,' Miles told him. 'We've found all the evidence. Did you really think you could get away with this? And hopefully by the time we get to court, we'll be able to charge you with a whole lot more.'

'What? What guns? Get out Mkazi, I want my lawyer,' he rasped, his voice laced with rage.

'That is one thing you will definitely need Dumeno, but there is so much damning evidence against you, that you may have difficulty in finding a willing lawyer. And after the events of this morning, you're probably going to have to liquidate all your assets to pay for one,' Miles smiled sadistically at him, the corners of his eyes crinkling with the effort.

Dante inhaled sharply. 'I'm innocent. I have been set up. I make millions every year, why would I jeopardise that detective?' Dante sneered. 'Do you know who I am?'

'I know who you were Dumeno,' Miles corrected. 'Who you were, how you have been protected by the police all these years. When I'm done with you everyone will know who you really are, even my prostitute superiors are turning their faces away from you. Good day, Dumeno. If it were up to me you would be receiving medical treatment in our cells right now, but it seems my superiors are still struggling to let your money go.'

'I didn't do what you think I did Mkazi.'

'You will have the rest of your life to prove that you're innocent Dumeno,' Miles smiled, the sneer a blight on his otherwise bright face. 'Now that we can finally do our jobs, When I'm done with you I'll make sure you have nothing left.'

Dante grunted as Miles sent him one last mocking smile and strode out of the room, the air around him resolute and confident.

'Smug bastard,' he muttered, pulling at the handcuffs. He needed to get out of here and salvage what he could before that bloody detective really made sure he had nothing left.

Farusja stared at the door in front of her, apprehensive. After shaking off the initial disquiet and shock, she had crept back up to Dante's hospital room, her steps getting heavier and heavier as she got closer to the door. A call from Sidney making her drag her feet.

Apparently after the guns had been found at DI Storage, HD Advertising was in an uproar; the police had swarmed to the company. Sidney had told her that Roberta seemed to be in charge of things. Sidney had paused, her breathing heavy after reciting the story. She had then asked Farusja where she was. Farusja had tiredly told her, her voice low and uneasy.

Farusja smiled ruefully as she subjected herself to yet another body search outside the door, ignoring the sneering tone on the police woman's face. She did not want to know how Hienry had got her permission to be in here, she was not even family. She stopped short inside the room, startled to see him conscious and propped upright in the bed. He had been stripped down to an indecent hospital gown, the bandage wrapped around his thigh the only thing indicating that he was not in good shape.

'Dante?' she gasped, the look on his face almost stopping her in her tracks. She moved to sit on the bed, facing him, laying her hand tentatively on his warm skin. His face was flushed and angry, and the liquid darkness of his eyes smouldered on every move she made.

'What in God's name are you doing here Mumba?' Dante asked her angrily, his dark eyes boring into hers. 'Why are you still in Namibia? Did I not tell you to leave? Well if it wasn't clear, I'm telling you now, leave!'

'I'm not your employee anymore. You cannot tell me what to do, and besides Hienry asked me to come,' Farusja clenched her teeth, her voice low and strained. She glanced down at his wrists encircled by handcuffs; she could see where his skin had broken as he fought against them.

Dante shook his wrist at her in a feeble attempt to shake her hand off, his eyes staring at the wall above her head.

'And again I'll ask why you're here Mumba,' he said shortly. 'Are you here to gloat? Or is it just the right thing to do? I told you I don't want you around me anymore!'

Farusja bit her lip, trying to stem the angry retort that threatened to spill from her mouth. 'I wanted to come. As incredibly impossible as it seems right now, even I don't know why, but I do care about you!'

'Well I don't care about you, I had my fun, so deal with it,' Dante was harsh, his eyes meeting hers. 'Now get your ass out of here, Mumba.'

Farusja sat, staring at him. Everything she had felt since the few wonderful days they had spent together and then that terrible phone call from him that day came rushing back. 'You're treating me like this? After everything that's happened between us?'

Dante laughed loudly, shaking his head at her in sympathy. 'You make it sound like it's so complicated. It's very simple. I got what I wanted, you got a few memories and a nice holiday at a lodge to show off to your other girlfriends that you slept with me, we all win.'

Farusja stared at him, the hurt rising in her chest in hatred. 'You're a mean son of a bitch. They should have locked you up in the cells.'

'I'm the one shot up in hospital,' Dante smirked at her. 'Some sympathy would be nice.'

'You don't deserve my sympathy,' Farusja hissed at him. 'You used me.'

'Used? You?' Dante raised his eyebrows, laughing out loud again. 'Since when were we a relationship Farusja? I thought we were just having fun?'

Farusja flushed, anger moulding her face. 'I hope gangrene infects that wound and you die.'

'Good intentions going astray?' Dante sneered. 'Fun, that's all it was. Did you forget? Was I so good that you forgot? I should have known you were this type of girl.'

Farusja pulled herself off the bed. 'You're an ugly bastard Dumeno, and as unpleasant as ever.'

Dante turned his face away, his chest heaving with the effort, his face shiny with sweat. 'As much as you hate me, and as big as a man I am, this wound is starting to ache and those bastards handcuffed me tightly. Could you give me some water?' he paused, taking another look at her face. 'And please, not over my head.'

Farusja snorted. 'Are you serious? You just insulted me and now you want water?'

'I'm at your mercy Farusja Mumba, as much as I hate to say it.'

Farusja looked at him, her face clearing itself of all anger, realisation dawning on her. 'You need me right now, and you know what, I'm going to help you simply because I want this moment and everything you said to me to haunt you for the rest of your life.'

She rounded his bed and grasping the water jug on the mobile counter on the side of his bed poured some water into a glass. She ignored him watching her as she put a hand behind his head and tilted the cup towards his mouth, only letting go of the cup when he had finished drinking.

'More?' she asked, laying his head gently back onto the pillows.

'Will you really haunt me for the rest of my life?' he asked quietly.

Farusja stared at him, not replying. She replaced the cup on the counter, disappearing into the little bathroom cubicle, emerging a moment later with a damp face cloth.

'You sweat like a pig.' She raised her hand to his face tentatively, ignoring his eyes as she gently wiped his face with the wet cloth, moving down to sponge his neck, pressing the cloth gently against his upper torso.

'Well, I'll be fine to continue were we left off, I might need you after all. No talking, no cuddling, just sex, you might be the only woman that comes close to me in this state. Well there's also that cute nurse,' he said thoughtfully as she lifted the cloth from his skin, satisfied with her work.

'You can no longer hurt me Dante,' she said softly. 'I'm done listening to your rubbish, this will be the last time you see me.'

'So you did come to gloat?'

'Wouldn't you after what you've just been saying to me?' Farusja said shortly, turning on her heel to return the face cloth to the bathroom.

Dante watched her go, his chest constricting. He thought she would have left days ago. Could she not see he was doing this for her own good? Even though he was doing his utmost to make her miserable enough to forget about him, he wanted her here, by his side, with him. He let out a long sigh, breathing out loudly as she came back into the room.

'Mumba.'

He was cut short by the ringing of her phone.

She raised questioning eyes up at him as she lifted the phone to her ear. He watched the expression on her face change as she listened to the person on the other end.

'You're outside?' she finally said, nodding her head. 'No, I'll come down and we can talk. Yes of course.' She nodded a couple of times, finally moving the phone away from her ear with a shrug.

'Friend of yours?' Dante raised his eyebrows at her nonchalantly, the look in his eyes betraying him.

She nodded vaguely, shrugging her shoulders.

'A male friend?' Dante asked her again.

Farusja raised her eyes to his, a smile tugging the corners of her mouth. 'You don't care, remember? '

'Get out of here Mumba,' Dante drawled, staring at her from under his brow.

Farusja smirked at him, walking towards the door. 'Always a pleasure Dumeno, always a pleasure.'

CHAPTER 28

*F*arusja exhaled noisily as she watched the elevator doors open. She had not wanted to see Sidney today, but Sidney had kept insisting and had already made her way to the hospital. Farusja walked out of the wide open doors and into the sunlight.

'Dear! Over here!'

She squinted into the sunlight, and seeing Sidney standing by her parked car, waved back unenthusiastically. As she picked her way down the steps carefully she wondered, and not for the first time, how Sidney had managed to afford such a car on the salary she was getting.

Of course notwithstanding savings and inheritance, for a woman in her position the car was an extravagance that could hardly go unnoticed. Her mini cooper convertible stood winking sky blue in the sunlight, cradled in its space snugly.

'*Eish* Farusja,' Sidney gasped at her, fanning her face with her hands. 'Would you believe this heat?'

'I thought you said you came from HD?' Farusja squinted at her, wondering at her attire. Sidney was always well-dressed and impeccably heeled. Her hair, if not in minute braids or delicately weaved across her head, was always pulled back in a sleek black ponytail, her face always made up, she had her suits tailor-made and styled to suite her tall frame, and heels to match.

Farusja was surprised today at the untidy ponytail Sidney's hair was in and the battered black tracksuit. 'What are you wearing?'

Sidney laughed, reaching down into the car to pull out a plastic drink carton sparkling with icy drops of water. 'I brought you something. Come sit.' Sidney slid into the driver's seat of her mini cooper, motioning Farusja to sit in the passenger seat.

Farusja sighed, and moving slowly to the car, opened the door, inhaling the scent of the black leather seats and gratefully accepted the icy cold drink.

'For a foreigner who might be out of a job, you seem awfully happy,' she murmured as she closed her lips around the straw, sighing pleasurably as the cold liquid trickled down her throat.

Sidney waved absently at her, her one manicured hand holding an exact replica of the plastic carton she had given Farusja. 'Let me tell you something, with people like Roberta Erlichmann and Dante Dumeno in charge, HD Advertising will be open for a very, very long time. Those guys are immune to the law, not to mention they have a hell of a lot of money at their disposal. So, how is our handsome head doing up there? I mean, what happened exactly? I heard he was shot!'

Farusja grimaced, sucking harder on the straw. 'Yes.' Farusja didn't want to talk about Dante.

'What are you doing here?' Sidney sneered at her good-naturedly, digging her in the ribs. 'Are you guys an item or what?'

Farusja tried to push her away. 'I'm not in the mood,' she exhaled noisily, trying to dig herself deeper into the seat.

'I'm sorry dear, I know that with everything you must be having a rough day?' asked Sidney quietly, reaching forward to brush a wisp of hair off Farusja's forehead.

Farusja nodded, her mouth opening wide in a yawn, her eyes closing involuntarily. 'I'm so tired, it's always so hard.'

She yawned again, her mouth opening so wide that she could feel the muscles in her jaw stretch individually. She shook her head sharply, she needed to stay awake, she wanted to check on Dante one last time … she yawned again, tears forming at the corners of her eyes.

'You seem exhausted dear,' Sidney said quietly. 'You have been here too long, let me take you home.'

Farusja shook her head again, putting her hands to her head, she could barely keep her eyes open, and her body felt like lead.

'Help me,' she whispered, covering her mouth with her hands. 'Need to stay awake.'

'Drink some more juice.'

Sidney's voice came to her from a distance, and Farusja tried to shake her head again, but it felt so heavy, her movements were slow and sluggish. The air seemed to engulf her and turn her to stone. She felt the straw touch her lips, and gathered up all her energy to suck some of that cool liquid down her throat again, sighing out loud as she watched the cup slowly fade in and out of sight.

'Sidney,' she whispered, her voice thick. 'Something's wrong.'

She tried to turn her head but the effort was just too much and so she settled back, moving slowly against the leather seat. She felt Sidney move into her line of vision, her eyelids too heavy to lift; she tried to form the words with her lips, her throat closing, the air escaping her lungs in a rush.

Sidney watched quietly as Farusja slumped against the seat, grabbing the plastic cup to prevent it from spilling on her expensive seat.

'Forgive me,' she said quietly. 'I didn't think we'd become such good friends.'

Naks was searched and allowed into Dante's room. He did not know how Hienry had managed this one. He sighed wistfully, missing the old days when things were less complicated. Now all Roberta could think about was HD and Dante, and all Dante could think about was DI Storage and his new girl. Naks had just seen a girl leave Dante's room, and couldn't help but wonder if this was indeed the woman whom Roberta found so threatening. The one that Dante seemed to be in love with. He could understand her appeal, the girl was curvy in all the right places. She was not tall or an obvious beauty, but she carried an air of confidence, even power around her. She was intriguing.

The security guard motioned him inside with a sneer. 'You people think you can just break the rules because you have high friends.'

'You mean friends in high places,' Naks laughed at him, getting great pleasure from the look on the man's face. Dante was propped up in bed, looking angry.

'It seems you got some comfort from that girl you like, I just saw her outside,' Naks said dryly.

Dante frowned at him. 'I didn't and I don't.'

'You keep doing this and you'll be back to selling drugs with me again.'

Dante sighed. 'I have no intention of letting whoever it is get away with this.'

'Provided you know who your enemy is,' Naks grunted, throwing himself into the chair by the side of the bed, adjusting his sunglasses on his face. 'Yo, what are you going to do, it's rough out there. Did Robbie tell you about what they did to HD?'

Dante shook his head, trying not to show the alarm he felt. 'What's up?'

'HD has been overrun by the police; Robbie closed the company for today. She sounded scared, and when Robbie sounds scared you know there is a hell of a problem.'

'Just take her into your bed as you usually do.'

'Jealous, bra?'

'No cause to be. Robbie and I have always had an understanding.'

'That's what you think. And that chick that just left, is she really the one Robbie is so jealous of?'

Dante shrugged.

'Sick fucking bastard Dumeno. When did we all change? When did we become the very people we were laughing at?' Naks said quietly. 'You were a scrawny idiot when I met you Dumeno, who knew both you and Robbie would rise to this?'

'It all had to change someday,' he said quietly.

'To this, man? Robbie running scared, stuck on two men that are supposed to be her brothers. You in cuffs, in a hospital bed. The businesses in ruins.'

'Robbie will be fine. She can always run to Germany. And what's life without a worthy opponent?' Dante grinned at him.

Naks shook his head. 'Whoever this guy is, I hope Hienry can find him before there's nothing left to mess up.'

CHAPTER 29

*H*ienry dusted himself off, squinting at the afternoon sun that continued its lukewarm washing over DI Storage. It was no longer a welcoming sight, what the light was revealing was eerie. It shone on empty storage lots and police vans parked haphazardly. The staff had left a long time ago, and only the supervisor of the security detail had stayed, hovering just out of reach of the commotion. The sun shone on the ambulance, the red and blue lights slicing through the air, leaving nothing to chance.

Hienry coughed suddenly, violently, his hands covering his mouth. What he had seen today he hoped he would never have to see again.

Detective Miles had ordered a clean sweep of the rest of the storage containers around the targeted one. Hienry had the feeling that eventually every storage box would be searched, but today was just the preliminaries. He did not want to see the repercussions once DI's clients found out that the police had gone through their personal belongings and opened their storage boxes.

Hienry could only imagine the state of the office after the policemen had ransacked it; search warrants had been obtained amazingly quickly and at the ready for anyone who might have the balls to ask them what they were doing. It had been almost noon and the activity at the park showed no signs of slowing down.

A macabre discovery was made in one of the other large storage areas in close proximity. Miles had stared at the deep grave that had been dug past the foundation and into the earth of the storage space for a full five minutes. The silence of the other police officers around him was deafening, and it was all Hienry could do not to vomit in the small space. He could hear the younger and weaker policemen behind him already dry heaving as they turned away from the tableau in front of them.

The glint of the metal links on the chains enveloping her wrists flashed in the light of the storage area, and Orabella Ricci stared up at them, her open dead eyes wide, the look of terror in them enough to scare even the strongest of men. Barbed wire had been wrapped tightly around her body, and Hienry could see the deep gouges that had been left when the wire had been dragged across her skin. Hienry did not even have to look closely at her to see that she had also been strangled.

Detective Miles had finally exhaled sharply, ordering his men to pull themselves together and call the ambulance. He had turned to Hienry, a look of steely resolve replacing his serious demeanour. 'I am going to throw away the key to Dante Dumeno's cell once I am done with him!' he snarled.

'Hienry?' Roberta's half hysterical voice shouted at him over the line. 'It's Orabella. I went to her house, something has happened, something is terribly ...'

'She's gone Roberta,' Hienry said quietly. 'Murdered. I'll arrange a safe house for you today still. The detective, he will come to you. He left here minutes ago. Say nothing!'

True to Hienry's word, Detective Miles Mkazi arrived at her house moments later. His tall, dark frame stood casually next to the white gate that closed her property, the police car parked haphazardly with two wheels off the curb and two wheels on the road. She walked down the driveway to meet him.

'Miss Erlichmann? Detective Miles Mkazi,' he extended his hand, and she was sure his eyes had taken in her flushed and nervous complexion. She nodded, not trusting herself to speak and not volunteering any information. Although she had nothing to hide. He motioned towards the house but she made no sign of acknowledging his meaning, and he chuckled.

'We shall do it outside then, right by your front gate. So you knew nothing of your partner's activities at DI?'

'I have no idea what you're talking about detective.'

'He's your lover too, am I correct?' Miles smiled at her, the smile frozen on his lips. 'And you stand here and claim you knew nothing of what he was doing?'

'I'm sorry detective; I really cannot say anything without my lawyer present.'

'Don't stand here and lie to me Ms Erlichmann!' Miles spat out at her, his anger showing on his face. 'Three women are dead! Three women! Are you not concerned for your fellow feminine?'

Roberta's lips quivered, she squared her shoulders. 'Dante did not kill those women!'

'He slept with all of them, they were in and out of his bed, they found out about what was happening. He even forced Orabella Ricci to commit crimes with him!' he had suddenly snarled, his face transformed within a matter of seconds. 'And you knew Miss Erlichmann!'

He had rounded on her, moving behind her and forcing her to turn around, to lose her centre of gravity. 'Orabella finally exposed him for the demon he was, the devil he is, and he had no other choice but to kill her!'

Roberta quailed inside, but stood her ground stoically, the only thing showing her nervousness was the quiver in her voice as she matched his snarl with hers. 'Where the fuck are you getting your information from detective? You're way off the mark! Are you arresting me? Otherwise this conversation is over.'

He sighed, the gleaming façade settling back into place on his face. 'Just tell me the truth Miss Erlichmann, and we can arrange a deal for you. There is so much overwhelming evidence against your partner, there is no probability of him being released, even on bail. And as his accomplice,' he paused, his dark eyes staring into hers fiercely, 'you are not going to be let off easily. Think about it Miss Erlichmann.' He smiled comfortably at her, his face nonchalant again as he casually strode back to his car.

She watched him jump into his car, his steps jaunty. He sent her a wave as he drove past, his smile glaring at her like a beacon. Despite Hienry's advice, she now knew she needed to stay visible, she needed to stay in the country; Detective Miles would be watching every move she made.

Farusja whimpered as pain exploded behind her eyelids, the feeling intensifying as she opened her eyes slowly. Darkness invaded the space around her; she could hardly see her fingers as she put them in front of her face. What had happened? The last thing she could remember was being at the hospital and drinking juice with Sidney ... Sidney?

She raised herself up slowly, straining her eyes against the pain to peer into the darkness, her hands digging into the mattress she was on, as she felt the space around her blindly. Placing one hand steadily in front of the other to guide herself, she crawled forward; her movement's jerky as she tried to keep herself balanced. Farusja was about to launch into the darkness when light flooded the room, her senses arrested in mid-movement as her hands rose instinctively to her eyes to shield them from the sudden glare. She was not prepared for the pain that exploded behind her eyes and moaned as she lowered her forehead to rest on the mattress, waiting for the fire behind her eyes to subside.

'Drink this dear.'

'Sidney?' Farusja whispered in shock as she uncovered her eyes and focused on the woman standing in front of her.

Sidney stood smiling down at her, holding out a Styrofoam cup. The strong aroma of filtered coffee wafting down. 'If you don't drink this, you will have the worst headache this side of the Sahara. Drink it.'

Farusja stared up at her in confusion, shaking her head slightly to make sense of the jumbled thoughts that were colliding in her brain. 'I was, we were at the hospital, in your car...'

'Yes.' Reaching down, Sidney grabbed hold of Farusja's hand, firmly placing the Styrofoam cup in it, folding her fingers around it until she was satisfied that it was in a firm grip. 'Drink it.'

Farusja complied, raising the cup to her lips and sipping the scalding liquid, sighing as the cobwebs in her mind cleared and the warmth reasserted itself into her limbs, the bright sparks in front of her eyes beginning to fade.

'Better?'

Farusja raised her eyes, bewildered and looked around her. She was lying on a thin, bare mattress. It was a small square room, the floor and walls of roughly plastered concrete. The only other thing in the room was a small blue bucket in one corner. There were no windows, only a single wooden door which was shut fast.

'Sidney?' she whispered, the tremor in her voice rising and falling. 'What's going on? Where are we?'

Sidney, who had knelt on her haunches in front of her, now stood up. She was still wearing the same tracksuit, her hair looking more untidy than earlier, spilling out of its tie.

'Do you want some more coffee?' she walked away from Farusja, moving to stand next to the wooden door.

Farusja placed the Styrofoam cup slowly on the floor away from the mattress, and placing her palms flat onto the floor she rose unsteadily to her feet, facing her friend across the room. The first goosebumps of fear dragged themselves rapidly across her arms. 'Sidney?'

'I needed the money,' Sidney looked at her and shrugged. 'I needed the money, my mother ... she lost everything when father died. I had to support her ... this was the only way ... I couldn't support anyone on the salary I'm getting.'

Farusja stared at her, comprehension slowly lighting its way across her face.

'The drink,' she shrieked, the pain of the betrayal laid itself heavily across her chest. 'You drugged me? You've kidnapped me? Sidney, where am I?'

'I'm sorry Farusja,' Sidney sighed, speaking quietly. 'I needed the money. But he promised that nothing is going to happen to you.'

Farusja put her hands up, palms facing Sidney, unable to prevent the anger lashing across her face. 'You despicable bitch!' she snarled, her face contorting. 'All this time! All this time! You were my friend!'

Sidney's face hardened, her mouth narrowing into a thin line, her eyes sparkling angrily in her face. 'We all do what we have to do, my dear.'

'You have no right to call me that!'

'Perhaps,' Sidney's voice was cold. 'Well, I cannot say it has been a pleasure, I have never met such a weak, simple minded and naïve woman since I left the rural areas of Nairobi, and such a bloody tease. You don't even know what to do with a real man.'

'You take that back!'

'Finish your damn coffee!' Sidney snarled at her, her face twisted in rage. 'It's over!'

Farusja screamed in fury as she lunged forward, knocking over the Styrofoam cup, her hands clawing and reaching for Sidney's throat. She hit her with a sickening thud, the anger from Sidney matching her own as they collided, their bodies smacking against each other as they went down. Farusja screamed as her hands closed around Sidney's neck, her rage blinding her, all the hurt and betrayal in her spilling out in the anguish of sound. 'You were my friend! And now you will have me killed? Did you help kill those girls at DI too? '

Sidney screamed back as she drove her knee into Farusja's stomach, digging her nails into Farusja's arms to loosen the hold her hands had on her neck, grunting and gasping for air. 'We d ... do what we have t ... to do ...'

Farusja tightened her hold on her neck, tears starting their long journey down her cheeks, the pain burning within her chest.

Sidney slapped at Farusja, clawing at her face and arms, her throat and chest starting to burn with the lack of air, she felt like she was moving in a sea of molasses.

'Farusja,' she whispered, 'please ...

Farusja sobbed, big gasping sobs that racked her body, leaving her gasping for air as she raised Sidney's head, preparing to smash it into the concrete underneath her, when suddenly she descended back into the darkness.

Sidney fell back to the ground, gasping and moaning for breath, her hands massaging her throat rapidly. 'That bitch!'

'Well, what did you expect? You pretended to be her friend, and then you drugged and kidnapped her. Some bloody friend you are,' Michael Katjihingua sneered at her, rubbing his hand where he had hit Farusja at the back of her head.

'Yes, but,' Sidney coughed, her body splayed flat on the floor, resting her head back on the floor.

Michael shook his head, reaching over her as he pulled the inert Farusja off the lower half of Sidney's body. 'You would think that by the way she looks that she'd be lighter.'

He half-lifted and half-dragged her to the mattress, throwing her down on it with relief and avoiding the puddle of coffee on the floor. He stared down at her, at the way her arms were flung haphazardly over her head, her face closed tight against the pain and the way her mouth opened and shut with laboured breathing; he could feel those lips full and pouting on his. His gaze raked over her body, devouring the white shirt and jeans hungrily. He was excited, aroused. She did this to him, he never wanted this; even unconscious she was such a tease.

Michael knelt down next to her face, smoothing away some stray hair, beads of perspiration starting to form on his forehead as he felt himself push against the zipper of his jeans. With a trembling hand he placed his index finger in her open mouth, shuddering with pleasure as the warmth and wetness of her mouth enveloped it.

'Enough you pervert.'

He jumped as Sidney hit him hard over the head, anger rushing to his face. 'You dare …'

'Yes I dare you, fucking pervert,' Sidney hit him again, this time pushing him forward on his knees. 'You cannot keep your hands to yourself can you? You disgusting piece of shit.'

Michael got up to face her, dusting his jeans, all evidence of his erection gone. Anger scrawled viciously across his face as it settled into a spiteful smile. 'That day you came to my house with him, yes him, he told me to kill you.'

Sidney froze, staring at him, trying to stem the bile that rose in her throat, the taste of fear. 'You're lying.'

Michael smiled, tucking his hands in his pocket. 'I hated you that day. I still do. And you thought you were his favourite? Who has been doing all the work? Who has he confided his plans to?'

'No he wouldn't. He promised!'

'Promised?' Michael chuckled maliciously. 'You're so naïve.'

'He wouldn't!' Sidney screeched at him, her head swivelling, looking for a way to escape. 'You can't!'

'If you cross me, I will!' Michael snarled at her, his face a mask of hatred. 'He changed his mind, but I can change his. Never interfere again, Aluna. Yes,' he smiled at her again, happy at the reaction on her face. 'I know who you are, who you really are.'

Sidney stared at him, her heart plummeting, her legs weak and almost crumpling underneath her in fear. 'You don't know.'

'He's waiting for you downstairs,' Michael cut her off abruptly. 'I don't care and I'm tired of hearing your voice.'

He sauntered past her, leaving her crumpled where she stood, opening the door, and glancing back over his shoulder at her. 'Pull yourself together, or you'll be useless to us.'

Farusja moaned, keeping her eyes tightly closed, trying to ignore the throbbing in her head. It had now settled into a steady, rhythmic thumping behind both eyes. What had happened? The last thing she remembered was the inky darkness, which had been a welcoming escape from the reality of her situation.

Sidney ... Farusja clenched her teeth at the stab of pain that squeezed her heart, it hurt to think about what her friend had done to her, all those secrets she had shared with her, what a fool she had been! Farusja clenched her teeth. Had she been the one who had helped put that bomb in Becca's car? What else had she done? Who was Sidney really?

Farusja strained her eyes to see through the darkness surrounding her. There was no light, only the bumpy mattress underneath her. She was still in the same room, which had now become her prison, no matter which way she looked at it. Farusja panicked – would she be found strangled just like the other girls?

She lowered her hands from her head, her body going cold. She realised that no one would miss her. Becca was living it up at the coast for the next week. Dante didn't care. No one would look for her. No one at all. Farusja fought the tears that flooded her eyes. She was utterly and truly alone.

She let the tears fall silently down her cheeks, her emotions spent and her mind numb. Nothing mattered anymore except staying alive and trying to escape. As her tears fell unheeded, she raised herself in a sitting position slowly. She raised herself to her knees and started to crawl forward, feeling blindly with her hands, the feel of rough concrete ugly to her knees. There! She drew back her fingers as they touched wet liquid and the outlines of the Styrofoam cup that she had been holding before she was knocked out. How long she had been unconscious? She screwed up her eyes, wiping the tears off her cheeks more in irritation than in anything else. She remembered nothing in the room except the mattress and the bucket, there had been no windows, but there had been light, so hopefully the light switch would be within the room.

She raised herself cautiously, standing on her tiptoes and placing her feet down gingerly, not wanting to encounter any nasty surprises.

She tiptoed forward, keeping her hands stretched out in front of her. If only she had known that joining HD Advertising would end like this for her ... she exhaled in relief as her hands touched the rough concrete of the wall; now just to find that light switch.

Sidney sat stiffly in the wooden high backed chair in Michael's garage, staring at Michael and staring at *him*, her protector ... *Diablo*. She was afraid for her life, for her mother. She needed the money, she had played her part, but now the novelty had worn off. Michael was right; she was useless. Her job, to befriend and kidnap Farusja Mumba, was over. There was nothing left for her to do here. Orabella Ricci and those two other girls were dead; by *his* hand. She trembled, digging her nails into her palm to calm herself.

She was scared. She had been reprimanded for not securing Farusja before she had woken up, and although that intensified the feeling that *he* would no longer need her on his side, it had been the least of her worries.

And so as she sat, watching Michael and *him* talking, no Michael listening, *him*, talking, hissing at Michael, she had decided to close her ears to what they were saying. She thought quickly, her mind confusing itself and thoughts jumbling in her head as she tried to formulate a plan to escape; she could be packed in an hour and across the border into Zambia in a day, where she could begin to make her way back home, back to her mother, to protect her ...

'Aluna.'

She gasped as *he* said her name, her trembling beginning all over again, guilty, as though her thoughts had been read out loud.

'*Bwana*,' she whispered, her head half-lowered in acknowledgement. 'I did everything you asked, I brought her here, I helped.'

'Yes,' *he* laughed heartily, it sounded cold. 'You did. Are you scared Aluna?'

'Please,' she raised her eyes to him, pleading, dropping all pretences. 'Please don't. I can be of use to you, I can help Michael. I can help.'

'Yes you can, and you have done your job excellently.'

She cowered from *his* eyes staring down at her and wrapped her arms around her body. She suddenly found herself wondering if all the money she had accumulated was really worth it.

'I still love you Aluna, just like I love Michael. You are my best daughter. Don't be afraid. I want you back here in an hour to take care of your friend.'

Sidney smiled back faintly, her legs beginning to gain back their strength. 'Thank you, *Bwana*!' she cried, reaching forward she grasped his arms in gratitude. 'I'll not fail you, I promise!'

He did not said anything, but smiled at her; a cold smile that chilled her to the bone but made her feel protected all the same. *He* was her protector, Sidney thought desperately. He would not do anything to hurt her, he *loved* her. *He* had brought her all the way to Namibia, had taken care of her, but she was still going to run.

'Go.'

She ignored the sneering look on Michael's face as she rose unsteadily to her feet, and grabbed her bag from the floor next to the door. Once outside she hurried to her car, which was parked across the street from Michael's house. She did not look back, swinging the iron gate closed behind her, her mind in overdrive. She thought furiously about what she could leave behind and what she really needed. She would go straight to the bank, withdraw all her money and leave for the Zambian border immediately.

Michael watched her leave through the garage door, a slow smile stretching its way across his face as he fingered something in his pocket.

'Do it quickly,' *he* said, turning back into the makeshift room that had once been the garage. 'She must not suffer. She will always be my best daughter.'

Sidney did not bother to put on her seatbelt, she was so intent on getting away that she did not bother to check her side mirrors or make sure that the bag she had so hastily thrown on the seat had not landed on the floor. If she had she would have noticed the small package wrapped in brown paper just behind her seat. She would have recognised it immediately and would have abandoned her car; she would have been free.

Her thoughts came to an abrupt halt as the bomb exploded; turning the small, expensive blue mini cooper into a miniature fireball, sending minute bits of her and it into the surrounding houses in the suburb.

Michael smiled lustily as he heard the muffled bang and saw smoke curdle into the sky.

'That is so fucking sexy,' he murmured.

Farusja trembled in the darkness. She had not been able to find the light switch, she was now certain that it was outside the room. Her hands felt raw from all the time she had spent trailing them up and down the concrete wall. She had sat, tired, on the cold concrete floor, hugging her knees and trying to infuse some warmth into her body. It was so cold! She had not noticed it in the beginning, but as she had started her slow movement across the room, the cold had crept under her clothing, through her skin and kissed her bones. The kiss had been light at first, but was now causing her to shiver uncontrollably.

The throbbing in her head had dissipated to a dull ache, and her mouth had become so parched and dry that she had started collecting saliva to swallow to relieve the tightness of it. Someone else had been here with Sidney, Farusja's teeth chattered.

Someone else…she remembered being hit over the head, she remembered that much, but who had it been?

Farusja shook her head slowly, unable to comprehend the situation she was in or the reason for it. Did she have any enemies? Was this part of the revenge on Dante? Was she going to end up strangled and tossed in some dirty hole?

Farusja strained to see in the darkness, if she could at least see, see her fingers in front of her, the mattress she had been so callously tossed on, her mind would stop to wander, the images flashing through her head would not be so ugly. She sighed, closing her mouth to stop her teeth from chattering, afraid that they would break against each other.

She stilled, there was a scraping noise above her head. It propelled her forward on her hands and knees in fear; she fell against the rough floor, wincing as it scrapped against her skin. She scrabbled on her hands and knees as far away from the sound as she could, stopping only as her head came into contact with the wall on the far side, causing the dull ache to explode into white stars of pain once again. It sounded like a key scraping in the lock. She had been sitting near the door.

Farusja shielded her eyes as the door scratched open in front of her, waiting for a burst of sunlight, and becoming anxious as darkness opened into even more darkness. A rush of warmth and heat surged through her as she shot up, adrenaline rushing through her body. She surged forward towards the now open door, her body coiled, and despite the fact that it was as dark as the room was, she released all her tense muscles on impact, slamming into the hard body of a man, hammering his hard torso with her fists and clawing whatever she could get her nails on. Her attacker had been caught off guard, and Farusja's heart leaped as she heard his yells of surprise and pain, until his hand grabbed a handful of her hair painfully and the flat of his other hand connected with her left temple.

'You bitch!' Michael growled as he pushed her away from him. 'You almost ruined my face!'

Farusja, who had raised her arms to cushion her impact against the rough floor, froze. 'Michael?' she whispered as light flooded the room, making her blink rapidly. 'Michael?'

Farusja could not prevent her face from contorting in shock then fear, as she swallowed convulsively. Nothing had been chance. Her friendship with Sidney, and her meetings and run-ins with Michael. They had all been planned, and the result was coming to its conclusion; she prayed that it would not end in her death. She stared up at him, taking in the half sneer on his face, the strange almost maniacal light in his eyes, and wondered why she had not at least told someone of her suspicions that day at the gym; and now it was too late.

He closed the door behind him, kicking at her leg so that she moved towards the mattress.

Farusja complied, her mind in overdrive and her body numb. 'Why?' she managed to croak out as she collapsed against the mattress on the floor. 'Who are you?'

Michael smiled, looking down at her, his teeth bared. 'You refused me Farusja, we were supposed to be together, we would have made a good team.'

Farusja bit down on her lip hard to stop the assault of fear on her senses. 'What are you doing here Michael? Why am I here? Let me go now! Did you kill those girls?'

He laughed, the sound hollow in the small room. 'I wish I had killed them, unfortunately I can only give that praise to someone else.'

'Sidney?' her voice wavered. 'She killed those girls? It's impossible …'

'Oh that one?' Michael dismissed her with a wave of his hand. 'Impossible? After what she did to you, you still think it's impossible? But she is no longer with us I'm afraid. She met with a small accident in her car.' He smiled at her lustily.

Farusja shrank away from the man in front of her, she could not think straight, there was too much going on, so much happening all at once. 'You …'

'Yes, she was no longer needed.'

'Why am I here?' Farusja whispered, her eyes on the mattress in front of her. 'Are you going to kill me too? Why are you doing this Michael? Why did you do this to Dante?'

'Eventually I'll kill you,' Michael winked at her. 'But if you're nice, we could think of ways to make your suffering less.'

Farusja shuddered and strained with every fibre in her being. She could feel his gaze on her, but she refused to look up. She knew what he wanted; she would die before she gave him anything. She turned her body away from him, moving towards the far end of the mattress against the wall, pulling herself in a sitting position. She had survived Dante Dumeno, how bad could this be?

'What have you done Michael? You'll rot in jail for all of this; you won't get away with it.'

He smiled, coming towards her and crouching on the mattress in front of her.

Farusja stiffened when she noticed the taser gun in his left hand.

'Be nice,' he murmured. 'Seeing your body in the throes of electric convulsions would be sexy for me but quite painful for you.'

He settled back on his haunches, staring at her, the hunger in his eyes obvious. 'A man with a higher purpose, a disgruntled employee. Call it whatever you want to. Seeing other people suffer at my hands satisfies me more than anything else ever could, not even the drugs were giving me this great feeling. Dumeno cannot save you here Farusja. Right now he cannot even save himself.'

Farusja glared at him as realisation dawned on her. 'You had something to do with the guns at DI Storage didn't you? It wasn't only the girls!'

'That pretty mouth of yours can be doing other things,' Michael interrupted her, his voice husky. He reached forward and massaged the swell of her right breast with the side of the taser gun, chuckling as she flinched away. 'You and me we're going to have so much fun together, just you wait and see.'

CHAPTER 30

Thursday, 17 May

oberta sat staring at Dante. It had been six days since the walls had fallen down. The moment Orabella Ricci's body had been found, Dante had been dragged into court to be arraigned.

Hienry had arranged the rest, and Roberta sent up a silent prayer, grateful for Dante's bodyguard. Despite their misgivings, a stream of defence lawyers had lined up wanting to take Dante's case.

Not only was it a high profile case that involved the CEO of DI Storage, but it had the potential of the company's board of directors implicated as well, which promised a hefty amount of money for the lawyer who managed to get the case.

The board had denied all involvement in the allegations; and they had vehemently protested that Dante had acted alone and that proceedings were taking place to relieve him of his position. DI Storage would no longer be his.

The board refused to assign its team of lawyers to the case, showing the public its unforgivable stance toward criminals of all kinds, playing to the press for sympathy for the hundreds of clients that now needed to be taken care of.

Roberta had not seen Hienry since Dante had been arraigned. He had acquired the services of a very promising young shark who had been on the company's retainer as one of the lawyers, and had quit as soon as he had established the amount of money he would be getting from the case. He was as cold to Dante's plight as he was as warm to demanding his salary. Hienry had chosen well.

The judge that had presided over the pre-trial had not been a coincidence either. Her name was Melanie Oko. A woman in her late thirties, her personality was well suited to the court and the cases she presided upon; she had none. She was as flat and as dispassionate about anything except the facts, impassioned pleas and cries from guilty offenders fell in the void between the prosecutor, the defenders benches and her stand. It was rare that anyone saw her in anything other than her judicial robes. Officially, she had no ties with Dante, but known only to Hienry and her, they had spent two passionate days together.

She was just as cold as the lawyer, but Hienry had made sure that her ruling would pass down his, Dante's and her throat, smoothly and easily. With Dante's bail paid, his trial had been scheduled to take place in three month's time. He had been arraigned for gun smuggling, and the police in their haste and excitement had decided to place the murders of Orabella, Frieda and Erica on his head as well. It was their biggest error, and Dante's attorney had a field day at the court hearing. No evidence had been found that connected Dante to any of the murders, despite him being intimate with all of them. But most importantly, the autopsy had shown that Orabella had been killed minutes after Dante had been shot and rushed to the hospital. The press had a field day, laughing at the ineffectiveness of the police for letting a probable murderer and gun smuggler go free.

Roberta sighed in regret, recalling the butt of their jokes, a certain Detective Miles Mkazi.

'What are you dreaming about?' Dante interrupted her.

'Miles Mkazi,' she answered quietly, resuming her staring at him from across the desk. 'You happy to be home?'

'Sad to be kicked out of that hospital, missing the morphine,' Dante mourned quietly.

'The house feels like a prison Dante,' Roberta said quietly. 'All these Smiths all over the place.'

'Well, I wouldn't need them if you and Jerome shipped yourselves off to Tanzania or somewhere else while all this nonsense dies down,' Dante smirked at her. 'Remember the press?'

'When I came here after you left the hospital, I couldn't get through to your gates,' Roberta said, annoyed. 'So many cars and cameras.'

'I thought you liked publicity Robbie.'

'Not like that,' Roberta whispered. 'They were all over, like ants, screaming questions, making it sound like we were nothing but murderers and money sluts. The only way I got to the house was when Hienry came to get me. Do you know what they're saying about us Dante?' she put her hands to her mouth. 'They think we're guilty as hell, that you killed them all, that we're both rich spoilt brats who will do anything for money!'

'Vultures, the whole lot of them.'

'And then you came back from the hospital, loud and angry, and went up to your room and fell asleep instantly,' Roberta laughed quietly.

Dante smiled at her. 'Thanks for being around Robbie.'

Roberta smiled. She had moved into the guest room, locked indoors, watching the news and leaving her answering machine to pick up and delete the countless of messages she was receiving from her colleagues at HD Advertising, the press and her friends. She had no desire to offer explanations and reassurances now, she had none. They both watched as Jerome sauntered into the room.

'I can't even go outside,' he grumbled. 'Freaking reporters still hanging about, those idiots even tried to get into the trees!'

'I told you to leave Jerome.'

'You want me to leave my only brother to go through this shit alone?' Jerome spat out angrily. 'Stop telling me what to do. I'm here, deal with it.' Jerome moved forward, angrily throwing himself on the couch next to Roberta.

Roberta stared at Dante, who stared back at her, then at his brother. Dante sighed. 'Thank you Jerry.'

'Ya that's right, recognise me' Jerome grinned. 'Now, what are we talking about?'

'Miles Mkazi,' Roberta said. He had been relieved of command, suspended and his name dragged through the mud. The press had been merciless. Everything about him was examined, from his childhood friends, to his years on the force and any misdemeanours that he had while he was growing up. Despite the threat he presented to her and Dante, she felt sorry for this particular campaigner of justice.

'Why the fuck are you thinking about that idiot? He got what he deserved the stupid bastard,' Dante growled, shifting himself into a more comfortable position behind his desk in the study.

'You know you don't mean that Dante. The evidence against you was so overwhelming, anyone would say the same.'

'He should have checked his facts first, the greedy bastard!' Dante sighed angrily, throwing the latest stack of papers across the desk, falling back into the cushioned chair that Hienry had conveniently moved into the study for him to sit on. He had just read the brief that Orabella had prepared on him for the third time, and he could not believe it, he would not believe it. Orabella. Hienry had not spared any details. Orabella Ricci had been strangled, her open eyes dull with the horror she had felt and seen in her last moments.

Dante replayed the scene he got from Hienry again and again in his mind, trying to work out why, how and who had killed her. She had been dead for only a few hours when they had found her, rigor mortis had not yet set in and as the policemen lifted her onto the ambulance stretcher; her body had still been slightly warm to the touch. What they had seen had rendered them all silent. She had been lying in the shallow grave on her side, her body naked. Both ankles and wrists had been handcuffed together, her arms held against her chest. Blood mixed with what was later found out to be urine had pooled under her, the earth underneath her drinking it up greedily, the blood still seeping from the numerous punctures and the deep scratches on her skin. From her ankles to her armpits, barbed wire had been lovingly wrapped around her skin, kissing it with deep, ugly red gouge marks and deep scratches where the sharp points of the wire had greedily sunk and torn into her, the thin trails of blood the only connection to dampness beneath her.

Her tongue hung out of her mouth, swollen to twice its size, a grotesque symbol of the strength with which she had been strangled. This time it had been ligature strangulation, the ligature in question still wrapped around her neck loosely; an obvious message to the police and their ineffectiveness. The autopsy had also revealed that the wire had been wrapped, no, dragged across her while she was still alive … Dante shook his head slightly to rid himself of the image, his chest on fire.

'Are you okay Dante?' Roberta asked quietly as she pushed the stack of papers that had fallen off the desk back onto the already overflowing table.

'She did not deserve this Robbie,' he paused, inhaling sharply to quell the tightness in his chest. 'She did not do this to me. She was killed to keep her quiet.'

Roberta nodded, agreeing with him. 'When I went to her house I knew something was wrong, horribly wrong, and then the last time I went there ...' Roberta raised her hand to her mouth, her face screwed up, remembering the smell, and the fear that assailed her on that day, sniffing back the tears that were threatening to fall. 'I'm scared Dante, I really scared. Who is doing this to us? What do they want? Are we next?'

'We never give into a fight, Aunt Roberta,' Jerome said quietly, laying his hand on her shoulder. 'We're all Dumeno's.'

Dante nodded, agreeing. 'He's right.'

'Orabella was killed, murdered!' Roberta shrieked, slashing at the pile of papers she had just replaced on the desk and sending them cascading back down to the floor. 'So were Frieda and Erica! They accused you of gun smuggling, you will go to jail for life! What is going to happen to us?' She sat back into her chair, her body slumped forward, sobs racking her body.

'Aww, come on Aunt Roberta,' Jerome patted her shoulder. 'Look at where we are now, we never give up.'

'Robbie ...'

He was interrupted by a knock on the open door and he glanced up, his face opening in surprise. John Oduraa, the chair of the board, stood at the door, with a wry look on his face.

'What a mess you have got us into Dumeno.'

Dante got up as fast as his leg would allow him, hobbling forward on his newly acquired crutch as he stepped around his desk and with both hands warmly grasped the hands of the older man, pulling him into the study.

John in turn grasped Dante's arm, steering him back to his chair and pushing him into it, looking down at him in disapproval. 'What a fine mess this is Dumeno,' John Oduraa, dressed in an open necked t-shirt and blue jeans, said again curtly as he lowered himself into the seat that Jerome had just vacated next to Roberta, nodding at Jerome and sighing in relief as he did so. 'I'm not staying long Dumeno, but I'll prolong my stay if it means getting through that group of vultures down there easily.'

'I was not part of it Oduraa.'

John grunted, nodding at Roberta who had been just as surprised to see him and was in the process of wiping her tears. 'Miss Erlichmann.'

She nodded back at him. 'John.'

He turned back to look at Dante, the look in his eyes stern. 'There was a murder on our premises Dumeno, there were guns smuggled into our premises.'

'I know that John.'

'No one will touch us anymore Dumeno.'

'I know that too John.'

'You know how many contracts have been nullified today? We're operating at a loss, our shares have plummeted. We have nothing.'

Dante sighed, staring at him quietly, their dark eyes meeting. 'It is still my company John.'

John harrumphed, the sound loud in the quiet room. 'That is why I know you had nothing to do with this.'

'The board at DI?'

'The board is a gathering of fools, and they will send you to the sharks, all the staff have resigned from DI. If you ask me I don't know what they are waiting for, we will probably have to declare bankruptcy in the next few days.'

'And you?'

'You think I'd let you get off that easy? You're going to have to rebuild this company with your own two hands, again.'

A tired smile tore across Dante's mouth, their eyes meeting.

'Who would do this to you Dumeno?' John shook his head, one large black hand rubbing his temples in bafflement. 'All this time, and right under all our noses. The security tapes are blank, erased. The guards, they don't know anything, have not seen anything. How a woman could be killed right under our noses, right under our noses Dumeno! And no one saw anything? In our own park? And all those guns … how?'

Dante stared at him, his mind rife with speculation. He did not know whether to laugh or cry at what John had just said. In some ways, John had become a second father to him, watching over the organisations interests like a hawk, even going the extra mile when it was needed. DI Storage had meant as much to John as it meant to him, and to see it in such ruins was nothing less than torture.

'We'll get to the bottom of it John, I can't promise you anything else, but I can promise you that,' he said quietly.

'It's too dangerous!' Roberta cried at them. 'What happens if the killer comes after us?'

'I cannot afford to not do it Robbie,' Dante said, his voice low. 'There is too much at stake. And if you haven't already noticed Robbie, he came after us a long, long time ago, when he first killed Frieda.'

'And how do you propose to do that Dumeno? With that electronic bracelet the furthest you can go from your house is two kilometres until the trial,' John said

Dante lifted his right leg slightly and glanced at the black bracelet encased around his ankle. A green light winked steadily at him.

'Once that thing turns red you know they will throw you straight into prison,' John paused. 'How you managed to avoid it in the first place is beyond me.'

Dante shook his head. 'I'm not planning to leave the house Oduraa, I have another pair of hands and legs.'

CHAPTER 31

Friday, 18 May

'What do you mean you can't find her?'

Hienry stared at his friend, his anger overcoming his composure. 'I cannot find the girl!' he roared. 'Exactly what I said! She has not been at the house, the last time anyone saw her was at the hospital! I cannot find her!'

'Maybe she's visiting someone. Maybe she's left the country?'

'No, we went into her house. Her passport is still here, her purse even, everything is in place. She did not return after visiting you in hospital. And remember we took both men tailing her and her friend off the moment you were admitted. We have no idea where she could be.'

'And what about that friend of hers, Rabecca?'

'She's on holiday at the coast; and not picking up her phone, who would bother to eh?'

Dante squinted against the early morning sun and looked at Hienry, refusing to believe what he was hearing. 'Maybe she's at a friend's house, there was this tall east African girl?'

Hienry settled his bulk comfortably in his chair. 'That Sidney girl? Here is the interesting thing, she's been found dead.'

'Dead?'

'She just happened to be in her car when it exploded.'

'Exploded? So what do you think has happened to Mumba?'

'I'd have found her body by now old friend,' Hienry said quietly. 'I think it's safe to assume that she is still alive somewhere.'

Dante had made a mistake. The day he had been in hospital, when she had left to speak to that mysterious caller; that was probably the day she was taken. He had just assumed she was just not coming back; after all he had treated her like shit.

After he had been dragged to court and released on bail he had expected to see her charge through the reporters and up his driveway to demand an explanation from him, if not to just pity him, but she had not come. A week had gone by and he had not heard from her. So he had sent Hienry to find her, and now realised that something was wrong, again. He had the same feeling about Orabella and he had rationalised his fears away and she had ended up dead. He was not going to do the same with Farusja.

He had lost his life, Orabella Ricci, his company and now his girl with the luminous eyes had gone missing. Dante continued squinting at the sun; he wondered how he could be so calm. 'Where do we start?'

'Where do I start you mean,' Hienry shifted his bulk again and looked around the garden, irritated. 'Does that thing on your ankle not itch?'

Dante stared down at the cuff embracing his ankle, the green light blinking merrily at him. 'Like hell.'

'You have been seen around the house for long enough, it is time to take it off.'

'You're right old friend. Orabella is dead Hienry, Farusja is missing. I'm more than prepared to meet our enemy head on.'

Hienry nodded. 'Shall we go inside?'

Ex Detective Miles Mkazi stared at the empty bottle leering at him from his bedside table; and with his bleary bloodshot eyes, he leered back. He was sprawled on his bed, which seemed to be moving under him at a nauseating pace. His home, what he had thought of as his refuge, had now become his prison. To go out would be to encounter the swarms of journalists waiting to descend on him, still sneering and laughing. Did these people not have anything better to write about? What a farce it all was. He had come across the case of his career, the case that would have got him a corner office with windows, a secretary and much needed accolades from the police chief, and what did he have to show for it? An empty bottle of tequila and a series of bad hangovers. He had fallen from grace quicker than a prostitute opened her legs.

He had made a grave error, a lapse in judgment, and with any other case it would have been overlooked, but with such a high profile case the police department had been ripped to shreds, and it had not stopped there. The task force assembled to find the murderer of the strangled women had been disbanded. Miles snorted, it had only been him and Philip, the others had never shown up for any of the meetings. They had called it gross incompetency and negligence.

Miles burped loudly; that had been the funniest part of this whole mess. As commanding officer, Miles had been hung out, wrung out and dried more than once over the past week. Dante Dumeno had not killed those girls. Though he hated to admit it, the Dante Dumeno he had come to know in the past few weeks did not strike him as anything other than being in the business of making money, of which

DI Storage made so much of that it would hardly need to add smuggling to the balance sheet.

The police force were as close to finding the girls killer as he had ever been, and despite Orabella Ricci's murder, he was sure that the gun smuggling would take priority due to the increase in crimes committed in the town involving the use of small firearms.

Miles reached out angrily and knocked the bottle of tequila off the bedside table next to him. Despite his suspension, he still was Detective Miles Mkazi, he had to put a stop to all the lies and the stories. Whoever had done this, whoever had killed those girls, was going to pay.

As for Dante Dumeno, he would get his just desserts for treating people like tools; it would just be a matter of time.

Farusja stared into the cold darkness, her eyes burning from lack of sleep, her body fatigued and hungry. She had not been given food since she had been dragged here by Sidney, and she managed to drink the cups of water given only if she did not accidentally knock them over in the dark. She did not know how long she had been here. Michael had come to her about seven times. The constant fear had kept her awake, her mind buzzing with possibilities of escape. She had made the mistake of falling asleep once and had woken up to find Michael hovering over her, her shirt unbuttoned and his hands squeezing her breasts, his breathing sordid in the enclosed space. She had fought him, screaming as she did so.

On another night she had woken up to a presence; she had cursed the pitch blackness of the room and had readied herself to scratch Michael's face if he had dared to come near her. But as the silence increased it had dawned on her that it was not Michael.

'Who's there?' Farusja's voice had wavered as her eyes strained to see in the darkness of the little room. Fear had kept her glued to her position on the mattress on the floor, and goosebumps had run rampant down the full length of her body. There was something terribly sinister about the feeling she got from the person in the room with her. Whoever it was had made no noise, but she could feel eyes on her, and the feeling they gave her was beyond terror.

'Who's there?' Farusja repeated as tears had rolled down her cheeks unchecked. The living shadow in the darkness with her stirred, and she felt the eyes close onto her once more. It had gone on for what had felt like a lifetime, and she had not dared breathe loudly until she had heard the scrap of the door opening and the sound of someone noiselessly padding out of the room.

She had to fight Michael off frequently, but the unknown person that had visited her that night had added a new meaning to the word fear. Farusja shivered as her eyes strained against the inky blackness. Whoever it was had not come back and despite dealing with Michael, she had felt relief. Michael had killed Sidney, she was sure about that, but there was somebody else, someone Michael was working for, who had orchestrated it all; the murdered girls, the guns at DI Storage. That terrible presence that had been in the room. That was the person who was in charge.

Farusja shivered; she had crawled on her hands and knees exploring every inch of the room, looking for any way to jam the door open and had found none. The room was a black hole; it closed and opened into darkness. The only light she ever saw was the glaring overhead light bulb that Michael turned on every time he came to assault her. Where was she? The one thing she knew was that she needed to get out of here, there had to be a way. Michael was getting bolder. She had realised that her fighting against him aroused him more than her body did; he had started slapping any part of her just to get that desired response. He had left just a while ago, and her head still rang where his hand had connected with it.

Farusja sniffed against the cold, despite what Sidney had said, despite what Roberta has said, what she was going through now was adding a whole new dimension to her personality. She wondered if Dante even knew that she was missing, whether he cared. If there was anyone who would have found her, it would have been him and Hienry. The longer she was kept here, the smaller her chances of survival were. She was running out of time, she could feel it.

CHAPTER 32

oberta watched as Naks filled her glass slowly. It was the first time the three of them had been together in a long while, and the familiarity of it was extremely comforting for her. There seemed to be no solution to what they were facing. They were sitting on Dante's balcony; the three of them perched on bar stools, the glasses of red and white wine and the bottles of beer littering the table between them.

'Just like old times,' Roberta sighed happily, raising her wine glass to toast her two companions; Dante and Naks raised their glasses to her, their wine sloshing over the top of the glasses. Naks was still wearing his trademark sunglasses; redeemed by the fact that it was a rainy and overcast day. 'So when are you opening up HD again?' Naks asked, raising the glass to his lips.

Roberta tried not to look wounded, shrugging her shoulders. 'Give me a break Naks, this is the first holiday I have had in years, I have no reason to run back to that office and clean the mess those bloody policemen made.' Once she opened the office again she would have to clean up the mess that had become her life and put some order to it. She hoped they would still have some clients left. The amazing tender they had won had been pulled a week ago; breweries and two ministries had been next. She wondered how many other cancellations were waiting in her inbox. She would have to open up HD after the weekend to do some damage control. 'You're asking me about HD? Ask your friend here what his bulldog did with that bracelet that's supposed to be wrapped around his ankle,' Roberta smirked at Dante. 'Do you want to ruin us?'

Dante shrugged, his other foot rubbing the spot where the bracelet had been. 'It was getting on my nerves, and besides I'm not leaving the property so what's the big deal?'

Naks shook his head. 'What I want to know bra, is how you managed to get it off without the pressure switch going off and alerting the police.'

'Hienry is good at what he does.'

'But it's impossible to get one of those bracelets off!'

Dante shrugged again. 'Hienry is good at what he does.'

Roberta shrugged her shoulders dismissively. 'As long as they still think you are here I don't give a damn how it came off.'

'Do you think we can bring DI Storage back from death?' Naks changed the subject quietly, his dark glasses immobile.

'Maybe we will shut down and open a gun assembling factory; we already have the stock on the premises,' Dante grinned.

Roberta looked at him worried. 'That's not funny Dante, what are we going to do?'

'Give it a bit of time to cool down,' Naks shook his head, 'and you'll be giving more time to this enemy of yours to make even more tracks.'

Dante shrugged. 'Board meeting, first priority, topic closed.'

Roberta sighed loudly making her disagreement known.

Dante ignored her, glancing at the watch on his wrist; Hienry was late.

'You said it was urgent, what's up bra?' Naks directed his dark sunglasses at Dante.

'I need you to keep Robbie in line, she listens to you more than she listens to me,' Dante grinned, turning to Roberta. 'You could at least fuck the both of us equally Robbie.'

Roberta stared at Dante. 'Well congratulations on getting jealous at this late stage in the game, all you've been concerned about is that fucking little doe-eyed sheep. I hope she's gone.'

Dante did not answer her, and instead stared at the glass in front of him.

Roberta made an exasperated sound, scrapping her bar stool back as she stepped off the stool. 'Reminisce with Naks if you like, I'm going to check on Jerome.' She stalked away from the table.

'What's up man?'

'She's missing Naks.'

'Who? Your special girl?'

'Yes, Farusja is missing.'

What you mean missing?'

'Missing, can't find her anywhere, dropped off the face of Windhoek.'

'But you dumped her man. Maybe she did leave, what you said to her was pretty harsh you know. Maybe she just wanted to get away or something?'

'She is missing Naks and she is in trouble. She hasn't been in Windhoek long, she hardly knows anybody here, where would she go?'

Naks shook his head. 'You're making a big deal out of nothing bra, the chick is probably living it up at the coast, she realised what a risky business you are and had to get away.'

Dante shook his head. 'She's not the type.'

'And you've known this girl for all of one month and now you know her?' Naks shook his head. 'Robbie was right bra, you're lost over this little sheep.'

Dante shrugged. 'I know what I'm talking about.'

Naks shook his head. 'Prioritise Dumeno, your business is in flames and you're worried about a woman?'

CHAPTER 33

Saturday, 19 May

*F*arusja woke up groggy, her head was pounding. She had lost all sense of time, it was just a never ending cycle of Michael and half sips of water in the dark. If they were trying to intimidate her through lack of food and light, it was working. She felt the weakness in her body every time she fought Michael off; she could not even add an angry scream to her fury anymore because of the dryness in her throat and chest. She grinned ruefully through the pain, licking her cracked lips hungrily. On the other hand her stomach had stopped complaining of its hunger and the big rumbles had been reduced to hunger pangs as her body began to slowly feed on itself.

Farusja dragged herself into a sitting position, holding her head wearily in her hands. She would have drank her tears gratefully if she had any water to spare in her body to start crying. At least they did not allow her to soil herself. Michael brought in a bucket every time he came into the room. Thankfully he left it there and only returned to empty it the next time he came, which she now assumed was in the evening. She hardly used the bucket; there was nothing she needed to get rid of. He had hit her harder than he usually did yesterday, her head felt dead on her. She sensed that the end was getting nearer. She dreaded the day she became too frail to fight him off, even when she knew that he let her get her way, every time.

Her hands froze as she heard the more than familiar scrape of the door opening, her body immediately tensing up. Not now, she thought desperately, please not now. She dropped her hands to her sides as she heard Michael's chuckle, and raising herself to her knees, she opened her eyes as light flooded the room again, refusing to shield her eyes from the searing pain; the constant switch between blinding light and pitch blackness had taken its toll on her body.

Michael recoiled dramatically, turning the basket he held in his hands away from her. 'Damn you don't look so good, what did I ever see in you?'

'Thanks to you, you fucking bastard,' Farusja croaked at him, pulling the tangled hair out of her face and falling back on her haunches in fatigue. 'I'm tired of these games, do what you have to do.'

Michael chuckled again, taking another step into the room and closing the door behind him. 'And you stink.'

'You're fucked up Michael; get the hell away from me,' Farusja stiffened as he came to stand in front of her, kneeling so that he stared straight into her face.

'So I guess you will not want some food then,' he slowly laid the basket he was carrying in between them.

Farusja's eyes hungrily followed the basket, was that chicken she could smell? 'Why are you feeding me now?'

'Are you hungry or not?' Michael, still staring at her, reached out a hand to pull the basket away from her.

Farusja reached out and grabbed his hand, her eyes still on the basket. She tossed his hand aside and grabbing the basket, retreating to the end of the mattress and devoured the contents of the basket. She wondered if it was her last meal. There were two bottles, one filled with juice and the other water, neither of which had never tasted as good as they tasted now. There were store bought buns, the ones covered in sesame seeds, and a few pieces of cold chicken, and to finish it all off a sweet sugary confection that brought tears to her eyes when she felt the sugar rush surge through her.

It was the best food she had eaten in years. She did not bother to keep an eye on Michael as he sat before her quietly, watching her finish the meal. Only as she was devouring the dessert did she notice what was dangling from his right hand. She paused, stuffing the last of the confection in her mouth and raising her head from the empty basket.

He was looking at her with a smile on his face, his eyes still staring at her with that look she could not quite identify in them; the look she had seen so many times on his face. In his hand hung a length of white rope, it gleamed merrily at her in the light.

Farusja's heart quickened, and with the realisation that her death would not be swift, grabbed the basket and lunging forward aimed it for his head, and managing to clip the side with the edge of the basket, ran past him as he raised his hands to shield himself; she scrabbled against the door which was half open, yanking it backwards and open she dove head first into a yawning cavern of darkness that opened up to her after she had been clothed in light. She was shocked; she had thought she would be outside in the sunlight! Farusja realised that she had been holding her breath as she landed hard on the floor, she could hear loud panting, and seconds later realised it was her own. She heard Michael's cry of rage and gasped as she felt his hand close over her ankle, yanking her back into the room. Farusja dug her nails into the concrete floor underneath her, sweat breaking out across her body as she strained to push herself forward and get away from Michael.

She was not going to end up as another one of Dante's murdered girls! She felt Michael stand up and grip her other leg and he yanked her back into the room, her bare arms scraping the concrete.

'No!' Farusja screamed at him, kicking her legs back in a swimming motion, trying to free her ankles. She felt the skin on her arms burn off as he yanked on her legs harder, and she looked around frantically, her eyes scanning the darkness for anything she could use or grab onto. She wrapped her arms around the small edge of the door frame, pulling her chest around the curve as he dragged her back into the room, hysterically looking around the darkness for anything that could help her, their panting and struggling loud in the enclosed area.

'You'll only make it last longer you stupid bitch!'

Farusja felt her chest burning as she struggled against him, tears bid farewell from her eyes and rolled down her cheeks unwillingly.

'You're a fucking bastard Michael! I'll haunt your fucking ass to the grave!' she screamed at him, straining her arms against the door frame that was now slipping out of her grasp. She did not see the shadow detach itself from the darkness before her, nor did she hear it move towards her and raise its arms. Her last view as she descended into darkness was of her fingers letting go of the door frame.

CHAPTER 34

ante looked at Hienry, it seemed that he was looking at his friend for the first time, and his respect grew. He knew that Hienry's past was shadowed but he had only realised how much he did not know about him when he saw the ankle bracelet safely on one of the Smiths' leg; he did not want to think about how it had got there. If Hienry and his group were capable of such intricate work, what else was his friend capable of? Although Hienry and his men had thoroughly searched Rabecca's house to find out where Farusja had gone, they were going to go there again. They had tried to get hold of Rabecca, but her phone had constantly been off, and there was no one else to call. Hienry had thrown his weight and numerous badges around and had appropriated the surveillance camera tape for the hospital parking lot. Dante had watched it in silence. He remembered the call she had received in the hospital, he had teased her about it. They watched as Sidney Kimani had spoken to Farusja outside the sky blue mini cooper she had come driving up in. A few seconds later they both entered the car and Sidney had driven off. That was the last time anyone had seen Farusja.

Hienry had not even had the time to trace Sidney's car before he had got the information that it had disintegrated into millions of flaming pieces. The last Hienry had seen of Sidney had been melded with the smoking shell that was her car. It had been difficult to determine what had simply been debris from the car and what had been Sidney. Hienry managed to get hold of Jaco from HD, who had told him that Farusja had been friends with Sidney and Rabecca, but that was all he knew about her personal life. As for Sidney, she was always impeccably dressed and a professional at what she did. Apparently Sidney had actually resigned on the day the news had broken about DI Storage. In all the commotion, Sidney's resignation had been forgotten. Jaco did not know if Sidney had any close family or relatives here, and despite her outgoing personality, she had hung around with Farusja most of the time.

Dante brooded silently; Farusja had now been missing for eight days, where was she? What had happened to her? He tried not to think of Orabella; will Farusja end up just as she did? Was she already dead?

'Come back from where you are Dumeno,' Hienry said quietly, watching Dante under hooded eyes. 'Because wherever you are, it does not look pretty my friend.'

Dante slowly, tiredly drew his eyes slowly back into focus, seeing the same look mirrored in his friend's eyes. 'Who is doing this?'

Hienry shook his head slowly. 'I wish I knew old friend, I wish I knew.'

'And this Diablo person?'

Hienry laughed shortly, the sound harsh in the silence. 'He's a ghost. We won't find him, he'll find us. And what reason would he have to come after you? You have nothing he wants.'

Dante shrugged. 'Apparently it does not take much anymore.'

He watched as another one of Hienry's Smiths left the living room, starting a long sojourn around the house and its grounds to show that Dante was honouring his house arrest and still on the premises. He looked down at his ankle. A pale band of skin gazed back at him mockingly; his eyes opened widely in shock as comprehension dawned on him.

'So stupid,' he muttered. 'So stupid, of course! Her husband!'

Hienry grunted, getting up to pick the surveillance tapes off the table. 'What are you talking about?'

'Orabella's husband!' Dante jumped up to his feet, grabbing Hienry's arms in excitement. 'What has happened to Orabella's husband? She's dead! No one has come forward to claim the body except her family. I have seen no pictures of him in any newspapers sorrowful, mourning, nothing!'

Dante started pacing the living room floor, his nerves on edge. 'Actually thinking back to it, Orabella started this reclusiveness when she met him, when she got married! She stopped seeing me; she stopped seeing anyone for that matter! Could it be?'

Hienry's eyes narrowed. 'I see.'

'Whoever this so called husband of hers is, maybe he's the one who is dead set against me?' Dante's movements became jerkier with the adrenaline surging through his body. 'All of a sudden she has this vendetta against me, and it was all after she got married! We need to find this man. I'm sure he will know what is happening, I think it's about time I left this house Hienry.'

Hienry smirked, his mouth turned down at the sides. 'Maybe you're in the wrong business old friend, from the way I have failed in my duties, maybe you should take over.'

Dante frowned, his thoughts in a whirlwind. 'He's dead?' His unvoiced concerns spread around the room, hitting the air and bouncing back towards him.

The face of the man in front of him fell, almost distorted by the look of grief that contorted his features. 'Our Orabella, she married without the families consent,' he said slowly, heavily. 'It was said that the marriage would not be blessed, but none of us thought that she would end up ...' he stopped, dragging his face across his hands.

Dante reached forward and touched the man's shoulder lightly, their grief connecting them together. 'I'm sorry Uncle, I did not do enough, I should have done more.'

Orabella's uncle shook his head slowly. 'No one could do anything, no one could tell her anything, and she would not listen.'

'I'm starting to think she did not have a choice Uncle,' Dante stared at the papers in front of him, and frowning he handed them to Hienry. He watched as Crescenzo Mancini walked away from them to stare out of the window, his thoughts with his dead niece. Dante sighed. The day he and Orabella had met for the first time, she had brought him to her uncle's restaurant, and Uncle Cenzo had welcomed him with open arms, stating that anyone who had a variation of an Italian name was ten times more welcome than anyone else in his restaurant.

Crescenzo Mancini's restaurant was a small, cosy family affair. The tables were booths upholstered in checkered picnic cloth, the red and white combined with the wide bay windows gave people the feeling that they had just headed outdoors to have a picnic. His love for food was translated in the wideness of his girth and the redness of his cheeks that came from being in the kitchen all day long. There was always a welcoming table for Dante at the restaurant and when Orabella had closed the Hunter deal there had been no question of him ever paying for a meal there again. They all looked at the papers in silence. There were pictures of Orabella's husband, although none of them showed the two of them together. He was English, of which they had all thought was a strange choice as they had known Orabella's character. Uncle Cenzo could not understand what had happened, even in her will all her personal effects had gone to him; with Orabella it was always family before anything else.

Dante picked up the marriage certificate. Mr Edward Ward had been a 34 year old English teacher from Devonshire, and he had married Orabella in Italy three months ago. The only publication of their wedding had been a notice in the newspaper. 'Did you ever see him?'

Uncle Cenzo walked back to the table, staring at the picture and shaking his head. 'She stopped speaking to us, even the wedding we heard about over email and then in the newspaper. They got married in Italy? When? I told the family! We tried to speak to her, tried to talk her out of it, but she would not take our calls; can you imagine we went to the house and were turned away by those ugly dogs!' Uncle Cenzo looked away, disgusted. 'This is the first I have ever seen of this Edward.'

Dante looked at the pictures again. Edward had been a tall, thin man, his brown hair thick and wavy, his complexion as grey as the sky behind him. The background of the picture was reminiscent of the English countryside; and taken against the backdrop of a wooden cottage, the green and rustic background was in direct contrast with the rumpled suit he was wearing, the wry smile on his face conveying more sarcasm for his surroundings than anything else. Orabella would never marry such a drab man.

'Exactly what I was thinking,' Uncle Cenzo huffed, reading Dante's expression. 'That man was like wallpaper to our Orabella.'

'And this man is dead now?' Dante directed his question to Hienry.

Hienry nodded. 'He was almost never here, they had gone straight on their honeymoon and then after that they were supposed to pack up his life in London and he was supposed to move here.'

'What a long honeymoon it was too,' Dante said quietly.

Hienry nodded.

'Where was he at the time of Orabella's death?'

'Apparently in England.'

'But they were on their honeymoon together for the past three months, no?' Uncle Cenzo looked at them in bewilderment.

'That was only on paper Uncle,' Dante grimaced.

'He died two days before Orabella did,' Hienry said quietly as he refilled his cup from the whisky bottle that was reclining on the red and white checkered table in front of him. 'He was killed in a car accident in South London, nothing was left of the occupants of either cars but their teeth. Damn accident held up the traffic up for hours.'

Uncle Cenzo raised his hands to his head, shaking it like he was in pain. 'What happened to my poor niece?'

'That's what we're trying to find out Uncle,' Dante walked towards him, stopping short of the window.

'She would never have done that to you,' Uncle Cenzo said quietly, still gazing out of the window. 'She loved you, you were family. She would never have hurt her family.'

'I know Uncle. This was nothing like her at all. I think she was in trouble a long time ago.'

Hienry nodded in acquiescence, the glass bobbing up and down in his hand.

'So we're back to square one,' Dante muttered.

'And you my son,' Uncle Cenzo turned to him, the look in his eyes so painful that Dante turned away in embarrassment. 'Your life has been ruined by false accusations, I have nothing to offer you but my support and more free meals for the rest of your life.'

Dante laughed heartily, the sound coming from deep inside his chest. 'I'm not destitute yet uncle, but the free meal I'll take any time of any day!' he sobered up. Your niece's murderer will not go unpunished.'

A faint smile creased Crescenzo Mancini's face. 'My wife and I, we would like that very much.'

CHAPTER 35

Farusja opened her eyes. The first thing she realised was that she could see. The light was on. Her breath expelled itself from her body in a gushing sigh of relief that she had not been killed by Michael and his invisible partner yet. Her mind was surprisingly clear and despite the constant hits on the head by Michael, her headache was not as bad as it had been previously. She tensed and could feel the bile and panic settling in her throat as her moving produced a rattle of chains and the scratch of the plastered concrete on her bare skin.

Farusja quenched the scream that rose in her throat as she realised she was naked and covered with a small brown cloth that smelled as though it had doubled as a dog blanket. She was lying on her side on the floor, her arms and legs behind her back. There were thick metal chains running from cuffs around both of her wrists, and twisting her head to the side she could see the small metal hoop through which the two independent chains ran through to attach themselves to her feet, which were also encircled with metal cuffs. Her arms were laid out behind her, and she could see that from the length of the chain it would be impossible to have any freedom of movement. Farusja cried out in anger, the pain leaving her body in sound. It was just one humiliation after another, she did not feel like she had been violated in any way but she just was not sure anymore; if Michael had been undressing her, his greasy hands would have been all over her body.

Angry tears came splashing down her cheeks, how did she allow herself to get into this mess? How had it gone so far? How could she be so trusting, so naïve? She let the tears fall as the pain started to creep in, she could now feel the soreness of her arms and legs as they were forced to lie in the same position hour after hour. Farusja did not want to get up. Her clothes had been taken and from her vantage point on the floor she could see no sign of her jeans or shirt; she was afraid that if she tried to move the small cloth covering her, the last of her dignity, would fall away.

She clenched her teeth, grinding them against each other; they had left the light on and she was sure it was so that she could see what was happening to her, so that she could see when they came, what they would do … she closed her eyes. She'd be damned if she'd give them the satisfaction. Making a decision, trembling at the sudden courage that gave her strength, she forced her hands flat against the floor as she raised herself to a half-sitting, half-reclining position, watching as the little brown cloth fell off her body to reveal her nakedness. The chains were heavy, and as she raised herself up she could feel them dragging themselves taut. She realised that the chains were shorter than she had thought and as soon as she tried to pull her hands any higher than her shoulders, they tightened and pulled her feet closer forcing her to sit with her front constantly curved to ease the tension in her arms and legs. Farusja lowered herself back onto the floor as the aching in her arms and legs gave way to tightening pain, her teeth clenched in anger. She knew what she had to do. She had been scared and fear had got her to this point, but she was going to die if she did not do something about it. She gave a small gasp as the light suddenly went out, washing her in darkness. Clenching her jaw resolutely, she lowered her head to the floor, and without blinking closed her eyes against the darkness. Even better, she thought, she would work faster in the dark.

Rabecca stared at the man in front of her; she was now in a panic. She had arrived from the coast back to Windhoek to find her house locked, with all Farusja's belongings in sight, her handbag still on the table as if she had just stepped outside to pick something up and was coming back; but there was no Farusja in sight. She had tried calling her numerous times and her phone kept going straight to voicemail. What had really set her in a panic was the fact that Dante Dumeno had called her and had asked where Farusja was. First of all, Dante Dumeno had never called her, and if he of all people did not have the resources to find her, then Farusja was in deep trouble; then he had shown her the video.

She was staring at him now; despite everything that was going on she was quite shocked to see him in such a comfortable setting. She had never seen him in shorts and a t-shirt before. He had nice legs, she could see why Farusja was attracted to him, she could clearly see what else Farusja was attracted to as well. Rabecca coughed, dragging her eyes back to his face. She had perched herself on the edge of a brown couch in his house, clutching her handbag tightly. 'So you have not seen her since the hospital?'

Dante shook his head. 'It looks like her abductor might have been Sidney, because the moment she got into that car she vanished.'

'And Sidney is dead, and Mrs Ricci is dead, and HD and DI are going up in smoke, and you're a gun smuggler,' Rabecca shook her head, her eyes wide open in wonder. 'What is going on Mr Dumeno? I went away because of all of this, I thought it would get better, but it's become worse, and now my best friend is missing!'

Dante sighed, scratching his head vigorously. 'Whatever you think of me, that's your opinion. But my priority right now is to find your friend.'

'My friend?' Rabecca shook her head, her anger visible. 'You were the one who was chasing her and stringing her around, now you act like she's a non-entity? You have some nerve Mr Dumeno! If she had never got involved with you this would never have happened to her! You cannot be stupid enough to think that her disappearance is not connected to the two murdered girls at DI? And Orabella Ricci?' Rabecca's chest heaved, her eyes shining with tears. 'You need to find her.'

'I'm trying Rabecca,' Dante said softly. 'I'm doing everything I can to find her. I do care about her, more than you know.'

Roberta knew that something else was going on. Hienry and Dante still thought they could hide things away from her, but she had spent her whole life working on some form of deceit or the other so she was not new to this game. She had just seen one of her employees, Rabecca, leave the house, and despite asking Dante what was going on he just shrugged off her concerns and headed to his study. She cornered Hienry as he entered the house, placing one hand on his shoulder, and pushing him against the corridor wall.

'You need to tell me what is going on,' she stabbed his other shoulder with her free hand, punctuating each word.

'I don't know what you're talking about Roberta,' Hienry started moving away from her.

'What are you doing to get us out of this mess? Wait a minute. It has to do with that girl doesn't it?' Roberta snorted, letting go of Hienry completely.

'I don't know what you're on about Roberta,' Hienry sighed, 'and I'd suggest you take care of your own life before you start with Dumeno's. Aren't you even interested in asking me to do something for HD?'

Roberta shrugged noncommittally. 'I still have some pretty good overseas clients who are immune to scandal, thanks to that useless father of mine. I'm not too worried about the fall out. But I think it might be time to move to a new country, Namibia is too small and this market can be very unforgiving. Stop changing the subject! I'm not letting you go until you tell me what is going on.'

Hienry sighed, watching the sharp nails stabbing at his shoulder again. 'I have to go somewhere with Dante, and you are holding us up.'

'This is despite the fact that Dante is supposed to be under house arrest?'

'What's going on?'

Hienry and Roberta both looked up to see Jerome, who had shown up in the foyer.

'What are you two up to? Don't try to disappear without me again bra.'

Hienry sighed. 'You two are both getting in the way, its time you both left it's not safe anymore.'

'I'm not leaving my brother.'

'I'm not leaving Dante, you bulldog,' Roberta hissed. 'Now tell us what's going on!'

Hienry sighed in frustration, staring at the two angry faces in front of him. 'Farusja Mumba is missing.'

Roberta pursued her lips. 'So that's what Dante is risking his life for?'

'Oh man, the pretty lady,' Jerome shook his head. 'No way! Why haven't you found her yet? I hope she's not in trouble?'

'That's who Dante is risking his life for Roberta,' Hienry shrugged her hands off him, smoothing out his shirt. 'Make peace with it. You might have been with him for most of his life, but Dumeno is in love with this woman. And you know it. Let him go.'

Roberta dropped her hands to her side, staring at Hienry.

Jerome stared from Roberta to Hienry. 'Sorry Aunt Roberta, I thought you knew by now.'

'Having some alone time?'

They all turned to see Dante standing in the corridor, ready to go out, a jacket held loosely in his hands.

'And where do you think you are going?' Roberta turned to him, hands on her hips. 'You know what trouble you two will get into?'

Dante shrugged, smiling at her. 'Keeps the blood pumping Robbie.'

'That girl is going to bring you nothing but trouble Dante, I told you!' Roberta hissed at him. Dante glanced from Jerome to Hienry, who threw up his hands in frustration.

'This woman is just like what she calls me, a bulldog. How can you expect me to keep anything away from her? How can you expect me to keep anything from the both of them?'

'Don't go out there Dante,' Roberta pleaded with him. 'The police will catch you, and whatever that girl is mixed up in, you will get caught up in that too.'

Dante stood staring at her, his hands loosely by his sides. 'I'm sorry for everything Robbie,' he said quietly. 'I wish I could have been the person you wanted me to be, but I'm not.' Dante moved forward, and took her hands in his. 'You know I have been by your side forever, and I'll continue to be by your side, but I'll never be that man; your man.'

Roberta stared up at the man she had loved for so long, tears springing into her eyes. She had finally got to the point she had always wanted to get to with Dante, but it was not going to play out the way she wanted it to. She could not imagine what Farusja Mumba had done in such a short time to get Dante to love her with such unconditional desperation; she had been trying for years, and she had failed. 'You're such a fool,' she whispered, tears starting their track down her cheeks. 'You are the biggest fool I've never known. You're going to be ruined and you're chasing a girl simply because of some stupid emotion?' Roberta sobbed, knowing her loss.

Dante smiled, wrapping his arms around her, hugging her tightly, he whispered in her ear breathing into the hair that tickled his nose. 'I love you Robbie, I always will. But I'm in love with Farusja, and I need to find her.'

'I'm coming with you bra,' Jerome said seriously. 'I like her too.'

'This is where I say no,' Hienry shook his head at the beginning of Jerome's protestations. 'Stay here and take care of Roberta, we have given you more than enough rope. Now it's time to listen,'

Dante nodded. 'Take care of your aunt.'

'But bra, she'll drive me crazy,' Jerome complained, annoyed. 'She's crazy!' He rubbed his shoulder where Roberta hit him.

Dante looked back as he and Hienry left the house, watching Jerome and Roberta scuffle in the foyer. It was a great sight in these troubled times.

CHAPTER 36

Sunday, 20 May

*E*x Detective Miles Mkazi smiled to himself. He had been a busy man. Despite his suspension, Philip had been giving him daily updates on the status of the case, and he had just been telling him about how an employee at HD Advertising, Sidney Kimani had died. She had not been strangled as the other girls had, but had met with an explosive accident in her car.

'Now the interesting thing is I found some rather exciting stuff in Sidney's house, on her calendar to be precise.'

'Calendar?'

'Yes, and you would think she would want to be a little discreet about it,' Philip had chuckled almost gleefully. 'There were red marks every Saturday on her calendar for the past month and written in tiny letters were the initials MK and DI.'

Miles grimaced. 'Well, we all know that DI stands for DI Storage, but MK could mean anything. Those were probably just her appointed Saturdays to head to her storage space. Remember most of the HD employees have storage spaces at DI for discounted rates.' Miles could hear his deputy rustling papers in front of him, what he had now come to recognise as the beginning of Phillips excitement.

'So I checked the sign-in sheets for Sidney on those dates. She was nowhere near DI, nowhere near her storage space which was empty anyway. So that left me with the question of what does MK stand for?'

'That is quite a stretch Philip, and what has this got to do with Dumeno and the guns or the girls' deaths?' Miles could hear Phillips now excited exhalations coming down the line at him, and goosebumps ran across his arms in anticipation.

'Well, you see sir,' Philip paused. 'I for one thought it would be ridiculous to try to find all her acquaintances with those initials, it is just not feasible. So I decided to cross-check the initials against all the people working at DI and HD.'

'And?'

'And I found seven names, of which only two signed in at DI on those specific dates.'

Miles sat up in his armchair, he could feel the excitement his deputy felt flowing through the line. 'And?'

This time Philip chuckled gleefully. 'And I checked the rest of her calendar, it goes back a month earlier.'

'Two people?'

'Even better, on some days three, but always the one name kept on showing up. He was there every day without fail: Michael Katjihingua. I saw the tapes, the footage is grainy but I think we have got our man.'

'What makes you so sure it is him?'

'He was the only one I spied on the surveillance tapes carrying black canvas bags into the park.'

'Did you talk to the security at the gates and the ones patrolling?'

'They claim he had nothing in the bags, except the menial household items people store there; I checked his storage facility it's just bits of kitchen equipment.'

Miles swore explosively, his anger barely contained. 'How often did they check?'

'The first three days without fail, I checked the tapes, and then they became careless because he always had the same type of things, so they just waved him through.'

Miles had almost thrown the phone against the wall in his anger. 'What of the surveillance cameras?'

'All blind. He knew where they were and he avoided them like the plague, turned his face away and everything,' Philip mused, 'he could have carried a nuclear warhead in there and no one would have been any wiser. The fact that they did not even bother checking his car boot after a while means he could easily have had Orabella in the back.'

Miles had clenched the phone in his hand angrily. 'So he could have been the one, all this time?'

'If not sir,' Philip said quietly, 'he knows something. But my bet is he's in this shit all the way up to his elbows.'

Minutes later, Miles sat at his computer and scrolled through the information that Philip had sent him on Michael Katjihingua. There was no blot on his record, no parking tickets, no drunk and driving charges, and no speeding fine, nothing. Miles was under the suspicion that this clean record was the result of his rich parents expunging it. There was nothing truly exceptional about Michael besides his riches; he was the perfect candidate for going unnoticed.

Miles scrawled Michael's address on a piece of paper, his jaw set in determination, and headed to the door in a hurry, dialling his deputy on his mobile phone as he went towards the back door to avoid the lingering reporters that still found him worth a few columns in their newspapers.

Michael's character also made him the perfect candidate for murder.

Farusja awoke slowly, something had woken her up. After the lights had suddenly gone off hours and hours ago, she had sat quietly waiting for them to come and get her. She had kept her eyes open for as long as she could and had finally ended up falling into a deep and dreamless sleep. Her headache was gone; her mind was so clear that she suspected that she had been given something in that last meal to slow her down. She dragged herself in the darkness into the only position her chains allowed, kneeling with her hands behind her back. She closed her eyes, relaxing her body, focusing on the plan formulating itself in her head. Startled, her eyes flew open again as she heard a sound in the darkness, the tinkling of chains against each other.

'Who's there?' she said sharply. 'If that's you Michael, you're not going to get away with this. I'll kill you with my own bare hands, you bloody bastard!'

She learned that holding onto her anger of what Michael had dared to do to her, gave her more strength than anything else and she had festered it until it had become a hard lump inside her chest, the lump fighting to get out with violence. She went rigid as she heard a slight moan and more chain rustling. Suddenly she realised that someone else had been taken, and the relief of finally having someone else to see and talk to was overwhelmed by her pity for the new abductee and what they were about to go through together.

'Who's there?' she said quietly. 'Please, we don't have much time. Who's there?'

Dante could feel every muscle in his body scream at him in pain. He had woken up because he had heard something; someone had been talking to him. He struggled to open his eyes and discovered that he could not move and was surrounded in darkness. What had happened? And he was cold, he could feel his bare skin scratching against a rough surface; even through the fog in his brain he realised that something had gone horribly wrong.

He peered groggily into the darkness around him trying to gauge his surroundings. What had happened? He and Hienry had been at Uncle Cenzo's restaurant again. He had remembered him and Hienry leaving the restaurant using the back door, Dante disguised just in case anyone recognised him. The rest had been a blur. He remembered hearing somebody shouting, but it had been a vague, rushed haze of trying to get into the car, of Hienry pushing him to hurry up and run; he had heard more running footsteps, someone had been after them, then darkness had swallowed him and now this. The last thing he remembered was Hienry falling; and now he had woken up here.

231

Dante grimaced, opening his eyes to their fullest extent as he moved slightly, testing his capabilities. He could feel his arms stretched behind him and the metal cuffs around them; his legs were pulled up to below his backside with the same metal cuffs encircling them. The more he moved them, the more he realised that there was a form of hook or loop they were attached to at his back that prevented him from standing up or from being in any other position than on his knees with his arms behind him, or lying on the floor on his side, which was what he had been doing now. He refused to do the former.

Dante froze as he heard a mirror of his movements in the dark, and his blood ran cold as he heard Farusja's voice call out to him tentatively.

'Who's there? Please, we don't have much time. Who's there?'

Dante, stunned, could only stare in the darkness numbly as he listened to her voice. He had found her, but he had found her in the worst possible way. All this time he had wanted to protect her, he had wanted her to be safe and so he had pushed her away, thinking that she would not be a target, but he had failed. Dante closed his eyes, thankful for the darkness. He did not want her to know that her potential rescuer was now going to be her death; he did not want her to know that it was him next to her in the darkness, just as helpless as she was. He had no illusions about where they were or what would happen to them.

'Hello? Who are you? Are you okay?' Farusja asked again, and this time Dante could hear the slight edge to her voice. He closed his eyes, hating himself for his weakness, keeping himself still to prevent her from hearing any noise from him. He grimaced as he heard her chains rattle as she moved, the joy he had of knowing that she was still alive was diminished by the pain of failure he felt at not protecting the woman he loved. He had admitted it to himself as he had watched that last grainy video of her being taken away by Sidney's car in the knowledge that he might never see her again.

'Please.'

Dante clenched his teeth as the rattling of the chains stopped and Farusja pleaded with him, her ghost in the darkness. 'We have no time left!'

He kept his eyes closed in shame. He was doing a foolish, stupid thing, but he could not let her see … He froze as he felt light wash the room, the knowledge more physical than mental as his body responded.

'Dante?'

He opened his eyes and allowed them to adjust to the light slowly. The room had no windows, just a door and a bucket. It was cold. From his vantage point on the ground he could see her knees. Dante, leaning on his elbow, pushed himself onto its knees; he had been right about the chains; they were attached to a hoop behind him, and any attempt at straightening his arms led to the chain attached to his legs being pulled taut. He finally raised his eyes to hers.

Farusja stared at him in shocked silence, unable to understand what she was seeing in front of her. He looked terrible, his eyes had shadows under them and she could see the fine stubble that dotted his cheeks and chin. There was still a bandage wrapped around his thigh where he had been shot. He was across the room from her, closest to the door. An incredible two paces away. He had been taken. Tears ran down her cheeks unchecked. She had so much unfinished business with him and she had wanted one more chance to be with him, even when he had treated her like shit, and she had been given that chance; here he was, dragged into the same dirty pit to die with her.

Farusja bowed her head, sobbing freely, her tears running down her cheeks and splashing onto the concrete floor.

'You bastard,' she sobbed, hiccuping and choking on her own tears. 'How could you let yourself? First you use me and then you dump me and then you come here to rub it in my face. You bastard.'

Dante looked at her, unable to say anything. She was a mess, the smell of the room was testament to it; her hair was all tangled up and in various positions around her head, she had bruises on her face, and around her eyes. He could see some faint ones beginning to darken on her body. Despite the dark circles under her eyes and the white cracked landscape that used to be her lips, her luminous eyes stared at him, glaringly bright and changing with the light. Her arms were pulled back behind her just as his were, and he could see the strain beginning to show. Anger stirred up inside him, whoever had done this would pay dearly. He opened his mouth and shut it again. Unable to look her in the eyes, unable to speak.

Farusja sniffed loudly, raising her head to the ceiling to stem the tears still flowing down her cheeks. 'You have some nerve Dumeno,' she said her voice louder and firmer. 'Showing up when you're not needed.'

Dante raised his eyes to her, finally finding his voice. 'And you have some nerve waiting around for people to put everything aside to come and look for you.'

'Who did this to you?' he growled, his eyes dragging across her naked body.

Farusja, stared back at him grimly. 'You got caught. How could you get caught? With all that talk about your fancy security and that Hienry, how?'

'Farusja,' Dante's voice was thick. 'There is something I need to tell you.'

'I don't care for your words Dumeno.'

'When I phoned you the other day, how I treated you in hospital, I was just trying to protect you. I thought they would leave you alone if you were no longer a person of interest to me. I was wrong. As inadequate as it is, I'm sorry.'

Farusja looked at him, avoiding what she could see in his eyes, trying to prevent her face from crumbling again into a million tears. In those few words so much had been said.

233

'Who did this to you?'

Farusja cleared her throat. 'You mean us? You're freaking employee Michael Katjihingua. And someone else,' she shivered. 'The one in charge. I don't know who he is, but he's the one in charge.'

Dante stuttered at her. 'Michael, the druggie?'

'He's not what you think he is Dante,' her voice went low as she recalled all those nights alone with Michael. 'He's a monster. He likes to see things destroyed, he likes to see suffering.' Farusja shivered, a muscle twitching in Dante's temple as he watched her. 'He enjoys pain.'

'He gave you those bruises?' Dante growled his anger barely contained.

Farusja's eyes clouded over. 'Let's not talk about it.'

'Did he touch you?' Dante asked harshly, the twitch in his temple more pronounced.

'We have to escape, that has nothing to do with ...'

'Did he touch you?' Dante growled, his eyes glowering.

'Yes he did,' Farusja stared at him. The expression in his eyes was dark, unreadable. 'I fought him for so long. He came in my sleep.' She spoke quietly, holding Dante's gaze. She watched his expression become thunderous. 'He violated me, but he was never inside me.' Farusja watched his whole demeanour almost sag in relief. 'I think he was planning to do that now.'

'Not while I'm here,' Dante growled venomously.

Farusja smiled slightly at him, her chains rattling behind her back. 'Well, that just makes a girl's day Dumeno.'

'Dante,' he said quietly, his voice low, his eyes staring at her. 'Call me Dante.'

Farusja rattled her chains some more, trying to keep her eyes on his shoulders, her body flushing warm.

Dante watched her closely, his eyes hooded under the weight of thinking how to escape. 'Are you okay?'

'Do I look okay?' she snorted at him, moving to try to find a comfortable way to sit, her knees aching.

'I missed seeing you naked.'

Startled Farusja glanced at him, and down the length of his whole body. Despite herself she felt a sharp twinge of pleasure slide between her legs. That time at the lodge, she had never felt him so, magnificent. Farusja cleared her throat, a grin curving her mouth as embarrassment crept up body in a hot flush.

Dante kept his eyes on her, his voice lazy. 'All those foolish games in the beginning, when we could have spent so many amazing times together.'

Farusja snorted, moving around to not have to look at him. 'Nice talk.'

'A lot has changed Farusja,' Dante said quietly, his demeanour serious. 'You know that just as much as I do. We don't have the luxury to ignore what's happening.'

Farusja stiffened, his words a verbal assault. 'You're a right bastard Dante,' she said quietly, her body crumpling gracelessly as she sat down on her heels, tired. 'You have some nerve to say that to me here. I've suffered a whole lot more for way longer than you have.'

'Farusja.'

'Just shut up and work out how to get us out of here,' she descended into silence, her eyes on the ground in front of her and the chains behind her rattling occasionally.

Dante watched her for a few moments, kicking himself inwardly. She was right, he was an insensitive bastard. He sighed and looked around the room. The room had been swept clean; there was nothing that they could have used as a weapon or that would have helped to get out of the room. He pulled at his chains again, hard, the hooks did not budge. 'How long ago where these hooks put in?'

Farusja pursed her lips at him. 'I was hit on the head and the next thing I know I wake up to this, overnight I guess.'

'Quick drying cement,' Dante murmured as he tugged at his hands again, the movements futile.

'There's a lock, a padlock on the metal rings surrounding our wrists,' Farusja said slowly, sweat breaking out over her face as it scrunched up in pain. 'That means we're going to be let go or at least unchained at some point.'

Dante nodded, looking at her in concern. 'Are you in pain?'

'Not anymore,' Farusja grunted, her whole chest heaving with the effort. She slowly straightened out her right arm, her wrist raw and bloody where she had scraped it against the metal in order to force it out. She sighed as she flexed her arm, wanting to get some feeling back into it. She had started last night; there had been no other way out of the chains. She was sure she had dislocated at least one finger but she had needed to fight. She rested it on her knee in front of her lightly, ignoring the raw and bleeding mess that had become her wrist.

'Full of surprises,' Dante watched her intently, trying not to look at her damaged wrist. 'Let's see the other hand.'

Farusja grunted, putting her right arm behind her again. 'You always have someone do all the work for you, don't you Dante?'

They both froze as they heard the door scrape open, admitting a very fresh looking Michael. Farusja frowned as she watched him step jauntily into the room. He was wearing a pair of black overalls, very old black overalls; a set of two small silver keys hung from a silver chain around his neck. She glanced at Dante, knowing that those were the keys to their chains. Dante smiled at her slightly, his eyes telling her in no uncertain terms that if she did not get the other hand out of those chains they were going to die today.

'Dante Dumeno,' Michael said, closing the door behind him as he sat on his haunches two paces away from both of them, staring at them in glee. 'I thought that by now you would have tried to escape.' He chuckled. 'I guess your reputation only precedes you, out of your comfort zone you're as useless as the rest of us.'

'You son of a bitch,' Dante said quietly. 'What did we ever do to you except give you what you wanted?'

Michael smiled, his eyes bright, too bright. 'You did nothing to me, except be an arrogant, self-centred bastard,' he spat out, spittle flying across the floor, his face contorting into an ugly mask. 'I hate people like you, and that bloody Roberta. And you.'

Michael turned his eyes on Farusja, who cringed, unable to tear her eyes away from his. This was the Michael that had visited her every night, and every night she had thought would be her last. 'You refused me, we were meant to be together. You saw that until he came and took you away.' Michael's face, still contorted in anger turned on Dante. 'She would have been with me if it weren't for you!'

Farusja looked away as she felt Dante's eyes on her, her skin flushing warm despite herself.

'And for that you kidnap and torture us? Let us go, Michael,' Dante's voice was quiet, low. 'I'll make sure you get a fair trial.'

Michael laughed, the sound ugly in the small room. 'Like you got a fair trial? With your troop of paid judges and crooked lawyers? Oh, we know, Dumeno. We know!'

'We?'

Michael laughed again, beginning to rock his body slightly. 'You're both such pawns you have no idea, yes we,' he gave Dante a mocking glance. 'You're ruined Dumeno. You will never walk these streets again with the same clout and conceit that you carried around with you all these years.'

'Who is we, Michael?' Dante asked again.

Michael moved fast, so fast that Farusja could only see the blur of his hand as it struck the side of Dante's face.

'Shut up!' he hissed, perspiration beading his face. 'Shut up! You're nothing here, I'm in charge!' He sat back on his haunches, rocking his body slowly, staring at Dante angrily, his eyebrows drawn together.

Farusja shivered, she did not want to see Michael pushed to his limit, and as she watched the expression on Dante's face remained neutral as blood trickled from a cut on his lip. She knew that that was exactly what he planned to do.

Michael laughed suddenly, his body still rocking. 'You have no idea, you both have no idea!' He half-crawled, half-shuffled to Farusja's side, his body right up against hers.

'Get away from her.'

'And what are you going to do exactly?' Michael sniggered. 'How the mighty have fallen. You can't even move!'

'I'll kill you if you lay another hand on her Michael,' Dante growled, his every muscle straining against the chains. Farusja felt Michael's hot breath against her cheek, cringing as his lips grazed it, their hot and hungry wetness an affront to the core of her being.

He laughed again, the sound sending chills down her spine. 'Do you know what your favourite toy and I got up to Dumeno? All this time,' Michael, still kneeling on his haunches, brought up his hand to touch the skin of her stomach, trailing it up and down slowly. 'We had so much fun, didn't we Farusja?'

Farusja kept her eyes on Dante, drawing strength from the thunderous expression on his face.

'Yes, all night I played with your toy,' Michael chuckled lustfully, his hand moving up and cupping her breast.

Dante, growling, lunged at him, the chains pulling him back sharply.

'Michael I'll kill you!' he spat out, enraged.

'I undressed her too last night you know,' Michael continued gleefully, beads of sweat now dotting his forehead. 'You're so warm and so soft,' he whispered at her, licking the side of her face.

Farusja kept still, her eyes on Dante. She did not want Michael to see what she had been up to. The less worked up he became, the better their chances were as long as he was near her.

Michael, disappointment showing on his face at her lack of reaction, smiled widely as he produced a key from his pocket. 'You will have to watch us consummate our relationship Dumeno, right here on the floor in front of you. I've been waiting for this day a long time.'

Farusja did not have to think twice about the look that Dante sent her. She knew now would be the perfect moment, but without her left hand free she would be severely handicapped and they would both be right back where they started. She shook her head slightly, pretending as if she was trying to get away from Michael, ignoring the incredulous look Dante gave her.

Michael had not noticed and instead rubbed his face against hers. 'We have all the time in the world Farusja,' he murmured. 'I wanted to keep you but he said I should kill you. What do you think?'

Michael's sentence finished in a scream as Farusja aimed for his eyes, the fingertips of both her hands digging deep into the soft tissue of his eyeballs mercilessly. With the chains now only on her feet she swiftly got up, shaking unsteadily on long unused feet, ignoring Michael who was writhing on the floor in front of her in agony as she yanked the chain and keys off from around his neck, hobbling across the room as the chains drew themselves through the hoop they had been threaded through, freeing herself.

'Come on,' Dante urged her as she fumbled with the padlock that was fastened on his chains, exhaling a sigh of relief as it gave way in her hands. Dante, shaking the cuffs off his wrists stood up swiftly, and mimicking Farusja's movements a minute ago he pulled the chains that were still attached to his feet through the hoop.

Michael's cries became louder, giving way to big sobs. 'My eyes, I can't see!'

Despite the chains on his feet, Dante strode over to Michael and with one well aimed kick, elicited another scream from him.

'I told you I'd kill you,' he growled, proceeding to kick the length of Michael's body. 'I. Told. You. I. Would. Kill. You.'

He punctuated each word with a kick, raising his leg and stamping down on Michael's arm repeatedly, feeling satisfaction as he heard the bone crack and renewed screams coming from him.

'Dante,' Farusja hobbled over to him. 'Dante!' She grasped his arm, shaking him. 'That's enough! We need to leave, now!'

Dante shrugged her arm off, giving Michael another kick. Farusja froze, loosening her grasp on Dante, goosebumps racing all over her body as she felt a presence behind her. It was the same feeling she had felt that night; the night she had woken up with someone in the room with her, the one she now called the main murderer. She turned slowly, her eyes widening in disbelief, her hands flying to her mouth in shock. She had seen this man on several different occasions around the hospital, around HD Advertising; and always with Dante.

Dante felt her stiffen up beside him, and pausing in his beating of Michael, looked up at Naks briefly, his face breaking into a smile. 'Naks is Hienry behind you? It's about time you both arrived. I had started to think the tracker we implanted in me had stopped working!'

Farusja collapsed to her knees, her head shaking itself from side to side, as if trying to deny the truth that stood in front of her. 'No Dante,' she gasped, fear shaking her body. 'He's not ... it's *him*.'

Dante looked at her puzzled, kneeling down next to her to put his arms around her. 'It's okay now, we can get out of here.'

'No!' Farusja cried. 'It's not, we're not, it's him!'

Dante looked from Naks to Farusja, bewildered. Naks was standing at the door, one foot halfway into the room; his glasses covering his eyes.

'Unfortunately she's right man,' he said mockingly. 'I didn't think you would make a mess of that fool over there like that, but you're always full of surprises aren't you, Farusja Mumba?' He moved into the room, his gait slow. 'I've been looking forward to taking these off.'

He reached up his right hand, taking off his sunglasses and throwing them to the corner of the room farthest to him. An ugly scar rippled its way across one eye, and where the eye was supposed to be a gaping hole peered back at them, loose folds of skin lay as if hung across the hole.

Farusja recoiled involuntary, her arms crossing themselves over her breasts. She could not prove it, but she knew that this was the other person that had been with her when Michael was not.

Dante stared at his friend, unable to speak, his mind unable to accept what was happening. Naks, the man who had given him a chance at a new life, albeit an illegal one, and who he had spent the last twenty years of his life calling his best friend; standing in his place was a kidnapper and a murderer. His mind refused to put the two together, and instead ripples of panicked unease ran through him. He was seeing the part of Naks who he had decided to ignore, the one who had beaten people up because they renegaded on a drug payment, the one who had knowledge of how to get into a place unobserved and how to deal with unwanted visitors without the help of any law enforcement authority. This is the Naks he was seeing now. The gaping hole where his eye had been made him look more sinister. Dante wondered when this had happened, and how he and Roberta had failed to notice. Why neither of them had ever insisted that Naks take his sunglasses off indoors. The smile on his best friends face was a slash across his mouth, an affront to the laughter they had shared over the years.

Dante stood up, pushing Farusja back on the floor as she tried to stand with him. 'Naks? What's going on? What happened to your eye?'

Naks ignored him, looking around him at Michael who was now mewling on the floor in pain, blood covering his hands that were still held up against his face. 'Michael, the most useless one of them all,' he murmured.

Michael, hearing his voice, cried out to him, starting a blind crawl across the floor towards Nak's voice, one hand still covering his bloodied eyeballs as the other one tested the ground in front of him. 'I'm sorry, I'm sorry. I cannot see. She did it, that bitch did it!'

'Then you're of no more use to me.'

Dante felt the air change inches away from his legs, heard Farusja scream as a small red hole blossomed in the middle of Michael's forehead, a thin trickle of blood running down the centre of the hole to his ruined and bloody eyes. Dante turned back to Naks, seeing the gun in his hand. Dante stared at him in shock, unable to comprehend what he was seeing. 'What have you done with Hienry?'

'Yes Dante!' Naks snarled, a mocking sneer on his face, pointing the gun at Dante, his hands shaking. 'It was me, it was all me! You took something away from me, and I'm going to take everything away from you!'

Dante spread out his hands sideways away from his body, shaking his head in disbelief at the betrayal he was witnessing.

'I don't know what you're talking about,' he rasped, his voice raw with emotion. 'I haven't done anything, you're the one who took me in, you're the one who started me off. I owe you everything!'

Naks laughed, the sound cold in the small room. 'Always shying away from your responsibilities,' he smirked, moving into the room to stand a few paces in front of them, the gun pointed at Dante's chest. 'Do you remember? Do you remember? Do you remember!' Naks screamed at him, his one eye rolling around in its socket. 'Do you remember the fire?'

Dante flinched. He had thought he could reason with the man who used to be his friend, but as he watched the fanatical light move and settle in Nak's solitary eye, he knew that it would be futile. He did not want to die today. He lowered his head.

'The fire was not my fault Naks. Things at DI were just starting up,' he sighed heavily. 'Your sister and mother were not supposed to be there that day, there was no way we could anticipate that a client would leave his chemicals in the reception and subsequently knock them over in his hurry to pay the taxi.'

The client was a chemist, and the resulting fire from the mixture of chemicals had ravaged the office building of DI Storage, laying it to waste. At that time Naks sister had been employed as a receptionist, and on that fateful day Naks mother had come to visit her only daughter at the office.

Naks shook the gun at Dante, the smile on his face terrible, his eyes bright. 'I had to kill them.'

Dante looked up. 'What?'

'You fucking bastard. You took her away from me!'

'Who?' Dante asked quietly. 'I did not kill your sister, Naks, or your mother, it was an accident.'

Naks smiled brightly, the slash in his face widening, his one good eye starting to roll around in its socket. 'I loved Lima, I tried to tell her, tried to get her to love me. But she refused. She said we were wrong for each other.'

Dante stared at him horrified. 'She was your sister!'

'I loved her,' Naks sighed, rubbing the gun against his temples. 'I showed her one day, in the house, I showed her. But then mother found out.'

Dante groaned, horrified. He could not believe what he was hearing. 'She was your sister!' he said again, his voice harsh.

'Then she told me she was in love with you,' Naks turned towards Dante. 'You took her from me, she loved you and not me! I had to set her free from you Dante. After you and Roberta abandoned me, left me alone to die with the drugs. You both did not care as long as your profit line was above the fucking red!' Spittle flew from Naks mouth, punctuated with the gun in his hand. 'The women were all drawn to you, Dante fucking Dumeno. You had the looks, the charm. You had the cars, the money, and I had nothing. I was always living in your shadow!'

'We didn't abandon you Naks, you refused to join us. I offered you a partnership. Roberta offered you shares. You're the one who wanted to stay dealing drugs. You're the one who wanted to remain a small time crook,' Dante said angrily. 'What do you mean; you set her free? I told Lima it would never work between us, you were my best friend, I could never date family!'

'Yeah that's right,' Naks whispered. 'She was dirty and rotten inside. Always trying to get you in her bed, she became ugly all because of you. All women become ugly because of you. I had to set her free, to send her to beautiful light. To cleanse her from the greedy and lustful being you had made her become. I gave her peace.'

Dante choked, looking at Naks incredulously. 'You killed Lima?' he whispered in shock.

'I did not kill her, I set her free,' Naks said. 'I set them all free from you. I tried to love them all like I loved Lima, and they refused. Each night I met one of them, they refused. So I let them go. I don't know why they struggled,' Nak's muttered to himself. 'I don't know why they struggled against something so beautiful.'

Farusja sat still, every muscle rigid as she heard the exchange between Dante and Naks. He must have been Dante's best friend. She could see the movie reel running through Dante's head, scrutinising everything he had divulged to his friend and more, and knew just how painful and how knowledgeable the memories were becoming. His enemy had been his best friend all this time. Farusja shivered. Even she did not know how they could get out of this one. She could see Dante trying to stall for time, but she now knew that their time had run out. She did not have to know Naks personally to know that he was extremely unstable, and very dangerous.

'You killed Frieda, Erica, Orabella. The guns. All this?' Dante whispered, almost to himself. 'You couldn't Naks, I know you. You could never.'

'Your girls are free from you don't you understand? I loved playing with them too.'

Naks nodded his head, the empty socket gaping at them. 'I left such a beautiful smile on Frieda's face, did you see it? I don't know why Erica struggled, she knew me. I did everything I could to keep her perfect. I didn't want to beat any of them. I wanted to free all the girls at DI,' he smiled, an almost serene look crossing his face. 'Them being with you was wrong, they would have all become rotten, just like my Lima.'

'Your mother, the fire?' Dante asked, horrified. The look on his face testament to his terror. 'You were the one who did that?'

'And that slut of yours, Orabella. Damn bitch was a tiger, took out my damn eye. I've been doped up on painkillers ever since. Felt good to finally get rid of her.' Naks massaged the edges of the gaping socket with his gun.

'You're crazy,' Farusja whispered, her hands to her mouth.

'Mother was not supposed to find out,' Naks whispered. 'I had to kill her too. If it makes you feel better they were both dead before they were burnt.'

'Strangled,' Farusja whispered, tears running down her face.

Naks grinned at her, the grin macabre and the folds of skin across his torn eye flapped as he moved his head from side to side.

'And Michael?' Dante said quietly, his body rigid. 'What was he doing here?'

'Just dredging up the remains of your rubbish,' he turned to Farusja. 'Just like Sidney, your friend. So desperate, so stupid. Everyone and everything turns to rubbish around you Dumeno.'

Naks took two steps away from them towards the open door, ignoring them as he leaned against it, his eye swivelling between the two of them. 'Not even your bulldog knew what was happening.'

'What have you done to Hienry?' Dante snarled at him. 'I'll kill you myself Naks!'

Naks laughed. 'People die so easily these days. All these years of plotting and planning, and building a reputation to get you off track. Diablo they seem to call me.'

'You were my brother,' Dante almost choked on the words, his shoulders sagging.

'You took Lima from me!' Naks levelled the gun at him. 'I had to marry Orabella to get your attention! I kept her locked in that filthy stinking house for months, writing emails and compiling that report. Stupid woman should have tried harder to escape.'

Dante roared at him, lunging forward, his hands reaching for Naks' neck, stopping himself short as he watched Naks move the gun slowly towards Farusja.

'I don't want to kill her so soon, so just step back to where you were.'

Dante, angry sounds of frustration leaving his mouth, stepped back to stand next to Farusja, his fists clenched at his side. 'You're crazy! You'll pay for this.'

Naks laughed, the maniacal light in his eyes shining brightly. 'I let Michael have a go at her after she took my eye. I was in such pain. You see Michael likes the ladies, but he just does not know when to stop. She was dead by the time I got to her, poor Orabella, and all that barbed wire … did you know Michael was a sadist when you employed him? The drugs just covered all that ugliness up.'

Dante's whole being shuddered, his shoulders drooping visibly. 'What did she ever do to you?'

'She loved you. But not even a snake could hold Roberta, she was my first choice you see but Orabella was easier prey and I was saving Roberta for last.'

'You love Robbie,' Dante said, his voice flat, not believing what he said.

'No one loves Roberta Erlichmann. Not even you,' Naks smirked, his gaze slithering to Farusja. 'All those years I had to listen to her whine about how she was so in love with you, and then jump into bed with me. I will kill her too just to teach her a lesson.'

'The bomb in Becca's car?' Farusja gasped out loud, her eyes widening.

'Yes, all those men were under my command, all of them. The men protecting your house; they planted the bombs around the house and in your car. You actually think that bulldog of yours handpicked those men? I picked them for him.'

'You sick son of a bitch,' Dante hissed. 'You killed them all!'

Naks shrugged, still looking at Farusja. 'Sacrifices need to be made for the greater good. It was necessary.'

Farusja placed her hands on her knees to calm their trembling. 'What about Sidney?'

'That was also a necessary sacrifice, she made so many mistakes. You really should revise your security procedures for DI Storage Dante; it was so easy for Michael to put those guns in the facility. Even moving Orabella's body to the park that morning was so easy. Don't you pay those men enough?'

'You were my brother,' Farusja turned away as she heard the pain in Dante's voice. 'How can you do this to your own brother? We started off together.'

'An eye for an eye my brother. You took what was mine and now I'm still taking all that is yours.' Naks grinned, his teeth bared.

'You killed all these people, just for revenge?' Farusja whispered as her hands clenched themselves into fists against her knees. She stiffened as she felt his eyes on her.

'They all deserved to die,' Naks whispered, staring at her. 'They were all prostitutes, prostituting themselves to the money and the greed that has become my so-called-brother. And I needed to hurt him where he would feel it most. This is your only ticket to freedom Farusja,' his voice went low, beseeching her. 'Once you're stuck to this monster you will have nothing left, and then he will abandon you and leave you truly alone. Be free and be at peace knowing that I saved you from the pain he would put you through. This is your chance. Don't move!' He turned to Dante suddenly, snarling and spitting as he pointed the gun at him again.

Farusja had not even noticed that Dante had taken two steps forward. From her vantage place on the floor she stared at the back of his bare calf muscles; she stretched her arm out and wrapped her hand around his right calf, breathing deeply as she drew strength from the hard muscle twined around his leg.

'My name is Naka Naks Shikongo. I hope your death is as painful as all the pain I have suffered all these years.'

Farusja stiffened, her body beginning to shake as Naks motioned Dante away from them both, gesturing for him to move to the opposite corner of the room. 'I'm tired of talking.'

'No, please,' Farusja cried as she grasped Dante's leg even harder, preventing him from moving.

'Move!' Naks snarled at him, the gun shaking in his hand.

Farusja let the tears fall as she scrabbled forward and wrapped her body around Dante's leg tightly. 'No, no!' She placed her head against his leg, smearing it with tears. She started as she felt his hand on her head, smoothing out her hair gently.

'Listen baby,' Dante reached down, separating her from him. He placed his hands on her shoulders, staring into her face.

Farusja grasped his arms tightly, letting the tears slide down her cheeks as she saw the pain in his eyes. 'Dante, he's going to …'

'Farusja,' Dante whispered, bringing his hand up to smooth her hair. 'Your hair looks terrible. You need a comb, and a bath.' He smiled at her, bringing his hand to her face to wipe the tears away. 'I'm not going far. You're one strong woman Farusja Mumba. Don't let anyone ever tell you otherwise.'

Farusja tried to smile at him, failing as her face crumpled into tears. 'You talk too much,' she whispered back, her arms trailing across his as he pulled himself away from her, her chest heaving with sobs.

'This is between you and me, brother,' Dante said quietly, sarcasm lining the last word as he moved slowly towards the opposite wall. 'Let's settle this the old fashioned way, like we used to.'

Naks laughed, striding forward towards Farusja he grabbed her hair, ignoring her as she clawed at him, screaming, yanking her head back. 'You'll watch me set her free first,' he whispered, his eyes glazed. 'I'll release her from you. You want to be free from this life of greed and lust and Dumeno, don't you Farusja?'

'No, I don't!' Farusja screamed as he yanked her head back again viciously; digging her nails into the skin of his arm, clawing her way down.

Naks did not flinch, but kept his eyes on Dante, keeping the gun trained on him with his right hand. 'I cannot believe they started calling me Diablo. Dante did not even notice when I was gone, that's how much of a brother he is. And it wasn't just the drugs I was dealing in, and it is not only five people that I have killed. I'm ten times richer than both he and Robbie, and they still have no clue who I really am.'

'You evil bastard!' Farusja screamed at him, her hands batting ineffectively at him, tears running down her cheeks as he yanked at her hair even harder. 'You're crazy!'

'Stay where you are!' Naks screamed at Dante, his eye rolling fanatically between the two of them.

'Let her go, it's me you want.'

'I said stay where you are!' Naks voice became shrill, his grip tightening on Farusja's hair. 'I'm really going to enjoy watching the expression on your face when this bitch dies!'

Farusja watched in slow motion as Dante lunged for Naks, his whole body, arms and legs stretching out for him, the look on his face resolute. The scene froze just before the lights went off. Why on earth that had happened at that exact moment she had no idea, but she was left with a nightmare tableau of Dante lunging forward and Naks turning the gun on him, the silent *phut* of a silenced gunshot filling the room.

'Dante!' Farusja screamed in the darkness. She had been knocked to the ground as Dante had come barrelling into Naks, his chest hitting them both so hard that the three of them toppled over, she thought she heard a second gun go off, but she was not sure. The lights were off for a little more than a few seconds before they flooded the room again. Farusja blinked, looking around her frantically, raising herself to her knees. She let out a cry as she saw another man standing in the doorway, surprise and shock registering on his face.

Ex Detective Miles Mkazi stared down at the scene in front of him, the expression on his face incredulous; a vein twitching in his forehead. He was dressed in a black tracksuit and in his right hand, his gun was still smoking.

He walked over to them, staring from Farusja, to Dante, and then down at Naks. 'I'm sorry I'm late,' he said quietly to Farusja, as he walked over to Dante and knelt next to him, feeling for a pulse with his left hand. Dante was lying at her feet, his body splayed out on the ground, his chest rising and falling steadily. Naks had fallen behind her, a red and white mess of blood and broken teeth splattered across his face, his eye wide-open and staring.

Farusja, sobbing loudly, scrambled over to Dante, kneeling at the base of his head. His eyes were open, and he turned to her as she reached under him and cradled his head in her arms.

Miles had already taken out his phone, his voice urgent as he called for an ambulance. 'They will be here soon,' he said quietly.

Farusja could not stem the flow of tears that ran down her face and splashed down on Dante's. She had seen the small hole in his side and she refused to watch as Miles had rapidly pulled off his tracksuit top and ripped the t-shirt he was wearing, holding it against the wound to stop the bleeding.

'Hey Mumba,' Dante whispered, smiling. 'I told you I'd save you, didn't I?'

Farusja half-laughed half-sobbed, her body shaking with the effort. 'Arrogant as always Dante.'

'I feel so heavy, I'm cold,' Dante murmured, his eyes closing.

'You still haven't got me out of here Dante.' She cradled his head in her lap, smoothing down his hair with her hands. 'You need to get me out of here.'

Dante, opening his eyes again looked up at her, the smile on his lips faint. 'You are beautiful.'

Farusja stared down at him, the dark eyes looking up at her were the eyes she had loved for so long. 'You are not too bad yourself,' she whispered, holding his gaze.

Miles, his hands pressed down on the cloth against the bullet wound, tried to hide the pool of blood that was collecting around his knees and soaking into his tracksuit. He turned his face away from them, bowing it heavily.

'I'm sorry Farusja, for everything,' Dante stopped as he started coughing.

Farusja's hands shook as she ignored the blood that dribbled out of his mouth. 'So am I.' she whispered. She leant down and kissed him, her lips smeared with his blood. 'You're going to be alright Dante,' she whispered, looking up again to gaze into his eyes.

He was smiling faintly at her. 'You know I,' he stopped as the coughing started again. 'I've loved you for so long.'

Farusja nodded, smiling at him through her tears, holding him as his body shook with the coughing, unable to contain the sobs that welled up from deep inside her. She lowered her head again, laying her forehead against his, inhaling his musky scent, the smell of him that had blossomed the attraction she had felt for him in the beginning. 'And I have loved you for twice as long.'

EPILOGUE

---

*F*arusja looked up at the sky, the dark sunglasses hiding the swollen puffiness that encased her eyes. Rabecca was by her side. The weather was the same as the day she had met Dante, bursts of sun with threatening clouds of rain; the hot air blowing over and covering everything with its static heat. Even standing where she was, she was still surrounded by the mourners that had congregated around the shining brown coffin. It seemed like the staff of both organisations and other friends and business acquaintances had shown up for the funeral. It was a very big crowd. She did not know whether they were all well wishers or whether they just wanted to be part of the drama that had surrounded DI and HD over the past month. All dressed in black, she watched silently as the women cried and the men bent their heads in respect. The coffin was closed, and she could see Roberta, Jerome and Cerise standing next to it. Cerise, her face blotched and swollen, was the only one wearing a bright red dress on her slight frame, testament to the passionate life that had ended. Jerome stood angrily by the coffin. His body rigid, his face twisted in anger and pain.

She and Detective Miles had sat there, talking to Dante, her cradling his head and babbling about anything she could think of to keep his eyes open. The ambulance had arrived, and horrified paramedics had bundled both Dante and her into the back. She had sat with him, the blanket the male paramedic had given her ignored on the floor, holding Dante's hands.

He had smiled at her all throughout and she had smiled back, whispering in his ear what she felt for him. She had watched as he had smiled at her one last time as she leant forward to kiss his forehead, and then suddenly his eyes had closed, refusing to open again. The rest had been a blur. She vaguely remembered meeting Rabecca, who had rushed to her screaming and crying in relief, her large arms wrapping around her, dressing her up, speaking to her, but it had all seemed like a dream.

She had sat next to Dante's comatose body at the hospital, and Rabecca did not leave her side. She briefly remembered a strange looking man who had spoken to her quietly as he picked dirt from under her nails and gently cleaned and bandaged the wounds on her wrists. The memory was vague.

Farusja watched from a distance as scores of uncles and aunties came wailing. It was on the second day she had sat with him, that Roberta, Jerome, Cerise and a tall black man had come into the room.

Farusja had watched silently as Roberta had screamed, crying and collapsing on the hospital floor; the woman was such a drama queen. She had to squint to see who it was; her eyes were so swollen from crying. Jerome had seen her and had come towards her, striding forward just like his brother used to do, and had wrapped his arms around her tightly, her tears beginning again as she felt his chest shake and the top of her head go wet with his tears. She had never seen Dante's sister Cerise, and her heart had ached for her as she had watched the young girl. Cerise had stood at Dante's head quietly and had touched his face.

She had found out later that the tall black man had been John Oduraa, one of the more influential members of the board at DI Storage and who also held shares at HD Advertising.

The only person speaking to her was Jerome. She had not seen Hienry. Roberta had loudly and shrilly proclaimed that she was the one to blame for Dante's condition, but Jerome had spoken up for her. Farusja had ignored them all, and had sat quietly staring at Dante, watching his chest rise and fall, until Rabecca had finally tugged her away, telling her quietly that they were going home. She had watched as she was taken away from Dante for a second time.

Once home, Farusja had fallen into a deep dreamless sleep, and had been woken up by Rabecca who had an apologetic look on her face telling her that Detective Miles was at the door. She had forgotten to thank him. She had dragged herself to the sitting room after Rabecca had woken her up, her limbs shaking and her chest heaving at the heaviness of the trauma of her ordeal. Detective Miles Mkazi looked apologetic; he was sitting uncomfortably on the couch dressed in his full police uniform, his hat complete with gold braid held in his hands between his legs.

'I'm sorry Miss Mumba,' he had said quietly, 'but I need to know some things, and there are a few things you need to know too.' He had sat quietly as Farusja had recounted her story. After she'd finished speaking, Rabecca had stood up and gone to the kitchen, coming back with a large plastic cup of water which she forced into Farusja's hand.

'After I was suspended, I continued working on the case with my deputy. We discovered Michael and his visits to DI Storage,' he sighed quietly. 'If this man was Dante's best friend then he knew the facility like the back of his hand, I'm sure he had full reign of the park, of Dante's house, he had access to his family. I actually saw him that day we came to the park, when we found the guns, but I assumed he was just one of the security guards, and in the chaos of what we found, it became hard to track who was coming and who was leaving.'

Miles reached into his pocket, and pulling out a black and white photograph, he handed it to Farusja. 'Do you by any chance know this man?'

Farusja took the picture from the detective, raising a hand to her mouth. Hienry's white and pasty face stared up at her; a circular hole decorated the space right in between his eyes, which were dead and unseeing.

'We found him yesterday hurriedly buried at the back of Michael's house. The same place we found you. Do you know who this is?'

'That's Hienry, he was Dante's unofficial head of his security,' Farusja whispered. 'He was supposed to keep Dante safe.'

Miles shook his head. 'Well, he failed miserably, and got himself killed during the process. Why was Roberta Erlichmann spared, I wonder?'

Farusja handed the picture back over to Miles, her hands shaking slightly. 'He was saving Roberta for last,' Farusja shrugged her shoulders. 'Naks wanted Dante to hurt, for the rest of his life.'

'He must have spared his brother and sister simply because he was more concerned with the women in Dante's life,' Miles mused. 'And Roberta Erlichmann did tell me the history between the three of them, and she was sleeping with him. Maybe he wanted to be the only remaining friend to comfort her and take Dante's place before he did?'

'Your guess is as good as mine Detective,' Farusja whispered. 'I'm sure Naks could have continued his charade if you had not come in when you did...' she trailed off, her hand tightening around the cup as it began to shake again.

'Miss Mumba,' Miles fixed his eyes on her, his voice urgent. 'The security detail that was at Mr Dumeno's house has disappeared. We could not find a single man that worked with this Naks person. I did not want to tell you this to alarm you during these past few days but Naks is gone. The skin under your fingernails is all we have to go on, and most of it seems to be from Michael. When the ambulance took Dante, my men were arriving at the house. They found only Michael's body and a pool of blood and tissue and some broken teeth.'

Farusja dropped the cup, ignoring the water that sloshed between their feet; her eyes open in shock. 'What?' she whispered.

'You're not serious detective!' Rabecca shrieked, as shocked as Farusja. 'How does something like that happen! How incompetent can you people be? So we have to live in fear for the rest of our lives hoping that he does not come back for us?'

Miles sighed. 'I thought I had hit him squarely in the head, but I'm assuming the bullet just broke his jaw and a few teeth and came out the other side. And forgive me but I must say this, Dante Dumeno cannot do anything in his state right now. He might as well be dead, so he might not come after you.'

'But wouldn't he be, he would be ...' Farusja trailed off as she clenched her fists against her knees.

'Only if the bullet hit his spine, which I doubt it did. We're searching for him but honestly Miss Mumba, this man is a ghost.'

'He's going to come back,' she said quietly. 'His work isn't finished yet. He needs to kill me. He wanted to free me from Dante, and as long as I'm alive, according to Naks, I'm still in pain and under Dante's spell, and so is Roberta Erlichmann.'

Rabecca put her hands to her head, a low sound coming from her throat. 'Please don't say that *mami*, please!'

'That is why I'm going to put you under protective detail until I deem you safe.'

Rabecca snorted. 'As if the police have done anything to prevent all the terrible things that have happened over the last few months!'

Farusja smiled at Miles, knowing that she would have to fight this battle herself. 'You have been reinstated?'

Miles shrugged his shoulders. 'Without even going before the panel, I have now become the man of the hour. I was the scapegoat for the police department less than a week ago.

'Have you told Dante's family all of this?'

'Yes, I also have to protect them. His brother will have nothing of it. He did not say anything, but he is determined to find his so-called uncle and bring him to justice. I just hope he brings him to my office at the police station first. I can tell you now that boy is just a smaller version of his brother. I am proud to have tangled with Dante Dumeno, he was an honourable man.'

Farusja smiled faintly, remembering Jerome's dark eyes, and Dante's even darker ones. 'He is an honourable man detective. I'll take care of Jerome.'

Miles dipped his head in acknowledgement. 'I came after Dante because I thought he was the one that had instigated all of this, instead of looking in the shadows, and I had an innocent man arrested. If I had not, all of this could have been prevented. I'd have caught the real killer. I'm very sorry for your loss Miss Mumba. If you could tell him that I'm very sorry. I'm sure that wherever he is, he is more likely to listen to you than to me.'

Farusja nodded, and she watched as Rabecca escorted the detective out. She sat staring down at the water puddle around her feet, raising her head as tears welled up in her eyes again, and trying unsuccessfully to keep them from spilling out over her cheeks. They had wasted so much time playing silly games, she and Dante, and now it was too late. She could feel the regret of all the things she had not done, and all the things she only had the courage to say as he was lying wounded in her arms, all those times her pride had kept her from the man she loved. And at the end of the day all she had were her memories, his body lying in the hospital and that little red Volkswagen beetle idling in Rabecca's driveway. Farusja put her hands to her head.

She knew that Naks would come after her, it was only a matter of time. She had to get ready, to prepare herself. She had stopped running, there was nowhere left to go, and no shadows left to hide behind.

Farusja stared up at the sky again, drowning out the crying and the words of the priest around her. There had been no question of her not attending Orabella's funeral. She had felt a measure of the terror Orabella had felt, and felt a kingship with the spirit of the dead woman.

She smiled faintly as she laid a hand on Rabecca's arm, pulling her with as she turned around, walking away and sidestepping the congregation of mourners.

She could see Dante's smile, and despite all the pain around her, it infused her body with warmth.

It was a beautiful day, Dante would have loved it.

TO BE CONTINUED

ABOUT THE AUTHOR

Sharon Kasanda

With an MBA, a degree in Business Administration and vast experience in various disciplines under her belt, Sharon Kasanda is a well rounded individual. She has had experience in sales and marketing techniques, operations support, assisting in global conference organisation, NGO development work, has worked in the freelance world as a business writer, and has also written for the worldwide magazine Suite 101; assisting in increasing the magazine's readership by contributing above par articles. Sharon has worked both in Namibia and in the United Kingdom, and has built on these experiences to add to the expertise in her fields. A flexible and dynamic individual, Sharon is the perfect embodiment of meeting ones potential in an ever changing environment.